New Market

A Civil War Novel

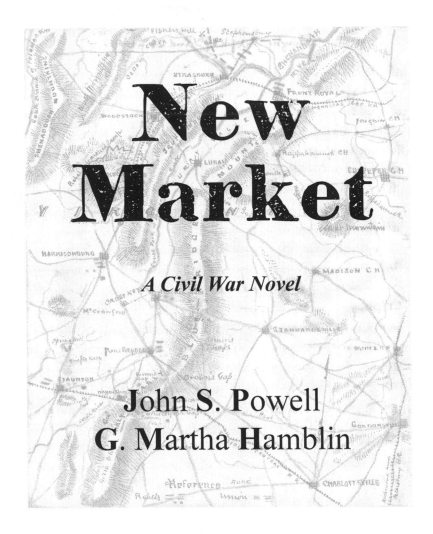

New Market

A Civil War Novel

John S. Powell
G. Martha Hamblin

HAWFIELDS PRESS
Mebane, North Carolina

Hawfields Press
P.O. Box 130
Mebane, NC 27302

Library of Congress Control Number: 2013958338

ISBN: 978-0-9629899-0-2

Images in this book are used with permission from
The Virginia Military Institute Archives, the Library of Congress,
Hagley Museum and Library, and New Market Battlefield Sate Historical Park.

Front cover: Painting by Benjamin West Clinedinst of the charge of the VMI cadets at New Market (detail). *VMI Jackson Memorial Hall*
Back cover: *Map of the Shenandoah Valley Campaign, 1864* by Robert Knox Sneden. *Library of Congress*

Maps by George Skoch

Cover design and layout by Photophish Imaging & Art

First Edition

To
Sophia P. Wolfe
Thomas E. Powell III, MD, VMI '57
James B. Powell, MD, VMI '60
William C. Powell, VMI '70
Samuel C. Powell, PhD, VMI '74
Annabelle "Beth" Powell, DPhil

To
Melissa H. Goslin
Mark C. Hamblin Sr.

Preface

This historical novel is a true story of real people and real events leading up to, and during the Civil War Battle of New Market. While
presented from different viewpoints, the part played by the teenaged cadets
at the Virginia Military Institute constitutes the main narrative. It is the
only instance in American history where the entire student body of a college fought as a single combat unit. With an average age of seventeen years
and eleven months, 258 cadets endured a casualty rate of 24.3% killed or
wounded. That was the second highest percentage for any Confederate
regiment on the field.

The engagement took place in the pouring rain on Sunday, May 15,
1864, in and around the small village of New Market, Virginia. The spring
of 1864 marked the start of the fourth year of carnage that President Abra-
ham Lincoln and many others had naively expected to last less than ninety
days. Near Richmond, the Overland Campaign was underway, pitting two
West Pointers against each other. One was "Unconditional Surrender"
Grant, fresh from the siege and capture of Vicksburg. He had been brought
in by Washington to try to conquer the South's "Marble Man" and master
strategist, Robert E. Lee. As the Overland Campaign degenerated into a
blood bath of brutal proportions, across the Blue Ridge Mountains in the
Shenandoah Valley, Union Major Charles G. Halpine (pen name: Miles
O'Reilly) could still write, "All the romance of the war is in this valley."

The number of troops engaged at New Market was relatively small.
The Confederates could field only 5,335 effectives. These troops were led
by Major General John C. Breckinridge, a Kentuckian and former vice
president of the United States. The commander of the 8,940 Federals was

Major General Franz Sigel, an émigré from Germany, popular with German voters whose support President Lincoln needed for re-election in November. The Germans, called Dutchmen in a rough translation of *Deutsch Mann,* marched forward singing, *Vot fights mit England long ago, To save der Yankee Eagle, To schlauch dem tam secession volks, I goes to fight mit Sigel.*

The importance of this one-day battle was derived from time and place. If Sigel could defeat the Rebel forces under Breckinridge he could combine his army with that of General George Crook's 12,500, cross the Blue Ridge, and strike Lee's exposed left flank.

This novel is not a history of the battle. Historical details have been covered in detail by William C. Davis in his definitive *The Battle of New Market,* and by other notable historians such as Charles R. Knight in his recent *Valley Thunder.* Instead, it is a simple narrative of events seen through the eyes of a few, select participants. Whenever possible the actual words and sentiments of those involved have been used. Where gaps exist in the records the authors have employed dialogue faithful to characters and times. As in all battles, some eyewitness accounts diverge in important particulars requiring a determination by the authors as to the most likely words spoken and actions taken. The authors have updated the language used, but have tried to be true to the sentiments and prejudices held by people in the mid-nineteenth century.

The cadets' viewpoints are presented in the main by John S. Wise, the 17-year-old son of a former governor of Virginia, and Moses Ezekiel, a state cadet with dreams of becoming a world renowned sculptor. Confederate officers' viewpoints are those of three men. One is Major General John C. Breckinridge, who ran against Lincoln in 1860 for the presidency. When Breckinridge tried to remain in Washington as a Senator from Kentucky, he was forced to go south and join "The Cause" to avoid being arrested for treason. Another is Captain Charles W. Woodson, a young Missourian and former bushwhacker who convinced Lee to assign him and his "Missouri Exiles" to the Shenandoah Valley. The third officer is Captain John Hanson McNeill, known as "Hanse." McNeill was a short-horn cattle breeder and lay-minister at the Sinking Wells Methodist Church in Missouri. A native of Hardy County, West Virginia, he moved back home to wage a guerilla war against Federal supply lines, Swamp Dragons, and the B&O Railroad.

Viewpoints for the Union are those of three officers. David H. Strother was a colonel with a touchy ego and no military experience who, before the war, had been the highest paid contributor to *Harper's Magazine*. Colonel George D. Wells, a former judge from Boston, commanded the 34th Massachusetts, the best regiment in Sigel's army. The third officer is First Lieutenant Henry A. DuPont, an ambitious artilleryman frozen in grade by lack of battlefield experience. DuPont graduated first in his 1861 class at West Point and was a scion of the DuPont gunpowder fortune.

There have been numerous accounts and articles written about the battle, its popularity due in no small part to the presence of VMI's cadets. Over the years their story of valor and sacrifice has become an important pillar supporting the mythology of the Lost Cause. It is a story carefully crafted and finely tuned to help a destitute South come to grips with the loss of a generation of men and the destruction of its culture.

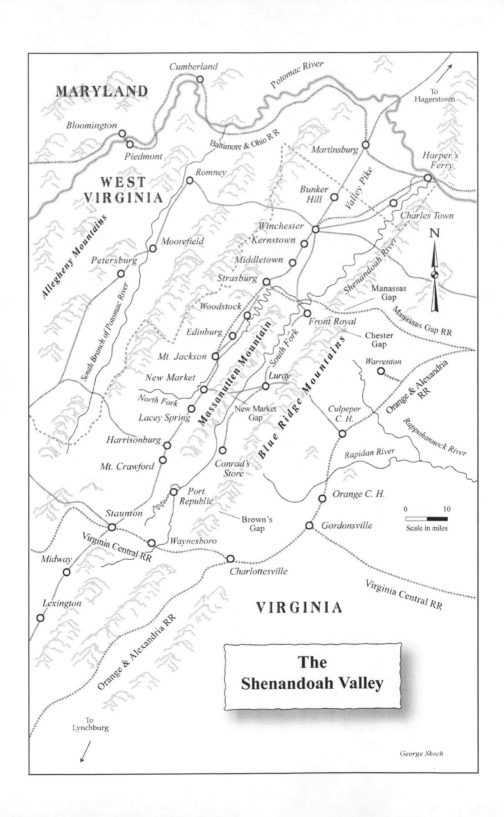

The Shenandoah Valley

Chapter 1

McNeill

Wednessday, May 4, 1864
Bloomington, Maryland

"What's got into Rufus?" grumbled the stationmaster as he fumbled for his pocket watch on the nightstand beside the bed. All that barking and scratching. Yesterday it was a deer. Now what? Locating his prized timepiece he ran his fingers over the case. On the back was an engraved Baldwin locomotive. On the front, in old English script, was his name, Obediah Q. Sledgewell. The timepiece had been presented last Christmas by the Baltimore & Ohio Railroad for twenty years faithful service at the Bloomington Railway Station. Now, 68, he was only staying on because of the war, *and* excellent pay. Lighting a lantern he held the watch to the globe. 4:55. Dagblame that Rufus and his yapping. With a yawn and stretch he pulled on his new slippers. Might as well get a move on. The 6:15 from Grafton would be here before long.

Obediah looked at Rufus who was standing stock-still, his hackles up and emitting a low, guttural growl while facing the east window in the cramped office. Slowly rising from bed, Obediah tried coaxing his reluctant body parts into working order. It wasn't easy, what with his rheumatism acting up from the sudden change in weather. Wobbling a little more than usual he shuffled to the window. He hoped it wasn't a skunk. Last New Year's day Rufus had gotten himself sprayed and had to sleep outside in the bitter cold for two weeks. "Serves him right," Obediah mumbled as he wiped the moisture from the window pane with the sleeve of his long johns. Squinting through the glass, he studied the rails as they disappeared into the fog rising from the North Branch of the Potomac River. Nothing.

There had been reports of bushwhackers prowling the tracks after midnight, but those were just rumors started by Jake Stillwater, the captain of the local home guard. "Jake and that fancy uniform of his don't impress nobody," Obediah muttered as Rufus wagged his tail in agreement. Anyway, everyone knew Jake was a Swamp Dragon who had probably stolen the outfit from some riverboat captain's house. Those Dragons were nothing but trouble, a bunch of cowardly chicken thieves who'd rather steal from civilians than tangle with Rebel guerillas. The worst part was that the Swamp Dragons were protected by the Union army. "That's sure 'nough a pact with the devil," Obediah mumbled, patting Rufus on the head. If it wasn't for his job—and age, he often fantasized about becoming a partisan ranger, one of those romantic will-o'-the-wisps who did what he wanted and made the ladies swoon.

Well, if there were any troublemakers out there, like that liar Jake claimed, they never came this side of the bridge. Just to be safe, Obediah decided to go investigate. If he didn't, Jake would blab to the Railroad bosses that he was too old and feeble to take care of business. He knew Jake wanted his job as stationmaster.

Once again, Obediah glanced out the window. Still foggy. He'd go as far as the bridge, but not all the way to the Piedmont train depot in West Virginia. That was a mile-and-half away and outside his jurisdiction. But dagnabbit, he wasn't gonna take that loud mouth Rufus. The mutt would just have to stay put. No more getting skunked and stinking up the stationhouse.

Before heading for the door, Obediah stoked the embers in the potbellied stove. Tossing in a few lumps of coal, he placed a kettle of water on top for some fresh coffee as soon as he got back. Putting on a set of ratty bib-overalls, he draped a wool blanket around his shoulders and stepped outside. Although the calendar said it was spring, the morning air was cold enough to cause the rails to be slippery and aggravate his chilblains. Holding a lantern in front, he carefully walked on the crossties as he trudged along the tracks. At the bridge a thick mist covered the tracks, cutting visibility to less than thirty paces.

Clump, Clump, Clump. "What was that?" Obediah paused, cupping a calloused hand behind his good ear. *Clump, Clump, Clump.* Sounded like hoof beats echoing off the planks on the bridge—and they were headed his way! Dousing the lantern, he slipped into the shadows behind a rotting tree stump, and hunkered down.

His heart quickened as ghostly figures emerged from the mist. The steam rising from the horses showed they'd come a long way. He counted—four—ten—fifteen. The riders were wearing dusters, slouch hats, and carried cavalry swords, and carbines. These weren't bushwhackers, but Rebel guerrillas. When the leader cleared the bridge he came to a stop twenty yards from where Obediah was hiding.

A rider galloped up, "Hanse, we're ready to cut the wires."

The hulking figure leaned forward in the saddle, "Hurry up. Can't wait no longer." He stared in the direction of the station. "Thought I saw a lantern…"

The stationmaster caught his breath. *Hanse?* It was that Rebel, Hanse McNeill. What was he doing this far north? It was over thirty miles across the Alleghenies to Hardy County where McNeill lived. While trying to decide what to do, Obediah heard Rufus barking. Hopefully, the yapping would distract the riders long enough for him to get back and raise the alarm. Removing his shoes, he padded away from the rails to the rocky footpath leading to the stationhouse. Crouching low, he crept along, trying not to step on a twig or branch.

"Quiet, Rufus!" he whispered as he slipped inside. With trembling fingers he felt his way along the telegraph table until he reached the familiar key set. Breathing hard he began tapping out a warning to the large Federal garrison nine miles away at New Creek. A minute later, the sounder began rattling, "m-e-s-s-a-g—-" Suddenly, the line went dead. The stationmaster slumped back in his chair, sweat rolling down his forehead. Had he gotten through?

Wham! The station door flew open as two dark figures rushed in. Shaking uncontrollably, Obediah stared into the muzzles of two large revolvers only inches from his face. Outside, horses snorted and stomped as riders circled the station.

The first rays of daylight began to light up the valley as a couple of riders dismounted, hitching their horses to the railing beside the station. A tall, erect, heavily built man with a full beard flowing down his chest climbed onto the station platform. He was wearing a Union-blue greatcoat over a grey wool jacket that had three horizontal bars on the collar. In the hat band was a large, black plume. A double-barrel shotgun was strapped across his shoulders. With a wave of his hand he motioned for the stationmaster to be brought outside. "What's your name?" he asked.

"I—I know y—you," sputtered Obediah while Rufus stood in the doorway, cocking his head and wagging his tail.

"You do?"

"You're that guerrilla, Hanse McNeill."

McNeill's dark eyes flashed. Did the Yankees already know he was here? "How…?"

"I s—seen you on the tracks a couple minutes ago."

"So, that was your lantern? You didn't…?"

The stationmaster crossed his heart and shook his head, "No sir, Mr. Hanse. I ain't said nothin' to nobody,"

"Good. Now, tell me your name?"

"It's Obe—Obediah. Obediah Sledgewell."

Towering over the 130 pound, five-foot-four stationmaster, McNeill looked him squarely in the eyes, "Obediah, I'm gonna need your help."

"Yes—yes sir, Mr. Hanse. Anything." Obediah's eyelids began to flutter, a sure sign he was lying, "I want you to know, s—sir, I ain't no Yankee lover. My cousin Caleb was with the Rebs, er, Confederates at Manassas. The Yanks shot him up real bad."

McNeill smiled, "Yep, Obediah. I'll bet you're a regular, fire-breathing Secesh. Now, tell me, when's the next train from Grafton?"

Obediah lowered his head and scratched his chin, "Cain't rightly say, what with the schedules all messed up by them bushwha…"

"Take a guess," growled McNeill, unslinging his shotgun and cradling it in his arms so it pointed at Obediah's chest. His scouts had informed him that east bound traffic from Grafton started early with trains passing through Bloomington every thirty minutes.

Obediah swallowed hard, "Oh, you mean the 6:15?"

"Yeah, that's the one. The 6:15."

The station door burst open and a clean shaven, young ranger with long, blond hair and fair complexion, bounded out. "Pa, look what I found. Just lying on the nightstand." He held up Obediah's silver pocket watch. "Can I keep it?"

McNeill took the timepiece and examined it closely. It was 5:43. "That's a mighty fine ticker, Obediah. I'm gonna use it to see if the 6:15 comes in like you say. If it does, you git it back. If the train's late, that means this here watch must be broken and I'll have to give it to Jesse to be fixed."

Clapping a hand firmly on the stationmaster's shoulder, McNeill signaled to Lieutenant B. J. Dolan, a tall, wiry ranger, to join them on the platform. "Take twenty men up the tracks and flag down the 6:15. Bring it to the platform. Obediah will go with you."

When Hanse and Jesse entered the station house, they could hear the kettle hissing. Rummaging through an overhead cupboard, McNeill found a can full of freshly ground coffee. That's what he liked best about B&O depots. There was always plenty of sugar and good, roasted, Yankee coffee available for the taking. He couldn't abide those cheap Confederate substitutes made from acorns, peanuts or okra seeds. Dumping a handful of grounds into the pot, he took an egg from a basket, cracked it open, and dropped the shells in to settle the grounds.

Unfolding a hand drawn map, McNeill spread it across the telegraph table. "Jesse, go fetch Captain Peerce."

McNeill relaxed as the aroma of fresh coffee filled the room. When it was ready, he poured himself a cup. Dumping in three heaping spoons of sugar, he sat down to rest. Quietly lying beside McNeill on a well-worn pillow was Rufus, who kept his head lowered and with large, soulful eyes watched the stranger's every move. Hanse leaned over, patted Rufus' head and tossed him a strip of beef jerky.

It had been a strange course of events that had brought McNeill full circle back to Virginia. Born in Hardy County in 1815, he moved to Missouri in '48 where he became a successful breeder of shorthorn cattle. A Knight Templar in the Masons, he spent time as a lay minister trying to save lost souls at the Sinking Wells Methodist Church. When war fever swept the state the popular McNeill easily raised a company of militia for General Price's Confederate army. He and his two sons, Jesse and George, fought at Carthage, Wilson's Creek and Lexington where Hanse was seriously wounded in the right shoulder. Unfortunately, George, his eldest, was killed at Lexington while on picket duty. After escaping from a POW camp, Hanse and Jesse returned to Hardy County. It didn't take him long to raise a company of partisan rangers attracted by the promise of excitement and booty. Operating behind enemy lines in an independent command and always keeping on the move suited McNeill's temperament. Within a year his ability to harass wagon trains and disrupt B&O's train schedules caught the favorable attention of General Robert E. Lee.

Unfortunately, Richmond's approval of his guerilla activities didn't prevent McNeill's superior, General John Imboden, from arresting him in '64. Use to operating under his own rules, Hanse had refused to hand over Confederate troops who had deserted from regular army units to join

his band of freewheeling partisans. After a quick trial McNeill was acquit-
ted and allowed to resume his sword. In appreciation for his early release,
McNeill immediately assembled a force of 60 rangers for a raid against the
Piedmont B&O railroad depot on the Maryland-West Virginia border.

After draining the last dregs of coffee from his cup, Hanse tossed Rufus
another piece of jerky. He was pleased Captain John T. Peerce had agreed
to take part in the raid. On detached duty spying for General Imboden,
Peerce was intrigued by McNeill's bold plan and welcomed the opportunity
to take part in a hit-and-run. Before the war Peerce had been a Justice of
the Peace and farmer in nearby Mineral County and had friends among
the locals who would provide shelter and information.

There was the jingle of spurs as Jesse and Peerce entered the station
house. McNeill motioned them over to the map. The station at Bloomington and depot at Piedmont were a mile-and-a-half from each other and
separated by the North Branch of the Potomac River. Located in a narrow
valley at the base of Backbone Mountain, the Bloomington station was at
the end of a steep 17-mile grade down from Grafton. By the time trains
reached Bloomington their brakes were hot and their engines needed water.

McNeill removed a small flask of apple brandy from his coat, took a
healthy swig, then passed it around. "We'll uncouple the engine from the
first train and run it over to Piedmont. I don't think they'll put up much
of a fight."

"How many men you reckon they got?" asked Peerce.

"Scout tells me there's a small provost guard of ten to twelve green
troops. No cannon. Our only problem's gonna be those regulars at New
Creek. With any luck we'll be in-and-out before New Creek knows we're
here." McNeill liked to time raids for first light. It caught the Yankees off
guard and added at least an hour to their reaction time. "Captain Peerce,
you stay here with ten men and stop all trains heading our way. I'll leave
Watkins and Sergeant Houck to help. Houck once worked on the railroad
and knows how to operate engines."

"What about the freight cars?"

"Bunch 'em up on the bridge and set 'em on fire. That ought to bring
down the bridge. If there's anything of value in the cars, let the citizens
help themselves." McNeill liked playing Robin Hood with Washington's
money. Such generosity helped keep the locals sympathetic and friendly.
"Trains will be coming along every thirty minutes, so be ready." He handed
the silver pocket watch to Peerce. "Give this back to Obediah and let him

remove his belongings before torching the building. No need to cause our new Secesh any more grief than necessary."

"Oh, and don't let anything happen to Rufus," added Hanse. "That mutt reminds me of Pokey." As a farmer before the war, McNeill had a soft spot in his heart for animals which often put him in conflict with anyone he saw mistreating a horse or dog. In January he was almost arrested when he reprimanded Confederate cavalry leader, General Thomas Rosser, for mistreating a horse. Rosser, a West Point graduate didn't take kindly to being scolded by an uneducated, backwoods guerilla. After the incident, Rosser fired off a recommendation to Richmond that all independent ranger commands be disbanded and absorbed into the regular army. When the Partisan Ranger Act was revoked in February, James Seddon, Confederate Secretary of War, specifically exempted McNeill's and Mosby's units, allowing them to continue operating as independent commands.

"What's the plan?" asked Peerce.

The corners of McNeill's mouth turned up in a wicked smile, "I mean to wreck the whole damn place. They've got all sorts of shops and rolling stock just waiting for a Confederate match. There ain't gonna be nothing left when I git done but twisted metal and ashes."

For over nine months McNeill had harbored a special grudge against the B&O. Last August when his wife, Jemima, and their young son were passengers on a B&O train in Maryland, they had been arrested and sent to prison at Camp Chase in Ohio. Jemima's only crime was being married to Hanse. After a month's confinement in a squalid cell, she was released. Punishing wives and children of soldiers for doing their duty was a serious violation of McNeill's personal code of honor, and he wasn't about to forgive and forget.

"The Yanks ain't gonna like it," mused Jesse. "Specially your old friend, Sigel."

"You know General Sigel?" asked Peerce.

McNeill nodded. It pleased him that Franz Sigel was the Union general in charge of all Federal forces in western Virginia. "We go back a long ways, all the way to Missouri. Three years ago at Carthage, me and Jesse stole two of his baggage wagons and captured one of his cannons."

"Along with 50 of his men," added Jesse. "We chased that damn Dutchman and his foreigners plum outta Missouri."

"Yeah. He ain't much of a fighter," observed Hanse. "But, enough about old times. Gotta get ready for…"

Wheeeee!

The shrill blast of a train whistle was accompanied by Rufus raising his head and howling. Stepping outside, McNeill watched the engine approach the platform. Inside the cab was Lieutenant Dolan holding a pistol to the engineer's head.

The train was quickly run onto the bridge and the engine decoupled. Two rangers were stationed in the cab with the engineer while Dolan tied a bed sheet to a broom handle for a flag of truce. When all was ready, Dolan signaled the engineer to slowly take the engine the mile and a half to Piedmont. Behind the engine trotted McNeill with 50 rangers.

Peerce watched the small detachment disappear into the fog. He then ordered the rangers to break open the freight cars and dump the contents beside the tracks. There were boxes of crackers, crates of canned ham, sacks of beans, blankets and barrels of flour. He called to Charlie Watkins, a ranger from Baltimore with relatives in Bloomington. "Tell your kin and their friends to help themselves. What they don't take gets burned or thrown in the river."

Twenty-four minutes later another freight train from Grafton pulled into Bloomington station, only to be welcomed by Peerce and his heavily armed men. Peerce ordered the engineer to place it on the bridge behind the first string of box cars. Without waiting for permission, the locals broke down the doors to the freight cars and emptied the contents. Peerce climbed on top of the caboose to watch flames rising from buildings and rolling stock in Piedmont.

With a whoop, an excited rider galloped up. It was Sergeant Pete Houck. Houck had been a cadet at VMI before the war and had gone with the Corps to Richmond in '61 to help train recruits. Instead of returning to the Institute when it reopened in January, 1862, he joined McNeill's rangers as a scout. "Cap'n, the engineer on that last train says there's a whole passel of Yankee infantry heading this way."

"From Grafton?" Peerce was puzzled. Had the stationmaster sent a telegram to Grafton? Why would troops come from Grafton, 40 miles away, when there was a large garrison at New Creek, only nine miles down the tracks?

"Yes sir. Engineer said they were loading soldiers on the mail train when he left. He claims they've got muskets and everything. He reckons there's more than a hundred infantry packed in the passenger cars. Kinda strange though, he says they weren't in any hurry. Maybe we oughta clear out while we still can."

Peerce ran to his horse and swung into the saddle. His mind weighed options as he peered up the tracks toward Grafton. Probably just a false alarm, but if the engineer was telling the truth, the rangers would be out-numbered 10-to-1. His first inclination was to immediately set the freight cars on fire and hightail it into the mountains. But that would leave McNeill trapped between the garrison at New Creek and the soldiers on the train.

Peerce pointed to a warehouse facing the tracks, "Gather the men in the corral behind that building. When the train's a couple hundred yards away, spike some flares on the crossties to slow it down. I'll place a man on the tracks with a lantern to signal it to stop. Let me know if you see any troops."

Peerce rode behind the station and positioned himself beside an out-house with a clear view of the tracks. Ten minutes later, he heard the high pitched squeal of metal on metal as an engine applied down-brakes on its approach.

In a flurry of hooves and lather, Houck galloped up, "*Train's loaded with soldiers!*"

As the train slowed to a crawl, then screeched to a stop, Peerce could see three passenger cars full of infantry, their rifles leaning diagonally across the windows. He quickly joined the rangers in the corral. "Watkins, take four men and work your way to the back of the train. Stay out of sight 'til I give the signal. Houck, you stay here with the rest. Space yourselves out so they think we've got a whole company. When I wave my hat, ride in yelling like demons. No shooting unless I fire first."

Galloping up to the caboose, Peerce spotted the conductor. "Where's the man in charge?" The startled conductor pointed a shaking finger at a figure who had just stepped out onto the platform. Peerce raced over, loudly jumping his horse onto the platform beside the officer. Aiming his pistol at the officer's head, he demanded, "Surrender your men Captain, or you'll all be killed." Removing his hat he waved it over his head.

On the opposite side of the train, Watkins rode up with his rangers, whooping and hollering. Rising in his stirrups, he turned back towards the houses and empty streets, "*Lynn, bring up the rest of the company! Crawford, cover me with those cannon!*"

Caught off guard, the Federal officer reluctantly raised his hands. In a pained voice he said, "*My God!* It's *damn* hard to be gobbled up like sheep, but we don't have any ammunition."

Peerce couldn't believe his luck. The soldiers were merely being transferred from Grafton to Washington. "Captain, tell your men to come out with their hands up."

"*Leave the guns inside!*" yelled Houck, pointing a shotgun at the captain's chest.

While the bewildered soldiers glumly filed out and lined up along the rails, Peerce rode to the back of the train. Inside the last passenger car were women and children, huddled together in small groups. Bowing slightly to the women, which included the wife of Union General Lew Wallace and two daughters of Ohio Congressman Robert Schenck, he assured them that unlike the Swamp Dragons, the rangers were gentlemen and wouldn't rob or harm helpless civilians.

When all the soldiers were out of the cars, Peerce sent Houck racing across the bridge to Piedmont to inform McNeill of the capture of two more trains and over a hundred prisoners with arms. Next, he directed Watkins to find horses and wagons for the captured muskets and accoutrements. In addition to rifles, the rangers found eighteen finely-finished, fully loaded revolvers inside the cars. The rifles and pistols were first class booty. Under the provisions of the Partisan Ranger Act, captured arms were sold to the government for full value and the money distributed among the men. For a private earning $11 a month, such a bonus could easily exceed a year's pay.

After forming the prisoners into a double line, Peerce detailed five partisans to march them across the bridge to the West Virginia side of the river. The passenger car with the civilians was decoupled and left at the depot while the rest of the train was pulled onto the bridge. When all was ready—and Rufus' food bowl and pillow had been carried outside—Peerce ordered his men to torch the station house, locomotives and freight cars. As the smoke swirled skyward, he saw a jubilant McNeill with the band of rangers returning from Piedmont. At the head of the column were thirty-four fresh horses which had been providentially delivered to the Depot just the day before. In addition, there were seven wagon loads of new Springfield rifles, saddles, munitions and supplies.

"Well, Cap'n, I see you bagged the whole lot," quipped McNeill, who had reason to be elated. In less than two hours his sixty rangers had captured a train full of soldiers from Grafton and the guard detail at Piedmont, all without firing a single shot. In addition, they had ripped up hundreds of feet of track and destroyed numerous buildings, trains and supplies. To slow the reaction from the Federals at New Creek, six engines under a full head of steam had been sent barreling down the tracks toward the garrison.

With no time to waste, Hanse, Peerce, Dolan and Jesse began paroling prisoners and lining up the horses and wagons for the return trip to Hardy County. While the flames from the burning freight cars rose to the top of the trestle, a satisfied McNeill spoke to Peerce, "We made the fur fly today. Sigel's going to catch hell from his overlords in Washington."

Peerce reached into his saddlebag and withdrew a bottle of whisky which he handed to McNeill, "A small token of appreciation from the citizens of Bloomington." Waving over a thin, stooped figure astride a mule, Peerce added, "Hanse, I want you to meet Joe Dixon. He's going to be our guide out of here."

McNeill's eyes narrowed as he warily sized up the elderly, diminutive figure.

Noticing McNeill's hesitation, Dixon said in a creaky, barely audible voice, "Don't you fret none, Cap'n. I may be ninety year old and ain't as spry as I once was, but I knows trails through these mountains the bluebellies never heer'd of."

Karump! A cannon shell exploded two hundred feet to the rear, stampeding several horses. Across the river, on a bluff overlooking Bloomington, a flash of artillery fire notified McNeill that the troops from New Creek had arrived. Unable to cross the Potomac because of the raging flames engulfing the bridge, the Federals watched helplessly while McNeill formed his caravan for an escape.

"You fellers follow me," called Joe Dixon, as he took a nip of corn liquor from an earthen jug. Patting his mule on the rump with a stick, he disappeared into a half-hidden trail leading into the mountains.

In less than an hour the telegraph line between New Creek and Washington crackled with news of the attack. West Virginia's Governor Boreman and John W. Garrett, President of the B&O, were demanding that Stanton and Halleck do something—now—to stop such depredations.

Unaware of the extent of rage in Washington over his raid, McNeill was leisurely winding his way over the mountains back to Hardy County. In two days they would be in Moorefield where they could take a much needed rest.

VMI as it looked in 1857
Valley Turnpike (The Great Wagon Road) is in the foreground
VMI Archives

Chapter 2

Wise

"Ellipse: a curve in the Cartesian plane…defined…defined by…" The squiggles and numbers in the geometry book were starting to blur. Wise closed his eyes and pressed a cool, damp cloth to his face. What use was book learning when the biggest event in his life—in all human history—was passing him by?

Lowering the soothing cloth, he stared blankly at the symbols and formulas. It was no use. His thoughts kept drifting back to the war. Everything would be over in a couple of months, maybe weeks, and what did he have to show for it? A notebook full of meaningless doodles, a few sheets of paper crammed with fractured French verbs, and the nub of a well-chewed pencil.

Drumming the pencil on the study table, Wise imagined the excitement swirling around Richmond. Bands were playing, soldiers parading through town, and pretty girls lined up along Broad Street waving flags made from silk petticoats. With a heavy heart, he closed the book. Here he was, stuck in room 56 on the 3rd stoop at the Virginia Military Institute. His head drooped as he thought of all the glory slipping away.

Gazing out the window he saw a hawk slowly circling, hunting for prey. At least being a cadet hadn't been a total loss. He *had* gone with the Corps into the mountains three times in the last nine months searching for General Averell and those Yankee marauders. But he still hadn't seen a single enemy nor fired a shot.

The outing in August had been a lark. The weather was perfect and there had been lots of apples hanging from trees. The Corps made it as far as Goshen before being ordered back. In Averell's second raid in November

the weather had turned raw and blustery, but it was still fun. His roommate, Jack Stanard, had gotten drunk and cremated a squirrel he was trying
to cook in a campfire. The Corps made it to Clifton Forge before being
recalled. Wise shuddered at the memory of the last call-out, the one in
December. The weather had been bitterly cold, the roads treacherous and
the icy rains made it impossible to sleep. Bivouacking in the open with no
tents and tromping around in slush for three days had worn out his shoes
and given him a severe case of sniffles. That last time they made it as far as
Cold Sulphur Springs before the inevitable order to return to barracks. In
spite of sore feet, wet clothes and tired muscles, the three marches had been
a welcome break from books and classroom boredom. They'd also learned
how to sleep in the rain, march on ice and load muskets in a downpour.
But, chasing shadows wasn't real soldiering. You couldn't claim bragging
rights until you had actually fired at the enemy. Since December there'd
been no more raids, no more breaks. Nothing but study, drill, eat, sleep,
and more study. Life had become a monotonous routine of shining shoes
and murdering the French language while the rest of Virginia sharpened
sabers, loaded muskets and prepared for battle. Now he would miss it all.

Rising slowly from his study chair, Wise returned the washcloth to the
rack beside the washstand. With nothing to do, he wandered over to the
peg holding his bayonet and cartridge box. Removing the bayonet he used
a wire brush to scrape off the streak of rust that had cost him two demerits
at yesterday's inspection. In a few minutes, he'd have to go back on guard
and prepare for another inspection by Andy Pizzini, sergeant of the guard.
Ordinarily he disliked guard duty, but since he had been scheduled for a
recitation in geometry it was salvation.

Moving to the open window, he held the bayonet up to the sunlight for
one last look. The fresh air drifting in from the pasture on the other side of
the North River refreshed him. Waving the bayonet like a sword, he fantasized about leading a cavalry charge against a company of Yankees massed
in the poplars at the end of the open field. They'd scatter like rabbits when
he thundered down on them riding a black charger and whooping *yee-aay-
eee!* When it was over, local newspapers would write glowing accounts of
his bravery. Polly Logan and her friends at the Ann Smith Academy would
be lining the road to hurrah him and his men when they passed in review.

Wise had often thought of running away and joining Mosby's Rangers.
But his father, the Honorable Henry A. Wise, former governor of Virginia
and now a Confederate general, wouldn't allow it. Besides, as a cadet, he

was already in the state militia and any unauthorized absence would be considered desertion. In seven months and twenty-four days, he'd be eighteen. Then his father would have to give his permission—but it would be too late. The war would be over and any chance for fame would be gone.

The faint smell of clover reminded him that it was spring. Spring, his favorite time of the year. In the distance, the leaves of the oak and apple trees were already budding out. White dogwood flowers and the brilliant pinks of redbuds dotted the landscape. In the last couple of weeks, the daytime temperature had risen ten degrees, warm enough for the Superintendent to issue a special order allowing those cadets with summer uniforms to begin wearing them. Spring meant flowers and pleasant weather, but this year it held a second, darker meaning. The warm breezes meant muskets were being oiled, Bowie knives honed and cannons tested. There were also ambulances being brought out of storage and coffins being built.

Returning to the study table, Wise picked up the April 25 issue of the *Richmond Dispatch*. The label was addressed to "Cpl. John S. Wise, Virginia Military Institute." He beamed at seeing his name and cadet rank in print. For the tenth time today he read the headline, "Major Battle Imminent. Grant's Forces On The Move." Standing at Attention, he raised the bayonet to his face and saluted the five bedrolls stacked neatly in the corner of the room, *"Corporal Wise, reporting for duty, sir!"*

With a heavy sigh, he brought the bayonet down and returned it to its scabbard. The only duty he'd be reporting for was classroom duty where he would "attack" the blackboard with stupid formulas. Holding the textbook so the worn spine wouldn't fall apart, he carefully wedged it into the bookrack mounted on the wall.

Wise especially envied cadets who had already seen action. A few had been in major battles and encountered famous Confederate generals. At sixteen, Carter Randolph had met Stonewall Jackson at Malvern Hill. When Jackson dropped his glove crossing a stile, Randolph had picked it up and handed it back. When Jackson asked, "Are you a warrior, sir?" Randolph had promptly answered, *"Yes, sir!"* Impressed, Jackson put Randolph on his staff as a special courier. After Antietam, Jackson, personally arranged for Randolph to attend VMI.

At fifteen, Johnnie Cocke had been with General Morgan on his famous cavalry raid through Kentucky, Ohio and Indiana. Almost captured, Cocke had plunged his horse into the Ohio River and swam to safety. And then there was George Raum. A smile crept across Wise's face as he thought of Raum, only four months older that he was. Everyone knew that Raum was a fabulist, but his outlandish tales kept them amused. In one story, he said he'd been at General Johnston's side when the general was wounded at Seven Pines. In another he told of having talked with John Brown after the raid on Harper's Ferry, then watched him hang at Charles Towne. Raum even claimed to have been close enough to Stonewall to hear his labored breathing while he lay dying at Guinea Station. All fancy lies, but still entertaining.

Wise brushed a speck of lint from his gray fatigue jacket. The ends of the sleeves were frayed and there were shiny patches on both elbows, but it was good enough for guard duty. Reaching into the pocket of his trousers he removed a leaflet. It was a program from last Sunday's tableaux at the Lexington theater. The show had been presented by the Soldiers' Aid Society to raise money for widows and orphans. He'd taken Polly and strutted around like a proud peacock until a private from Rosser's Laurel Brigade heckled him. The cavalryman, no older than eighteen, was drunk and singing, *If you want to have fun, just jine the ca-val-ry*. When Wise sneered, the youngster turned to a comrade and exclaimed in a loud voice that it was a dirty, rotten shame that a pretty girl like Polly had to waste time with a *boy* when there were so many *real* men around. Wise would have laid into him then and there had it not been for his cousin and roommate, Louis Wise. Louis saved him from further humiliation since Wise weighed only 128 pounds and stood five-feet-five, while his opponent was big with a bull neck and massive fists. The worst part was that Polly had giggled. She didn't think he had noticed, but he'd seen her covering her mouth and nudging Constance Shriver with an elbow. In church last Sunday a cadet overheard Shriver whisper, "Cadets are so insipid when cavalry are about."

Wise pounded the desk with his fist. Girls are *so* fickle. Just last October he had run the blockade to see Polly and been caught out of limits. For punishment the Commandant gave him thirty demerits, a month's confinement and four extra tours of guard duty. And, for what? Did she care? Not a bit. When he got the chance he'd show them.

Wise read the leaflet again. His favorite scene had been the one depicting Stonewall Jackson's body lying in state at the Institute the night before burial in Lexington's Presbyterian cemetery. That was twelve months ago, almost to the day. Wise had been a member of the honor guard which escorted Jackson's remains from the canal terminus at Jordan's Point to the Institute. With muffled drums and reversed arms, they had solemnly marched beside the caisson. When they reached barracks Wise had helped carry the casket to room 39 on the second stoop where Stonewall had once taught natural philosophy.

If only Wise could remind Polly of the important role he'd played in the procession—without seeming to brag. Maybe work it into a conversation during next week's flag raising ceremony. He would mention how he'd been close enough to the coffin to smell the lilacs and spring flowers. She would be impressed. Girls liked sentimental stuff like flowers and funerals. He remembered how everyone in Lexington had been moved by the spectacle. Grown men and women, even Presbyterians, wept openly as the body lay in state. Some of the women kissed the coffin, then fainted. It was as if the general's death had been a personal affliction.

As Wise folded the leaflet and returned it to his pocket, the door to the room flew open.

"Johnny, it's come."

"What?"

"Lee's response," said Louis, stopping just long enough to catch his breath. "Old Spex sent it to the Commandant. Hanna's seen it."

Johnny's eyes grew wide with anticipation. Just last week the First Class had asked the Superintendent for their diplomas early so they could join Lee's army in time for the spring campaign. If their request were denied, they planned on requesting a furlough for the duration of the war. However, before they could act, Lt. Colonel Ship informed them that their services had already been offered by the Superintendent. Now the reply was here. If accepted, the Corps could leave immediately and be in Richmond within a week. "Where's Hanna?"

"In the Commandant's office," said Louis, pressing his finger to his lips. "Mum's the word. Colonel Ship doesn't want a mob scene."

Wise grabbed his forage cap and headed out the door. "Any idea…?"

"Nope," replied Louis, as they ran along the stoop, down the stairwell, and across the courtyard to the Commandant's office. Cautiously peering through the glass panes of the door they saw John Hanna, First Lieutenant in Company D and officer of the day. He was standing beside Lieutenant Colonel Ship and they were reading the reply. Louis rapped lightly on a pane.

Glancing up, Hanna motioned for them to go next door.

With hearts thumping, Wise and Louis bounded across the sally port into the guard room, almost colliding with Andy Pizzini, sergeant of the guard. Sam Letcher, a new cadet from Lexington who had only been at the Institute since February, stood quietly in the corner. He was adjusting the sling on his musket while waiting to be posted on guard.

"Come in Suggs-J," said Pizzini. "I was about to fetch you." He glanced at Louis, "You too Suggs-L."

"W-well?" asked Johnny, pointing toward the Commandant's office. Both Louis and Johnny smiled at Pizzini's use of their nicknames, Suggs-J and Suggs-L. Since they were cousins with the same last name, fellow cadets had christened them "Suggs" after a third cousin, William Wise, entered the Institute. While Suggs-W was not the best of students, he had managed to read Hooper's *Some Adventures of Simon Suggs*, which he quoted endlessly. This led all three to be tagged Suggs, with only the initials of their first names used to tell them apart.

"We'll know soon enough," Pizzini said, calmly checking the guard roster.

Johnny and Louis eased down on a wooden bench against the wall. Johnny fidgeted with his kepi while Pizzini prepared the daily drill schedule. Andy's father, Juan Pizzini, a native of the Isle of Corsica, had served in Richmond as Italian consul. Once his assignment was over, Juan decided to settle in the Confederate capital as a permanent resident. At fourteen, Andy had joined the First Virginia Infantry as a private, and fought at the Battle of First Manassas. Because of his age the secretary of war ordered his release so he could attend VMI. Although Andy was still only 17, his bearing was that of a much older cadet. Wise was impressed at how unconcerned Pizzini appeared in the face of such momentous news. But that's the way it was with veterans. They never seemed to be in a rush to trade three meals a day and comfortable quarters for the excitement and privations of camp life. Their eyes would glaze over whenever a cadet mentioned wanting to see the elephant. Only George Raum ranted on about the glories of combat and what havoc he'd wreck on any bluebelly unfortunate enough to meet him in battle.

"Mr. Wise, sir?"

"What is it Rat?" asked Johnny, as he glanced in Sam Letcher's direction. Like Wise, the 16-year-old was the son of a former governor of Virginia, but more important, Sam's father was the War Governor, the one in office when Virginia seceded. Wise was also envious that Sam's father had allowed him to serve in the trenches around Richmond at fifteen. But the fact that Sam lived in Lexington and had a pretty sister named Lizzie helped soften Johnny's attitude.

"I heard you were born in Brazil, Mr. Wise," said Sam.

"That's right. Rio de Janeiro. My father was US Envoy for Brazil in '46."

Louis chuckled, "Envoy? Go ahead Johnny, give him the full title."

Wise grinned, "Envoy Extraordinary and Minister Plenipotentiary to the Empire of Brazil from the Republic of the United States."

Louis laughed, "Sounds like some character in a minstrel show. Now tell him the rest of the story."

Wise looked in Pizzini's direction, pleased at the chance to brag about his family. When he noticed a flicker of interest, he started, "On the day after Christmas in 1846, my father was walking along the docks in Rio with an assistant surgeon from the US Navy. As they strolled along, they met two young West Point lieutenants out sightseeing. The officers were from a ship named "Gloria" that had just docked. The lieutenants were on their way to California to join American forces fighting in Mexico."

"I know the landing," said Letcher. "I was in Rio at the beginning of the war." Sam and two friends had been traveling in Brazil when they learned that Fort Sumter had been bombarded and Virginia had left the Union. Catching the first available steamer back to the US, they landed in Baltimore just before the Battle of First Manassas. Stranded in Union territory, they met a sympathetic boatman who smuggled them back into Virginia. When they reached General Longstreet's Division they were invited to supper with the General. With no place to stay, they spent the night in General Beauregard's tent before returning home to Richmond.

Wise cocked an eyebrow, annoyed at the interruption. "Since it was the day after Christmas, my father invited the two young officers to his home for dinner. When they arrived at the legation they were seated on the veranda with the Russian minister for Rio. After a couple of rum swizzles, everyone began discussing the Mexican war. Everyone that is except my father who kept excusing himself, then returning. The young officers noticed my mother wasn't there, but said nothing. When they finished their meal, they returned to the veranda for cigars and coffee. Around 11:00pm a Brazilian doctor joined them but was too busy for idle chat. Both the doctor and my father immediately went upstairs. The two lieutenants sensed it was time to go and left at once. As it turned out, the doctor was there to see my mother. At 1:33am on December 27, I made my entrance into the world, kicking and screaming."

"And you haven't stopped," said Louis. "Now, tell Letcher who the lieutenants were."

Wise waited a few seconds for maximum impact. "Union Generals William T. Sherman and Henry W. Halleck."

"And who's your uncle?" quizzed Louis, wagging his finger.

"Union General George Meade," said Wise. "General Meade married my mother's sister."

"I swear, Johnny," said Louis. "You're more Yankee than Rebel."

The door to the guard room swung open. The Commandant stepped in, followed by Hanna.

Pizzini snapped to attention.

"At ease," said Lt. Colonel Ship. The Commandant was a large man with dark eyes, deep voice and neatly trimmed beard. Only 24, he had the bearing of an overworked, thirty year old. He held up a piece of paper. "Lee's answer."

Wise glanced at Hanna. He could tell from the frown the news wasn't good. Like Wise, Hanna also had family connections with Philadelphia. The 20-year-old had attended Gonzaga College and Georgetown University before entering the Institute. His parents still lived in Philadelphia, near the house where Wise had spent several summers visiting his grandparents. Although staunch Unionists, Hanna's parents supported their son's decision to remain at VMI and, if necessary, fight for the Confederacy.

The Commandant handed Lee's letter to Hanna who read it out loud:

Genl. Francis H. Smith, Supt.
Hdq. Va. Mil. Institute
Genl. I desire to express my appreciation for the patriotic spirit that actuates you in tendering the services of the Corps of Cadets at the Va. Mil. Institute for the approaching campaign. I do not think, however, it would be best at this time for the Corps to be called to this army. It is now in a situation to render valuable aid in defend-ing our Western frontier which may be menaced simultaneously with the general advance of the enemy in the East. It will thus prevent the necessity of detaching troops from the army. I think it would be advisable for you to hold the command in readiness to cooperate with Genl. Breckinridge and Genl. Imboden in case of necessity, and notify those officers of the fact. Should it at any time become necessary or

expedient to have the services of the Cadets with this army, it is very gratifying for me to know that they are so freely placed at my disposal.
Very Respectfully,
Your obedt. servant
R.E. Lee, Genl.

"Shucks," mumbled Wise. Now there was no way out. He would have to make a recitation in geometry on Friday.

The Commandant patted Johnny on the shoulder. "Don't take it too hard. It's quite a compliment that General Lee trusts us to protect the Valley. Once the battles start this spring, there'll be enough fighting to go around."

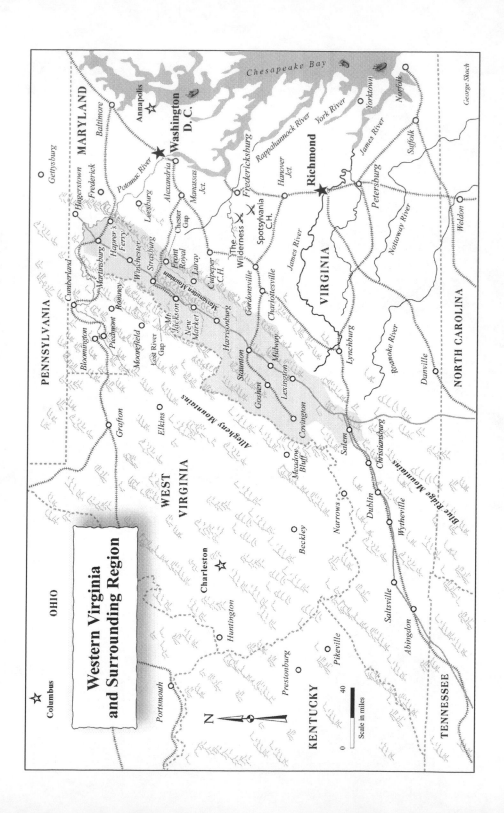

Western Virginia and Surrounding Region

Chesapeake Bay

George Skoch

MARYLAND

OHIO

Columbus

PENNSYLVANIA

WEST VIRGINIA

VIRGINIA

NORTH CAROLINA

KENTUCKY

TENNESSEE

Gettysburg
Hagerstown
Frederick
Baltimore
Annapolis
Washington D.C.
Alexandria
Leesburg
Chester Gap
Manassas Jct.
Fredericksburg
Hanover Jct.
Richmond
Yorktown
Norfolk
Suffolk
Petersburg
Weldon

Cumberland
Martinsburg
Harper's Ferry
Winchester
Strasburg
Front Royal
Luray
Culpeper C.H.
The Wilderness
Spotsylvania C.H.
Gordonsville
Charlottesville
Lynchburg
Danville

Romney
Piedmont
Bloomington
Moorefield
Lost River Gap
Mt. Jackson
New Market
Harrisonburg
Staunton
Goshen
Midway
Lexington
Covington

Grafton
Elkins
Meadow Bluff
Beckley
Charleston
Huntington
Narrows
Dublin
Wytheville
Christiansburg
Salem

Prestonburg
Pikeville
Saltsville
Abingdon

Portsmouth

Potomac River
Rappahannock River
York River
James River
James River
Roanoke River
Nottoway River

Massanutten Mountain
Allegheny Mountains
Blue Ridge Mountains

N

40

0

Scale in miles

Chapter 3

Breckinridge

Wednesday, May 4
Dublin, Virginia

> *I think it would be well to have everything prepared to meet them, and,*
> *in conjunction with General Imboden, destroy them....Gen. Crooks'*
> *movements in the western department will probably be simultaneous*
> *with the attack here by Grant.*

Breckinridge gazed out the window of his office as he mulled over Lee's telegram. The hills and valleys around Dublin reminded him of Cabell's Dale in Kentucky where he had grown up. Those had been the happy years. The time before going to Washington as the youngest vice president in the history of the US, and watching the country torn apart by warring factions.

Lost in his reveries he was startled when a cool breeze blew the telegram off the table onto the floor. Seeing Lee's name on the message reminded him that he was no longer a civilian but a major general in the Confederate army in charge of the Department of Southwestern Virginia.

He re-read the telegram. It wasn't going to be easy preventing Crook from capturing the Virginia and Tennessee Railroad depot at Dublin. In addition to guarding the railroad Breckinridge was also charged with protecting the critical lead mines in Wythe County and the salt works at Saltville.

The Federal forces opposing him were formidable. Grant had handpicked Brigadier General George R. Crook as their commander. Crook was a seasoned veteran who still carried an arrow in his hip from a pre-war scrape with Indians in Oregon. An 1852 graduate of West Point, he had been at Second Manassas, Antietam and Chickamauga, and wasn't likely to make mistakes.

Confederate spies in Kanawha reported Crook with 10,000 infantry and an additional 2,500 cavalry under Brigadier General William W. Averell, another West Pointer. Against this Breckinridge could muster only 4,000 infantry and 2,600 cavalry. By concentrating his several commands and using scouts to keep him informed of Federal movements, he felt reasonably confident he could hold back the Union tide.

In January when Davis had asked Lee who to put in charge, Lee had responded, "*So important do I consider western Virginia to the successful conduct of the war that I will relinquish any of my officers you may select for its command.*" After due consideration, Davis had chosen fellow Kentuckian, Major General John Cabell Breckinridge. The 43-year-old former politician had earned his military spurs at Shiloh, Baton Rouge, Stones River, and Chickamauga. Now he was being "rewarded" with one of the most difficult assignments in the Confederacy.

Breckinridge tacked the May 1st telegram to a cork board on the wall of his first floor office in the Dublin Hotel. Despite the limited space, he had selected this hotel as base of operations since his wife, Mary, was with him. The barnyard smells drifting up from nearby stables and the constant noises of clattering trains, braying mules and rattling supply wagons were bothersome, but the hotel had decent food and was centrally located. It also had easy access to the all-important telegraph office. For the past several days, cables from Richmond and Lee had arrived hourly as Grant's spring offensive got underway.

On a small desk in the cramped office were two detailed maps of the western Virginia mountains. They had been drawn by Claudius Crozet, the "Pathfinder of the Blue Ridge." Crozet was a graduate of France's prestigious military school, *Ecole Polytechnique,* and had been an officer of artillery in Napoleon's *Grande Armee de la Russie.* When Bonaparte invaded Russia in 1812 Crozet had been captured at Borodino. After spending two years as a POW teaching a Russian Count's children how to read and speak French, he had been released. In 1814 Crozet immigrated to the US and taught engineering at West Point. Well-versed in the structure and operations of French and American military schools, in 1837 he helped found the Virginia Military Institute.

Next to Lee's message, Breckinridge pinned a copy of the May 2 telegram assigning Brigadier General John H. Morgan to his command. The two men had fought together at Shiloh and Nashville and were close friends. In December 1862 Breckinridge had served as an usher at Morgan's lavish wedding to society darling, 21-year-old Martha "Mattie" Ready. General Leonidas Polk, a graduate of West Point and the former Episcopal Bishop of Louisiana, performed the ceremony. Among the guests were Generals Bragg, Cheatham and Hardee. Some wags cautioned that the marriage by the 38-year-old Morgan to the "trim figured Southern Belle with dark brown hair, fair complexion, rosy cheeks and gray eyes," would rob him of any enthusiasm for combat. But Breckinridge knew better.

When Morgan arrived in the area from Tennessee he'd bring additional cavalry. On a pocket calendar Breckinridge circled May 7. That was the earliest date Morgan's men could reach Saltville.

Next, Breckinridge tacked up a May 3 cable from Brigadier General John Echols. In it Echols reported that his best scouts had confirmed that Averell's cavalry was planning on striking the salt works and lead mines at the same time Crook attacked Dublin Depot. More ominously, Crook's troops were now calling themselves the right wing of Grant's army. Breckinridge was pleased to have Echols in charge of one of his brigades even though the 260 pound general suffered from neuralgia of the heart. Echols, a graduate of the Virginia Military Institute was experienced and had commanded the 27th Virginia at the First Battle of Manassas and during Jackson's Valley Campaign.

A major problem was the confusion in the chain of command. Breckinridge was in charge of the Department of Southwestern Virginia and General John D. Imboden was in command of the Shenandoah Valley District. Both had been ordered to report directly to Jefferson Davis. If Davis wasn't available, they were to communicate with James A. Seddon, Secretary of War. If Seddon was busy, they were to report to Breckinridge's old nemesis, General Braxton Bragg.

With a pocketknife Breckinridge cut off part of a plug of chewing tobacco and wedged it in the corner of his mouth. Stepping out on the porch, he settled in a rocking chair. A frown darkened his features as he thought of the approaching campaign and how it would result in another, long separation from Mary. It would also mean days, if not weeks, of bivouacking in wet, spring weather and subsisting on salt pork, cornbread, beans and molasses. Turning his face to the warm sun, he closed his eyes and relaxed as nicotine slowly seeped into his system. As he was about to drift off, he heard the *thump, thump, thump* of approaching boots. It was the telegraph operator with a new cable.

> *Richmond, May 4, 1864*
> *General BRECKINRIDGE, Department of Southwestern*
> *Virginia*
>   *Information received here indicates the propriety of your*
> *making a junction with General Imboden to meet the*
> *enemy on his movements toward Staunton. Communicate with*
> *General R.E. Lee and General Imboden.*
>   *JEFFERSON DAVIS*

Breckinridge sat bolt upright. Staunton? What about Crook and Dublin? Was this a change in orders? Who was "the enemy" mentioned in the cable? Was Major General Franz Sigel's army heading toward Staunton? Lee had said he didn't think Sigel was ready to move, but now—? Earlier, Imboden's scouts had reported Sigel settled down in Winchester, ninety-five miles north of Staunton, with an estimated 9,000 infantry and 4,000 cavalry. The only Confederate troops currently between Sigel's army and Staunton were Imboden's 1,600 cavalry. Breckinridge hastened back inside to study the maps.

Dublin was over 145 mountainous miles from Staunton. Not only was Sigel 55 miles closer, but he had better roads. If Breckinridge immediately sent his infantry to Staunton it would take them several days to get there. Glancing at the scribblings in his notebook, he re-examined the numbers. The total Confederate force in western Virginia was less than 8,400. Against that, Sigel and Crook had more than 25,500 effectives. Fortunately, the Federals were scattered across the mountains from Harper's Ferry to Charleston, West Virginia and Sigel was known for being disorganized and slow.

Breckinridge knew that if he sent half his small army to the Shenandoah Valley to stop Sigel, it would violate the basic military maxim that warned against dividing a smaller force in the face of a numerically superior enemy. But Jackson, when outnumbered more than three to one, had divided his forces and defeated Fremont, Banks and Shields. Lee had done the same at Second Manassas and Chancellorsville. If he could just keep Crook from joining up with Sigel, then maybe, just maybe...

Two hours later, while Breckinridge was packing saddle bags for the move to the Narrows, there was another telegram from Lee.

Orange Court-House, May 4, 1864
Major-General BRECKINRIDGE, Dublin
The President informs me that you will report to me. For the present you will take the general direction of affairs and use General Imboden's force as you think best. He has been ordered to report to you. I trust you will drive the enemy back.
R.E. LEE

Breckinridge was pleased that Jefferson Davis had placed him in charge of all Confederate forces in Western Virginia. He was also officially part of Lee's army and he didn't have to report to Braxton Bragg. From the brevity of the message it was clear Lee was under tremendous pressure. He had written, "...*as you think best*." Granting a subordinate blanket authority for operational decisions was an unusual step for Lee. The only other commander so entrusted had been Stonewall Jackson.

There was a knock on the door. It was Major Charles S. Stringfellow, Breckinridge's energetic, bespectacled, assistant adjutant. "Courier from Lexington, sir. Dispatch from General Smith, Superintendent at VMI."

Breckinridge scanned the letter. Stringfellow had already underlined the important points. "...*available for such orders as the emergencies of the approaching campaign may call for... The Corps of Cadets numbers an aggregate of 280...fully equipped... We have an abundance of ammunition, tents, knapsacks, shovels and picks, and will be prepared to march at a moment's notice.*"

"Well, General?"

Breckinridge slowly shook his head. "No, Major. We'll have to make do without the cadets." The thought of sending school boys into battle against hardened veterans was not acceptable. The situation was serious, but not so desperate as to justify that kind of sacrifice. His thoughts drifted back to his own son, Cabell, who had run away from home at sixteen to join the Second Kentucky Infantry, a unit in the Confederate army. At the time, Cabell had been the same age as many VMI's cadets. Breckinridge remembered Mary's anguish when she learned what Cabell had done. Later, after Cabell's capture at Missionary Ridge, and return unharmed, Mary had written, "I just made a promise that if I could hear Cabell was not wounded I would never shed another tear. But sometimes in the silent hours of the night, unbidden tears will steal down my cheek." No. This wasn't a boys' crusade. He thought of his two cousins currently at the Institute. William H. Cabell, 18, and Robert G. Cabell, 16. He was determined to spare their mothers from the torment Mary had suffered.

Breckinridge handed the letter back to Stringfellow. "Send General Smith a reply. Tell him we may need the cadets to protect the iron furnaces at Botetourt, or in Buchanan, but not here." He didn't want to give offense by implying the cadets weren't qualified. Still, they were *so* young. "Advise the Superintendent we'll keep him informed of our progress. There's no telegraph in Lexington, so send the reply by courier." He left the wording up to the major who had entered college at William and Mary at fifteen and was teaching Latin and Greek at a private school in Williamsburg at seventeen.

Breckinridge, who held a BA from Centre College in Danville, Kentucky, an LL.B. from Lexington's Transylvania University, and had spent six months as a resident graduate at Princeton, prized education and intelligence among his staff. At Centre, the popular, athletic 6-foot-2 student had excelled at classics, history and oratory. In law school he had received high marks for scholarship, industry, and behavior. During the boring gaps between campaigns he enjoyed stimulating conversations with his staff on government, history and Greek literature.

Before leaving, Stringfellow paused, "Every time I hear 'VMI' I think of Stonewall Jackson. If the war hadn't come along when it did he'd still be a major in the state militia, boring cadets with mind-numbing lectures."

"And Grant would be in Galena, Illinois, selling saddles to the local gentry at his father's leather shop."

"I guess it's a matter of being in the right place at the right time," mused Stringfellow.

"Good thing Stonewall also taught artillery tactics," added Breckinridge, thinking of the many VMI graduates in his command who had received instructions directly from Jackson.

"Funny, the way things work out. Didn't Grant own slaves?"

"He had one in St. Louis when he was a farmer trying to scratch out a living on a rocky farm called 'Hardscrabble.' The slave's name was William Jones. Grant's wife owned four dowager slaves. When he went belly-up in Missouri and moved to Illinois he had to sell them."

Stringfellow chuckled, "So if he'd been a better farmer he might've wound up a slave-holding bushwhacker killing Jayhawkers for the Confederacy. Now he's the darling of the abolitionists. As I recall you got into trouble with voters in Kentucky who claimed you were an abolitionist."

Breckinridge smiled, "In politics you're damned if you do, and damned if you don't." He'd learned long ago to keep his opinions about the South's "peculiar institution" to himself. During his campaign for President he had declared such details personal and not open for public discussion, but that hadn't prevented his enemies from attacking him on the subject.

"If it hadn't been for slavery, there might not have been…"

"Slavery wasn't the *casus belli*," interjected Breckinridge. "The real cause was the refusal of honorable men to seek compromise. When the planters lost control of Congress, they packed their bags and went home. Virginia and North Carolina both voted against secession and didn't break away until Lincoln's call for troops." Breckinridge shook his head, "It all could've been settled so easily had the politicians just been patient. Now it's treason to talk compromise."

Breckinridge had always considered slavery an evil which was spiritually and morally degrading to both slave and master. In his opinion the Founding Fathers should have taken care of the problem when they had the chance. Recently he had supported Generals Cleburne and Hardee in their proposal to recruit 300,000 slaves as soldiers in exchange for freedom. Unfortunately, the diehards in Richmond decided the plan was too radical and forced Davis to stop the conversation.

"General, you're a Presbyterian. What's your view on predestination?" asked Stringfellow. "Stonewall said, 'My religious belief teaches me to feel as safe in battle as in bed. God has fixed the time for my death. I don't concern myself about that.' "

Breckinridge smiled, "When the lead starts flying, I still duck." Although the product of a staunch Presbyterian upbringing, he didn't attend church on a regular basis. But, as leader of men who believed in the power of Divine Providence, he couldn't afford to discourage their faith since it gave meaning to their privations and sufferings.

"So do I," replied Stringfellow, on his way out the door. "As an Episcopalian I'm allowed to drink whiskey and dodge bullets."

Breckinridge stood over Crozet's maps and stared out the window at the mountains. How peaceful they seemed. He wondered if history would say he had done all he could to prevent the madness of war. After serving as Buchanan's vice president, he had allowed himself to be listed as a candidate for the presidency by the breakaway Southern wing of the Democratic party. Although he came in second to Lincoln in electoral votes, the Democrats lost the election by fielding too many candidates.

When the election was over Breckinridge had remained in Washington until after the Union defeat at First Manassas. He hoped that being a

Senator from Kentucky would give him some protection from the fury of the radicals. But neither his friendship with his cousin Mary Todd Lincoln, nor his frequent visits to the White House had held the jackals at bay. By daring to talk compromise and reunion he put himself at risk of being arrested without warrant and being held in prison indefinitely while his property was confiscated. When he learned that Union General George Thomas, a Virginian, was on his way to arrest him for treason, Breckinridge reluctantly "went south" and joined the Confederacy.

At first, Jefferson Davis, a fellow Kentuckian, considered appointing Breckinridge Secretary of War. But it was decided that because of his popularity he would be more useful as a brigadier general recruiting troops from the bluegrass state. In November, 1861, he was placed in command of the First Kentucky Brigade, a unit composed entirely of volunteers from a state still in the Union.

Although he wasn't a graduate of West Point, he did have some basic military training. During the Mexican War he was appointed a major in the 3rd Kentucky Volunteers and sent to join Winfield Scott's command in Mexico City. Arriving too late for action, he used his six months in Mexico to meet and socialize with the US army's rising, young officers. As a 26-year-old major of volunteers, for a time he technically outranked such regular West Pointers as lieutenants U.S. Grant, George B. McClellan, Richard Ewell, P.G.T. Beauregard and captains Robert E. Lee, William J. Hardee and James Longstreet.

The transition from politician to fighting general had been rocky, but once committed, he'd thrown himself into his new role with his usual determination and enthusiasm. Shiloh, Baton Rouge, Stones River, Chickamauga, Chattanooga, all stepping stones along a difficult path. As he gained experience his efforts began winning recognition and praise from those who mattered: Lee, Beauregard, Hood, Hardee, Johnston and D.H. Hill. After Shiloh, he was promoted to major general, the only "political" general in the Confederacy to earn such high recognition.

Fortunately for Breckinridge, many of the officers in his small command were VMI graduates with extensive combat experience. In addition, he had the services of two seasoned West Pointers. The rest were bootstrap officers like himself who had earned high rank because of merit.

He was especially pleased to have the services of John D. Imboden as commander of the important Valley District. Before the war, Imboden had attended Washington College in Lexington, Virginia, then read law in Staunton. Although he was without formal military training he was appointed Captain of Staunton Artillery and helped capture Harper's Ferry for the Confederacy. After the battle of First Manassas Imboden returned to the Valley and organized a battalion of partisan rangers. On the retreat from Gettysburg he earned accolades from Lee for successfully escorting a wagon train of Confederate wounded safely back into Virginia.

While waiting, Breckinridge walked across the room to a double breasted frock coat hanging on a wooden peg by the door. It had been a special gift from Mary in recognition of his new assignment. Tomorrow he would wear it in the field for the first time. The coat was an extravagance but he liked to dress well when meeting new troops. As a politician he had learned the importance of first impressions. Two years ago, Confederate General John B. Gordon had written a friend, "Breckinridge is tall, erect and excellent in physique and would have been selected in any martial group as its leader." After Chickamauga when an observer complimented Union General John Beatty on being the handsomest mounted figure he had ever seen, Beatty replied, "Sir, that's because you've never seen Confederate General Breckinridge on a horse."

While Breckinridge was examining the coat, the door to his office swung open and Lt. Colonel J. Stoddard Johnston strode in with a telegram. The 205-pound chief of staff was a graduate of Yale and the University of Louisville Law School and a close friend from pre-war days.

There was a frown on Johnston's round, normally jovial face as he handed Breckinridge the cable. "Bad news from Grumble Jones."

> *Glade Spring, May 4, 1864*
> *Major-General BRECKINRIDGE*
> *I am ordered by General Bragg to push my cavalry forward to Tennessee. I have notified him of the state of affairs here and asked if I must withdraw my support to you. My brigade is near Jeffersonville. Morgan is at Saltville. Both will move to you if needed.*
>
> *W.E. JONES, Brig. Gen.*

Breckinridge's eyes flashed with anger as he crumpled the telegram in his fist. "Bragg's meddling again. He's not going to get away with it this time."

Johnston nodded reassuringly, "Don't worry, Breck. Grumble won't let you down."

Breckinridge could read between the lines. Jones was asking for tacit permission to ignore Bragg's order. If there was anything the irascible Jones detested, it was an incompetent like Bragg trying to interfere with his command. A native Virginian and West Point graduate, Jones was Old Army to the core and harbored a veteran's disdain for high ranking martinets like Bragg who tried to run field operations by telegraph. Unburdened by social graces or any desire to please superiors, Jones had been banished to southwest Virginia after a run-in with JEB Stuart, who court-martialed him for disrespect.

This wasn't Breckinridge's first run-in with the vindictive, autocratic Braxton Bragg, who at one point had declared all Kentuckians, "Nothing more than cowards not worthy of being liberated." By 1863 Breckinridge had served in Braggs' Army of Tennessee for seventeen months and gone from golden boy after Shiloh to scapegoat following Stones River and Chattanooga. Bragg's troubles with subordinates were legendary. During the Mexican War there had been two attempts on his life—by his own men. In little more than a year-and-a-half as commander of the Army of Tennessee, he had managed to alienate most of his generals, especially Leonidas Polk, D.H. Hill, James Longstreet and William Hardee. In an unusual display of insubordination these officers had petitioned Davis to have Bragg removed from command. After Chattanooga, General Nathan Bedford Forrest, the best and most feared cavalry leader in either army, confronted Bragg and to his face called him a "damned scoundrel and coward." Forrest warned, "If you ever try to interfere with me again or cross my path it will be at the peril of your life." Wisely, Bragg chose not to report the incident to Richmond, or test the resolve of a man who had personally killed over twenty men.

Early in his career, Breckinridge had made it a policy to avoid all forms of petty scheming and political bickering. It had been said of him, "Breckinridge is difficult to anger and impossible to provoke to revenge. He makes few promises and breaks none. As a citizen and statesman he is stainless and incorrupt." But Breckinridge found it impossible to deal civilly with Braxton Bragg. When Bragg ordered him to execute a Kentuckian wrongfully convicted of desertion, a permanent breach erupted between them that never healed. Now, Bragg was trying to send Grumble Jones back across the mountains to Tennessee to face an imaginary enemy. Fortunately, Breckinridge had an important ally. Scribbling a telegram message to Bragg, he handed it to Johnston for review.

The corners of Johnston's mouth turned up in a wicked grin as he read, *"General Bragg. Will answer as soon as General Lee responds to my dispatch of this date. Have advised General Jones to wait until I hear from General Lee."* Johnston waved the note over his head, "Bragg won't dare go against Lee."

There was a light rapping at the door as Major Stringfellow entered, "Message from General Lee."

> *Verdierville, May 4, 1864-5pm*
>
> Major General BRECKINRIDGE
>
> General Imboden reports that Sigel will probably cross at Chester Gap and move upon our left. If you cannot by counter moves occupy him in the Valley, leave sufficient troops to guard against movement from Kanawha, and push your troops to Orange Courthouse if Sigel moves in that direction. Grant's whole army is moving on our right, and I am following.
>
> R. E. LEE

Breckinridge noted the time of dispatch. 5pm. He tugged on the ends of his mustache. How accurate was Imboden's intelligence? There'd been several conflicting reports from Imboden in the last couple of days. Unsure of what to do, Breckinridge prepared a response. *"Is Staunton the point threatened? Shall I send Echol's, Wharton's and McCausland's infantry to Imboden at Staunton? This would leave Jenkins and Jones with some 4,000 cavalry and 600 infantry and a good supply of artillery. Will sit up tonight to hear from you."* He realized that 600 infantry wouldn't be enough to stop Crook, but if Jenkins fought part of his cavalry as infantry, he might slow Crook down long enough for Breckinridge to deal with Sigel.

While Breckinridge was mulling over his options a telegrapher came in with another telegram. It was from Imboden. *"Sigel's cavalry at Maurertown today, but have fallen back to Strasburg. Sigel has moved to Front Royal and is doubtless going to Grant via Chester Gap…"*

Just as Lee had feared, but still—Imboden said "cavalry," not "infantry." Breckinridge looked at the map. If Sigel's *infantry* was at Front Royal, then he was definitely heading across the Blue Ridge. But why tarry so long at Winchester if that was his objective? In spite of Imboden's warning, it looked to Breckinridge like Sigel planned to join Crook in Staunton.

Now it was a race against time. Breckinridge motioned to Stringfellow, "Send a telegram to General Jenkins. Tell him he's in charge of defending

Dublin, the salt works and lead mines. He'll be low on infantry so he'll have to dismount some cavalry. Tell him to do what he thinks best. If he can't buy enough horses for his artillery, impress them."

Albert G. Jenkins, a Harvard educated lawyer and two-term US Congressman was another boot-strap officer. A native Virginian he was familiar with the mountainous geography of western Virginia and was good at raising volunteers. A quick study, Jenkins had learned his craft as a partisan ranger in the Valley with Stonewall. Although Breckinridge had only met Jenkins a couple of times he was going to have to rely on him to make the right decisions. Beginning tomorrow, both men would be in the field and telegraphic communications between them would be impossible.

Examining the numbers in his notebook, Breckinridge underlined the "what ifs." *If* Jenkins could slow Crook down. *If* Sigel wasn't heading across the Blue Ridge at Chester Gap. *If* Breckinridge could reach Staunton before Sigel.

When Stringfellow re-entered, Breckinridge placed a hand on his shoulder. "Major, I want you to stay in Dublin and keep an eye on things. Most important…" his voice trailed off as a rush of emotion swept over him.

"I understand," said Stringfellow. "Before the fighting starts, I'll make sure Mary leaves for Salem."

It had been a godsend to have Mary with him, but now he was worried about her safety. The choice had been hers and he knew she wouldn't have it any other way. If he or Cabell were wounded, their lives could well depend on her being close at hand. She had nursed Major Rice E. Graves back to health after Stones River. For this kindness Major Graves had given her the ultimate soldier's tribute by naming one of his cannons "The Lady Breckinridge." Last year while she was staying at a plantation near Tuskegee, Mary had suffered a near fatal bout of malaria. That brush with death made her more determined than ever to spend as much time as possible with her husband and son.

As the last rays of daylight streaked through the window in Breckinridge's office, Stoddard Johnston stuck his head in the door. With an "I told you so" smirk he handed Breckinridge a cable from Bragg. "*General Jones will not move so as to endanger the iron or salt-works…*"

Breckinridge smiled, then slumped into a nearby chair. With less than six hours sleep in the past two days, the headaches had returned and he was having trouble concentrating. He rubbed his eyes with the back of his hands. "We'll have to notify Echols, Wharton and McCausland of the change."

"I'll take care of it, Guv," said Johnston. "You go upstairs and get some rest. Mary will be expecting you." "Guv" was Johnston's nickname for Breckinridge when he wanted to lighten the mood. It had originated with the delusional ramblings of a San Francisco character who called himself Norton I, Emperor of the United States and Protector of Mexico. On December 2, 1859, *The San Francisco Herald* reported that Norton I had issued a decree dismissing Virginia Governor Henry A. Wise from office for hanging John Brown. In Wise's place, the Emperor had appointed, "John C. Breckinridge, of Kentucky, to said office of Governor of our province of Virginia."

Breckinridge raised his head, "But Stoddard, I've got to . . ."

"What you've *got* to do is get some sleep. We have a long ride ahead of us tomorrow." He hesitated, "Remember Missionary Ridge."

Breckinridge sighed, "You're right, as usual. I'll go." The memory of Chattanooga still haunted him. After his men had been routed from Missionary Ridge, Breckinridge, pushed to exhaustion by tension and lack of sleep, had sunk to the floor at Bragg's headquarters and fallen into a trance-like slumber. Misinterpreting fatigue for intoxication, Bragg, ever eager to find a scapegoat, reported to Jefferson Davis that for four days "the Kentuckian" had been unfit for duty because of drunkenness.

Removing a silver flask from his coat pocket, Johnston poured a generous shot of whiskey into a tin mug. "Scrounged some first class O-Be-Joyful from a Kentucky sergeant here at the depot. Claims it's 110-proof sour mash whiskey from a secret family recipe. Wouldn't hurt to try a little sip."

Breckinridge waved it away. "Thanks, Stoddard, but I'll have to take a pass. Got to stick with sassafras tea, at least until this is over. If the wrong person smelled alcohol on my breath..." To insure against such rumors he'd promised Mary to abstain from strong drink until the campaign was over.

Johnston nodded and screwed the cap back on. "When this is over, Guv, we'll have ourselves a good, old fashioned bluegrass jubilee."

Breckinridge rose from his chair, then slowly climbed the stairs as he thought of Mary and what might be their last night together.

In the morning, while it was still dark, Stringfellow knocked lightly on the hotel kitchen door. He could smell fresh coffee and see a light flickering under the threshold. Entering, he was greeted by Mary who had personally prepared a hearty breakfast of ham, eggs, and pancakes. Breckinridge, Stoddard Johnston and Cabell were already seated around the table.

"Please join us, Major," said Mary, as she set another place.

"Thanks, ma'am," he said, as he handed Breckinridge a new telegram.

> *Orange Court-House, May 5, 1864 - 4am*
> *General BRECKINRIDGE, Dublin*
> *I don't know whether Staunton is the threatened point, but all the forces sent west seem to have returned east, and are now coming up by Front Royal or the Valley. These are the forces I wish you to meet, or by some movement drive back before they get on my left. Communicate with Imboden and try and check any movement in the Valley as soon as possible.*
> *R.E. LEE*

Now Breckinridge knew what to do. He felt guilty about bothering Lee at such a critical time, but he wanted to know Lee's priorities. Finishing the last bit of eggs, he handed the cable to Johnston. "It's time." He called to Stringfellow, "Saddle the horses and pack five days' rations on the mules." While Stoddard and Cabell wolfed down the remainder of their breakfast, Breckinridge and Mary retired upstairs, arm in arm.

Twenty minutes later when they came back down, Breckinridge wore his new coat. With a heavy heart he walked outside and mounted Old Sorrel. Turning in the saddle he waved a final farewell to Mary. She had stayed in the doorway, afraid of breaking down if she went further. As the little group disappeared into the morning mist, Breckinridge wiped his eyes with a handkerchief then reached into his coat pocket for the ever present plug of tobacco. Beside the tobacco was an envelope. When he opened it a dozen dried rose petals tumbled out. He held the paper up to the morning light, "Darling Husband. Remember that little two-room cottage we shared in Tennessee? The pretty rose bushes beside the porch? Whenever I think of our time together at that beautiful, peaceful place, it brings joy to my heart. Someday I would like for us to return to that cottage. I love you and Cabell more than life itself. May God watch over and protect you both. Love always, Mary."

Chapter 4

Ezekiel

Moses pulled his forage cap down to the bridge of his nose to shade his eyes from the noonday sun. With his left hand he carefully spread his last clean sheet of paper on a makeshift drawing board. With a penknife he painstakingly trimmed the pencil nub so only a small tip of graphite was exposed. He didn't want to waste the precious lead since it would have to last until the quartermaster's store was open Saturday morning.

Removing a crumpled passbook from his pants pocket, he examined the balance. Two dollars and thirty-five cents. A frown crossed his boyish face. The seventh child in a family of four brothers and nine sisters, he dreaded having to ask his grandfather for more money, but if he didn't he'd run out before the end of the month. Sometimes he envied cadets from wealthy families who could buy whatever they pleased, but it was best not to dwell on such things. When he was 12, his father had guaranteed bonds for relatives who were unable to pay them off. The resulting financial loss forced Moses to drop out of school. To make ends meet he was sent to live with his grandparents where he worked as a bookkeeper in the family's dry goods store. As he approached his eighteenth birthday, his grandparents decided he should continue his education. With the blessing of a strong-willed mother, Catherine de Castro Ezekiel, who let it be known she wouldn't tolerate a son who refused to fight for his home and country, Moses enrolled at VMI. As one of the Institute's 76 state students, his tuition, room and board were paid for, but not drawing supplies.

Sitting outside barracks on a plank balanced between two packing crates, Moses studied the front of the building. Beside him sat four classmates from Section 1 of Colonel Williamson's Drawing class. Their assignment today was to sketch the rectangular, four-storied barracks, with its fortress-like crenellated towers and roof line. All that was needed to complete the image of it being a castle was a moat full of alligators, a drawbridge and a fair-haired damsel in distress. In the center of the wall facing the road was the sally port with its high, central arch. Across the road from the entrance was a life-size, bronze sculpture of George Washington. Moses held his pencil at arm's length and closed one eye, measuring the building's dimensions. If he had time he would add Washington's statue to the drawing for extra credit.

Of all classes, he liked Drawing best. It was the one course at which he excelled. Due to a lack of formal education, it had been a struggle to keep up in Geometry and French, but he was at the head of his class in Drawing. This natural artistic talent not only bolstered his confidence but gave him extra time for the other courses. As a state student he couldn't afford to be thrown in *any* subject since the Institute's policy was clear, "*Whenever any State Cadet shall be found deficient in any one of his studies for two successive years he shall ipso facto stand dismissed.*" If he was sent home a failure he'd never be able to face his family.

Moses rose from his seat and walked over to Washington's statue. It was a bronze copy of the original, marble masterpiece by Jean-Antoine Houdon. He strolled around the base, running his fingers over the cool metal, admiring the fine detail. It was an inspection he'd performed dozens of times. In the library he'd read that Houdon had based his work on actual measurements taken of Washington. Moses admired the way the sculptor portrayed the general as an ordinary human and not a god. To accomplish this, Houdon had dressed the general in a revolutionary war uniform, then placed his right hand on a civilian walking cane with his left hand resting on a fasces, the Roman symbol of civil authority.

Moses was determined to someday become an important painter or sculptor. At thirteen he had received praise for a clay bust done of his father, which started him thinking seriously about art as a career. He had tried painting with oils, but the cost of supplies was prohibitive. His drive for success was based on an overwhelming desire to impress his cousin, Leonora Levy, the love of his life. She was the most beautiful girl he'd ever seen, and the thought of pleasing her determined his every action. One reason for attending VMI was to become an officer like Leonora's favorite brother, Ezekiel "Zeke" Levy. Captain Levy was placed on a pedestal by all the members of his adoring family, especially Leonora. Maybe, when Moses had proven himself on the battlefield, the Levy family would welcome him as a son-in-law.

Returning to his seat, Moses deftly began sketching the outline of barracks, shading in the windows and free-handing the curvature of the arch. While other cadets struggled with perspective, Moses easily drew in roof lines and towers. By the time the pocket watch Professor Williamson had loaned him read 12:45, Moses had finished drawing barracks and had completed a basic sketch of Washington's statue. He swelled with pride as the other cadets gathered around and mumbled approval of his artistic talent. He would send the drawing to Leonora after Professor Williamson graded it. Forming his section into line, he marched them back inside barracks to the classroom.

When class was dismissed, Moses raced to his room on the second stoop. Bounding through the door, he almost collided with Tom Jefferson, his roommate. Jefferson was room orderly for the week and was sweeping the floor and checking the pitcher for water.

With a broad grin, Jefferson pointed to a large box on the study table. "Packet boat just came in. After lunch in the mess hall we'll have some of mom's apple pie."

Although Jefferson was a fourth class "Rat," and Moses a third classman, they were best of friends. Jefferson, a distant cousin of President Thomas Jefferson, was the eldest son of a prosperous tobacco and cotton farmer who lived at Winterham plantation near Richmond. When Jefferson's mother found out they were roommates, she asked Moses to look after her son. As a token of appreciation, she always included a treat for "My Special Friend, Mr. Ezekiel" in the food parcels which arrived monthly. She had also invited Moses to stay at Winterham, the family estate, whenever he passed by on his way home.

The contrast between the two cadets was striking. Moses, 19, was five-feet-four, with jet-black hair and dark eyes. Jefferson, 17, stood five-feet-eleven, had relaxed blue eyes and straight, light-brown hair. Because he had dropped out of school at 12, Moses found class work challenging while Jefferson, the product of privilege, had been privately tutored. Moses, the first Jewish cadet at the Institute, had to ask for a furlough to attend Passover services in Richmond, while Jefferson, although not yet baptized, easily fit in with Lexington's Christian community. In spite of these differences their temperaments were compatible and over time their friendship only deepened.

Rat—a—tat—tat—tat. The kettle drum sounded the call to lunch. Leaving the room, the two roommates trotted along the stoop, down the stairwell to the ground floor, then out the sally port to the road. As the drum finished with three longs rolls, the high-pitched voices of company first sergeants rose above the chatter. "*Com-pan-ee A! Fall in! Com-pan-ee B…*" With two final taps, the drum fell silent. "*Front!*" snapped the sergeants as squad leaders checked for absentees and gave their reports.

When all cadets were accounted for, First Captain Collier Minge barked, "*Battalion! Ten—shun! Left—face! For—ward! March!*" With two drums beating cadence, the cadets trooped along the road in front of barracks for the short trip to the mess hall.

As each company reached the steps the cadets broke ranks and made their way to their assigned seats. By the time Moses reached the 12-man table, Fourth Sergeant William M. Patton, was already standing behind his chair. At the head of the table stood a tall, erect, Confederate colonel.

When everyone was in their place, the first captain read a special order suspending classes on May 10, the first anniversary of Stonewall Jackson's death. Once the cheering died down, he announced that there would be a special flag raising ceremony in the Presbyterian Cemetery attended by the Corps. After the chaplain offered a prayer, Minge ordered, "*Seats!*"

All eyes at Moses' table were fixed on the mysterious colonel with the neatly trimmed beard, black wavy hair and weathered face. While the rest of the mess hall echoed with excited voices, no one at Moses' table made a sound.

"Hope you men don't mind my joining you," said the colonel, glancing around the table at the eager faces.

"*No, sir!*" came the reply in unison.

"He's my brother," explained Will, barely able to contain his pride. "Colonel George S. Patton, commander of the 22nd Virginia."

A murmur of appreciation arose from the cadets.

"Class of '52," explained Colonel Patton. "Twelve years ago, I was sitting right where you are now, complaining about the food—and professors. I'm just passing through on my way back to the regiment. Thought I'd stop in to see Will and get a good meal." He nodded at the nearest cadet, "And your name is…?"

One by one the cadets introduced themselves. The last to do so was 15-year-old Charlie D. Walker, who had been a cadet for less than three weeks.

"Any kin to Jim Walker, from Augusta County?" asked Patton.

"Not that I know of, sir. I'm from Richmond."

"Too bad," said Patton, with a wink. "Jim was a real rounder."

Will leaned forward, "Walker's the one who challenged Stonewall to a duel."

Moses' eyes grew large. He'd heard a lot of strange tales about Jackson's time at the Institute, but had dismissed as rumor the one claiming a cadet had actually challenged him to a duel. "Colonel, would—would you tell us what happened?"

"Soon as we're finished eating," said Patton, surveying the food with a practiced eye. "Right now, I could eat a mule."

"That may be what you're eating," quipped Will.

In front of each cadet sat a tin cup, a tin plate, a fork, knife, and half a loaf of bread. In the center of the table was a pitcher of milk and one of water. At the head of the table was a large bowl of beef stew mixed with turnips, potatoes and onions. It was the infamous "growley" that Patton remembered from his days as a cadet. At the opposite end of the table was a small bowl of sorghum molasses.

"Sure looks good," said Patton, tucking a napkin into his collar. "If this war keeps up you'll see the day when you dream of growley."

After the cadets had wolfed down their food they sat on the edge of their chairs, waiting on the colonel. Although only 30, to his attentive audience the colonel could pass for Methuselah.

With the last piece of bread the colonel wiped the remnants of stew from his plate. Grunting with satisfaction, he pushed back in his chair. "Well, it was like this. Jim Walker and I were classmates in '52, with two months left 'til graduation. It was May—yeah, May 4th. We were both in Old Jack's Natural Philosophy class when Jim was sent to the board to find the hour angle of the sun. No big deal. Just routine. Now, Jim was book smart, but had a temper that ran right over him. Anyway, he failed to solve the problem to Old Jack's satisfaction, so was sent back to his seat. Well, instead of just letting it go, Jim sat there stewing and fuming. Wasn't long before he blurted straight out that it was the major's fault. Claimed that Jackson hadn't explained how to solve the problem in the first place. He even told Old Jack that he was a poor teacher, and had to change." Patton burst out laughing, tears rolling down his face. "Can you imagine that? A cadet telling Stonewall Jackson to his face that he's a poor teacher?"

But he *was* terrible, wasn't he George?" asked Will, wanting to show he could call the colonel by his first name.

The colonel chuckled, "The worst. The nicest thing you can say is that Stonewall was—eccentric. We used to make fun of him—behind his back of course. Called him 'Square Box,' 'Tom Fool,' and 'Old Blue Lights.' Had the damndest blue eyes I ever saw. Now don't get me wrong. We respected him for his service in the Mexican war, but that didn't make him a good teacher. Nope. He'd just memorize his lectures and recite them like he was reading an obituary. If you interrupted to ask a question, he'd just mumble, then start over from the beginning. We had a little ditty, 'The VMI, / Oh, what a spot. / In winter cold, / in summer hot. / Great Lord Almighty, / what a wonder, / Major Jackson, / Hell and thunder.'"

"You mentioned a duel," said Moses.

Pouring himself another large glass of milk and stirring in a spoonful of molasses, Patton continued, "Well, next day, Jim was still riled up. Just couldn't let it go. When the major sent him to the board to solve the same problem, Jim crossed his arms and refused to go. Got all red in the face and started rattling on about poor teaching and how *he* deserved an apology. Old Jack ordered him to sit still and shut up, but Jim's jaws kept moving. Finally, the major placed him under arrest and confined him to his quarters. Next day, Jim was court-martialed for conduct disrespectful to a superior officer, found guilty and dismissed. But before he left barracks, Jim sent Old Jack a note challenging him to a duel. Stonewall was going to accept, but General Smith stepped in. You can't allow that sort of thing. Nope. So Jim was hustled out of town on the next stage—without a diploma."

"What happened to him?" asked Charlie Walker.

"Funny how life plays out," replied Patton. "When the war started, Jim wound up in Jackson's command. Things were a mite testy at first, but Jim was a natural born fighter and that's all Stonewall ever cared about. He even court-martialed his best friend here at the Institute, Colonel Gilham. Colonel Gilham's a good teacher, but didn't live up to Stonewall's expectations in the field—but that's another story. Anyway, Jim was with Stonewall at Harper's Ferry, Falling Waters and during the Valley campaign. Wasn't long before Stonewall took a real liking to this troublemaker. At Chancellorsville…"

"That's where Stonewall was shot, wasn't it George," interrupted Will.

"Yup. By his own men. Now where was I? Oh yeah—Chancellorsville. Well, when Bull Paxton, commander of the Stonewall Brigade was killed, someone asked Jackson who to put in charge. Without hesitating he replied, 'Give it to Walker. I don't know a braver officer.' So, Jim the challenger, the loudmouth, got promoted to brigadier general of the famous Stonewall Brigade. Wasn't long before his men started calling him 'Stonewall Jim.' Right now the brigade's down east with Bobby Lee getting ready for a showdown with Grant. Sure hope Jim survives."

After lunch, Moses rushed back to barracks, eager to tell his roommates about Colonel Patton. On entering his room he found Jefferson and Oliver "Big" P. Evans gorging themselves on apple pie. Lined up on the study table was a turkey, a large chunk of cheese, several small molasses cakes, apples, pickles and preserves. Jefferson held up a slice of pie. "Special gift to you from mother. Thought we'd better test it to make sure it's not Yankee contraband."

Evans sheepishly wiped apple filling from the corners of his mouth, then flashed a thumbs up. "Passes inspection." A second classman from Jackson Court House, Evans was second sergeant in Company B. Nicknamed "Big" because of his 6-foot-2 frame, Evans had a broad, full face offset by deep blue eyes and curly, blond hair. Before entering the Institute, he had served seven months as a private in the 22nd Virginia. Like Moses, he came from a humble background and was a state cadet.

In a corner of the room sat a third roommate, John "J.C." Early, a 16-year-old Rat from Lynchburg who had entered the Institute on January 14. Before enrolling, the diminutive Early had been with Lee's army in Maryland and Pennsylvania. At Gettysburg he served as a special courier but was sent home by his uncle, Lt. General Jubal Early, to look after his father who had been seriously wounded in the Wheatfield on July 2.

Helping himself to a second piece of pie, Jefferson nodded toward Early. "J.C.'s still feeling poorly. I offered him some dessert, but he turned it down."

At Gettysburg, Early suffered from dysentery. Still feeling the debilitating effects he had just returned from a fourteen-day medical furlough. In a weak voice he said, "My corporal, Mr. Ridley, wants me to come to his room after lunch. He found out I haven't been bucked and said, 'Every Rat in my squad's gets bucked, and you're no exception.' "

"That so?" piped up Evans. Clearing the food from the study table he patted Early on the back. "Don't worry, J.C., we'll take care of it right now." While Big didn't think it necessary to buck Early since he'd been at Gettysburg, he understood the importance of tradition and knew it would be easier on him if bucked by friends. Motioning to Moses, Evans called out in a low, officious voice, "Mr. Ezekiel, would you help me buck this mean, little Rat?"

"Aye, aye, sir," replied Moses.

"Sit here, Mr. Rat," said Evans, pointing to the study table. "Hold out your hands." Taking a bed strap, he gently wrapped Early's wrists together. "Now draw up your knees and place your arms over them." When this was done, Evans slid a ramrod under the Fourth Classman's knees to lock his arms in place, then rolled him on his side. "Have you a bayonet scabbard, Mr. Ezekiel?"

"I have."

Evans stepped back, "Then do your duty."

Moses grinned, "What should we spell, Sergeant? Name, county, state, class, and Virginia Military Institute?"

"His middle initial's C," said Evans. "That must stand for C-o-n-s-t-a-n-t-i-n-o-p-l-e. We'll use that."

With the scabbard, Moses lightly rapped Early on the rear, one tap for each letter. When he'd finished, he stood back and saluted. "Bucking completed, sir. Rat has been taught a lesson."

Untying Early, Evans said, "Now, tell your corporal you've been bucked. If he has any questions, tell him to come see me."

"Now for more serious matters," said Moses as he carved out a large slice of pie and wolfed it down. After math class this afternoon, Company C was scheduled to go to the firing range for an introduction to the new Austrian rifled musket. The new muskets had been delivered in April to replace the old model, smoothbore Springfields the Corps had been using for the past twelve years. Unfortunately, there were only 200 rifles for 275 cadets. A shooting competition had been scheduled for the following weekend to decide who would get one. For the past several days Moses had been busy in the library reading about the Austrian musket hoping it would improve his chances. If he could win a new rifle it might help him gain promotion to sergeant in July when next year's rankings were announced.

It was 4:15 by the time the 57 cadets from C Company were lined up along the open field behind barracks. A wooden silhouette of a soldier was placed at 50 yards, one at 100 yards, and a final one across Woods Creek at 250 yards.

Each cadet was handed a cartridge box with nine rounds and a dozen caps. The lead instructor was Captain Benjamin "Duck" Colonna. Colonna had used the rifle in Richmond three years ago to help train recruits. Assisting him were Andy Pizzini, first sergeant of Company B, and John Stuart, first sergeant of Company C. Pizzini had been armed with an Austrian musket at First Manassas, and Stuart had drilled with it during his nine months with the 52nd Virginia.

"Attention, men," said Colonna, raising a musket. The cadets liked calling each other "men." "This is the Lorenz rifle. It weighs eight pounds and has a fixed rear sight. It fires a .58 caliber Minie ball and in the right hands is accurate up to 600 paces." He then held up the old cadet smoothbore. "This is our regular musket. As you know, it fires a round ball which is accurate at 50 yards or less."

Colonna held up a cartridge. "The Lorenz is loaded the same way as the old Springfield—with one important difference." He surveyed the expectant faces. "Pour the powder down the barrel as usual, then ram the bullet home, but do *not*—I repeat—do *not* cram the paper down on top of the Minie ball. The stiff paper will cause a misfire."

While Pizzini climbed a nearby tree, Colonna picked up a musket. "Pay close attention to what I'm about to tell you. To hit a target at 50 to 250 yards, you need to understand how gravity works."

When Pizzini reached 16 feet, he sat on a limb and faced Colonna who raised his hand. "The muzzle velocity of a bullet from this rifle is 325 yards per second." He then dropped his hand to signal Pizzini to release the lead slug. Colonna counted, "One-Mississippi." At the end of the count the bullet struck the ground with a thud. "That's how far a bullet will fall in one second when the rifle is fired horizontally." Colonna tapped the rear sight. "To counter gravity, this rifle has been sighted for 250 yards. If you aim at a man's belt buckle who's standing 250 yards away you'll hit him squarely in the gut. Does anyone know what happens if you aim at the belt buckle of someone 50 yards away?" Impatiently patting the gun's stock he waited for an answer. "Anyone?"

Moses raised his hand. "It'll hit the target 18 inches above the belt buckle, probably on top of his head."

Colonna nodded, "Thank you Mr. Ezekiel. And at 100 yards?"

There was silence. Colonna pointed to Moses.

"It'll go 33 inches higher than the belt buckle, and miss the target completely." Moses preferred using the word "target" rather than "man." It bothered him to think of actually killing a person.

"And at 150 yards?"

"Forty-three inches higher," said Moses, who had obviously done his homework.

"Excellent, Mr. Ezekiel," said Colonna. "That's why you'll hear officers cautioning their men to aim low. To hit a man's head at 100 yards, you aim for the knees. If he's 150 paces away, you aim for the feet." Handing Moses the demonstration musket, he said, "It looks like Mr. Ezekiel just won a new rifle."

Chapter 5

Strother

Friday, May 6
Winchester, Virginia

Shivering in the cool morning air, Colonel David Hunter Strother bent over a porcelain wash basin and splashed cold water on his face and hair. The makeshift bath was next to a large, stone grist mill on Abram's Creek. The mill, used by Strother for sleeping quarters and eating facility, was built in 1833 by David Hollingsworth and was still being used for grinding corn and wheat when not overrun by invading armies. Fifty feet away was a two-story, blue-gray limestone house known locally as Abram's Delight. It was the finest residence in Winchester—a fact which had not escaped the notice of the Federal commander, Major General Franz Sigel. Although a member of General Sigel's staff, Strother hadn't been invited to stay or mess with the other staff officers in the large, imposing mansion. This slight to Strother's touchy ego caused him to note in his diary, "General Sigel surrounds himself with a set of low-life scouts, spies, detectives, and speculators. He keeps these fellows next to him while his loyal staff officers are forced to remain outside...." This was not a flattering observation from someone selected by the commanding general to write a glowing chronicle of the campaign for the Secretary of War.

After patting his face dry, Strother ran a fine-toothed comb through the tangled, twin peaks of beard jutting below his chin. The handlebar mustache and oversized beard were carefully fashioned trademarks meticulously cultivated to help appreciative readers of *Harper's New Monthly Magazine* recognize the famous author. Strother had also written two popular travel books, *The Blackwater Chronicle* and *Virginia Illustrated*. Small of stature with piercing blue eyes, a stern face and small voice, he needed all the trademarks he could muster to stand out in an army full of towering egos and creative facial hair.

Before the war, Strother, a native Virginian from Martinsburg, had been the highest paid contributor to *Harper's*, averaging two lead articles a year. A master illustrator, he populated his narratives with woodcuts of fictional characters and rural landscapes. At a time when most people never travelled more than twenty miles from home in a lifetime, his travelogues of rural life in the Shenandoah Valley were a huge success. Publishing under the pen name, Porte Crayon, Strother filled his sketches with folksy, back-woods characters with names such as Little Mouse, Jim Bug, Billy Devil, Squire Broadacre and Mrs. Trollope.

A keen observer of the human condition, Strother employed satirical wit to skewer southern fire-eaters and northern abolitionists who constantly stirred the sectional pot with their prejudiced, holier-than-thou rantings.

"Is this a—?" he muttered as he held the comb up to the light. Clinging to the tines was the small body of a blood-sucking louse. "Damn," he grumbled, snatching the tiny bug and cracking its head between thumbnail and forefinger. Jerking off his cotton nightshirt, he shook it over a newspaper. Out tumbled four more adult lice which quickly scrambled for cover. Pouring more water over his head and face, he again worked the comb through the matted hair. Examining the tines closely, he sighed with relief. There were no nits. Maybe he'd caught the infestation in time.

He ran his hand behind his neck to check for telltale lumps. There they were, little itchy spots just below his right ear. Peering into a small mirror he surveyed the area. He could see welts rising on the sun-burned skin. In disgust he slammed the nightshirt on the ground. Now he'd have to soak his whole body in a tub of scalding water and scrub down with lye soap. He'd also have to boil the cotton clothes in hot, soapy water and smoke the wool ones. All this because he hadn't been offered a cot at Abram's Delight. Frowning, he glanced up at headquarters. Where was Major Smyth, the chief medical officer? He hadn't seen the Major in a couple of days and now needed mercuric oxide powder for his hair and sulphur with lard to stop the itching. If left unchecked, these little vermin could cause all sorts of diseases. In an army where more men died from illness than battle wounds, the 48-year-old Strother had no intention of wasting away from typhus, the bloody flux or some other camp malady. His half-hearted attempt at studying medicine thirty years ago had at least taught him how to recognize and treat an invasion of these little greybacks.

No wonder that lumpy sofa in the mill had been vacant. The lice had probably hopped off some Johnny Reb bugging out ahead of Federal cavalry. But, who knows? Winchester had changed hands so many times in the last two years they could've come from anyone.

Maybe the lice had been put there by locals to spite the Yanks. Yesterday, three houses on Main Street were torched by drunken soldiers. Was it revenge? During General Nathaniel Banks' retreat two years ago several civilians had taken potshots at soldiers passing through town—some shooters were rumored to have been women—still, that didn't justify burning private homes or stealing private property.

Yesterday afternoon, when he called on his old friend, Nan Burns, to barter two cans of real coffee, eight pounds of sugar and a sack of dried beans for some of her fried chickens, country ham and apple pies, he'd been surprised at her reaction. "I guess it's better to trade vittles then have 'em stolen by your Yankee white trash." Calming down she informed him that her last hog had been taken by scavenging troops. "You know, don't you," she said, the disgust making her eyes twitch, "that Miller's storeroom was burned to the ground."

When he offered to help find the missing hog, she just glared. "Too late now. It's done been butchered and et. Probably by some of your high and mighty officers." She glared at Strother, "This war ain't nothin' but a sorry excuse for your Yankee friends to run honest people off'n their land and steal what ain't theirs." She mentioned that several Rebel women in Winchester, especially his mother's distinguished relatives, the Hunters, Cookes and Dandridges, considered him a turncoat and Judas. Many held him personally responsible for the worst Yankee outrages. On parting, she cautioned him against trying to contact old acquaintances, or wandering too far from camp. Several death threats had been made should he return and be captured.

Strother really didn't blame them—well, not much. As the war dragged on there'd been a noticeable shift in sentiment by Federal soldiers in dealing with citizens. As days turned into months, and months into years, the treatment had become more callous. Last year, when General Milroy was in control of Winchester, he'd written his wife, *My will is absolute law— none dare contradict or dispute my slightest word or wish—I confess I feel a strong disposition to play the tyrant among these traitors.* When challenged by several local women on his arbitrary rules and curfews, he replied, *Hell is not full enough, there must be more secessionist women from Winchester to fill it up.*

In the spring, Milroy, a radical abolitionist, had instituted a draconian policy of forcibly evicting "disloyal" Winchester families from their homes, stealing their houses and contents, and warning that if they dared return they would be hanged as spies. One such unfortunate was Mrs. Lloyd Logan who had the bad luck of owning an elegant home coveted by Mary Milroy, the General's overbearing wife. Claiming that Mrs. Logan, who was an invalid, dealt in contraband, Milroy had her, along with her two young daughters, forcibly evicted. They weren't even allowed to take a change of clothes or morsel of food. While Mary Milroy waited impatiently in her carriage to take possession of *her* new house, Mrs. Logan and family were hustled aboard a crude cart, driven six miles outside town and unceremoniously dumped on the side of the road.

Strother had tried to distance himself from such brutality but his close association with Federal officers had branded him a Benedict Arnold. His efforts at being fair-minded had been colored by the rough treatment accorded his pro-Union father, John Strother, after his arrest for treason against Virginia in 1861. Colonel Angus McDonald, a former close family friend, and Confederate provost, had jailed the 70-year-old John Strother for five days before releasing him. When he died shortly after from pneumonia, Strother blamed McDonald. To add insult to injury, two years ago when Stonewall's men took over the family's hotel at Berkeley Springs, they trashed the building, stole and smashed tableware and dishes, and burned Strother's personal papers. They even stabled horses inside Strother's cottage, wrecking the furniture and causing it to stink like a barn.

When Strother called on Aunt Sarah Strange to inquire about hiring a cook, she warned him away. No one in Winchester wanted to be seen fraternizing with "Damn Yankees" since Confederate troops would soon be back.

The only help Strother could find was Tom, a raw-boned 16-year-old, cornfield mulatto he had hired in Martinsburg and who agreed to stay on as body servant as long as he was paid in Yankee gold. Untutored in such basic skills as cooking, washing clothes and cleaning, Tom's salvation lay in his natural talent for foraging—or, more precisely—stealing. He was an expert at liberating chickens, milk, butter, eggs and fence rails from their owners. Although Strother condemned petty larceny in principle he knew he'd have to rely on Tom's special talents as the army moved deeper into the Valley.

"Boss, I knows where thar's an ant hill," volunteered Tom. "I kin kick it up and put yer clothes on top. Dem louses'll be gone in no time. Ants love to eat dem fat little bugs and they small eggs."

Strother smiled indulgently. Perhaps he'd been a little too hasty in failing to appreciate the true value of Tom's homespun education. "Just boil the cotton and use the ants on the wool," he cautioned. "Be sure to put salt in the water."

After a hot soak in a horse trough, a hard scrub with lye soap, a cup of sherry and two mugs of strong coffee, Strother felt better. As was the case with most army issue, too much ash had been mixed in with the lard, making the lye soap much too caustic. But, the temporary burning sensation was a small price to pay for good health. Two years ago when he was in Winchester with Banks he had suffered a near fatal case of dysentery. He didn't want a repeat performance.

After drying off, Strother checked his pocket watch. 9:30. Might as well meander up to headquarters for the daily staff briefing. Putting on his last set of clean clothes, he shook out his boots and brushed his hair. Glancing toward Abrams Delight he noticed a formation of cavalry beside the stone house. On the steps leading to the first floor were three men engaged in an animated conversation. One was General Sigel, his left hand jabbing the early morning air. Another was Major General Julius Stahel, chief of cavalry, and the third, a stout, cavalry officer.

Strother's eyes lit up in anticipation. With all those horses, he might be able to scrounge a mount. Before leaving Martinsburg, Sigel had taken away his black colt and given it to one of his favorite civilian scouts. What particularly galled Strother was that 45 days ago he had been chief of cavalry under General Kelley, and while only a paper assignment it had at least provided a fine mount. Now, even though a colonel in the 3rd West Virginia Cavalry, and a member of Sigel's personal staff, he had no means of transportation. How would it look to other officers if he had to begin the campaign perched atop a commissary wagon like some low-level, file clerk?

When Strother first met Sigel, he held high hopes the general was honest, patriotic and a leader of men. Now he was convinced the Prussian Kriegmeister was merely a military pedagogue given to technical shams and trifles. Physically unimpressive and incapable of speaking plain English, Sigel failed miserably in measuring up to Strother's idea of what a general should look and act like. At five-feet-seven, 140 pounds, with a square jaw, angular cheek bones, and small face fixed in a permanent scowl, Sigel reminded Strother of nothing so much as an unhappy shoe clerk. In addition, since the general had chosen to surround himself with lowlife, it was clear he was wanting in any practical capacity. Two of Sigel's regiments, the 1st New York Cavalry and the 28th Ohio Infantry, were composed entirely of Germans who prattled on in their native language. To make matters worse, whenever he became excited—which was often—Sigel lost the ability to speak properly and issued orders in pidgin English.

As Strother neared headquarters, an unpleasant odor stung his nose. It was the familiar *Bouquet de Rottenhoss* mixed with swamp gas that pervaded old battlegrounds. The miasma came from carcasses of dead animals left in the open to rot. On the march down from Martinsburg the troops had passed many broken, shallow graves of soldiers killed in previous battles. From the road they could see exposed arms and leg bones, and remnants of shoes filled with decomposed feet. One particularly gruesome site contained a grinning, sun bleached skull with clumps of hair still attached to the crushed head. There was no way of telling if the body was Union or Rebel without digging for belt buckles or buttons, and no one had the stomach to find out. Since Strother was here two years ago with General Banks the whole region had become desolate. Fields were left unplanted, farms were deserted and fences torn down. Instead of making the troops angry, these broken graves with grinning skulls only disheartened them since it foreshadowed their own fate.

Immediately to the left of headquarters at Abram's Delight was a small, log cabin used for tool storage. Next to it stood a cipher tent which belonged to the telegraph service. Two guards manned the entrance of the tent to keep out the idly curious and prevent spies from reading dispatches. Standing in front of the tent was Major James Lyon, one of the few staff officer's Strother liked. The bright, young major, who had been with Sigel for two years, was leaning against a battery-wagon and talking with a middle-aged, heavy-set man dressed in civilian clothes.

Strother strolled over. Although running cable slowed the army's movement, he understood the importance of good communications with Washington. The downside was that it allowed General Henry Halleck and Secretary of War Stanton to meddle in operations. To prevent army commanders from interfering with his telegraph service, Stanton had set the system up as a civilian bureau reporting directly to him.

Seeing telegraph equipment and spools of wire reminded Strother of the old days when he was an art student of Samuel Morse's, the developer of the Morse code. In 1836, Morse, president of the National Academy of Design, and the most accomplished portrait painter in the US, had attempted to teach Strother the art of painting portraits. Along with three other pupils, the 20-year-old Strother had lived and studied with Morse. Never able to master the use of oils, he did learn how to sketch images in ink and crayon, a talent he used to advantage in illustrating his articles published in *Harper's*. Once when Strother fell behind in a quarterly payment of twenty-five dollars, Morse wheedled ten dollars for food and drink. Sharing his simple meal with his pupil, Morse told Strother, *"This is my first meal in twenty-four hours. Strother, don't ever become an artist. It means beggary if you do. Your whole life will depend on people who know nothing of your art and care nothing about you. A house dog lives better. The worst part is that the very sensitiveness that stimulates your work as an artist, keeps you alive to your suffering."* Strother was pleased when Morse later gained financial independence with royalties from his code.

Approaching Major Lyon, Strother lightly tapped the wheel of the battery wagon, "Major, any chance of my getting a hors…?"

"It's started," blurted Lyon, his face flushed. "Grant's in the middle of it now. Lee's attacking on all sides."

Strother let out a low whistle. "Where?"

"In the Wilderness. Near the old Chancellorsville battleground."

"How's Grant doing?"

"Don't know. There's no telegraph on the battlefield. A few reports have come in, but they're sketchy." Lyon forced a smile, "So far, Grant seems to be holding his own—maybe even winning."

"How about us? Is Sigel ready to join in?" asked Strother. He knew Grant's plan called for a coordinated push on all fronts once the main attack began. He nodded towards the nearby cavalry detachment. "Are they headed south?"

"Not yet," replied Lyon. "All hell's broken loose at the War Department. Some bushwhacker named McNeill attacked the B&O Railroad in Piedmont, West Virginia. Wrecked and burned everything. The President of the railroad complained to Stanton, and…" He pointed toward the three men standing on the porch, "That's Colonel Higgins with the General. He's going after McNeill with 500 cavalry."

Strother arched an eyebrow. Now wasn't the time to be sending men into the mountains after guerrillas. They should be concentrating forces and advancing on Staunton. Recent reconnaissance patrols at Strasburg and Front Royal met no serious resistance, but that wouldn't last long. He checked his watch. "When's the staff meeting?"

"Been called off," replied Lyon. "Too much going on." He held out a telegram, "This just in from General Weber at Harper's Ferry. Halleck's transferring all troops guarding the railroad to General Kelley, but Weber's refusing to hand over his command until Sigel gives him a direct order to do so."

Strother shook his head. The campaign was just beginning and Washington was already interfering by shifting men away from Sigel's army to General Kelley. As it was, Sigel had less than 13,000 effectives, far fewer than Banks, Fremont and Shields had two years ago when they were routed by Stonewall Jackson. The newspapers were starting to call the Shenandoah the Union's "Valley of Humiliation." Now the telegraph service was proving more of a hindrance than help. Four days ago when Mosby's raiders captured eight wagons from Sigel's private baggage train, Washington ordered that all large wagon trains must have an escort of at least 400 cavalry.

"What about battalion drills?"

"They're still on," replied Lyon. "As long as we're waiting for instructions from Washington, the general wants to stick with the training schedule. He says it keeps the men occupied and out of trouble."

Strother had heard about yesterday's fiasco on the drill field. "Let me know when you find an extra horse," he told Lyon. Still scratching lice bites, he turned and headed back to the grist mill.

While Strother prepared to feast on the food supplied by Nan Burns, Tom stuck his head in the door, "Boss, they's two mens headin' dis way."

Strother's first instinct was to hide the baskets. Wouldn't do to have to share. At headquarters the staff had been reduced to eating hardtack, beans and pickled beef and there were many hungry officers prowling around camp looking for something better. Peering out the door, he was relieved to see that one of the men was Major Lyon on a small, sorrel pony. Beside him, riding a black stallion was an older officer with receding hair and neatly trimmed beard.

Strother stepped outside, closing the door behind him. "Lyon, Any chance…?"

Lyon grinned, dismounted and handed Strother the reins to the pony. "Consider it a loan from Captain Prendergast. He's down with the flux and won't be needing it anytime soon." Lyon stepped aside, "This is Colonel William Lincoln from the 34th Mass."

Lincoln dismounted and grasped Strother's hand. "Pleased to meet you, Colonel. I'm one of your biggest fans. I've read every one of your articles in *Harper's Monthly*. When Major Lyon told me Porte Crayon was in camp, I asked for an introduction."

Elated at finally having a horse, Strother now felt generous. He was pleased that Lt. Colonel Lincoln was close to his own age, not one of the uneducated young officers who hadn't read any of his articles. Leading both men inside the mill he pointed to two baskets, "Compliments of a loyal Union supporter." He directed Tom to place a couple of straight backed chairs and a spare nail keg beside a mill wheel.

"Got to get back to the telegraph tent," sighed Lyon, wistfully eyeing the fried chicken and apple pie. "West Virginia's governor Boreman is demanding more troops to protect Weston. That damned McNeill's got the governor so spooked he's seeing bushwhackers in his sleep. We're going to send the 4th West Virginia along with a gun or two from Maulsby's battery." He paused at the door, his eyes fixed on the food. "If there's anything left, could you save me a leg and a slice of pie?"

"Better take it with you," said Strother, wrapping two chicken legs, a large serving of pie and a generous wedge of cheese in a piece of cloth. It was the least he could do for someone who had found him a horse.

With time to spare while Sigel fiddled with the drill schedule, Lt. Colonel Lincoln settled into a chair. "Awfully kind of you to share your bounty. Things are tough in camp. All the chairs and tables have been taken away, so we sit on the ground balancing plates of beans and hardtack on our knees, trying not to think too much about what we're eating. Don't know how much more rancid beef my system can stand." As Tom dished out fresh bread, cheese and fried chicken, Lincoln continued, "The officers are limited to one small valise and have to carry their own blankets. We don't have cots so we sleep on the ground. At least I've found a dry space in a tent with the surgeon and his two assistants."

Strother nodded sympathetically while he helped himself to a slice of pie. Now he knew where to find a doctor for his lice medication.

Lincoln scowled, "Don't know why General Sigel's confiscated all our creature comforts. The only thing we have a lot of is red tape." He waved a drumstick in the air. "Day before yesterday one of the men collapsed from heat stroke while on picket duty. In the old days the surgeon would've simply sent an ambulance to pick him up. Not now. We had to fill out a form asking headquarters for *permission* to bring him in. Poor chap. It took two hours before the correct forms were found and filled in. He's lucky to be alive."

Strother had complained to General Stahel about the red tape, but there was little he could do. Out of habit from his days in the Baden army, Sigel had placed the whole army under the thumb of pencil-pushers.

Strother walked over to where Tom was smashing coffee beans on the mill wheel. It had been a real challenge teaching his young helper how to make coffee that didn't taste like burnt corn. Rubbing the coarse grounds between thumb and forefinger, he sniffed the latest attempt. Not gourmet, but it would do. Returning to his guest, he asked, "Lincoln. You're not by chance—?"

Lincoln chuckled, "Related to Honest Abe? Afraid not. Some of my kin claim a distant connection through a common ancestor in 17th Century England, but that's just wishful thinking."

As they talked, Strother learned that Lt. Colonel Lincoln was 52, had been born in Worcester, was the son of a former governor of Massachusetts and a graduate of Bowdoin College. At an early age he had been attracted to the military life by the uniforms and patriotic speeches. At 22 he was elected captain of the Worcester Light Infantry. Trained in law, Lincoln caught "western fever" at 26 and moved to Alton, Illinois where he became the town's attorney. In 1837, he witnessed what many considered the real beginning of the war. The Reverend Elijah Lovejoy, a Presbyterian minister and newspaper editor, rashly published his abolitionist views in the *Alton Observer.* For this he had been shot and killed by a pro-slavery mob, making him the radicals' first martyr. Ten year later Lincoln returned to Worcester where he combined law with farming. In May 1862, he was appointed Lt. Colonel of the newly formed 34th Mass Infantry Regiment and had been with them ever since.

"Tell me a little about your Colonel," said Strother, as he opened a box of cigars and offered one to his new acquaintance.

"Colonel Wells? He's a good Bay Stater. A graduate of Williams, he studied law at Harvard. When the war broke out he was judge of Boston's Police Court. Now only 38, the Colonel's very mature and intelligent." Lincoln thought for a moment while he devoured another piece of fried chicken. "He was a Free-Soiler in '52, but isn't too keen on the President's Emancipation Proclamation. Says the furor over slavery only muddies the water, that he's fighting to preserve the Union, nothing else." Licking the tips of his fingers, Lincoln reached for a piece of pie. "He's seen his share of combat. Was with the 1st Mass at Bull Run, Yorktown and during the peninsular campaign." With a devilish gleam in his eyes, Lincoln added, "I'm afraid you won't be seeing much of Colonel Wells for the next couple of days."

Strother sensed a good story behind that comment. Eager for all the details, he had Tom carry two chairs outside and place them by the mill pond in the shade of a willow tree. Since morning, the weather had turned a balmy 70 degrees with a gentle breeze which kept the flies and camp smells at bay. While Tom poured two mugs of coffee laced with brandy, Strother settled back in his chair, "Anything to do with yesterday's drills?"

Lincoln laughed, almost spilling his drink. "Bad news travels fast. Tell me Colonel, how long have you been with General Sigel?"

Strother leaned forward, "Only two months. To tell the truth, he only put me on his staff to get his name in print. Thinks I'll write a glowing article for *Harper's* that makes him look good to Stanton. Fancies himself an Übermensch whose every word has to be recorded for posterity." Glancing around to make certain there were no unfriendly ears, he continued, "He was only given command to secure the Dutch vote in November." Strother had heard that in spite of Halleck's warnings, President Lincoln had insisted that Sigel be placed in charge of the Department of West Virginia. With general elections only six months away, and 150,000 Germans in uniform, the administration was willing to sacrifice the new state for the "greater good." "It's amazing how Dutchmen treat him like the second coming. There's even a song—"

Lt. Colonel Lincoln wagged his head from side to side, "*Ja. 'Ish Goin' To Fight Mit Sigel.'* It's a big hit in camp. The men strut around in fake lederhosen balancing plates of fake sauerkraut on their heads while singing it. Have you ever listened to the words?"

"On and off," replied Strother. With so many Germans at headquarters, it was politically risky to make fun of Dutchmen.

"Vell, it goes like dis, *'Dem Deutshen mens mit Sigel's band, At fighting have no rival; Un ven Cheff Davis' mens we meet, Ve Schlauch em like de tuyvil.'* "

Strother burst out laughing, "You sound just like one of them." Turning serious, he asked, "Tell me, what's Colonel Wells' opinion of this army?"

"Unfortunately, not good. He says there're *way* too many Germans. Half the time he doesn't understand a thing they're saying."

It amused Strother that Germans were called "Dutchmen." It was a popular corruption of "*Deutsch mann.*" "How's he rate the regiments?" Strother was concerned that the language barrier would cause major problems on the battlefield.

Lincoln took a long drag on his cigar. "I guess you could say he considers the 54th Pennsylvania the best of the lot. The rest…?" He shook his head.

Strother nodded agreement. "I can personally vouch for Colonel Campbell of the 54th. He's been fighting guerrillas in these mountains ever since Stonewall's day." Strother sat back, "I heard that yesterday's drills were a trifle…"

"Confusing?" snorted Lincoln. "They were a farce. Fancy foreign soldiers playing at war. Where did they learn such stupid maneuvers?" Without waiting for a reply, he continued, "That sort of stuff might've worked in Germany, but not here, not with Americans. Someone said Sigel graduated from a military school in Germany. Is that true?"

"The Karlsruhe Military Academy in Baden. It's an excellent school. In '48 he fought as a Baden revolutionary which has made him extremely popular with German immigrants in Missouri."

"I heard he didn't do so well three years ago against General Lyon in Missouri."

"He was routed at Wilson's Creek. Some say he abandoned his troops and beat them back to Springfield."

"What about General Stahel?"

"Not a bad sort, actually. Very polite, very mannerly. Born in Hungary, possibly to nobility. Has a solid military background in the Austrian army. Got a commission here when recruiting foreigners was all the rage." Strother was still irritated at Stahel for replacing him as chief of cavalry, even though the Hungarian was clearly more qualified. When Stahel first arrived in Martinsburg he had tried to make friends by visiting Strother in his tent and discussing American literature and Hungarian wine. "I'd say he's honorable enough, not a political hack like…" Strother jabbed his thumb in the direction of headquarters. "But enough about those two. You still haven't told me what happened yesterday."

Using sticks for infantry, rocks for artillery and chicken bones for cavalry, Lincoln arranged them on the ground. "First Sigel lined us up in columns with artillery to the rear. The cavalry were placed on the flanks. Then he rode over with his top officers to inform Colonel Wells that the 34th was to act as skirmishers.

When the drill started, our bugler sounded "Forward" and *tromp, tromp, tromp* off we went. Behind us, the artillery boomed while officers pointed this way and that, shouting orders in German—which no one understood." Picking up a rock Lincoln dropped it on the stick representing the 34th regiment. "Good thing for us the cannon weren't shotted or we'd been blown to bits." He chuckled, "It was quite a sight. The cavalry galloping all over the place, the infantry marching and countermarching. Unfortunately, in all the confusion no one noticed that we had disappeared over the horizon. On we marched, *tromp, tromp, tromp*, crawling over fences, sloshing through swamps, stumbling down ravines, moving past the outer picket line. Occasionally Colonel Wells dropped off a bugler to relay orders, but none came."

"Go on," said Strother, his shoulders shaking with laughter.

"Well, sir, after attacking briars, mosquitoes and bushes we ran out of buglers, so Colonel Wells finally ordered a halt. We stacked arms and waited. Nothing. Four hours later, a courier rode up, calling us back. It was well after dark before we returned to camp."

Strother poured another shot of brandy into their coffee mugs.

Lincoln continued, "This morning Colonel Wells put his name on the sick list. He told me 'Take your regiment, Colonel, and do with it what you please. I've lost all interest in it, and the service.' " Lincoln flicked the ash off the end of his cigar. "When I asked him when I should form the regiment for drill, he answered, 'I don't give a damn. Do with it what you please. I won't serve under such damn fools, and *you're* a fool if *you* do.' " Lincoln sighed, "Can't blame the colonel. Two days ago Sigel ordered him to perform a complicated maneuver ending with 'right face.' When the colonel pointed out that the last command should be 'left face' the General exploded. 'I don't vant no suggestions from regimentals!' says he. 'All I vant is fer dem to listen keerfully to der orders and repeat dem to der troops *exactly* as dey're received.' "

"I'm afraid we're headed for trouble," said Strother. Although Sigel had a reputation for personal bravery, and showed occasional flashes of intelligence, his inflexibility and failure to adjust to the American military culture was costing him the loyalty, respect and support of his non-German officers.

After a few moments silence, Lincoln said, "I was fascinated by the articles you wrote on your travels in the Shenandoah Valley. It never occurred to me that one day I'd be here with a gun and sword." He gazed at the storm clouds on Massanutten Mountain, "It's all rather biblical."

"How so?" asked Strother, who because of his mother's rigid Presbyterianism and father's dogmatic Episcopalianism, had lost all interest in organized religion.

"The 23rd Psalm. 'Yea though I walk through the valley of the shadow of death …' When I saw the desolation on the march down I had the eerie feeling I was stepping on someone's grave." He pointed towards the mountain, "That ridge looks like it's frowning at us, brooding, warning us not to trespass." He brushed an ash from the sleeve of his coat, "But enough of that. Tell me how you wound up in Yankee blue?"

Strother shifted uncomfortably in his chair. It was a question he'd been asked many times. "Really quite simple. In Martinsburg, where I grew up, most people were—still are—strongly pro-Union. When the state voted on secession, Berkeley County went against it six to one. The Blue Ridge separates us from the tobacco and cotton planters down east. We identify with Washington and Baltimore, not Richmond. My father fought for the Union in 1812. When the President called for troops to put down the rebellion, he rushed to Washington to volunteer. He even spoke with President Lincoln who commended him for his patriotism. Of course, at 70 he was too old, but like father, like son. His love of the Union helped convince me to go with the stars and stripes."

Strother didn't mention that when he was 23 he'd been denied an appointment to West Point because his father was a prominent Whig. When he visited the Secretary of War to plead his case, he quickly learned that cadetships were only granted to those with correct political connections. At the end of the interview, when it became obvious he wasn't going to get an appointment, he declared, "I now understand, sir, that I'm denied the privilege of serving my country in arms because my father is not a subservient partisan of the Democrats. I am prouder of this disability than I should ever have been of your appointment. *Good day, sir!*"

"I was especially intrigued by your articles on John Brown's raid at Harper's Ferry. Your pen and ink sketches were very informative."

"I was lucky," replied Strother. "When that greasy old thief attacked the arsenal, I was in Martinsburg only twenty miles away. I caught the first train to Harper's Ferry and was the only reporter there. Unfortunately, the marines had already stormed the engine house by the time I arrived. I talked with Brown while he lay wounded and made some sketches of him and his sons. I also met J.E.B. Stuart and Robert E. Lee who was in charge of the marines." It had been the scoop of a lifetime and made Strother even more popular with *Harper's* readers.

"I take it you don't consider Brown a martyr," chided Lincoln, remembering how Strother had labeled Brown and his men as "outlaws" in his articles.

Strother's eyes flashed, "Osawatomie Brown was a delusional, cold-blooded killer. That old man was hell-bent on starting a servile insurrection to drown Virginia in a sea of blood. In Kansas he dragged five citizens from their homes and hacked them to death with broadswords in front of their families." Strother spat on the ground, "Your Secret Six in Massachusetts played thunder sending that madman those military pikes and .52 caliber 'Beecher's Bibles.' If it hadn't been for Brown—and his radical backers—this war might never have happened. What was it that Massachusetts abolitionist, Stearns, wrote?"

Lincoln sat back, surprised at the depth of Strother's hostility.

"Why sir, he had the impudence to write, 'I consider it the proudest act of my life that I gave good old John Brown every pike and rifle he carried to Harper's Ferry.' " Strother paused, "He and the rest of that gang of six should've been strung up and had their heads stuck on their own pikes. What they did was treason and murder, plain and simple." Strother's eyes narrowed, "Colonel, I hope *you're* not a radical."

Lincoln straightened and blushed, "Not at all, sir. But I—I am against slavery. How can we claim to be a righteous and God fearing Country when we're weighed down by the curse of slavery? England, Ireland, Scotland and France, all banned—"

"And, they did it without killing each other," snapped Strother.

"True," said Lincoln. "Actually, slavery wasn't much of an issue in Massachusetts until Washington tried to turn us into slave catchers." He had personally witnessed a riot in Boston in 1854 when an angry mob stormed the courthouse to rescue a fugitive slave.

Strother waved his hand at a nearby encampment. "You think those Dutchmen give a continental damn about the colored man? That they felt so sorry for the poor slaves that they came all the way to Virginia to fight and die for them?"

"But here they are," said Lincoln.

Strother sneered, "That's because of the draft, or they're bored at home and want the bounty and three meals a day. Most can't afford the $300 commutation fee or don't have enough money for a substitute. 'It's a rich man's war and a poor man's fight.' " Strother's good friend, William Luce, who was captured at Berryville and spent five months as a POW in Salisbury, North Carolina, told him that Union privates kept coming up and asking, "What's this war all about?"

Grinding the stub of his cigar into the ground, Strother continued, "The pettifoggers on both sides started this butchery. Slavery's just a catch word to fool the simple and stupid, and God knows there're enough of them around." During John Brown's trial Strother had been approached by Edmund Ruffin, James Mason and Virginia's Governor, Henry A. Wise, who wanted him to join their scheme to seize the Federal arsenal at Harper's Ferry in anticipation of secession.

"But could it have been avoided?" asked Lincoln.

"Certainly," replied Strother. "It was the President's call for troops that forced Virginia and North Carolina to join the Rebels. Without those two states, there would've been no Confederacy capable of waging war."

Lincoln took a long drag on his cigar, and blew a perfect smoke ring. "Slavery may not have caused the war, but it's going to help end it."

"How so?"

"When slaves desert the plantations they deprive the Rebels of what they need most—manpower."

"Good point," said Strother. Not only had the blacks proven to be good soldiers but every runaway was one less field hand growing food for Richmond.

In the distance a bugle sounded Boots and Saddles. Taking his leave, Lincoln mounted his horse and doffed his hat, "Ya, Herr Keronel! Das if drue, I shpeaks mit you, I'm going to fight mit Sigel."

Later that morning, at the daily staff meeting, Sigel announced that the move up the valley would take place the following day at 6:00 a.m.

Strother was worried. Still no word on Crook and only sketchy information about how Grant was doing in the Wilderness. Initial reports had been optimistic, but early rumors were often based on hope, not facts. To determine what was actually taking place you had to read between the lines and look for telltale signs. While at the telegraph tent that morning he saw an ominous message from the Secretary of War to Major General Augur, commander the 22nd Army Corps in Washington. The dispatch reeked of desperation, *"All stragglers and deserters will at once be brought before a drumhead court-martial and if found without authority, be immediately executed."*

The conflict was now in its third year and the butcher's bill was running high. States were dredging the bottom of the barrel for cannon fodder and had to pay large bounties to fill quotas. All hopes for a quick, easy victory had vanished. Strother remembered how naïve he'd been last year in New Orleans when he felt there was still some honor and romance left in the war. Just yesterday he'd re-read his idealistic ramblings, *"War is a business as natural to man as hunting squirrels or tilling the soil…the peace loving man is simply a poltroon and coward. Roll your drums, flaunt your banners and advance to the battlefield. War is a joy and the glory of our race."* Had he really written such drivel? Must have been the absinthe.

While watching lightning bolts dart along the peaks of Massanutten Mountain he was gripped by a foreboding. He packed his precious diaries in a saddlebag and handed it to Tom to send back to his wife in Martinsburg.

Chapter 6

Wise

A hush settled over the court as the jury of six cadets slowly filed back into the hall and took their seats. Each wore a homemade, black armband over his left shirt sleeve. As the court was called to order by Presiding Judge, George Macon, second corporal in Company A, rays of early morning sunlight cast an eerie glow on the walls of Society Hall where the court-martial was taking place. Two alert sentries armed with muskets and fixed bayonets stood guard at the entrance.

"Has the jury reached its verdict?" asked Macon, his voice lowered to underscore the gravity of the occasion.

"We have," answered a somber Jack Stanard, foreman of the jury.

"Is it unanimous?" asked the judge.

"It is," replied Stanard, as he cast a pitying glance at the accused.

"The foreman will hand me the verdict," said Macon, reaching for the piece of paper. He sadly shook his head as he saw the results. Placing a black handkerchief on top of his head, he ordered, "The accused will rise."

With help from Corporal Johnny Wise, his cadet attorney, Clyde E. Crump, slowly got to his feet. As a Rat from Norfolk who had only recently entered the Institute, Crump's real crime had been to refuse an order from third classman Bolling Barton to stop talking in ranks. As if that weren't serious enough, two nights later, in the mess hall during supper, Crump had called third classman Francis Lee, a "two-bit, tinhorn soldier." Later, he'd been overheard boasting about the insult to fellow Rats. The prosecution had also pointed out that Crump was a "Mink" who had attended Washington College for three months prior to becoming a cadet. This only compounded the evidence of guilt.

Judge Macon rapped the table with the butt of a bayonet. "Mr. Crump, you have been found guilty of willfully, and without excuse, deserting your post on the north corner of barracks while standing guard between the hours of 9:00 to 11:00pm on Sunday, May 8."

There was a murmur of disapproval from the fifteen third classmen gathered together in the room. Echo's of "shame, shame," bounced off the bare walls.

Judge Macon raised the bayonet, signaling for silence. When the room was quiet, he continued, "There can only be one punishment for such a grave offense." He paused, "And that is death."

An audible gasp rose from the hall.

The Judge banged harder on the table demanding silence. Turning back to Crump, he said, "You are to be taken beyond the parade ground within the hour and executed by firing squad."

"No. No. Not that!" someone shouted. "Give the Rat a second chance," pleaded another.

Judge Macon rose from his seat, posture erect. "Men! Men! Control yourselves. You've got to bear up. The country is at war and you're acting like civilians. You mustn't give way to your sensitive feelings in such a case."

Unable to stand, Crump slumped in his chair, burying his head in his hands.

Judge Macon turned to Wise, "As counsel for the condemned, does the convicted man have anything to say?" Receiving no reply, he continued, "Would he like to write a final letter home to his family? Maybe cut off a lock of hair for his poor mother?"

Wise whispered into Crump's ear, and helped him to his feet. "Your honor, the Rat—er—the condemned would like to make a statement."

With quivering lips, Crump sputtered, "Y—your honor. I—I'm just a ne—new cadet. I didn't know—no one told me. Please, sir. I—just give me another chance. I promise to—oh, my poor mother…"

Unmoved, Judge Macon beckoned to Patrick Henry, sergeant of the guard. "Take the prisoner into the next room, give him a pencil and piece of paper and let him write home." While the prisoner was out, Macon reminded the cadets that it was 7:45 a.m. The matter would have to be disposed of quickly, since formation for the flag raising ceremony at Jackson's grave was scheduled for 9:00. He commended the participants for missing breakfast to take part in the trial.

Fifteen minutes later, with wobbly knees and head bowed, Crump was escorted back into the room. Wise rose to address the court. Nodding toward Crump, he said, "We petition the court to grant the unfortunate prisoner a ten day reprieve so he can prepare to meet his fate." His voice shaking, he asked, "Have we no pity? Surely, ten days is not too much to ask for a fellow cadet, even a lowly Rat." Heads bobbed and there was a general murmur of approval.

After a brief consultation, the jury agreed to the request and passed a note to the presiding judge. Calling the court to order, Judge Macon said, "Then it's decided. The execution will be held at sunrise ten days from today, provided the prisoner can secure approval for the delay from the Superintendent." Motioning to Patrick Henry, he ordered, "Sergeant of Guard, post two sharpshooters on the roof at each corner of barracks. Don't let the condemned talk to anyone, or try to escape. Take a detail of six men and march him over to Old Spex's…er, the Superintendent's quarters and let him plead his case."

With guards on all sides, Crump was led out onto the third stoop, down two flights of stairs, then out of barracks through the sally port. The unusual detail drew stares from curious upper classmen as it grimly made its way along the south side of barracks to General Smith's quarters.

While the cadets waited for the guard's return, Stanard, the jury foreman, opened Crump's letter and read it aloud. The room erupted with snickers and guffaws when he got to the part where Crump told his sister that when he kissed her goodbye at their last meeting, he never thought he'd disgrace the family name in such a dishonorable manner.

"I commend the Judge for that bit with the black handkerchief on top of the head," said Wise.

"That's how they do it in England," replied Macon, pleased with his improvisation.

"And the lock of hair?" chuckled Stanard. "That was touching. Did you see the Rat's face?"

Twenty minutes later, the sergeant of the guard returned with his detail, but no Crump. The guard filed into the room with muskets casually slung over their shoulders and bayonets back in their scabbards.

"Well?" inquired Judge Macon, as the rest of the cadets gathered around.

Unable to contain his laughter, the sergeant of the guard started to speak, then stopped, his body shaking. "You should'a seen Old Spex's face when the Rat begged for mercy. He babbled on 'bout how he was gonna be shot right now unless the General showed mercy and postponed the execution. Crump was white as a ghost and shaking like a leaf. Old Spex just stared at the Rat, then us. First time I've ever seen him crack a smile. When tears started running down Crump's face, Old Spex patted him on the shoulder, 'Son, don't worry about this. These cadets are just greening you.'"

At that, the cadets roared with laughter, clapping their hands and stomping their feet. On the way back to their rooms, they whooped and hollered along the stoop chanting "Third Class! Third Class!" They wouldn't have any more trouble from Crump, or any other Rat—for awhile. Greening new cadets was a heck of a lot more fun than simply bucking them.

By the time Wise and Stanard got to their room, "Squirrel" Overton had a special breakfast laid out on the study table. Since classes had been suspended for the day in honor of Stonewall's death, Squirrel had gone foraging last night for a couple of nice, fat chickens. At twenty past midnight he returned with a pair of plump hens whose heads had been bashed in by a rock. He claimed it had been a matter of self-defense. Jim, a cook in the mess hall, fried them up, and for the usual remembrance, brought the chickens to room 56 for breakfast, along with butter, molasses, and warm biscuits. Squirrel had carefully divided the pieces into five equal portions so each roommate would have a share. As procurer, who risked dismissal if caught, Squirrel was granted first choice, plus an extra piece of white meat. Next came Louis, a second classman. Then Johnny Wise and Stanard, both thirds. Although Stanard had flunked his freshman year and was having to repeat his courses, he was still considered a Brother Rat by fellow classmates. The fifth roommate, Willis Harris, a Rat from Powhatan County, was lucky to get a wing.

"I think counsel for the defense should get to choose before the foreman," said Wise as he surveyed the three remaining portions. "Besides, I'm a corporal."

"Motion denied," snorted Stanard. "Rank means nothing among roommates. I was foreman so I should go next." He reached for the last piece of white meat.

"Cut for it," said Louis.

"Agreed," replied Wise. "Agreed," said Stanard, disappointed at the possibility of winding up with two thighs and a leg.

From the bookshelf, Wise pulled down a copy of MANUAL OF INSTRUCTION for VOLUNTEERS AND MILITIA by Major William Gilham, a VMI professor. Holding the book behind his back, he randomly opened it to pages 44 and 45. With his forefinger he scrolled down to the second letter in the second line on the left page. It was a "d." Confident he'd won, since "a" was the best and "z" the worst, he beamed as he handed the book to Stanard. With his head turned, Stanard opened the book to pages 56 and 57. On the left page, the second letter on the second line was a "b." Pleased, Stanard grabbed the last piece of breast.

Envious, Wise, who had to settle for a leg and two thighs watched as Stanard slowly devoured the prized piece of white meat. Savoring his victory, Stanard leisurely sopped up the last dabs of gravy with a warm biscuit, then licked his fingers.

Wise shook his head. Sometimes it seemed like Stanard had all the luck. Nineteen-years-old and the youngest boy in a family of six siblings, Jack had been shamelessly spoiled by a doting mother. Having lost her husband in 1862, she constantly petitioned the Superintendent for furloughs for her "darling boy." Although Wise considered Stanard a "momma's boy," always complaining about the food, the classes, and the drills, they were best of friends. Wise liked Jack's quick wit, uncompromising loyalty and generosity in sharing all worldly possessions—especially food parcels from home.

As soon as they finished eating, there was knock on the door. It was John Hanna, First Lieutenant of Company D, holding a long, wooden box.

"Good," said Hanna, seeing both Wise and Stanard. Walking over to Stanard, he handed him the box. "Picked this up in the guard room. Packet boat just came in."

"Manna from heaven," said Stanard, as he cleared the study table, and placed the heavy box in the middle. With the tip of a bayonet he pried open the lid. Inside, were two weeks of newspapers full of war news, a neatly folded flannel shirt, a box of gingerbread, a small ham, lemons, two jars of damson preserves and a heavy duty cavalry saber in a metal scabbard. Removing the saber, he handed it to Hanna.

"Thanks, Jack," said Hanna, his face beaming. Sliding the sword from its scabbard, he held it up to the light, running his fingers along the sharp edge.

While on furlough, Stanard had taken delivery of the saber for Hanna. Because of erratic train schedules, the Confederate mails had become unreliable, so Jack had volunteered to act as postman. Unfortunately, at the last minute hen had left the box behind, but a family friend sent it on by the next canal boat.

Hanna passed the sword around for inspection. This was a genuine fighting saber, not a flimsy, cadet dress sword. The guard was stamped "m1860 Ames" and the scabbard "3/NY/Cav." Nicks on the 35-inch blade showed it had been used.

"Where'd you get it?" asked Wise, as he lifted the heavy weapon.

"Will got it from one of Mosby's rangers," said Hanna. "It was captured from a Yankee baggage train outside Winchester." As a cadet officer, Hanna would be armed with a sword when he went into combat. For the past few weeks, he'd been practicing Patton's "Saber Exercises" with his ornamental, cadet sword but it wasn't the same. He had asked Will to look for a pistol also, but the prices had been too high.

While the cadets played swashbuckler with the saber, Hanna handed Wise a sheet of paper with a diagram of Jackson's grave site. "You, Ross, Pizzini, and that new cadet, Letcher, will be honor guards at the flag raising." Hanna had been sergeant of the guard at Jackson's burial a year ago and had done such an outstanding job that the Commandant had placed him in charge of today's ceremony.

"But Letcher's a Rat," protested Wise, who didn't want to share the honor with a lowly fourth classman.

"Yeah, but he's also the son of the War Governor who's the main speaker. Pizzini's in charge of the detail. Suggs-J, you'll be carrying the new flag. When we get to the cemetery, hand it to Pizzini, and take your position at the southeast corner of the metal fence. The ceremony's going to last a couple of hours so make sure you don't pass out."

"What's so special about a new flag?" asked Louis.

"It's from a gentleman in Liverpool, England," said Hanna. "He sent it to Richmond to be raised over Stonewall's grave when the old flag gave out. Said he had the greatest admiration for General Jackson and wanted to honor him with a flag."

When Hanna left, Wise gave his shoes one last buff. He'd hoped to have a new uniform by now, but the ship carrying the cloth had been captured outside Wilmington. Polly Logan and her friends from the Ann Smith Academy would be at the ceremony and he wanted to make a good impression.

As Stanard removed the flannel shirt from the box, an envelope fell to the floor. It was addressed, "For Miss B c/o My Darling Boy."

"What's in the envelope?" quizzed Wise, scooping it up. "Who's Miss B?" He shook a finger at his roommate. "Don't tell me you're sweet on Mollie Bull, Captain Bull's daughter?"

"Never you mind," replied Stanard, his face flushing crimson. When he made a grab for the envelope, a daguerreotype tumbled onto the table.

It was a photo of Stanard seated on a stool. He was dressed in a new, tailored uniform with six brass buttons running down the front and a black stripe down the leg. His hair neatly combed, he was looking at the camera with a pleasant, relaxed expression. "It's for, uh—mother. I forgot to give it to her before I left." Although it was a feeble explanation, it did contain a grain of truth. During his visit home his mother had insisted he pose for a photograph so she'd have a memento in case anything happened to him.

"To 'Miss B' from mom?" said Wise, smiling broadly. Just then the *rat-tat-tat* of the first drum sounded in the courtyard. Grabbing his musket Wise headed for the door. He called over his shoulder, "Hey, 'darling boy.' Don't forget mom's picture."

By the time the Corps reached the cemetery there were hundreds of visitors and dignitaries surrounding Stonewall's grave site. Two white marble headstones inside the enclosure stood sentinel. Eight young women from the Ann Smith Academy dressed in fashionable black mourning dresses gathered around Stonewall's marker. Their long hair was parted down the middle and tied back in a tight bun. Four girls sprinkled flower petals over the grave while the rest held their hands in front while they bowed their heads. An additional ten students outside the fence gazed at the grave with studied melancholy.

Posted at a corner of the metal fence, Wise straightened his shoulders and held his head erect. He was proud to be part of such a grand tableaux. The weather was perfect, sunny and cool. The faint smell of flowers drifted in from the fields as the crowd jostled for position near the speaker's platform. Out of the corner of his eye Johnny noticed Polly Logan standing by the fence, ten feet away. She was looking in his direction and whispering to Olympia Williamson. To Wise, the rays of sunlight highlighting her blond hair made her look like a forest sprite. As he watched, she started giggling at something Olympia said. Although she tried her best, Polly, a 16-year-old refugee from Fredericksburg, was too cheerful and full of life to look "wistful," even at Stonewall's grave.

"Guard, 'ten-shun!" ordered Hanna. "Present arms!"

Wise smartly brought his musket front and center. Slowly, the old flag was lowered while the fifer played a solemn hymn and the muffled drums beat a slow cadence. After it was folded and presented to Jackson's widow, the fifer began playing "The Bonnie Blue Flag" as the new flag was run up the staff. As if on cue, a gentle breeze caught the folds and the flag fluttered in tribute.

Returning to parade rest, Wise began planning the afternoon's activities. With classes suspended he would have until evening to be with Polly. In the background, he heard former Governor Letcher launching into his oration. "The presentation of this flag, and the duty assigned to you in connection with it, is without parallel…" Wise watched the flag sway hypnotically in the wind. As a member of the honor guard, he'd been invited to the Governor's garden for light refreshments after the ceremony. "… cherish it and honor it, and should any vandal's hand assail it, protect it with your lives…" But first, he'd have to take his musket back to barracks, then go to the garden.

After all the luminaries had been introduced, speeches made and egos massaged, Hanna formed the honor detail for the return to barracks. Just before marching off, Polly eased up beside Johnny. "I'll be in the garden at the Governor's house in thirty minutes—in case you're interested."

Wise's heart skipped a beat. It was indeed a glorious day.

By the time Johnny reached the garden, Polly was already there. She was standing beside Lizzie Letcher, who was busily arranging a large vase of daffodils. Both girls had changed out of their mourning clothes into bright, spring dresses. Slightly out of breath, Wise tried to think of something clever and witty to say. Walking over to Polly he picked up a daffodil, "I wandered lonely as a cloud / That—uh—floats on high o'er vales and hills, / When all at once—uh…"

"I saw a crowd, / A host, of golden daffodils; /… And then my heart with pleasure fills, / And dances with the daffodils," said Polly.

"Would you like some lemonade, Mr. Wordsworth?" asked Lizzie, trying to hide her amusement at Johnny's bumbling recitation. "We also have lemon pound cake." It had been her idea to serve lemon refreshments in honor of Stonewall, a hypochondriac who had been extremely fond of lemons. Taking Johnny's hand, Lizzie led him to where her father was standing. The former Governor was chatting with VMI Professor, "Old Ball" Preston, a friend from pre-war days. Tugging at her father's sleeve, she said, "Papa, this is Johnny Wise, Governor Wise's son. The one Sam mentioned."

Johnny blushed at Lizzie's having interrupted two such important people to introduce a mere cadet.

"Pleased to meet you, son," said Governor Letcher, graciously extending a hand. Letcher, tall, thin, balding with a florid complexion, had recently left the governorship to return to Lexington and renew his law practice.

No longer the hard driving politician, his current activities consisted mainly of delivering morale boosting speeches and re-connecting with former acquaintances. "I knew your father quite well. We had our differences, but I always respected him for his honesty and integrity." Before the war, Letcher had been strongly pro-Union, while Governor Wise had been a fire-eater who beat the drums for secession. On April 4, Letcher's Unionists defeated an ordinance of secession by a two-thirds majority. But when Lincoln called for troops from Virginia to quash the rebellion, the irate delegates felt betrayed and voted to secede by a margin of 88 to 55. Defeated in his attempt to keep Virginia in the Union, Letcher had dutifully written to the President, "…the militia of Virginia will not be furnished to the powers at Washington for any such use…Your object is to subjugate the Southern States…an object, in my judgment, not within the purview of the Constitution…You have chosen to inaugurate civil war, and have done so…" He patted Johnny on the shoulder, "Look after Sam for me. He always wanted to be a cadet and can be a little headstrong."

"Come along, Johnny," coaxed Lizzie, leading him to the lemonade table. "Mustn't keep Miss Polly waiting."

Balancing two plates of cake on top of two cups of lemonade, Wise rejoined Polly who was not at all pleased at having been left waiting.

At the far end of the vine-covered garden, John Hanna played a violin duet with Mary Compton, daughter of a local merchant. Hanna, one of Lizzie's good friends, was a frequent visitor to the Letcher home where he and roommate, Tom Davis, often entertained the family with their violin duets. In his diary Hanna noted, "Miss Letcher has a merry, merry laughing face and travels on the Sunny Side of the pathway of life. By her cheerfulness, she induces others to follow suit."

With refreshments in hand, Polly and Johnny joined a small group of cadets and girls sitting on blankets spread on the lawn. The cadets flirted and tried to act sophisticated while the girls whispered, giggled and attempted to look fetching and demure.

When the impromptu concert was over, Duck Colonna and Erskine Ross strolled into the garden accompanied by a pair of girls tugging at their sleeves. "Please, Erskine. Please, Duck. Tell us what happened with the flag."

Feigning reluctance, Ross halfheartedly raised a hand in protest. Grabbing his outstretched arm, Clara Davidson pleaded, "Tell us—tell us Erskine. You and Duck were there." Without waiting for a reply, each girl latched onto an arm and pulled the smiling cadets to a bench.

"Okay, okay," said Ross, "But I'll need Duck's help."

"Everyone gather together," announced Clara as she dashed around the garden, corralling an audience. "Erskine and Duck are going to tell us about the time the cadets almost went to war with local boys over a flag."

It was a tale told many times, but one that always found a ready audience. Both Ross and Colonna had been cadets in the early spring of 1861, when Stonewall Jackson was an unknown professor and Virginia was still a bright star in the Union flag.

After gulping down a large glass of lemonade, Ross cleared his throat. "Three years ago, when Duck and I were Rats, there was a flag raising in town. It was a whole lot different from the one today. It took place at the Courthouse on Saturday, April—er—"

"The 13th," said Colonna.

Ross nodded, "Back then, most everyone at the Institute, cadets and professors, were hell-bent for secession . . ."

At the mention of "hell" the girls blushed, covering their mouths with their hands and looking at each in amusement. The cadets smiled knowingly, showing that they were hardened soldiers use to such strong words.

" . . . While most of the people in Rockbridge County were pro-Union, tempers were short. Arguments for and against secession caused neighbors to fall out with each other. In April, the Seceshs got the bright idea of holding a rally on the Courthouse steps to show support for the new Confederacy. They scheduled a rally for 11:00am on a Saturday, our day off. To show their support for South Carolina they decided to raise a homemade flag with fifteen stars and the motto 'Union of the South' painted on one side. Duck and I heard about it and were curious, so we went to the courthouse to hear Major Colston, J.G. Paxton, and a few others give speeches and see the new flag. Everyone was cheering and…"

"And drinking John Barleycorn," added Colonna.

"Yup," agreed Ross. "People were celebrating and some drank too much. After the flag was run up the pole, there was some hurrahing, then we broke into small groups and wandered around town."

Handing an empty glass to Clara for a refill, Colonna took over. "Not to be outdone, the Unionists decided to raise their own flag at four o'clock that afternoon. Their pole was a lot taller, but Put Thompson and Danny Lee had snuck into town the night before and cut small holes in the sections near the top. When they—they—" Duck was laughing so hard he couldn't continue.

"As soon as they began to raise their flag—Boom! The pole snapped into three pieces and their flag tumbled to the ground," said Ross. "The Unionists were mighty peeved."

"Is that when the fighting started?" asked Nannie Williamson.

"Not right away," replied Ross. "But, it set the wheels in motion. Some rowdies from House Mountain, who'd been guzzling corn liquor all day, went around town trying to pick a fight and shouting insults at the cadets. By then most of us were back in barracks getting ready for Saturday afternoon inspection. But Put Thompson and," he turned to Colonna, "—who was the other—?"

"Chuck Flowerree," said Colonna.

A murmur of recognition swept through the small gathering at the mention of Flowerree's name. The former cadet was something of a celebrity at the Institute. Having entered VMI the same time as Ross and Colonna, he'd gone to Richmond with the Corps in 1861 to help train recruits. When the Institute reopened in January, 1862, he'd stayed with the 7th Virginia as a Second Lieutenant. Rising rapidly through the ranks he was appointed a full colonel when the commanding officer was killed at Gettysburg in Pickett's charge. That made Flowerree, at 20, the youngest regimental commander in Confederate service. As a full colonel, he even outranked Lt. Colonel Ship, VMI's Commandant.

Ross continued, "Both Flowerree and Put were still in town when they ran into a local tough named Mule Davis, who, with some drunk buddies, started taunting them. Well, Put was a big farm boy with a wicked temper and powerful right arm. He took all the guff he could, then jumped Mule, sending him sprawling to the ground with a broken nose and busted lip. Several of Mule's friends joined in and pummeled Put and Flowerree."

A girl sitting at Ross's feet sighed and shook her head sending dainty curls swaying back and forth. "Were the poor cadets hurt?"

"Nothing serious," said Colonna. "Bruised egos and a black eye, but that was about it. But, in all the excitement some troublemakers fired their guns in the air. Little Andy Summers, the smallest cadet in the Corps, saw the ruckus, heard shots and went running back to barracks. Rumors started flying that Put had almost been killed and Flowerree was seriously hurt."

While Ross and Colonna caught their breath, Clara Davidson passed around more slices of lemon cake.

After taking a bite, Ross continued, "When the guard raised the alarm, Tom Galloway, who was First Captain, ran through the courtyard yelling

'All cadets turn out under arms!' We grabbed our muskets and rushed out-side. We'd been target practicing all week so had plenty of ammunition. Loading on the run, we headed for town." Rising from the bench, Ross pointed to the front of Governor Letcher's house, "When we got about there, we saw some armed townspeople coming down the street straight at us. We weren't sure what to do. If we fired we might hit innocent civilians. When we formed a battle line, Captain McCausland and Old Polly came riding up and got between us and the town folks. While they held us in check, the Superintendent rode up, breathing hard. You could see the sweat running down his face."

Wise had heard several versions of the incident but never from a par-ticipant. "Were the people in Lexington going to attack the Corps over a fight started by a few drunks?"

Colonna took a deep breath. "Hard to say. Things looked pretty bad. The Mayor was there but didn't do his job. He should've just arrested the troublemakers and thrown them in jail to cool off, but when he heard the cadets were armed, he panicked."

"You mentioned that some town folks had guns," said Clara.

"The local militia, the Rockbridge Rifles, were armed. They held drill every Saturday afternoon and had just finished."

"My uncle Sam was head of the militia," said Lizzie. In a firm voice, she declared, "He would never have fired on the cadets."

Ross frowned, "Maybe not. But the situation was explosive. All that was needed was for some drunk to pull a trigger. Fortunately, no one did. Once we were assured by the Mayor that Put and Flowerree were OK, we settled down. General Smith quickly formed us up, turned us around and marched us back to barracks."

"When we got on Institute property, we fired off our muskets," added Colonna. "That rattled the Superintendent who ordered the whole Corps to go in barracks and assemble in Major Preston's section room. He lectured us for half an hour on the duties of a soldier and the seriousness of what we'd just done. When Major Jackson entered, the cadets chanted, 'Old Jack, Old Jack.' He wasn't much of a teacher, but everyone knew he was a first class fighter. When Old Spex finished talking, he turned to Stonewall, 'Major, I've driven in the nail, but it needs clinching. Speak with them.'"

Ross's face brightened at the memory. "When Jackson got to the lec-tern, you could've heard a pin drop. He wasn't one to waste words. Got right to the point in that high pitched voice of his. 'Military men make short speeches. The time for war has not yet come, but it will, and that soon enough. When it does, my advice is to draw the sword and throw away the scabbard.'"

A murmur of appreciation rippled around the garden.

"When did everything finally blow over?" asked Wise.

"The flag raising was on the 13th," said Colonna. "On the 16th the city councilmen heard about Lincoln's call for troops. They immediately sent a delegation to the Institute to ask for a state flag. Several cadets went along as an honor guard and the town council raised it at the Courthouse. On the 17th the state voted to secede and that was it."

"Those were exciting times," added Ross. "All people could talk about was how we'd whip the Yanks in one big battle. Classes were suspended on the 20th and the next day the Corps left for Richmond. The new Confederacy needed drillmasters and we were the best they had."

Colonna chuckled, "Our first days at Camp Lee were crazy. The farm boys had no concept of discipline and what a military life was all about. Most had brought flintlocks, squirrel rifles, shotguns, bowie knives, or whatever they could find. Some had large trunks full of clothes, others had servants to cook their food."

"How did the volunteers like taking orders from cadets?" asked Clara Davidson.

"Wait a second," said Lizzie, holding up her hand. "I've got something y'all have just got to hear." Running into the house, she returned shortly with an article by George Bagby, a southern journalist who had been at Camp Lee when it opened. It first appeared in the 1862 Christmas edition of the *Lynchburg Virginian*. With a grin and a wink, she began reading:

> *Reveille was a misery. When I arrived at Camp Lee I was thirty-three years old, a born invalid, with a habit of rising late, bathing leisurely and eating breakfast after everybody else was done. To get up at dawn to the sound of fife and drum, to wash my face in a hurry in a tin basin, wipe down with a wet towel, and go forth with a sense of uncleanliness to be drilled by a fat little cadet from the Virginia Military Institute, young enough to be my son, was indeed misery. How I hated that little cadet! He was always so wide-awake, so clean, so interested in the drill; his coat-tails were so short and sharp, and his hands looked so big in those white gloves. He made me sick.*

Howls of laughter echoed through the garden.

"That must've been Cookie Johnson," said Ross. "Cookie was 5-foot-3 and looked 12. He kept a haversack full of small cakes he snacked on all day."

"Johnny, let's go for a walk," whispered Polly as she rose from the blanket. Wrapping uneaten pound cake in a paper napkin, she said, "It's such a beautiful day, and I—" She hesitated, "I have something special to show you."

As they slipped away, Wise's heart began to race. This was the first time he'd been truly alone with Polly who looked more beautiful than ever.

Taking his hand, she led him along a well-worn path into the woods, past the ruins of the old Liberty Hall Academy, toward Cave Springs. As they approached a bend in the trail, she stopped and held a finger to her lips. "This place is secret, very secret. Cross your heart and hope to die you'll never reveal it to anyone—ever."

Wise smiled, and with a flourish crossed his chest with his right hand.

"I'm serious, Johnny," said Polly, her brow knitted in a frown. "No one must ever know."

"I swear—"

"Don't swear, Johnny," said Polly. "Just promise."

"I promise."

Passing around a curtain of wisteria vines in full bloom, Polly led Wise along a faint, moss covered path which meandered between a row of small bushes with bright yellow and white flowers. Rounding a corner, they approached a small, gurgling spring enveloped in green, leafy ferns.

A large, flat, moss covered rock sat near the edge of the spring. Polly spread the blanket near the boulder and unwrapped the pound cake. Breaking the cake into small pieces she piled them in little mounds on the rock. Gathering flower petals, she sprinkled them around the cake. Noticing Wise staring, she said, "It's for the fairies. At night they come out to play and dance. When they get hungry, they eat the cake."

Without comment, Wise sat down beside her and watched the water swirl down a narrow, fern bedecked creek. As flashes of sun danced off the clear water it wasn't hard to imagine fairies playing on the moss in moonlight.

"When I come back in the morning, the cake is always gone," said Polly, as if no further proof were needed. "When I'm sad, I think of the fairies and it cheers me up. If I leave a note and ask them to look after you, they'll make sure no harm comes to you."

Wise could only nod. He'd heard that her home had been destroyed in the battle of Fredericksburg and that her parents were living behind enemy lines. He was grateful that she had found a way to cope with so much uncertainty and stress.

Smoothing out the edges of the blanket, Polly's eyes brightened. "Oh look, Johnny, shamrocks. Let's find a four-leaf clover. It'll bring us luck."

"Pshaw, that's just superstition," he murmured, not mentioning the lucky, white rabbit's foot he always carried in his pocket.

"Not so, Mr. Smarty," replied Polly, as she kneeled and began examining a patch of clover. She paused, unsure whether to share a secret. "When I was seven, Josephine, my oldest sister, came down with typhoid fever. She suffered terribly for four weeks. Finally, the doctor told mother he didn't think she would survive the night." Polly's face clouded, "But I found a four-leaf clover and put it under her pillow. That night—" she faltered as emotion caught in her throat. "That night, the fever broke. Next morning she was completely well. The doctor said it was a miracle." A moment passed. "But I know why."

"I—I didn't mean to—" sputtered Wise.

"Here's one, Johnny," she said, happily plucking a small clover and holding it up to a ray of sun streaming through the trees. With her right index finger she pointed to the leaves. "This one's for hope. That one's faith. The third is for good luck. And, the fourth—" she lowered her face.

Wise waited as she shyly raised her eyes, "It's—it's for love, Johnny. For love."

Wise felt his face turning warm.

Handing him the four-leaf clover, Polly said, "Promise me you'll keep it with you if you're ever in danger."

"I promise," he said.

Taking his hand she pulled him closer.

Chapter 7

Breckinridge

"Well, Breck, you were right. Sigel didn't cross the Blue Ridge," said Stoddard Johnston, as he gobbled down a second country ham biscuit. On the plate before him were the remnants of a late breakfast of scrambled eggs, stone-ground grits and red-eye gravy prepared especially by the staff of the American Hotel. Using his thumb he pushed the last bite of grits onto a fork. "I don't know how they do it, but this food beats anything we've had since leaving Kentucky." He was still trying to make up for the scant rations endured during the grueling, 145 mile horseback ride from Dublin Depot.

"We can thank Dame Fortune Sigel has the slows," said Breckinridge, relieved that the Federals hadn't beaten him to Staunton. After refilling his cup with leftover coffee, he walked out onto the balcony overlooking the railroad marshaling yard.

Johnston stuck his head out the door, "Are you finished?" There was still an uneaten ham biscuit on Breckinridge's plate.

Breckinridge waved his hand, "Help yourself. Tell the kitchen to remove the plates, then go get Major Gilmor."

In ten minutes Major Harry W. Gilmor was standing in front of Breckinridge and Johnston who were sitting behind a hastily arranged table. On top of the table was a lengthy court-martial report.

"At ease, Major," said Breckinridge as he casually leafed through the papers. After a few minutes underlining words and scrawling comments in the margins, he passed the report to Johnston.

While Johnston scanned the document, Breckinridge sat back and watched the sweat bead up on the Major's brow. Not wanting to make eye contact, Gilmor was staring straight ahead while fidgeting with the ornate buckle on his black leather belt. The Major was outfitted in a full dress uniform with polished leather knee-high boots, bright yellow waist sash, and white kid gloves. By his side dangled an engraved, light-weight French sword presented to him by the ladies of Winchester. Looking at Gilmor, it was easy for Breckinridge to believe the rumors he'd heard that this high-spirited officer had received numerous proposals of marriage from women he'd never met. The same romantic mystique had swirled around Colonel Turner Ashby, the "Black Knight of the Confederacy," before his death two years ago at the Battle of Good's Farm.

There was no need for Breckinridge to spend more time reading the report. He was familiar with Gilmor's background and reputation as an aggressive partisan ranger. Born in 1838 into the landed gentry of Baltimore County, Maryland, the Major had grown up at Glen Ellen, the family estate. Educated in classics by a Harvard trained tutor, Gilmor had tried his hand at farming but quickly decided he had no talent for cleaning stables and shoveling manure. When the Federals began arresting anyone in Maryland suspected of having southern sympathies, he'd been detained and imprisoned for two weeks at Fort Henry. After release, Gilmor had quietly slipped into Virginia, and attracted by dreams of honor and glory, joined Ashby's cavalry in the Shenandoah Valley. By 1864 the Major was an experienced veteran having taken part in Jackson's Valley Campaign, the Battle of Brandy Station and Gettysburg. At Gettysburg, he served briefly as provost marshal for the town.

Unfortunately, on a recent raid against the Baltimore and Ohio Railroad, some of his men had stolen cash and jewels from several passengers. This robbery of citizens was strictly against Lee's policy of treating civilians with respect. Although Gilmor had issued orders "not to molest citizens or ladies," he'd been arrested, court-martialed and tried in Staunton. Found not guilty he was waiting for Lee's approval of the verdict before being allowed to resume the sword.

Turning to Johnston, Breckinridge winked. "Well, counselor, what's it going to be?" Now wasn't the time to let legal niceties stand in the way of returning to the field one of the Valley's most effective guerillas. While Gilmor languished in legal limbo, 40 of his rangers stood idly by, drinking, playing cards and waiting for orders. In addition, the Major was well known among the 25,000 Marylanders in the Confederate army and smearing his good name over a trifle wouldn't be popular back home. Besides, Breckinridge had a soft spot for anyone from a state where he'd received 42,482 votes for President compared to Lincoln's 2,294. Although protocol called for Lee's approval, necessity dictated an immediate resolution to the problem. The only Confederate troops currently between Staunton and Sigel's 13,000 were Imboden's 1,600 horsemen, and three small bands of guerillas under Gilmor, McNeill, and Mosby. With the situation deteriorating hourly, Breckinridge couldn't afford to let red tape interfere with military imperatives. He needed men, and needed them *now*.

Johnston placed the record of trial back on the table, "Seems to me the Major's a brave officer who should be commended for his actions, not court-martialed."

"My thoughts exactly," said Breckinridge, as he stood and with a warm smile extended his hand. "Major Gilmor, you're officially released from arrest and restored to full command. When your men are provisioned I want you to take them down the Valley, get in Sigel's rear and raise hell with his communications and supply lines. Keep the Federals off balance while we gather our forces here at Staunton."

Grinning broadly, his white teeth flashing, Gilmor snapped to attention and saluted. "Yes sir, General. You can count on me."

"And, Major, try to keep your men under control. You and I both know how much we need the goodwill of border states. Robbing their citizens doesn't help." Breckinridge turned to Johnston, "Stoddard, make sure the Major's men get plenty to eat and all the equipment they need, then report back on the double."

Johnston lingered behind as the jubilant major bolted from the room, literally skipping down the hotel's steps. When he was out of sight, Stoddard said, "One of Gilmor's men said the Yanks are causing trouble in Winchester. They've burned a couple of private homes, looted businesses and expelled whole families on the pretext they're aiding bushwhackers."

"They're just making enemies," said Breckinridge. "Lee's right. Only fools harass women and children."

"Guv, there's a question I've been meaning to ask. After this thing's over and *if* we have to go back into the Union—and I'm just saying *if*—any chance you'll run for office again?"

Breckinridge shook his head. "I'll be lucky if they don't hang me."

Johnston chuckled, "If the Radicals get their way, they'll string us all up."

"Stoddard, go see if there's any word on Jenkins and Crook." Not knowing the whereabouts of Crook's army was making Breckinridge edgy.

If he marched north to meet Sigel, and Crook was near Staunton, there would be no way to keep him from simply walking in and taking over. But if Breckinridge waited for Crook to show up, he might have to fight both armies at the same time. With their three-to-one advantage in troops and cannon he wouldn't stand a chance.

After Johnston was gone, Breckinridge walked over to three large maps tacked to the wall of his office. Drawn on linen, they each measured 8.25 by 3.5 feet, and stretched from floor to ceiling. These were the same maps used by Stonewall in 1862 in his Valley campaign to outmaneuver Banks, Shields and Fremont. The fine, detailed charts were the handiwork of cartographer Jedediah Hotchkiss and depicted important natural barriers and defensive positions from Lexington to Harper's Ferry. Hotchkiss, a native New Yorker, had moved to the Valley in 1848 and taught school. To supplement his meager income he worked part time as a mining geologist. Since there were no dependable maps of the Valley and neighboring mountains, he made his own. Before long his reputation as a map maker spread and his hobby turned into a profitable business.

For a moment, Breckinridge stood back and admired the beauty of the cartographer's art. The rivers and streams were sketched in blue, the trees in green, and important roads in red. Then he stepped forward and with a finger traced the two branches of the Shenandoah River as they meandered north, down the Valley from Port Republic to Front Royal.

Breckinridge repeated the term, "Down the Valley." In reading maps he had always considered "down" to mean south, and "up" to mean north. But, since the Shenandoah River flowed north to the Potomac, Valley usage had reversed the meaning. Between the north and south forks of the river lay Massanutten Mountain. It was divided into two sections, with north and south separated by New Market gap. The mountain formed a natural barrier which had been used by Stonewall to keep three Federal armies off-balance while defeating each in detail. Breckinridge hoped it could be used again to help keep Sigel and Crook apart.

The Massanutten also provided a series of excellent observation posts for monitoring Sigel's every move. Just this morning, Captain Davis, in charge of the signal station at Buzzard Rock, had reported Sigel's infantry going into camp at Strasburg. Now the question was, "Which way would they head next?" South to join Crook at Staunton, or east across the Blue Ridge to threaten Lee's left flank? With a ruler Breckinridge measured the distance from Sigel's headquarters at Strasburg to Staunton. It was eighty miles. If Sigel maintained his usual slow pace it would take him five days to reach Staunton. "Just stay put 'til I'm ready," Breckinridge muttered.

Tacked beside the maps were two telegrams from Lee. The first was the May 5 message ordering Breckinridge to stop Sigel's forces from crossing the Blue Ridge. The second had arrived three days ago when Lee had been battling Grant in the Wilderness. It read, "*Your movements proposed in the Valley, if made, must be made at once.*" That was a clear mandate to confront Sigel before Grant realized the situation and ordered Sigel to march his army across the mountains.

Current battlefield reports mentioned a major engagement taking place at Spotsylvania Courthouse. The Spotsylvania battlefield was 60 miles east of Sigel and 90 miles from Breckinridge. If Sigel force-marched his infantry across the mountains he could be on Lee's left flank before Breckinridge even got started. That might be all the edge Grant needed for complete victory. Breckinridge studied the calendar. Once Echol's and Wharton's brigades arrived at Staunton they would need at least a full day's rest before continuing.

Breckinridge paced the room. He still hadn't fully recovered from the weary ride from Dublin. In addition, he hadn't been sleeping well lately. Last night's rest had been interrupted by a recurring nightmare of Chickamauga. Stretching out his hands, he stared at the rough, weather-worn skin. There was a slight tremor in the fingers he hadn't noticed before. Were these the hands of the peacemaker, the family man who had tried so hard to prevent war? Was he the same man who had stood in the moonlight at Chickamauga gazing down on the ashen faces of the silent dead, their eyes open, staring at *him*? Now, whenever he tried to sleep he was haunted by the stench of death and ghosts of battered men. Was this the same world? The here, the there?

Needing fresh air, Breckinridge returned to the balcony. The Virginia Hotel on Greenville Avenue had bigger rooms and was more elegant but the American Hotel overlooked the vital Virginia Central switching yard and military warehouses. Leaning against a railing, he pulled out the ever present plug of tobacco and cut off a corner. The nicotine-rush would help sooth his nerves so he could concentrate and plan the next move. Below, wagons rattled back and forth while sweating teamsters cracked whips and swore at balky mules. He watched one mule try to kick its tormentor only to become entangled in the traces. In the last three years he had gained new respect for these irascible, bad-tempered animals. What was it about these critters that he admired so much? Maybe it was their stubbornness and absolute refusal to obey commands they didn't like. Or, being a cross between a horse and donkey, it might be their lack of pride in ancestry or concern for offspring. Willing to plod along all day with a 300 pound load chafing its back, the mule was too intelligent to charge men armed with long, sharp bayonets. "Smart thinking, Private Mule," he muttered. If only men were as smart.

He reached in his vest pocket for a rumpled telegram. It had been sent two days ago by Major Stringfellow in Dublin. *"Enemy advancing on this place about ten miles distant. Has five regiments of infantry and twelve pieces of artillery."* The next sentence was the one he was searching for. *"Mrs. Breckinridge left in ambulance this morning for Salem."* His eyes misted over. Embarrassed by the sudden rush of emotion, he glanced around to make certain no one was watching. As a young boy in a house full of women he had become overly sensitive, easily hurt and brought to tears. Other boys teased him unmercifully, but the women had been sympathetic and supportive. Now he had to hide the gentle side of his nature lest it be taken as a sign of weakness. Refolding the telegram he slipped it back in his pocket.

"Poor Mary," he sighed, gripping the railing. What would become of her if the Confederacy were defeated and he was arrested for treason? The hardcore abolitionists were a vicious, vindictive lot who cared nothing for justice or reunification. They only sought revenge and were determined to crush the old southern society and anyone who supported it. The harsh wording of a December 9, 1863, editorial in the *New York Times* had given him some idea of what lay ahead if he were ever captured. He had tried to hide the article from Mary, but knew she'd seen it. In responding to a rumor that Breckinridge had been killed, the editor opined, *"If it be true that a loyal bullet has sent this traitor to eternity, every loyal heart will feel satisfaction."* After expressing limited sympathy for Stonewall Jackson's death, the editor continued, *"We know that it's not easy to draw distinctions between the shades of this black treason against the Union…Of all the accursed traitors of the land there have been none more heinously false than Breckinridge…none whose memory will live in darker ignominy."* Drawing a deep breath, he closed his eyes. He hoped such venomous tirades didn't upset Mary too much. But, she was strong and would survive. His family would make sure of that.

With the toe of his boot, he slid a brass spittoon closer to the railing. Recent northern newspapers obtained by scouts had reported Halleck's lack of confidence in Sigel. They had reported that Sigel's only goal was to demonstrate against Staunton while Crook attacked the railroads. If that was true, it helped explain Sigel's reluctance to act on his own initiative. It was clear that Grant had planned on a quick victory, but the fighting had now bogged down into a grinding war of attrition.

Breckinridge gazed east at the Blue Ridge Mountains. It had been two years since Stonewall drove the Federals from the Valley. Two years of relative peace and prosperity during which time Staunton had become *the* major lifeline for Richmond. Running through the center of town was the Valley Turnpike, an all-weather, macadamized road between Lexington and Harper's Ferry. The town was also home to five stagecoach lines and served as the main depot for the Virginia Central Railroad. In addition, it had three banks, two newspapers and eighty businesses providing food, clothing, shoes, horses and wagons for Lee's army. No wonder Grant wanted the town captured, its military stores burned and train tracks torn up.

The sound of heavy boots on wood announced Stoddard Johnston's return. In his hands was another ham biscuit which he offered to Breckinridge, who politely declined.

"Message from General Imboden," said Johnston. "Six days ago one of his rangers, a Captain Hanse McNeill, wrecked a big B&O depot in West Virginia. The whole place was burned to the ground and all the rolling stock destroyed. The partisans captured over a hundred Yankee prisoners with equipment and some horses."

"Excellent," replied Breckinridge, who needed all the good news he could get.

While downing the last biscuit crumbs, Johnston continued, "When Sigel got word of the raid, he sent 500 cavalry into the mountains after McNeill. Imboden thinks he can head the Yanks off if he moves fast. Says it won't take long, four or five days at most. He's leaving Colonel Smith with the 62nd Virginia at Mount Jackson to block any Federal cavalry who might venture this way."

Breckinridge raised an eyebrow, "Hope Imboden knows what he's doing. How many men does Smith have? Seven hundred? Eight hundred?

"More like 450, plus some field guns."

"Not many. Not many at all," said Breckinridge, pursing his lips. With Imboden in the mountains and Echols' and Wharton's two brigades still not at Staunton, a quick strike by Federal cavalry could wreak havoc.

"Don't worry Guv," said Johnston. "The Dutchman's lying low at Strasburg. If he breaks camp, our scouts on Massanutten will let us know."

"Too risky," said Breckinridge. "Even if Imboden bags all 500, they're still going to outnumber us two-to-one in horsemen." Checking his pocket watch, he glanced up the tracks. "Sure hope the infantry gets here soon." Just that morning Wharton had cabled from Jackson River, "*…men getting very sore footed. We will reach Staunton.*"

"I figure 24 hours for Echols. Maybe two days for Wharton," said Johnston.

"Any news from Jenkins?"

Johnston shook his head. "Just that telegram from Stringfellow." Pulling a cable from his pocket, he handed it to Breckinridge. "*Enemy descending Cloyd's Mountain. Pickets been firing for two hours. Six or eight cannon shots just heard. Will be two hours before the fight opens fairly. Our men in splendid spirits. Anxious for the fight. Will telegraph from the field.*"

"Too bad we had to leave McCausland behind," said Breckinridge. "We could use his men." At the last minute, Crook's rapid approach to Dublin had forced Breckinridge to leave McCausland's 1,500 infantry with Jenkins to help defend the depot and New River bridge. "Maybe, if we…"

Tweee—Tweee—Tweee. Three faint blasts from a train whistle drifted in from the west.

Breckinridge cocked his head, "Did you hear that?"

"Could be one of our brigades," said Johnston, as he jumped to his feet, leaned over the rail and peered down the tracks. "Can't see a thing from here."

Grabbing his hat and heading for the door, Breckinridge called over his shoulder, "Stay here while I check it out. Let me know if you hear from Jenkins." Hurrying downstairs he directed an orderly to saddle Old Sorrel. Ten minutes later he was cantering west along the tracks towards the sound of the whistle. Eight hundred yards away, chugging around a bend was a large locomotive pulling a string of flat beds and freight cars. On the cars were hundreds of soldiers waving hats and echoing the Rebel Yell. On two flat beds men held tightly to ropes securing four artillery pieces.

As the engine wheezed and coughed to a stop, Breckinridge could see an officer standing in the cab beside the engineer. He immediately recognized the tall, lanky frame of General Gabriel "Gabe" Wharton. A Virginian and 1847 distinguished graduate from VMI, Wharton had extensive combat experience fighting in the mountains of east Tennessee and western Virginia. For a brief period he had been Commander of the Shenandoah Valley District and knew the area well. Rumors stated that Jefferson Davis held a special grudge against Wharton that had resulted in his slow promotion to brigadier and banishment to southwestern Virginia. Breckinridge, no stranger to political intrigue, was just thankful to have Wharton in charge of one of his two Brigades.

Energized by the sight of so many soldiers, Breckinridge galloped up. "Howdy, Gabe. Didn't expect you so soon."

"Stroke of luck, General," said Wharton, as he nimbly jumped to the ground, dusting clouds of soot from his uniform. "Just as we were preparing to hoof it all the way, along came this beautiful train."

Breckinridge nodded towards the troops, "That your whole brigade?"

"Not quite. Just the 51st and 30th plus Jackson's four-gun battery. The rest will be arriving by foot. Should be here no later than morning after next." He looked at the smoke rising from the hotel's chimney, "Wouldn't happen to have any extra rations lying around? It's been nothin' but corn-pone crawling with weevils, mealy bacon and water for the past few days." After telling a sergeant to remove the artillery horses from the freight cars, he added, "Our animals need forage real bad. They're jaded from pulling cannon over those mountain roads and not getting enough to eat."

"We've got all the fodder you need. You can draw provisions and pasture the horses as soon as you reach your bivouac area." Leaning forward with his hands resting on the pommel of his saddle, Breckinridge watched the two veteran regiments forming for the short march to camp. He was relieved they seemed in high spirits despite all the privations. As he watched, a wave of confidence swept over him. When Wharton started to leave, Breckinridge called out, "Have the men get plenty of rest. We'll be heading north in thirty-six hours.

As he nudged Old Sorrel toward headquarters, Breckinridge saw Stoddard galloping toward him. It wasn't like Johnston to be in a rush. Reining in his mount, Breckinridge waited.

Waving a telegram, Johnston shouted, "Bad news, Breck. Message from McCausland."

The blood drained from Breckinridge's face. McCausland? Where was Jenkins? The muscles in his jaw tightened as he reached for the cable:

> *Jenkins wounded and in Federal hands. Enemy under Crook drove me from the New River bridge. I have fallen back to Christiansburg. Will oppose their advance toward the east, but my force is inadequate to keep them back. The enemy has twelve regiments of infantry, two of cavalry and fifteen pieces*

of artillery. Cavalry under Averell is operating independent from Crook and headed toward Saltville.

Breckinridge took a deep breath. That was more than twice the number of regiments reported by Stringfellow. "Any word from Grumble Jones or Morgan?"

"Nothing yet. But they're more than a match for Averell."

"*Men*, Stoddard, we need *more* men," exclaimed Breckinridge. Now that Crook had taken Dublin and the bridge, he'd be heading for Staunton. Breckinridge *had* to prevent the two Federal armies from joining forces. Rummaging through his pocket he withdrew a scrap of paper listing the troops available. With Echol's and Wharton's brigades, Imboden's cavalry, and the rangers, the best he could come up with was 4,500. He turned to Johnston, "What're the chances of reinforcements from Richmond?"

"Snowball's in hell."

"Am I overlooking anything?"

"Well," said Johnston, "There's the Rockingham reserves. You could call on them. That's about 500."

"They're just civilians. They mean well, but they would only use up our provisions and get in the way."

"Well—there's VMI—"

"No, Stoddard," said Breckinridge, emphatically shaking his head. "They're just boys."

"Boys with rifles—and cannon. By my count the Corps has 280 infantry and two 3-inch field pieces. They could be here in two days."

"Stoddard, I just *can't*—"

"Use them as a reserve—like Stonewall." It pained him to see Breckinridge struggling so hard to keep from having to involve the cadets. "It'll add to our numbers and make the Yanks think we have more veterans."

After a minute's silence, Breckinridge lowered his head, "Don't see we have any choice. Send a courier to the Institute. Have them join us here at Staunton."

Maj. Gen. John C. Breckinridge, CSA
In charge of Confederate army
Library of Congress

Brig. Gen. John D. Imboden, CSA
Library of Congress

Capt. John H. McNeill, CSA
Library of Congress

Maj. Henry W. Gilmor, CSA
Library of Congress

Lt. Col. Scott Ship
VMI Commandant
Photo ca. 1865
VMI Archives

Maj. Gen. Francis H. Smith
VMI Superintendent
Pen and ink sketch by
Cadet Moses Ezekiel, ca. 1875
VMI Archives

Cadet Moses J. Ezekiel
Photo ca. 1866
VMI Archives

Cadet John S. Wise
VMI Archives

Cadet J. "Jack" Beverly Stanard
VMI Archives

Cadet Thomas Garland Jefferson
VMI Archives

Cadet Andrew Pizzini Jr.
VMI Archives

Cadet Benjamin A. "Duck" Colonna
VMI Archives

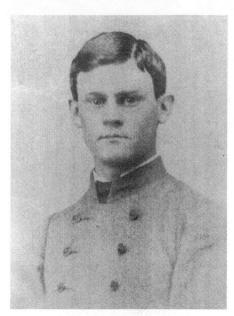

Cadet John F. Hanna
Postwar portrait
VMI Archives

Cadet Samuel H. Letcher
VMI Archives

Students from Ann Smith Academy at Stonewal Jackson's grave
Lexington, Virgina
Photo ca. 1866
VMI Archives

Maj. Gen. Franz Sigel, USA
In charge of Union Army
Library of Congress

Brig. Gen. George Crook, USA
Library of Congress

Col. David H. Strother, USA
Library of Congress

Chapter 8

Stringfellow

"There were—just too many," rasped Colonel Smith. The wounded officer was propped up on a blood-soaked stretcher in the front parlor of Hans Meadow, the elegant home of 23-year-old Mary Taylor Craig. With a shattered right elbow and gaping foot wound, Smith waited patiently for another turn at surgery. As commander of the 36th Virginia, the colonel had been in the midst of the carnage at Cloyd's Mountain before being carted off the field to the relative safety of Christiansburg. It had been over 20 hours since his injury and he was drifting in and out of consciousness. "They had us better'n three to one. Kept coming—on, forcing us back. It's—it's—"

"When was General Jenkins hit?" asked Stringfellow, as he eased a flour sack stuffed with hay under Smith's head. He was trying to piece together a situation report for Breckinridge to help him determine which way Crook's army was headed.

"I—we were sent to support the right flank when Jenkins—went down. Then I got hit. Don't remember much after… The Yankees must've got him. I—I just don't know."

Leaving the colonel in care of a medical orderly, Stringfellow walked out onto the porch of the two story brick home which had been converted into a makeshift hospital. Dozens of wounded were crowded in the yard under a canopy of large elm trees. Rattling along the dirt road in front of Hans Meadow was a continuous stream of wagons packed with refugees heading for Salem, nineteen miles away.

While Stringfellow jotted notes on a crumpled pad, three cavalry officers galloped up. They were looking for Colonel McCausland. From them he learned more details about yesterday's battle. The good news was that Morgan and Jones had stopped Averell's raids against the important salt works at Saltville and lead mines at Wytheville. The bad news was that Dublin Depot had been captured and Crook's army had burned the New River Bridge. Because of faulty intelligence, Jenkins had been forced to divide his small force which left him with only 2,400 infantry against Crook's 6,500. The vicious battle lasted an hour and fifteen minutes resulting in over 1,200 killed, wounded and missing, one of whom was General Jenkins.

When Crooks' forces reached the depot they ripped up the railroad tracks, looted tobacco warehouses and burned military buildings. This morning they attacked the New River railroad bridge which was now engulfed in flames. The Federals were expected to be across the river soon and headed for Christiansburg.

Before returning to the telegraph office, Stringfellow chatted briefly with Mary Craig. He warned her that if McCausland decided to make a stand at Christiansburg, the houses and community buildings would be hit by artillery shells and small arms fire. When the Federals took the town she could expect the livestock to be stolen and vacant homes looted. Fortunately, General Crook had a reputation for being a fair and reasonable officer who maintained discipline among his troops and respected citizens' private property.

Mary's hands shook as she gave hurried instructions to field hands to scatter the cattle in the hills and take the pigs and chickens to remote farms north of town. She ordered the house servants to hide the bacon, ham and flour in the attic of the main house, then put the family silverware and valuables under the floor boards. Personally strong and determined, she had decided against abandoning the property and fleeing to Salem. By staying at Hans Meadow she hoped to keep the property from being sacked and burned. She wasn't concerned for her own safety, but was worried that a few stray artillery shells might land among the wounded, or strike the house and buildings. Hans Meadow had been in the Craig family for over 90 years. Her brother, John Craig Jr., had been killed a year ago at Chancellorsville while serving in the Stonewall Brigade and was buried in the family cemetery behind the main house. To surrender his grave to the mercy of invaders would be a sacrilege. As a constant reminder of John's sacrifice she wore a mourning locket with a lock of his hair around her neck at all times. Resolute, Mary clenched her fist and with the back of her hand wiped away tears of frustration.

At a loss for words of comfort, Stringfellow was relieved when a lanky, barefoot boy came running toward him, feet flying, arms flailing.

"I'm looking for Mr. Strangefeller?" he blurted.

"You mean String-fellow?"

"Yeah, that's it. Strange-fell-er. There's a Mr. Pennytown at the telegraph office. Says fer Mr. Strangefeller to come quick as a rabbit." When he'd finished delivering his message, he waited, stubbing his bare toes in the red dirt.

"You've come to the right person," said Stringfellow. Noticing the boy still watching him intently, he asked, "Is there something else?"

"Mr. Pennytown—said you'd give me a piece of hard candy."

"Oh, did he?" laughed Stringfellow. Now he knew the message was from Nat Pendleton, Dublin's telegraph operator. Only Pendleton knew the Major always carried a small supply of horehound candy wherever he went.

After handing over two sticks of the prized sweet, the Major headed for the telegraph office at a trot. Located on the west side of Main Street it took him four minutes to reach the communications center. Tied to a hitching post in front of a shed was a mule-drawn wagon piled high with wooden crates and rolls of copper wire. When Stringfellow entered he saw a thin, short, bespectacled civilian hunched over a telegraph key. It was Pendleton, his sensitive fingers expertly tapping out a message. Standing beside him was Jinny Beckley, the pretty, young, war widow who was the local operator.

"I was getting worried they might've bagged you," said Stringfellow. "Any trouble getting out?"

Pendleton stood and extended a bony hand, "Damned close. Waited as long as I could. Kept trying to send word to Lynchburg and Richmond but couldn't reach 'em. The lines must be down." He spat a well-aimed stream of tobacco juice into a stained can. "A few seconds longer and I'd be picking off bed bugs in a Yankee jail."

"Were you able to—?"

Pendleton's eyes lit up, "Just like we planned. Kicked over a few chairs and burned a couple of important looking papers in the fireplace. Left the first fake telegram beside a trashcan near the sounder. Ciphered it to look like a real dispatch. Even jotted a couple of keywords on the side, then crumpled it up and tossed it on the floor." As a member of the Confederate telegraph service it was part of Pendleton's job to collect and transmit military intelligence. Gifted at math, he was a natural at coding messages and had a professional's disdain for the Confederate's cumbersome Vigenere system. He knew the Yankees had long ago broken the Vigenere code, but he wasn't sure how savvy Crook's operator was, so he'd given him a little help.

"How'd you word it?" asked Stringfellow.

"Well, we had that information from Richmond saying Lee's forces were driving the Yanks so I put that in. Course, that doesn't mean Grant's army has been defeated, but if we don't know, neither does Crook. I didn't want them to have any doubt so I laid it on nice and thick. 'Grant's forces crushed in the Wilderness with great loss. Meade's army in full retreat back across the Potomac. Federals being pressed hard on all sides by Hill and Longstreet.' I signed it, 'R. E. Lee, General Commanding.' Thought it would carry more weight if it came from Bobby Lee." Pendleton frowned, "Hated leaving that key set and all the wire at the depot, but wanted it to look like we left in a rush."

"Excellent," said Stringfellow, pleased at the mischief his little plan would cause. If he could just convince Crook that Grant was retreating, Crook might turn around and head back to West Virginia. That would give Breckinridge some much needed breathing room. "I left the main telegram behind the stove. Mixed it in with some old dispatches before scattering the whole lot on the floor and grinding it into the wood with the heel of my boot."

"How'd you word that one?" asked Stringfellow, as he glanced at Jinny. It was a shame how many young war widows there were in southwestern Virginia. A lot of good men had been lost in the past three years and he wondered how much grief her husband's death had caused. Fortunately, she was bright and pretty, with no children. It wouldn't be long before she found a new suitor.

"I addressed it to General Jenkins and signed it with General Breckinridge's name. Worded it like you said." He pulled out a worn notepad and read aloud, "When Union forces reach Dublin, put up a token resistance, then fall back to Staunton. Try to get Crook to follow. Gen. Early has been dispatched to Lynchburg with 12,000 men and 19 cannon. Will try to trap Crook's army in the mountains."

"Good," said Stringfellow. It just might work. He knew the first thing Crook would do when he reached Dublin was head for the telegraph office looking for messages. With his supply lines stretched thin and 150 miles of mountain roads separating him from his home base at Kanawha, Crook would be concerned about being cut off and captured.

While they were discussing the cables, the sounder began to rattle, *Click—click—clack—click—*

"It's him," said Pendleton as he slanted his good ear toward the sounder. "It's that Yankee operator traveling with Crook. I'd recognize his signature anywhere." Two days earlier Crooks' telegrapher had tapped into the Dublin line and tried to get information by impersonating a Confederate operator. Pendleton hadn't been fooled for a second and had answered, "Hello, Yank." After a brief exchange of pleasantries, Pendleton invited Crook to supper in Dublin. Crook accepted but requested that the invitation be postponed for a couple of days. Now the same operator was trying to reach Lynchburg. "He's asking if the reinforcements have arrived from Richmond."

Stringfellow rubbed his hands together, "They've taken the bait."

Pendleton pulled his chair closer to the key set. There was nothing he liked better than matching wits with Union operators. He held his fingers over the key set, "Don't want to respond too quickly. Might spook 'em."

Standing next to Jinny, Stringfellow studied her soft, full face set off by a pair of dimples. He admired the smooth skin, clear blue eyes, and sleek, auburn hair gathered on top of her head. Even in a faded cotton dress, she looked beautiful. He wondered how old she was? Twenty? Twenty-two? Maybe only eighteen. How long had she been married? Where had her husband been killed? Stringfellow had a lot of questions, but few answers. The blacksmith at the livery stable had mentioned that Jinny's husband had been an officer in Stonewall's army and had died fighting in the east, but that was all. If it wasn't too forward, he would call on her before he left, maybe take her a pound of real coffee and ask her out for a stroll. But he had to be careful. A gentleman shouldn't push too hard, but these weren't normal times. Things had changed and there was no going back.

"They're repeating their request," said Pendleton, his eyes riveted on the sounder. "What's our reply?"

"Tell him that 6,000 of Early's infantry and ten cannon have already arrived by rail and the rest are expected any time." Crook would learn that fighting Indians out west wasn't the same as playing bluff with Confederates on their own turf. He glanced at Jinny. There it was again, that smile. She blushed and quickly looked away. When the war was over he was definitely going to come back to see her.

Chapter 9

Ezekiel

Moses' face blanched as he read and re-read the devastating words. Collapsing in a chair, his mind reeled while his arms fell limply to his side as the letter fluttered to the floor.

Tears pooled up in his dark eyes as the significance of what his sister had written sank in. What would happen now? Taking long, measured breaths, he fought off a panic attack. With a wet towel he dabbed at his face and looked around, thankful no one else was in the room. Bending over, he retrieved the sheet of paper. It smelled faintly of perfume, belying its crushing contents.

Holding it at arm's length, he squinted at the words:

> *It is my duty to inform you that rumors have reached Leonora*
> *Levy that you have fathered a child with a mulatto slave girl in*
> *grandfather's employ. Two days ago, in strict confidence, Miss*
> *Levy called on sister Ester and me to inquire if the rumors were*
> *true. We, of course, strongly denied them. Ester and I feel that*
> *if this gossip reaches her father, he would forbid Leonora, or*
> *any member of his family, from having contact with you, or us.*

Moses exhaled. Rebecca hadn't meant to hurt him, but, as eldest daughter it was her duty to protect the family's reputation from even the hint of scandal. She and Ester were merely trying to help. When the slave girl, Isabella Johnson, first told him she was pregnant with his child, he immediately informed Rebecca who had confided the awful news to sister Ester, their mother, grandmother and grandfather. They were the only ones who knew. He had wanted to tell his older brother Michael, but his mother had said no. Michael was in the Confederate army, and didn't need to be worried about Moses' indiscretion. Moses had also wanted to tell his father, but again his mother had said no. As a prominent member of Richmond's Kahal Kadosh Beth Shalome congregation, he would be deeply embarrassed by such news.

Four years ago when Moses was only 15, Isabella, a bright, beautiful mulatto housemaid had aroused his passion beyond the breaking point. How could he have been so stupid? So blind? They had only been together twice, but that was enough. Now, he was the father of Alice, a pretty little three-year-old. Whenever he gazed into her round, innocent eyes he was overwhelmed with guilt. To think that this cute, vivacious child was a slave was almost too much to bear. His grandmother had assured him that both Alice and Isabella were better off in bondage. She promised that when the gossip died down, they would both be quietly manumitted. As it was, Alice's light skin and the preferential treatment given her mother had caused too many tongues to wag. If they were suddenly freed and allowed to stay with the family, it would create a scandal.

Swishhh. Moses jumped as the door to the room swung open. It was Tom Jefferson, his roommate.

"Come on Moze, the girls are waiting," Jefferson pleaded, shifting weight from foot to foot. Noticing Ezekiel's lack of response, he walked over and tapped him on the shoulder. "Are you all right?"

Moses slipped the letter into his geometry book, then stood up, trying to regain his composure. "I'm fine. Just let—let me get my pencils and drawing pad." Still shaky, he collected the art supplies that had arrived yesterday in a food package from Jefferson's mother. With a heavy heart, he followed Tom who happily bounded down the stairwell and out the sally port.

At the edge of the road beside Washington's statue, four young girls preened and giggled. They were students from the Ann Smith Academy who had been at the morning's flag raising ceremony in Lexington and had returned for evening dress parade. Now outfitted in colorful, airy spring dresses, their fresh faces beamed with the exuberance of youth. The leader was 17-year-old Juliet Howlett, an attractive blond with a slim figure and mischievous grin. Juliet was Jefferson's "date" but they were friends, not lovers. Before the war they had grown up in Amelia County as brother-sister playing Annie Over and Graces while their parents gossiped and complained about the high costs of silk and imported glassware. Standing beside Juliet were the 16-year-old McPherson twins, Ellen and Cornelia. With them was 15-year-old Sarah Kursheedt, whose likeness Moses had promised to sketch.

The girls whispered and flirted with passing cadets while Moses positioned Sarah on a bench with the sunlight streaming over her left shoulder. She wore a long sleeved, bright yellow cotton dress set off by a white lace collar and starched cuffs. On her head was a straw bonnet encircled by a wide, blue silk ribbon.

Moses sat across from Sarah and carefully lined up his pencils on a nearby plank. There was only time enough for a quick sketch. He studied her face, noting the high cheekbones, delicate neck, pert, straight nose, and the firm chin. He admired her luxurious, shiny black hair, and doe-like eyes which reminded him of Leonora's. He wondered if they knew each other since they were both from prominent Jewish families in Richmond. He liked Sarah's quick, easy smile and gentle manner. With a pencil he began drawing lines and shading in details. How would Leonora's family react if they found out about his daughter? He couldn't bear to think of rejection. With everyone caught up in the war, maybe his indiscretion would be overlooked, he lied to himself.

In fifteen minutes he had finished the sketch. The girls clustered around, signaling approval with smiles and nods. Moses handed the portrait to Sarah whose eyes sparkled with appreciation. She squeezed Moses' hand then kissed him lightly on the cheek, making him blush.

"Draw us, Moses, draw us!" chanted the other three girls.

After glancing at Jefferson, who beamed with pride at his roommate's artistic talent, Moses eagerly agreed. Drawing portraits would help take his mind off his problems at home. "Later. Maybe this weekend."

"Sunday afternoon. We'll be here Sunday afternoon," said the McPherson twins in unison.

Ratta—tat—tat. The sound of a drum beckoned the cadets back into barracks to prepare for dress parade. After shining shoes, adjusting belts, polishing cartridge boxes, combing hair and checking muskets, the Corps formed in front of Washington Arch. The first sergeants shouted their reports and the captains ordered companies to attention. With the fife playing *When Johnny Comes Marching Home* and drums beating cadence, the cadets headed for the parade ground. Something about the rhythm of a drum and a spritely tune from a fife always quickened Moses heartbeat and lifted his spirits.

As Company C marched onto the parade ground, Moses felt a surge of pride as small groups of visitors applauded while the cadets went through battalion drills. This was the first dress parade in which he carried the new Austrian rifle and the heavy weapon with its long, sharp bayonet made him feel like a real soldier. Standing beside the Guard Tree were Jefferson's four friends from Ann Smith Academy. They gaily waved handkerchiefs as the Corps passed in review. Clutching the prized sketch next to her heart, Sarah waved her bonnet when she recognized Moses.

At the close of dress parade, the flag on top of barracks was lowered and the evening gun boomed to signal the end of the day. When he returned to his room to prepare for supper, Moses warily glanced at the geometry book with Rebecca's letter tucked inside. His appetite vanished quickly as he thought of the troubles he'd brought on Isabella, his family and himself. When the Corps reached the mess hall, Moses took his seat and stared glumly at the empty plate. Instead of the usual growley with turnips and mystery meat, this evening's fare was a real treat. To honor the memory of Stonewall the cooks had prepared turkey, lemonade, butter beans, soft white bread and lemon pie. Unable to eat, he watched other cadets gobble down their meal. In addition to his problems with Isabella, Moses was scheduled tomorrow for a recitation on his most difficult subject—geometry. Since he was already border line deficient, if he did poorly he might be expelled.

When the Corps marched back to barracks, Moses immediately fell out and went to his room. While cadets strolled on the parade ground with friends and sweethearts, he was stuck at the study table cramming for tomorrow's test. But it was hopeless trying to concentrate with the sounds of laughter and horseplay echoing throughout barracks. By the time the drum beat evening tattoo his eyes were tired and his mind exhausted. While he lowered his wood bed frame and unstrapped the bedroll, his stomach began to rumble. Now he was hungry. If only he'd eaten some turkey or at least brought a piece of white meat back to the room. But taking food from the mess hall was a serious offense and he was already in enough trouble over his grades.

When his roommates finished putting down their beds and the lights were put out, Moses lay on his back, his eyes wide open. As he tossed and turned he listened to the sounds drifting in through the open window. Down by the river, frogs croaked their lonely mating calls while crickets chirped at the darkness. If he failed geometry he would be a further embarrassment to his family and Leonora would avoid him like the plague. If only time would stand still.

Clip—clop—clip—clop. The sound of a horse approaching the sally port caught his attention. Muffled voices outside the guard room engaged in a hurried conversation, then silence. He was just drifting off when a drum began the long roll.

Jefferson bolted upright. "What was that?"

"We'll know soon enough," said Moses, as he lit the lantern and swung his legs to the side of the bed. Recently, these middle of the night call-outs had become more frequent. Three weeks ago, there'd been a fire in the woods behind barracks. Last week, the long roll had summoned them to search for deserters and bushwhackers.

After pulling on their pants and fumbling with shoe laces, the cadets filed out of their rooms, down the stairwells, and out of barracks. Near Washington's statue a group of officers surrounded the Commandant as he held a lantern to a piece of paper. When the Corps was formed, Lt. Colonel Scott Ship handed the paper to Cary Weston, cadet-adjutant. Weston stepped forward and in a loud voice began to read:

"Attention to orders. The Institute has just received the following message:

> *To: Maj. Gen. F.H. Smith, Supt. VMI*
>
> *Sigel is moving up the Valley and was at Strasburg last night. I cannot tell you whether Staunton is his destination. I would be glad to have your assistance at once with the cadets and the section of artillery. Bring all the forage and rations you can.*
>
> *Yours respectfully,*
> *John C. Breckinridge, Major General*

A murmur of excitement rippled through ranks as all eyes focused on the officers huddled with the Commandant. After muted orders, the cadet officers returned to their companies.

First Sergeant Andy Stuart from Company C, who had served for seven months as drillmaster with the 52nd Virginia, began reading from a list. "The following men will immediately report to Captain Minge for artillery detail. Taylor Smith—Stuart Davis—"

Moses listened closely for his name. He enjoyed working with cannon and it would be exciting to fire the big guns in a real battle. Even if the rest of the Corps were kept in reserve, the artillery was certain to see action. Why had they selected Stuart Davis? Heck, Davis was only 15 and hardly big enough to shoulder a musket. But, he *was* tough and wiry, and knew how to handle horses.

"Andy Davis—Archy Overton—Chuck Tate…"

When the last name was called, Moses' heart sank. It would no doubt have impressed Leonora, if he'd been chosen. She was always bragging about her two brothers, Captain Ezekiel "Zeke" Levy and Isaac J. Levy, both in the Confederate artillery.

Stuart continued, "Everyone else return to your rooms and prepare to move out tomorrow morning at 8:30 sharp. Bring muskets, bayonets, cap and cartridge boxes, canteens, knapsacks, haversacks, oilskins and blankets. Put the rest of your gear in a trunk and leave it in barracks. Each man will be issued 40 rounds and 60 caps prior to departure. Breakfast is at 5:30. While in the mess hall, pick up a two day supply of cooked rations."

As soon as the Corps was dismissed, Moses joined the others in a wild cheer. Here was salvation. In a matter of minutes his world had turned completely around. There would be no recitation in geometry and he had a chance to impress Leonora.

No one slept that night as cadets packed and repacked knapsacks and haversacks. Jefferson distributed the leftover ham, cheese, cake and bread from yesterday's food parcel. Jackets and pants were checked for holes, ripped seams, and missing buttons. Moses examined the shabby condition of his shoes and clothes. Worn, but they would have to do. After three years of blockades the cadets' fancy uniforms with shiny brass buttons had given way to plain, gray fatigue jackets, worn shoes and patched pants. Only the black stripes down both legs marked the outfits as uniforms. The forage caps were blue or gray with leather visors. Around the waist was a leather belt for attaching bayonet scabbards, cartridge and cap boxes.

A little after midnight, Andy Stuart came to Moses' room to inform J.C. Early he'd be left behind to help guard the Institute.

Crushed, Early collapsed on his bed. "Tom, you can take back the food. I won't be needing it."

"Big" Evans walked over and put his hand on the despondent cadet's shoulder. "You're in no condition for a hard march, J.C. You need rest. Somebody's got to stay and look after things while we're gone. Yankee cavalry could attack here any moment, so be on the lookout. You'll go with us next time, when you're feeling better." He hesitated, noticing the lack of response, "Besides, we probably won't even see action. They'll just hold us in reserve, like always."

Moses stopped packing, "Think it's gonna be just another wild goose chase like December?"

"Probably more like two years ago when Stonewall called on us to help stop McDowell near Staunton."

"How long you figure we'll be gone?" asked Jefferson, thrilled at the prospect of a springtime lark in the Valley.

"Well," said Evans. "In '62 we left barracks on the first of May and didn't get back until the 20th. So, two, maybe three weeks."

"What's it like?" asked Jefferson, as he stuffed a change of underwear into his knapsack and rolled up his blanket in an oilskin. "Did you see any Yankees?" Jefferson had been with the Corps on the last three call-outs but those excursions had been uneventful and they hadn't been gone long.

"Mostly blisters and sore feet," said Evans. "Marching. Lots of hard marching. Stonewall kept shifting us all over the Valley. One day we covered forty-four miles in twenty-two hours. That was brutal. This could be just as bad. It's thirty-six miles from here to Staunton, and that's just the start."

"But, did you see…?"

Evans paused, "Any Yanks? Yeah. Lots of Yankees—dead ones anyway." The experience still made him shudder and he didn't like talking about it. While in one camp, the cadets were given the grim duty of burying twenty-six Union dead. In a small farm house was a wounded Federal from Ohio lying on the dining room table with a triangular hole knocked in the top of his head. His brains were running out on the floor with the front half of his skull completely empty, but he was still alive, noisily sucking water from a sponge. Later, after burying him under a sugar maple by a river, Otis Glazebrook, who always carried *The Book of Common Prayer*, held a brief Episcopal service over the grave.

"What about rain?" asked Moses, concerned about the poor condition of his shoes. He'd been promised a new pair by the quartermaster but it would be a couple of weeks before they were ready.

"Rain and lots of it. Make sure to take an oilskin or poncho." Standard issue didn't include a poncho, but some had one from home or had bought it in Lexington. The large tents carried on the wagons were reserved for protecting ammunition and provisions.

"Now pay attention," Evans said as he held up a leather brogan. The coarse shoe reached just above the ankle and was fastened across the instep by a short leather thong. "Your biggest problem will be shoes, and feet." Looping the ends of the laces into a knot, he pulled it tight. "Always use a square knot. It keeps the shoe from slipping and blistering your feet, especially in thick brush or mud." Noticing the worn soles on Moses' shoes he added, "Whatever you do, don't wear *new* shoes unless that's all you've got. Better to go barefoot than try to break in new leather. It'll cut your ankles and rub your heels and toes raw. And socks. Wear thick high-tops and take an extra pair."

"Anything else?" asked Jefferson while wedging a block of cheese in his haversack.

Evans shook his head. "Shoes and food. That's about it. Oh yeah. Take some twine. It'll come in handy." Juggling an apple, he said, "Trust me, you'll never have enough to eat. After a week of bacon, beans and cornbread, you'll be dreaming of growley."

There was a knock on the door as Sprigg Shriver, Captain of C Company barged in. "Big, you've got a new assignment. Shaw's on medical leave, so you're the new color bearer. Go to the quartermaster and pick up a pistol." Turning to Ezekiel, he said, "Moze, you're a member of the color guard which means a temporary promotion to corporal." Continuing to check names off his list, he said, "Go find Dinwiddie, Julian Wood and Garland James and tell them to report to me in the guard room."

Evans beamed. Carrying the flag was the ultimate honor. At six-feet-two he could hoist the colors high enough to be seen by the whole Corps—and enemy snipers.

Moses was elated. Although the promotion to corporal was only temporary, it meant that he'd been noticed. Being a member of the color guard was an important assignment and came with serious responsibilities. If Evans was shot or disabled, it would be up to the nearest member of the guard to grab the flag and carry it until killed or disabled. If he did a good job it was almost certain he'd be promoted to sergeant at makeovers in July.

Wednesday, May 11

At a hurried breakfast by candlelight Moses wolfed down a double serving of milk, coffee, bread, eggs, butter, and molasses. After packing two days cooked rations in his haversack he returned to barracks for his most prized possession—the small portrait of Lenora Levy he'd drawn the last time he was in Richmond. Rolling it up, he placed it in a short waterproof tube which he wedged in his knapsack. He thought about taking his pencils and drawing paper to make sketches of the campaign, but decided against it since there was no way to protect them from the elements.

Once his gear was assembled, Moses joined the other cadets walking along the stoop and filing down the stairwells. Shriver had told him to stay with Company C until the color guard was formed on the battlefield. As the cadets milled around Washington's statue waiting for the order to form ranks, Moses noticed Sam Adams, a Rat from Arkansas, struggling with his blanket roll. Moses watched as Adams tried to balance his musket between his legs. Leaning his own gun against the statue, Moses caught Adam's firearm just as it was about to hit the ground. "It's easier if you tie the ends of the blanket together before draping it over your shoulder."

"Thanks Mr. Eze—Ezekiel," said the flustered cadet. When he pulled the blanket roll over his head, he knocked off his cap.

Retrieving the kepi, Moses placed it firmly on Adam's head. Patting Adams on the back, he said, "You'll do fine, Sam. Just relax." One of six 15-year-olds in Company C, at five-foot-two and 110 pounds Adams was the smallest and least soldierly cadet in the unit. Because of his diminutive size, he'd been issued a cut-down version of the old model Springfield, but it was still too large.

While waiting, the four companies were brought together for an explanation by the Commandant on a change in command structure. To provide experienced leadership during the campaign a tactical officer was assigned to each company as "First" captain. The cadet officers normally in charge were designated "Second" captains.

The tactical officer in command of Company A was First Captain Henry A. Wise, brother of cadet Sergeant Louis C. Wise and cousin of Corporal John S. Wise. Captain Wise was no stranger to combat. A recent graduate of the Institute he'd marched to Richmond with Stonewall in 1861 to help train new recruits. After appointment as adjutant of the 46th Virginia he had participated in several battles and skirmishes in the Valley before being captured at Nags Head, North Carolina. After release on parole, he joined VMI's faculty as Assistant Professor of Mathematics and Latin. When his exchange came through, he managed to remain at the Institute as a teacher. Though only 21, the Corps had nicknamed him, "Old Chinook."

The tactical officer in charge of Company B was First Captain Frank Preston. A graduate of Washington College and Instructor of English, Latin and Tactics, he'd been wounded by a Minie ball and shell fragment at the First Battle of Winchester. After the amputation of his left arm by Federal surgeons, Preston managed to escape and returned to Lexington where, no longer fit for field duty, he joined the faculty.

First Captain Archibald Hill headed up Company C. An 1859 graduate of VMI and veteran of the Peninsular Campaign, in 1862 he had been appointed as Instructor of French and Tactics.

The sub-professor assigned to Company D was First Captain Thomas B. Robinson, Instructor of Mathematics. Robinson was the only tact officer who hadn't seen combat. The second captain of Company D was 20-year-old Duck Colonna who had been drill-master at Camp Lee and knew more about battlefield maneuvers than most professors.

There was no tactical officer assigned to the two 3-inch rifled cannon section. Nineteen-year-old Captain Collier Minge from Mobile, Alabama, and the highest ranking cadet officer in the Corps, was placed in sole charge of the 32-man unit. Minge, whose ancestor James Minge had been clerk of Virginia's House of Burgesses in 1676, was considered mature and intelligent enough for independent command.

At 8:30 a.m. the drums began their *ratty-tat-tat* for assembly. After roll call, the Corps was brought to attention and faced left. At the head of the column was Colonel William Gilham, acting Superintendent for General Smith who was ill and staying behind. Next was the Commandant, Lt. Colonel Scott Ship, followed by the four companies of 226 cadets and six wagons of provisions. Because of the difficulty in impressing enough horses, the artillery section would have to stay behind and catch up with the main column at the first night's bivouac.

Standing in his stirrups, the Commandant held his hat high in the air, *"Corps! For-ward! Marr-ch!"* Immediately the line moved out at a brisk pace. Passing over the wooden bridge spanning the North River, the students stomped on the planks, causing the rickety structure to creak and sway. When the Institute's turrets were only faintly visible, the Corps halted and turned about. Waving their kepis over their heads, the cadets gave three hearty cheers, *"Hurrah for VMI!"*

It was 2:30 by the time the column reached Midway, 18 miles north of Lexington. In the hot, dusty weather the active pace resulted in the cadets' uniforms being soaked with sweat. As soon as they were released the cadets set off in small groups searching for a suitable spot to cool off and spend the night. While Evans secured the colors in the quartermaster's tent, Moses and Tom began scouting for level ground, free of rocks and roots. Finding extra lumber and poles piled behind a small Presbyterian church, they built a lean-to which they covered with pine branches.

Gathering an armful of straw and leaves, Moses sprinkled the cushioning over a grassy spot inside the lean-to. Unrolling his oilskin he laid it on the ground, and placed his blanket on top. He removed his shoes to inspect the soles for wear. After shaking out loose sand and gravel from the flaps, he reinforced the insides with strips of rawhide and cotton cloth. From his haversack he took out a mashed, cheese and ham sandwich, then joined his roommates at a large, communal campfire.

Several cadets cut slits in their brogans to relieve pressure on swollen blisters. New leather and ill-fitting shoes were taking their toll. Some cadets cut out the top half over the toes for much needed breathing room. Most walked around barefoot. Beside the campfire sat a large, tin kettle of water for making coffee. Next to the kettle was a cast iron skillet for cooking rations. To help restore flagging energy the cadets brewed a pot of dark, strong coffee while waiting their turn to use the skillet.

At 6:30 p.m. the cadets had finished cooking the next day's rations and eating leftovers from food parcels. With full stomachs and rested feet, they began to plan the evening's entertainment.

From his knapsack Evans removed a large, metal flask of applejack brandy from a parcel he'd received from his uncle Abner, a noted Botetourt County bootlegger. It was labeled "Dr. Abner's Magical Restorative, For Medicinal Use Only." After taking a swig, he passed the flask to Jefferson. "Here Tom, have some Dutch courage."

"But, I don't—"

"Relax, Tom," said Moses, as he winked at Evans. "We're on campaign and you can drink whatever you want. It'll make you feel better."

"Can't be too careful," cautioned Evans. "You know what they say about catching camp fever."

Taking the flask and lifting it gingerly to his nose, Jefferson sniffed the opening, then hesitated. "What would mother...?"

"She's not here," said Moses, mischievously nudging his roommate's elbow. "She wouldn't want you to get sick, would she?"

Jefferson nodded, "Guess not." Holding the flask in both hands he took a small sip.

"Not enough," chided Evans. "Take a swig like a real fightin' man."

Closing his eyes, Jefferson took a mouthful, then sputtered as the fiery liquid coursed down his throat.

"That's the way," chuckled Evans. "C'mon, soldier, have another."

Moses poured three ounces of brandy in a tin cup and added some sugar water. "Try this."

Jefferson slowly drained the cup. "Say, that's pretty good." He held out the cup for a refill.

"That's enough," said Evans, popping the cork back on the flask. "Gotta save some for tomorrow."

Several cadets with decks of cards were trying to drum up interest in a game of poker. Since no one had money they'd have to play for dried beans and bragging rights. As daylight faded, small groups sat around campfires, trading rumors of coming action and boasting of manly prowess. On the horizon, a bank of dark clouds moved toward them.

"Gonna rain," observed Blair Taylor, a third classman from Caroline County.

"Says who?" responded his roommate, Charlie Fulton.

"The signs," replied Taylor, with a knowing smile. Having grown up on a farm he had learned early how to read the weather.

"What signs?"

"See that ring around the moon?" asked Taylor, pointing overhead. Gathering his gear, he started for the church. "Yup. Gonna rain for sure, and it ain't gonna be long gittin' here."

Overhearing the conversation, Jefferson, a little tipsy from his encounter with the brandy flask, tugged on the sleeve of Moses' jacket. "Shay, Moze, I shink we'd better go shleep in that church."

As the winds picked up, a bank of fast moving clouds soon covered the moon. Moses glanced at the church, now barely visible. Behind the building were three rows of headstones which looked like ghostly sentinels. Reluctant to leave the lean-to he'd worked so hard to build, he said, "Don't know, Tom. The locals might not like us breaking into their church."

"Don't pay it no mind, Moze. I'm a Pressby…Pres—be—teari—a member of that kinda church. You can be my guest."

While Moses pondered his next move, a strong breeze swept by, blowing sparks from the campfire into his face. Without waiting, Evans ran to the lean-to, grabbed his gear and headed for the church. Following close behind, Jefferson fumbled with his bedroll and called out, "Come on Moze. If'n it rains we gonna get whet out heer. Ish's dry inside."

Reluctantly Moses rolled up his blanket, picked up his knapsack and grabbed his musket. In the distance, a bolt of lightning streaked to the ground, followed by a clap of thunder.

"It's getting closer," observed Taylor, who had returned for the coffee pot. "Reckon it's about a mile away."

With no time to waste Moses dashed after Evans and Jefferson. Using his bayonet, Evans pried open a window and the cadets scrambled in. Wedging a lighted candle in the open end of his bayonet, Moses searched for a suitable place to spend the night. Noticing a ladder leading to a loft, Moses, Jefferson, Taylor and Evans climbed up. In the corner of the small room was a pile of corn shucks which the cadets spread over the rough, wooden floor.

"Don't think the good Calvinists will mind us sacking out in their church," said Evans, as he adjusted his pile of corn shucks.

"Stonewall was a Presbyterian," said Taylor. "He'll square it with the Man upstairs."

As rain splattered on the tin roof, and wind blew the window shutters back and forth, Moses reached inside his knapsack for the tube with Leonora's portrait. Gingerly removing the sketch he held it close to the candle light for one last look. Returning the drawing to his knapsack, he blew out the candle and lay down to think. In less than a minute he was fast asleep.

Chapter 10

Strother

Thursday, May 12
Woodstock, Virginia

With rain drumming against the canvas, Colonel David Strother poked his head outside his tent. Overnight, spring thunderstorms had turned the campground into a quagmire of mud and ruts. At least it helped cool off the unseasonably hot weather which had killed one soldier from Massachusetts. In yesterday's march down from Strasburg, not accustomed to hard marching in a wool uniform, he had died from heatstroke.

Peering through the downpour at the telegrapher's tent, Strother wondered if the operators had established communications with Washington. The telegrapher's tent was adjacent to army headquarters, which was located on the first floor of a large clapboard house owned by the widow Cheney. To avoid conflict and confiscation, Madam Cheney had been pressured into taking the loyalty oath. Crossing her fingers, she had claimed to be pro-Union even though her husband, Jason Kilpatrick, had been killed by a cannon ball while fighting for JEB Stuart at Chancellorsville.

It infuriated Strother that once again he had to fend for himself in finding space for his cot and mess facilities. Since he didn't bow and scrape, or *sprechen Deutsch*, Sigel hadn't encouraged him to mingle with the chosen few.

Last night, as soon as the supply wagons reached Woodstock, Strother and Major James Lyon found space inside a hospital tent for their accommodations. The tent would be needed later for wounded, but was now being used as a storeroom for boxes of crackers, barrels of flour, salt pork and other quartermaster provisions. Crowded, stuffy and claustrophobic, at least it kept out the rain and furnished enough room for two cots, a couple of saddlebags and a few personal items. Even Tom, Strother's body servant, had found a place among the boxes for his blanket roll and a homemade haversack. It secretly pleased Strother that Lyon, one of Sigel's fair-haired wonder boys, was having to sleep in a tent like an ordinary mortal.

Strother watched two men roll a large spool of cable from the battery wagon into the telegraph tent. To find out what was going on, he would have to navigate the mud puddles between the tent and him and read cables as they trickled in.

Pulling his head back inside, he rummaged through his saddlebags for a cavalry poncho. Finally locating it tucked away at the bottom of his saddlebag he jerked it out and pulled it over his head. While searching for his hat, the tent flap flew open and Major Lyon scurried in, trailing water onto the dirt floor.

"Telegraph's up and running," said Lyon, removing his slouch hat and slapping it against a flour barrel.

"Any news?"

"Grant's in a life-or-death struggle with the Rebels at a place called Spotsylvania Court House. Casualties are running high. General Sedgwick's been killed. Shot by a Rebel sharpshooter."

"Did you find out what that racket was last night?" Bone tired from the move down from Strasburg, and after a cold, tasteless dinner of beans and hardtack, Strother had collapsed on his cot at 9:00pm only to be awakened by creaking wagon wheels, braying mules and cursing mule skinners.

Lyon chuckled, "You're not going to believe it. Those were our supply wagons heading back to Martinsburg."

"Pretty late at night to be heading back for supplies. But, if we're out of—"

"That's just it," said Lyon. "The wagons were full of provisions."

"Whoa," said Strother, holding up a hand. "Who was stupid enough to send—?"

"The division wagon master got what looked like an official order from the chief quartermaster. It said to rush all wagons, empty or full, back to the depot at Martinsburg. No explanation, just an order. It was written on headquarters stationary and appeared authentic."

"Was it signed?"

"Yep."

"Where'd it come from?"

"A man riding a Federal horse and dressed in the uniform of a Union major delivered it." Lyon chuckled, "He even spoke English with a German accent."

Strother grunted, "Damned guerillas." After a moment's reflection, he added, "But, a small band of Rebels wouldn't be able to take it from the escort." He recalled the standing order prohibiting supply trains from traveling in enemy territory unless guarded by at least 400 cavalry.

"That's just it. There *was no* escort. The order said to move out at once, that a detachment of cavalry would catch up. Lucky for us the chief quartermaster heard about it in time. He chased them down and brought it back."

Strother could only shake his head with admiration at the Rebels' audacity. It was a bold plan and would've meant real trouble had it succeeded. Now Mosby, McNeill and Gilmor were ordering around the army's wagon trains.

"Time to check telegrams," said Lyon as he and Strother pulled their ponchos tightly around their bodies and stepped out into the rain. As they splashed through puddles, Strother noticed two thoroughbred horses tied to the tongue of a battery wagon outside the cipher tent. The animals were guarded by a rough looking cavalry sergeant mounted on a sturdy horse and cradling a carbine. Strother recognized the black horse with a silver trimmed saddle as belonging to Major General Julius Stahel, chief of cavalry.

"Poof, just like dat! Gone. Into tin air," exclaimed an excited voice from inside the tent.

As Strother and Lyon drew nearer, the flap flew back and out came two officers draped in cavalry ponchos.

"Strother," called the smaller of the two, "Can you beleef what jus' happened?" It was General Stahel. As he removed his kepi, the rain splattered over his neat, wavy hair. "My best horsemens. *Poof.* Gone like a piece of smoke."

Strother bit his lip to stifle a grin as water cascaded down the center-part in Stahel's hair, and dripped off the ends of his mustache. Having worked as a teacher and journalist in London and New York, the Hungarian was perfectly capable of speaking correct English if he took his time, but was now clearly flustered.

"Was it Higgins' detachment?" asked Strother. Before leaving Winchester he'd seen Colonel Higgins with 500 horsemen heading into the mountains after the partisan, Hanse McNeill. Four days later a telegram arrived from General Kelly stating that Higgins' detachment had been attacked by General Imboden and driven back toward Romney.

"Damn right it was," said the man standing next to Stahel.

Despite the broad brimmed hat pulled low, Strother easily recognized Colonel John Wynkoop, commander of the Second Cavalry Brigade. Wynkoop, a large, imposing man of 38, stood a head taller than Stahel and had a receding hairline set off by an oval face and neatly trimmed mustache. Now his normally pleasant expression was flushed with anger as he struggled to control his temper. A native of Pennsylvania, Wynkoop was a veteran cavalry officer who had fought with distinction at Gettysburg and had extensive experience skirmishing with guerillas in the Valley. When asked, he had strongly advised against sending cavalry into the mountains after partisan rangers, but Washington had been embarrassed by McNeill's attack and demanded action.

There was a rustling sound from the tent as an operator leaned out and waved a new telegram. "This just in," he said, handing it to Stahel.

The General read the cable, then slapped his kepi against his leg. Staring first at Wynkoop, then Strother, he sputtered, "It's—it's from General Kelley. Higgins jus' reached Cumberland. Dat Colonel abandoned all his mens, horses, wagons—everything. Kelley says dat Higgins is badly broken down."

"Just what I expected," grunted Wynkoop. "Now I'm out 500 good men—all for nothing. He paused, "I hope the same thing doesn't happen to Boyd."

Strother nodded in agreement. Yesterday, at Woodstock, another 300 of Wynkoop's men had been sent east over the Blue Ridge to scout for Rebels. Crossing at Ashby's gap they were to patrol down the east side of Massanutten Mountain to prevent Imboden's cavalry from circling behind the Federal position. The plan called for them to re-cross back into the Valley at New Market gap where they would rejoin the main body of Union troops. To Strother it was a mistake to send such a large detachment beyond supporting distance where they could be cut off and defeated in detail.

As Stahel and Wynkoop mounted their horses, Stahel motioned for Strother. "Colonel, let me know as soon as you hear anything from General Crook."

As they rode off, Strother turned to Lyon, "Any idea where Crook is?"

"Nope," said Lyon. "Last message from him was six days ago when he was heading for Dublin depot."

"I don't think he's close to Staunton," said Strother.

"Have you heard something?"

"Just those Rebel telegrams." The day before, when Union cavalry swept into Woodstock they captured several important dispatches from Breckinridge. One, dated May 5, said he was leaving Dublin for Staunton with 4,000 men. That meant the Rebel army was somewhere in the Valley with a sizeable force. Another dated May 10, reported Lee driving the enemy at all points at Spotsylvania Court House. A third telegram wanted to know if Sigel was moving across the Blue Ridge toward Grant's army.

"But there's no mention of Crook," said Lyon.

"Exactly. Not a word. If he were near Staunton, Breckinridge would've said something."

"Guess you're right." As the rain slackened, Lyon turned toward Cheney house. "I'd better go give the General the bad news about Higgins. He's not going to like it."

As Strother threaded his way around the mud puddles on his way back to his tent, he noticed a rickety, two-man cart heading his way. The swayback mule pulling the cart had one ear standing mostly upright, the other flopped over. The cart's two wheels were slightly bent causing it to sway from side to side as it lurched through ruts in the road. Perched on the seat were two figures. One was Strother's young servant, Tom.

"Found him, Boss," called Tom, motioning with a thumb toward a tall, lanky, black man driving the cart. The driver was dressed in tattered coveralls held in place by a single strap over the left shoulder. The soles of his shoes dangled by a few threads. On his head was a generous crop of curly, gray hair which was topped by a ratty, narrow brim straw hat.

Strother walked over. "That you, Pastor John?"

"Sho is, Mr. Porte," said a low, rich voice. Jumping down from the buckboard, Pastor John removed his hat. "I'se de same ole me."

Strother extended a hand, "It's been a long time." It amazed him how little his friend had changed. It had been four years since he last saw the kitchen manager, general greeter and entertainer for the Inn at Narrow Passage. The Inn, a well-known watering hole and overnight accommodation along the Great Wagon Road, was two miles south of Woodstock at a point where the roadbed was only wide enough for a single carriage.

While traveling through the Valley before the war, Strother, writing under his pen name "Porte Crayon," had frequently stayed at the Inn gathering country fables for his articles in *Harper's*. Pastor John's folk tales of animals and characters who inhabited the ever-sunny "Sassafras Springs" were a rich source of mountain lore which Strother mined with enthusiasm. One of Porte Crayon's main characters, Little Mice, had been patterned after Pastor John.

"How do you stay so young?" asked Strother. He knew Pastor John to be at least 70, but he still had the quickness of a 50-year-old.

"De Lord hath watched over me," said the spry, elderly Negro. "You looks the same as you did las time I saw you, three-fo years ago. Maybee a lil older. Maybee a lil scrawnier." Pastor John stepped back and looked Strother up and down. "Must say, I'se surprised to see you dressed in dat Yankee uniform. I always thought you wuz a real southeren gentleman."

"Don't be too hard on me, Pastor John. After all, I'm fighting for your..." The words trailed off when he saw the look of disapproval on the stern face. Pastor John wasn't a slave, hadn't been for over thirteen years, ever since Philip Stover died and willed him his freedom. As storyteller and head cook at the Inn he had managed to fit in with Valley culture and made a good living entertaining guests while dishing out heaping portions of regional specialties. Pastor John owned his own home, was main preacher at the Ebenezer Valley church, and patriarch of an extended family. It was no use explaining to Pastor John how the war benefited him. He'd adapted and had no desire to see his life torn apart by marauding armies and hard times.

Before the war, Strother's family had owned the large Pavilion Hotel in Berkeley Springs and both he and his father had been good friends with Miss Ann Elizabeth Ruddell, proprietress of the Inn at Narrow Passage. Known affectionately to the locals as "Miss Daisy," the quick-witted, intelligent Ann Elizabeth had been educated in France. When her foster mother died in 1855, Ann Elizabeth inherited the inn. Returning to the Valley at 19, she decided to keep the inn open and operate it herself. With the help of Robert McGinnis as general manager and Pastor John, who ran the kitchen and entertained the guests, the inn prospered until the war drove away the customers.

Strother was amused at Pastor John's use of the slave's patois. He knew Pastor John could speak as "white" as he wanted, that he slipped in and out of the slave's vernacular when telling stories, or as a defense against suspicious strangers. Five years ago Strother had seen him do a scrape and shuffle when a pair of vile looking slave catchers stopped by the inn. Pastor John later explained that it wasn't wise to speak too "high" when dangerous, greedy men were lurking about, looking for a black to kidnap and sell south. "They ain't searchin for runaways who got owners," he'd said. "No, siree, not dese men. Just some poor person of color like me who won't be missed when dey snatches 'em up an' sends 'em off." He always carried his Certificate of Freedom in his pocket, but knew that a piece of paper wouldn't carry much weight on a sugar plantation a hundred miles down some nameless Louisiana bayou.

Strother nodded toward the rickety cart, "That's some rig."

Pastor John grinned broadly, "Body cain't be too careful, what with all dem Yankee soldiers milling around. Dey's not God fearin' men like you and me. Dey'd sooner steal a fancy workin' rig den snatch a fat chickin." He pointed toward Tom. "Your boy says you want to ax me somethin." He took off his battered straw hat, and absentmindedly straightened the brim, "Might it be dat you got a hankerin for some of Pastor John's secret recipes?"

"Just might be," said Strother, hoping to make an arrangement for eating at the inn while at Woodstock. He planned to invite Lt. Colonel Lincoln and Colonel Wells from the 34th Massachusetts to join him. They would make good company and he wouldn't be "casting pearls" like he frequently did when talking with uneducated, junior officers. In addition, if the going got rough it wouldn't hurt to have friends in high places. He also planned to ask Lyon to tag along since the major was the only one privy to conversations inside Sigel's headquarters. Hiring Pastor John would be expensive, but it might be his last chance for anything other than hardtack and mealy bacon. "I don't suppose you can—?"

"Yep, kin do, Mr. Porte," said Pastor John. "The inn's closed for bisness right now. But I already discussed it wif Miss Daisy, and she says—since it's you—if you kin git a guard for de inn to keep looters away, we kin take keer of you."

"How's Miss Daisy? Married yet?" If she was still single, Strother knew it was by choice. When he last saw her four years ago she was 23, vivacious and extremely attractive.

Pastor John hesitated. He didn't want to mention that McGinnis, her beau, was a captain with Mosby's Rangers. "She's doin' jest fine. But cain't really say if she has a boyfriend. Some say she do, some say she don't."

Strother turned to Tom. "What unit's camped near the inn?"

"It's them Massatoosets fellas," said Tom. "Your good friend, Mr. Lincoln's there."

"Fine," said Strother, relieved it wasn't cavalry or one of the German regiments. He turned to Pastor John, "If you can feed four of us every night while we're here, you can tell Miss Daisy I'll get her a guard."

Pastor John nodded, then stared at the ground. Speaking slowly, he said, "Now less see. What kinda—food—you got in mind?"

"What's available?"

"Well, dat depends," Pastor John replied as he thoughtfully puckered his lips. "What wit everthin' bein' so hard to git—an 'spensive."

Strother tried to look serious, but knew he was being played by a master. Pastor John was one of the smartest businessmen he'd ever met, a real genius at separating gullible, hungry travelers from their cash. Although Strother was wearing the fancy uniform, he knew it was this sly, black man, dressed in poor-man's rags, who was really in control. "I'm willing to pay . . ."

With long, delicate fingers Pastor John scratched his chin. "Is we talkin' paper money—or gold?"

"Gold," Strother quickly answered. For the past two years he'd been converting his army pay into one dollar gold coins. Gold had no political agenda or conscience and was readily accepted everywhere. The current exchange rate was four dollars Federal paper for one dollar gold. In the South the conversion rate was 20 dollars Confederate paper for one dollar gold. In a tight situation having the right amount of gold could save your life.

"Gold—de Lord be praised," said Pastor John, raising his hands skyward. "Now, how many folks we talkin 'bout?"

"Four. For supper."

"Well, if'n you kin see your way clear to makin a small contribution to the church . . ."

Strother cringed. He knew that whenever "The Church" was mentioned, things got expensive. "Now, what I want is—"

"Le's see, two—three nights?"

"Probably three." It looked to Strother like Sigel had settled down at Woodstock and wasn't going to move until ordered to do so by Washington.

"Well, ain't gonna be easy, what wif all de soldiers scrounging around, stealin' everything dat ain't nailed down. I'll haf to go into the mountins for de good things. But if de Lord be willin'. . ." He held up a forefinger missing an end, "Firs night,—fresh fried fish." He stared into the distance as if trying to conjure up a menu from the swirling storm clouds. "Wif enuf of dat gold I kin git some real nice shad. Den succotash—canned by my wife. Spoon bread wif real butter, watermellen rind pickles, and persimmon puddin for dessert."

"Excellent," said Strother, closing his eyes in anticipation. It'd been a long time since he'd eaten at Pastor John's table and it surprised and delighted him that here, in the midst of all this deprivation, it was still possible to eat well.

"Secun night, hmmm." Pastor John glanced sideways at Strother to dangle the hook. "I'm thinkin'—gud country ham and a big servin' of hot grits wif lots of red eye gravy. Candied sweet taiters, and fresh collard greens—seasoned with side meat." Now for the clincher, "Fer dessert, some of Pastor John's famous strawberry short cake with real whippin' cream." He smiled at the look of pleasure on Strother's face.

"You still haven't said how much."

"Well, in de old days, I'd hadda charge a lot. But since we's sech good friends, I kin let you have it fer, say, three dollahs gold." He monitored Strother's expression closely, "—each night."

Strother knew he should haggle, at least a little, but was relieved it wasn't more, much more. The variety and abundance of food pleased him. "Tonight at seven-thirty," he said, rummaging through his purse for coins.

Pastor John cleared his throat, "Fer another one of dem gold coins, I kin git you some of Pastor John's 'Special Reserve.' "

Strother nodded and fished out another gold piece. Pastor John's Special Reserve was known to be the finest homebrew in the Valley. Made by the legendary moonshiner, Elmer Creech, at Mudhole Gap, the corn liquor was over 120 proof and had a smooth finish that didn't scorch the enamel off your teeth or cause you to go blind.

Satisfied, Pastor John placed the coins inside a leather pouch tied to a leather shoelace around his neck. "Tell yer friends to bring dere own cups. All de glasses at de Inn were snatched six months ago by some cavalry."

"Not ours I hope?"

"Don't know. Now days, cain't tell. De riders was dressed in Yankee blue, but uniforms don't mean nothin. Coulda been bushwhackers or Yankee scouts jist passin thru." With that, Pastor John hitched up his pants, jumped on board his dilapidated rig and with a sprightly "giddy up" pointed the mule's nose toward home.

Fifteen minutes later, Strother mounted his pony and headed south to find Lt. Colonel Lincoln. It was only two-and-a-half miles to the 34th's camp, and he could've walked, but it was muddy and he didn't want to leave his pony unattended. One of Stahel's scouting parties might scoop it up and he would be back riding a commissary wagon. On the outskirts of town he passed troops from the 18th Connecticut. They were huddled around a smoky camp fire, picking off lice and setting them on tin sheets held over an open flame. He could hear shouts of encouragement as the greybacks scurried around the hot tin race track. Further on, he saw men from the 123rd Ohio gathered around a pit betting on a cockfight. From the commotion it sounded like "Old Abe" was battling "Jeff Davis." Unfortunately for the Union, after a flurry of spurs and feathers, Old Abe wound up *hors de combat* destined for the evening's supper table.

Nearing the campground of the 34th, Strother saw several rows of tents neatly aligned in an open field. In the distance was the Inn behind a line of trees bordering Narrow Passage Creek. Despite the rain and mud, he noticed the regiment going through close order drill. That was a good sign. While men from other units were betting on lice races and lounging in their tents, Colonel Wells had his troops out marching. Spotting a picket draped in a poncho, Strother asked where to find Lt. Colonel Lincoln. With droplets of water dripping from the end of his nose, the sentry pointed to a tent on the river bank at the far end of the field.

As he rode along the edge of the camp Strother noticed a man dressed in rags walking among the tents, picking up scraps of paper. For pants the man had his legs thrust through the arms of a blouse tied loosely around the waist by a dark blue cloth. Small pieces of red flannel were attached to his shoulders by brass buttons.

As he neared the tent Strother saw four men standing at the entrance. One was Lt. Colonel Lincoln conversing with two armed guards. Between the guards was a bare headed prisoner whose legs were shackled by a heavy chain.

When Strother rode up, Lincoln waved him over. After he dismounted the two went inside. Half the tent was being used to store commissary supplies. The other half held two cots and two small valises. Set up near the entrance as a table was a large wooden cracker box. Two seats fashioned from nail kegs had been placed behind the table.

Unable to control his curiosity, Strother said, "I couldn't help but notice the rather unique uniform of that man policing the grounds. Is that a new style Zouave outfit?"

Lincoln looked puzzled, then grinned, "Oh, you saw Private Anderson."

"That's quite an outfit."

"It's his own design."

"And the red cloth on the shoulders?"

"Some kind of exalted rank. I think the brass buttons are stars. He won't say exactly, just 'exalted.'"

"It looked a little breezy in the back. Hope you don't entertain high hopes that Washington's going to approve it as a regimental uniform."

Lincoln chuckled. "Yesterday morning, Anderson showed up at sick call. Claimed to have stomach cramps so severe he couldn't stand up. The only thing that could cure him was that new outfit. When Doc Lindley examined him and couldn't find anything wrong, I recommended a strong purgative. After spending last night with his rear end hanging over a bucket, Anderson says he's feeling better and would like his old uniform back. Unfortunately, we're not issuing new clothes until tomorrow morning."

It didn't take Strother long to outline Pastor John's offer of special food from the inn in exchange for a guard detail. Lincoln was quick to accept for himself and Colonel Wells. In fact, Wells had already posted a guard at the inn since two rooms on the ground floor were being used as a hospital for men suffering from heatstroke and typhus.

"I need to be clear on one point," said Lincoln. "Is the food paid for?"

"As compared to—liberated?" asked Strother.

"Exactly. Colonel Wells has a strict policy against stealing from citizens. In fact, he's quite adamant about it. He says we're fighting to bring the Rebels back into the Union, not drive them out."

"Hope he's not *too* picky," said Strother, who wasn't bashful about living off the land while on campaign. "Not even a stray chicken?"

"Not even a stray egg," replied Lincoln. "The Colonel's a man of principle. When he was provost in Martinsburg he spent a lot of time listening to weeping women complain about being robbed by soldiers. Their tales of woe made a strong impression on him."

"I can assure you it's all fully paid for."

"Good. Just checking. Colonel Wells would rather starve than eat stolen food." Lincoln motioned toward the prisoner waiting outside. "Care to sit in on a small matter?"

Strother nodded.

Lincoln opened the tent flap, "Bring in Private Treadwell."

Lincoln and Strother sat in the chairs behind the makeshift table and poured themselves two cups of cold coffee from Lincoln's canteen. Roughly pulling the prisoner inside, the guards brought him to an abrupt halt in front of the two officers.

"Unshackle him," ordered Lincoln. When that was done, he told the guards to leave.

While the man stood, head lowered, Lincoln read aloud from the charge sheet. "Private Joseph Treadwell, Company A. You're accused of cowardice in the face of the enemy." He raised an eyebrow, "Well, Private. What have you got to say for yourself?"

"Not—not much, Colonel."

"Not much, indeed," snapped Lincoln, waving the charge sheet at Treadwell. "It says here, 'When stationed on picket duty with two fellow soldiers, Private Joseph A. Treadwell did break and run when attacked by six Rebel cavalry. Had a relief column not come along in time, the two soldiers left standing bravely at their post might have been captured or killed.' " Raising his head, he asked, "Do you know the penalty for cowardice in the face of the enemy?"

"It—it ain't good," was the barely audible reply. Still looking down, Treadwell said, "But, Colonel—I ain't to blame."

"Not to blame? What do you mean by that?"

"Why, Colonel, I had on a new pair of shoes, and try as I might, I could *not* make them stand still. They just up and run away, taking me right along with 'em."

Strother snorted, spewing coffee over the table.

Lincoln tried to stifle a grin while he wiped coffee from the charge sheet. "Fortunately for you, Private Treadwell, the men you deserted were not hurt, and your company commander states you've been a good soldier until now." He hesitated, "Because of that, I'm going to give you *one* last chance."

"Yessiree," came the reply, as Treadwell raised his head and straightened his back. "I won't let you down again, Colonel. You've got my word."

"It's not me you're letting down. It's your fellow soldiers whose lives depend on you doing your duty." He leaned forward and looked down at Treadwell's feet. "Best get rid of those shoes, Private, or the next time you're brought up on a charge of cowardice those shoes are going to march you right in front of a firing squad." Lincoln slammed the charge sheet on the table, causing the coffee mugs to rattle. "Now, get out of here before I change my mind."

As soon as Treadwell was gone, Lincoln pushed his chair back. "Just don't know what came over him. He's been one of our best." As he ripped the charge sheet into little strips, he added, "I don't want to send this sort of thing to headquarters. It would only hurt the regiment's reputation. Colonel Wells thinks whippings, brandings and firing squads are bad for moral. Better to handle such matters inside the regiment.

"We're all cowards at one time or another," said Strother. "You'll know soon enough if Private Treadwell has backbone."

"Hope I haven't made a mistake," said Lincoln, as he strapped on his sword and pulled a poncho over his head. "Time to check on the men."

As the two officers walked out into the rain, Strother said, "Couldn't help but notice that your regiment's the only one going through drills in this weather."

"The men have to learn how to keep their powder dry and rifles working regardless of the rain. The Rebs aren't going to stop fighting just because we might get our feet wet."

"Seven-thirty sharp then, in front of the inn," said Strother, as he climbed into the saddle. In the distance he could see smoke rising from the kitchen chimney at the rear of the inn. Pulling the brim of his hat low to keep out the rain, Strother headed back to camp. Still tired from last night's fitful sleep, he decided to get some rest. Since Sigel was only communicating with his German officers, there was no need to check in at headquarters.

When he reached his tent, Strother switched into dry clothes, poured himself a shot of brandy, then sat down to write Mary about the day's events. When the campaign was over he planned to use the letters to complete his diary. He gave Tom instructions to wake him at 6:00 p.m.

After a short, dreamless nap, Strother felt a tugging on his sleeve. "Time, Boss."

Strother looked at his watch. 6:03. Splashing cold water over his face he had Tom saddle the pony. By the time he reached the inn, the rain had slowed to a steady drizzle. The sturdy, two story structure was as he remembered it. Thick log walls, heavy shutters and a stone foundation built in 1740 as a stronghold against Indian attacks. A wave of nostalgia swept over him as he recalled the good times spent at the inn as a guest. With rum punch in hand he had whiled away many nights relaxing by a roaring fire and listening to fellow travelers spin outlandish yarns.

When he rode up two guards from the 34th Mass were stationed at the steps. Good. That would keep the bummers at bay. After tying his pony to the iron hitching post, he walked around back to check on Pastor John's progress. The large kitchen was behind the main building and was constructed from hand-hewn oak logs chinked with clay. Seeing light streaming through cracks in the walls, Strother went to the door and knocked.

"Dat you, Mr. Porte?" called a voice. "I'se coming."

The inviting, yeasty smell of freshly baked bread wafted into the outside air as Pastor John opened the kitchen door and stepped into the yard. "Try dis," he said and handed Strother a hot cheese biscuit dripping with fresh butter. Strother nodded approval as he devoured the biscuit.

"Gud—real gud," he mumbled, as he licked the butter from his fingers. "Where's Miss Daisy?"

"Upstairs. She'll come down when yo guests gits here. Come on in and check out de special room I got for you." Pastor John led Strother through the back door into the main dining room, which was empty except for two plank tables and eight, hardback chairs. The largest table was set with four mismatched plates, spoons, knives and forks. On a small side table a pitcher of water, a pitcher of fresh lemonade, a bowl of ice and an earthen jug full of Pastor John's Special Reserve were laid out. "Dat's de best I can do fer eatin' utensils. All that I had befoe done been stolen by men with sticky fingers."

"Everything's top rail," said Strother as he viewed the simple but functional arrangement. It had been a long time since he'd tasted fresh lemonade—and ice? What a nice touch. He'd almost forgotten you could have ice in such warm weather. There had been an ice house at his family's hotel in Berkeley, but Stonewall's troops had used it for a trash dump.

"You said this room's special?" asked Strother.

"Sho is. Genr'l Stonewall Jackson used dis very same room fo' his head-quarters when he was here in '62." He pointed to a Bible on the fireplace mantel, "Dat's his Bible. He was a good man. A God fearin' man. A fine Christian gentleman. He gave me dat Bible for use at my church. It's my most prized possession."

Next to the Bible was a cross made from interwoven vines and two homemade candles. The candles had burned down so that all that was left were two globs of tallow. Noticing Strother looking at the candles, Pastor John said, "I lit dose candles on the tenth of May. It was a year ago on the tenth that Marse Jackson died. De flames carried my prayers fo' him up to de Genr'l in heaven."

"Well, gotta git back to my fixin's," said Pastor John, as he dusted specs of flour from his apron. "Let me know when yo friends gits here. You kin hep youself to the drinks. Tell 'em to go easy on the Special Reserve or dere eyes'll cross and dey won't be able to find dere way back home."

After Pastor John left, Strother walked around the room trying to shake an eerie feeling that there were ghosts looking over his shoulder. For fresh air, he unbolted the front door and stepped outside to chat with the guards.

It wasn't long before he saw three riders approaching. The collars on their raincoats were turned up to the ears and their hats were pulled low. As they drew nearer Strother recognized Major Lyon and Lt. Colonel Lincoln.

The third horseman was mounted on a handsome bay, the sleek black mane and tail contrasted sharply with the rich mahogany of its body.

"Finally, I get to meet the famous Porte Crayon," said Wells, as he pulled up and dismounted.

"It's a pleasure, Colonel," said Strother, as he patted the horse's neck. "That's some animal." While Wells tied the reins to the hitching post, Strother sized up his new guest. Of normal height and build, Wells had a broad face, high forehead, kind eyes, erect bearing, and full beard. More important, he had mentioned Strother's writings. Just the kind of attributes Strother looked for in a commanding officer.

Wells beamed, "He's a gift from the local bar when I joined up. I call him 'Boston Bar.' Not too original I know, but it reminds me of home." Affectionately stroking the horse's mane, he said, "He's the closest thing to family I've had for three years."

Ushering the men inside, Strother explained the room's connection with Stonewall Jackson and how Pastor John had turned the room into something of a shrine.

"I'm surprised Sigel didn't commandeer this place for his headquarters," said Wells.

"He doesn't know about it," said Strother. "Anyway, it's not big enough for him and his German staff." Strother led his guests to the drink table, "This isn't the bar at Willard's, but it's the best corn liquor in the Valley." As the men poured themselves cups of lemonade laced with Special Reserve, Strother helped himself to a glass of ice filled part way with the private homebrew. "Watch out for this stuff. It'll make your knees go wobbly."

The men stood by the fireplace and relaxed over small talk. Strother learned that Wells was a dutiful son, wrote frequent letters home to his mother, wasn't married, liked pretty women, enjoyed the soldier's life, and was well thought of by his men and the legal fraternity in Boston. Because of his sense of fairness, the Colonel also had a good reputation among citizens in Rebel areas where he'd been in control. He understood that people had long memories when it came to humiliation and thievery. It was his opinion that if the radicals in Washington adopted a scorched earth policy, the Republican party would pay for it at the polls after the war.

Gradually the conversation shifted to Sigel's plans for advancing on Staunton. Strother's face flushed when he had to admit that as a non-German speaking outsider, he wasn't privy to the details.

"I overheard General Stahel say we'll be here at least a couple of days," volunteered Major Lyon. "We're waiting on orders from Washington."

To show he wasn't totally uninformed, Strother added, "The general thinks we've already accomplished our main objective."

"Which is…?" asked Lincoln. "We haven't beaten Breckinridge."

"All Grant wanted us to do was draw the Rebels away from Crook while he wrecked the Virginia and Tennessee Railroad in Dublin."

"And that's it?" asked Wells, surprised that so little was expected.

"There aren't any new orders," said Major Lyon, defensively.

"Orders?" snapped Wells. "Grant's locked in a death struggle with Lee at Spotsylvania Court House and we just sit here? Whatever happened to plans for a coordinated attack? What more do we need? Couldn't we show a little initiative?"

Strother poured himself another touch of liquor. "One of the telegrams we captured said the Rebels are worried we might cross the Blue Ridge and strike Lee's left flank."

"Yet we just sit," muttered Wells. "Breckinridge hands us a battle plan and we hunker down and drill. In a couple of days any chance we have of making a difference will be gone."

"General Sigel doesn't think we're strong enough to attack Lee's flank without Crook's infantry," said Lyon. "If we head east we'd have Breckinridge in our rear, Mosby on our flanks and Lee in front. It seems only prudent to wait."

"Indecision is the enemy of victory," said Wells, brushing off Lyon's comments. He looked directly at Strother, "Someone ought to tell the commanding general what needs to be done." It had been over two years since the 34th had been organized and Wells was eager to test his men in combat. Even though they'd received high praise for parade ground appearance, rumors were starting to circulate that the regiment was nothing but a band-box outfit full of paper-collar soldiers.

"They'll have to tell him in German," said Strother, with a smirk.

"Keerfull, mein herr," cautioned Lincoln, in a perfect imitation of Sigel's high pitched voice. "Ish don't vant nein suggestions von regimentals." He held his cup aloft, "Yah! Das ist drue, I shpeaks mit you. Vile vee sits hier on our hands, der Rebels runs from Deutscher manns."

Strother and Wells roared with laughter. Even Lyon had to smile.

There was a light tapping on the door leading to the second floor as Ann Elizabeth "Daisy" Ruddell entered. She was wearing a plain, dark blue dress trimmed in white that showed off her shapely figure. All conversation stopped.

Strother stepped forward, and took her hand. "Ann Elizabeth, you've made time stand still. You haven't changed a bit."

"How many years has it been, Mr. Strother? Four? Five?"

"Too long." Still holding her hand, Strother introduced her to the officers. When he got to Wells, the Colonel blushed and was so taken by her beauty that he could hardly remember his own name.

"It's—it's a real pleasure Mi—Miss Ruddell."

"Please Colonel. Call me Daisy, it's my *nom de guerre*."

"*Nom de guerre*?" asked Strother. "I hope that doesn't mean you've joined the Rebel army."

"Why, Mr. Strother, didn't you know? I've always been a participant in the battle—the battle of the sexes," she said as she cast a fleeting glance in Colonel Wells direction.

Wells' face turned scarlet red. "If all the ladies in Virginia were as fair as you, I'd—I'd . . ."

"Secede, Colonel?"

Wells was too smitten to reply.

"Ann Elizabeth, would you care to join us?" asked Strother. He knew the officers would enjoy dining with this delightful, quick-witted woman who wasn't at all bashful about stating her opinions. "From what I've heard, the food at the Inn is still the best in Virginia."

"Even better than your Berkeley Hotel?" asked Daisy. "But I forgot, you're a *West* Virginian now. I'd better be careful. Colonel Wells might think me a spy if I showed too much interest in your man-talk. Then he'd have to shoot me at sunrise. And I must confess that I'm not an early riser."

Wells smiled but couldn't help staring. "Miss Daisy, I—I can assure you . . ."

Ann Elizabeth turned to Strother, "I just received a note from Mary Hollingsworth at Abram's Delight in Winchester. She wrote that General Sigel and his staff recently took over her home and after eight days of trashing the property and butchering all her animals, paid her a paltry five dollars in Yankee paper." She sighed, "I ask you, Mr. Strother, is that any way to treat a lady?"

Now it was Strother's turn to blush. "I wasn't part of that—"

Daisy held up her hand, "I don't blame you, Mr. Strother, even though you *are* dressed in that outfit. It's the ill-bred Dutchmen and their lack of manners that are to blame. They show no respect for our simple country ways and treat us like peasants." She reached over and patted Wells' arm. "Colonel, I've heard you're a man of quality. A Yankee who doesn't steal chickens and who respects citizens' rights." She gazed into his eyes, "If only you weren't an *invader.*"

Wells felt a sudden urge to protect this independent woman whose life had been turned upside down by the misfortunes of war. "I—I'll keep a guard at the inn, at least until we're ordered to move out."

"Thank you, Colonel," said Daisy. As she prepared to leave, Wells rushed to open the door leading to the stairs. She nodded her appreciation and turned to Strother, "Please ask General Sigel to send some hay to the inn. His Yankee horses have eaten all we had and before long your doctors will need lots of hay to keep Yankee blood from staining the floors."

After Daisy left, each man's thoughts drifted to the coming campaign as he wondered if it would be his blood soaking the floors. The somber mood quickly vanished when the back door swung open and Pastor John came in carrying a tray heaping with food. The delightful smells of fried fish, spoon bread, and steaming, hot succotash filled the air.

"Gentlemen, I present Pastor John, storyteller and chef extraordinaire," said Strother with a wave of his hand.

Placing the tray on the side table, Pastor John, who was dressed in a tattered, clean, white jacket and tall, starched white hat, said, "Gentlemens, please be seated." Walking over to the fireplace he removed Jackson's Bible from the mantle. "Befo' we partakes of de Lord's blessin's, le's bow our heads and give thanks."

When all was quiet, Pastor John began, "De Bible says, 'Thou shalt not kill.'" Frowning, he slowly shook his head while patting the Bible, "In Matthew, Jesus tells us dat whosoevah liveth by de sword, so shall he *die* by de sword."

Strother winced. He'd neglected to warn his guests how religious and pro-Confederate Pastor John truly was.

Wells immediately thought of home and his mother. What *were* his chances of dying by the sword in the coming battle? Two weeks ago he'd written his sister, *"My only care is for mother. If I fall, it is of her I shall think, first and last. Tell her this if the time comes."*

Opening an eye, Pastor John peeked at the officers gathered around the table. "Furthermo', de Bible says blessed are the peacemakers, fo' they shall be called chilren of God. Blessed are de merciful, fo' they shall obtain mercy." He raised his right hand, "God, grant fogiveness to dees men for dere *many, many* sins. Protect dem as they passes thru the valley of the shadow of death. Sho Your mercy to those who have caused so much sufferin' in this, Your peaceful valley. Grant dat these mens, humbled befo' Your almighty hand, may dwell with You in Your heavenly kingdom." He held the Bible over his head, "Amen."

"Amen," replied the officers.

Chapter 11

Wise

Friday, May 13
Staunton

It was still dark when the Corps formed into ranks for the first roll call of the day. Low lying clouds drifted over the camp sending down a light drizzle which only added to the penetrating chill. After last night's bountiful hospitality by the citizens of Staunton, more than a few heads were throbbing from too much liquid refreshment and too little sleep. Having to bivouac without tents, the cadets had spent the night huddled in wet clothes, on wet ground, under wet blankets, and with wet knapsacks for pillows. Only an oilskin offered any protection from the elements and that wasn't much. Yesterday, several cadets with friends in town had run the block and hadn't been heard from since. As each company called out names of the missing, Wise looked around for Jack Stanard. If he didn't show up for the 6:00 o'clock departure, he would be declared a deserter and arrested.

While first sergeants passed out tin pots for coffee, Second Captain Duck Colonna read General Order Number 1 which had been tweaked by the Commandant for use by the Corps:

> *Attention to Orders! The Corps will form at 5:50 for the march to Harrisonburg, 18 miles down the Valley. Each man will carry his personal equipment, plus two days cooked rations. Canteens will be filled with water—repeat—water—only.*

The following Order of March will be observed:
   Wharton's Brigade,
   Echols' Brigade
   Corps of Cadets,
   Reserve Forces,
   Artillery
VMI's artillery section will travel with the main artillery battalion under the command of Major McLaughlin. If you have any questions, ask your first sergeants.
   Corps! Dismissed!

Wise returned to the campsite. Using the light from a lantern he rolled up his blanket, checked his knapsack and draped his oilskin over his musket. While Louis gathered sticks and limbs for a breakfast fire, Johnny balanced his musket on his blanket roll and trotted over to the pike to search for Stanard.

Yesterday, when the Corps marched through town, they passed three girls' schools. As the fife played "*The Girl I Left Behind,*" pretty students leaned from windows and waved embroidered handkerchiefs at the giddy cadets. When they passed the Virginia Female Institute, Stanard spotted a familiar face. Grinning broadly, he whispered in Johnny's ear that as soon as the Corps was settled in, he planned on running the block for a rendezvous with a "friend."

Concerned that his roommate didn't know about the early departure, Wise tried to think of some way to cover for his absence. Up ahead six figures gradually emerged from the mist. As they drew nearer he could make out three pairs of cadets with dates. The couples leisurely strolled along, holding hands and exchanging intimate glances. Johnny recognized Stanard who limped while carrying a knapsack, a bulging haversack and a cloth bag.

"Better get a move on," yelled Wise. "Formation's in forty minutes."

"Looky here, Johnny, fresh eggs," called Stanard, as he held up the cloth bag. Stepping aside, he added, "I'd like you to meet Becky Gregory, a *good* friend of mine. She's a refugee from Alexandria." He pulled her close, "She wants me to protect her from the big, bad 'ole Yankees heading this way."

"No, silly," said the attractive, fair skinned, redhead as she playfully rapped Stanard on the shoulder. "You're the one who needs protection. At least from camp food." She extended a warm, slender hand, "Pleased to meet you Johnny. Bev's said a lot of good things about you." She waved toward town, "I'm a student at VFI."

"Is this the mysterious Miss B?" asked Wise, remembering the daguerreotype from Stanard's mother.

Becky glanced at Stanard, "Miss B?"

"It—it's a long story," sputtered Stanard, motioning behind Becky's back for Wise to shut up. "I'll tell you all about it when I get back." Changing the subject, he said, "Becky wants me to join the church. The Episcopal Church." He held up the haversack and bag, "To help me 'see the light,' she bribed me with this fried chicken, cookies and fresh eggs."

"Baptism will have to wait," said Johnny. He winked at Becky, "If you can get this sinner confirmed it'll make his mother happy." He reached inside Stanard's haversack for a drumstick. "She's been trying to get him sprinkled with holy water ever since he was knee-high to a grasshopper, but he still plays cards on Sunday and drinks strong spirits." Grabbing Stanard's sleeve, Wise gave a hard tug, "Now, Becky, if you'll just excuse Sir Galahad while he takes his place amongst the heathen."

The tears welled up in Becky's soft, blue eyes as she gave Stanard one last hug. "I'll wait here with the other girls. Until you leave."

"No tears. You promised," said Stanard, holding her tightly while trying to control his own emotions.

"It's just the mist," she said, dabbing her eyes with a crumpled handkerchief.

As Stanard hobbled back to camp, he waved a perfumed letter under his roommate's nose, "She's the one, Johnny. I've never met anyone like—I thought I was up the spout when you rattled on about 'Miss B.' You know doggone well that's Mollie Bull." When they reached their campsite, Stanard handed the fresh eggs to Louis, then whispered to Johnny, "I don't care what mother says. Soon as this campaign's over I'm going to break out of that dagblamed prison for good. All I need is a few more demerits and they'll have to kick me out. Then I can come back for Becky and—" He caught himself mid-sentence. He was sounding sappy over a girl, a high crime in cadet society. "Now don't you go blabbing what I just said."

While Louis scrambled the eggs, Stanard gingerly removed his shoes and grimaced as he peeked at his swollen feet. Two days ago, when the Corps left Lexington, he'd made the mistake of wearing new shoes. The stiff leather hadn't hurt so much at first, but that soon changed. Big, puffy blisters covered the toes, heels and soles of both feet. Just the thought of having to limp to Harrisonburg with leather rubbing his skin raw made him cringe. It would be better to go barefoot, but his feet were no match for the hard surface of the pike. Becky had found some soft leather to wedge in the heels but he needed more room. With a pocket knife he slit the upper part of each shoe from instep to toe. Pulling on two pairs of cotton socks, he worked his feet into what was left and wriggled his toes. Although the shoes now looked like sandals, at least he could walk.

At 5:50 sharp, the Corps lined up beside the pike in company formation. It would take ten minutes to reach their assigned position at the rear of Echol's brigade. As the cadets marched in double column along the turnpike, they passed two regiments of regulars standing by the road. When they were less than ten feet away, the veterans started their heckling. Cradling muskets in their arms they began singing "*Rock-a-bye baby, in the treetop, when the wind blows, the cradle will rock...*"

Pointing to James Baylor in Company D, who stood 5-feet-3 and was armed with a cut-down version of the old model Springfield, a vet called out, "Look at that 'un. He's marching in a hole. Naw. Naw he ain't. He's jest walkin' on his knees." When the laughter died down, another regular joined in, "Is that a real shootin' arn, sonny, or a pop-gun yer paw give ya to shoot baby rabbits?"

Seething with rage but unable to reply, the cadets kept their heads down and eyes straight ahead. In Company B, First Sergeant Andy Pizzini cautioned, "Easy, men, easy. Don't let those bumpkins upset you. Our time will come."

"Thar they go," called another vet. "Headed to the rear to guard the baggage wagons—like they always duz."

"At least back thar they'll be fust in line when it's time to bug out," chimed a soldier leaning on his musket.

Wise gritted his teeth. He knew the regulars didn't mean any real harm and were just funning. Still, the taunts cut to the quick. Their gibes were partly in response to all the attention lavished on the cadets by the citizens of Staunton. The sight of fresh-faced schoolboys going off to fight Yankee invaders had gained their admiration. Yesterday afternoon, when the Corps first arrived in town, curious townspeople had flocked to the camp to inspect the students and watch dress parade.

Even more irksome to the regulars was the attention given the cadets by the students of the female academies. They had greeted them with pitchers of lemonade and homemade cakes. Invitations to private homes soon followed and dances were arranged in their honor. At a dance at the Augusta Female Seminary, Wise had snatched a pretty eighteen-year-old out from under the nose of a big, blond captain. The perplexed officer couldn't understand why anyone would prefer a downy-cheeked boy to a real man sporting a fierce mustache, polished boots and fancy uniform adorned with gilt aiguillettes.

At 6:00 a.m. the Confederate column began snaking its way north. On the outskirts of town an old Irish butcher lining up hogs for the day's slaughter, noticed the youngsters approaching. Hanging over a gate with a corncob pipe stuck in his gap-toothed mouth, he scratched his head and exclaimed, "Begorra, an' it's no purtier dhrove ave pigs hev passed this gate since this hog-killin' began."

Every hour mounted couriers clattered by, looking for General Breckinridge to report on Federal movements. It was early afternoon by the time the Corps reached its bivouac at Mount Crawford, a little south of Harrisonburg. As soon as the cadets were dismissed, Johnny and Louis began searching for a dry spot for the night. A hundred and fifty yards east of the pike was a small, dilapidated barn with two broken doors and a couple of large, boarded windows. Rushing over they claimed three spaces in a stall under a leaking tin roof. The dirt floor was covered with a mixture of moldy hay and dry cow dung which gave off an unpleasant, musty smell. To make their accommodations more habitable, they pried off the boards covering the windows to let in fresh air, then stripped needles from a nearby pine tree to spread on the floor.

Hobbling up, Stanard sat on the edge of an empty water trough and removed his cramped shoes. With a pocket knife, he carefully lanced two large blisters, sighing with relief as the clear fluid ran down his heels. Reaching in his haversack, he rummaged around until he found a small flask of peach brandy wrapped in a sock. When he noticed Johnny staring, he held up the flask, "Snake bite medicine." After pouring himself a hefty portion, he waved the flask at Wise, "Want some remedy?"

"Thanks, but it's a little early."

"Not with these blisters," replied Stanard, slowly sipping the strong libation while waiting for the burning in his feet to subside.

"I'll go get our allocation of coffee, beans and bacon," said Louis. "What else do we need?"

"Let's take inventory," said Wise. Since they had just been in Staunton, their haversacks were full of delicacies which were subject to the unwritten rule of share-and-share-alike. He also remembered Stanard's haversack full of fried chicken, his favorite.

Placing a blanket on the ground, they gathered the knapsacks and haversacks and opened the flaps. As each item was carefully removed and placed on the blanket, there were nods of appreciation and grunts of approval. Fried chicken, cake, biscuits, country ham, cheese, boiled eggs, and five flasks of assorted spirits.

With a practiced eye, Johnny assessed the bounty, "We don't want to eat it all at once. No telling when we'll get more."

"He's right," said Louis. "I vote that each day we eat a third of what's left. Perishables go first. We'll take inventory just before supper and make the division. Camp rations will be eaten as a last resort."

"What about the hootch?" asked Stanard, who had provided two of the five flasks.

"Share equal," replied Louis.

"Agreed," chimed in Evans and Johnny.

At 7:00 p.m. the Corps formed for the last roll call. Since it was raining no cadets had wandered off and there were no absentees. Lt. Colonel Ship handed a copy of Breckinridge's General Order Number 2 to Duck Colonna to read to the Corps.

> *Attention to Orders! The army will form tomorrow morning at daylight for departure down the pike. The order of march is as follows.*
> > *Echols Brigade,*
> > *Whartons's Brigade,*
> > *Corps of Cadets,*
> > *Reserve Forces*
> > *Artillery*
>
> *The order of march must be closer than it was today. Straggling and wandering into houses and grounds by the roadside will be stopped at once. Medical officers will march with their commands and allow no one to fall behind without a surgeon's certificate.*
> > *Corps! Dismissed!*

It didn't take long for Johnny, Louis and Stanard to make their way to the barn and lie down on their bedrolls. Exhausted from the days march and tired from last night's partying they ignored the musty smell and steady *drip, drip, drip,* of rain trickling through the holes in the tin roof. Within five minutes they were all asleep.

Saturday, May 14

After a hurried breakfast of hot coffee, ham and boiled eggs from his haver-sack, Johnny rolled up his blanket and prepared for departure. Draping his oilskin over his shoulders, he fastened it into a cape. It wasn't as waterproof as a cavalry poncho, but it was better than nothing.

"Don't know what the almighty obsession is about leaving so darn early, especially in the rain," grumbled Stanard, who was having a hard time wedging his swollen feet back in his shoes. "Rush, rush, rush, just so we can get to the next campsite and stand around in the rain. Hurry up and wait. For what?"

When the Corps was ready, more taunts were hurled at them as they made their way past Wharton's Brigade to the end of the column. "Hey, look at the new issue," called a vet. "Them purdy uniforms look a mite soggy to me. But, don't worry none, boys. You kin dry 'em out when you skedaddle back to them pretty girls in Staunton." A voice from the rear of the brigade rang out, "Does yer mammy know her little boy's out in all this rain? Land's sake. She's gonna be plenty worried. Best git on home and leave the fightin' to *real* soldiers."

At 6:45 a.m. Echols brigade led off, moving down the Valley at a leisurely three miles-an-hour pace. The usual light-hearted banter among the cadets had been replaced by tired faces and sore feet. As the day wore on, the column encountered more evidence of the approaching Federal army. Overloaded carts of every description rattled past as civilians fled south with whatever household possessions and livestock they could manage. The creak of wagon wheels mixed with the noise of squawking chickens, squealing pigs, and bellowing cows made the pike sound like a barnyard.

Occasionally a weary cavalryman would trot by with the latest news on how Imboden's thin line was holding out. Early in the day they reported Yankees, *near Mount Jackson.* Then it was, *this side of the Shenandoah.* By noon it had become, *Yankee scouts seen on the outskirts of New Market.* When the Corps passed a stone church beside a spring the cadets saw their first Federal prisoners. The glum, surly-looking Germans stared at the cadets and muttered among themselves, unable to make out the flag or uniforms.

When they reached Lacey Springs, seven miles south of New Market, the Corps was assigned a campsite in a small body of woods east of the pike. Pleased that the rain had finally let up, the cadets built fires to dry clothes and cook rations. Spotting a church seventy-five yards away, Johnny,

Stanard and Louis sprinted ahead to claim space on the floor or in a pew. When they went back outside, Duck Colonna, and First Sergeant Will Cabell were waiting.

"Hold up, Stanard and Suggs-J," said Cabell.

From the official tone of Cabell's voice, Johnny knew something was up. The expression on the first sergeant's face told him it wasn't good.

"Don't make yourselves too comfortable," said Cabell. "Starting at sundown, you're both going on guard duty. When we move out tomorrow morning you'll travel with the baggage wagons. Suggs-J, you're in charge of the detail."

"For how long?" asked Johnny, realizing that his plans for sitting around tonight's campfire, sipping brandy and swapping stories had just vanished.

"Until relieved," said Cabell. "The other two members of the guard are Woodlief from C and Redwood from B."

"All day tomorrow?" asked Johnny, not wanting to acknowledge the prospect of having to guard baggage while everyone else took part in the action.

"Until tomorrow night when we change guards."

"But, I—"

"It's not a request, Suggs-J," snapped Cabell, clearly irritated at Johnny's reluctance to do as ordered.

Turning to Colonna, Wise pleaded, "Duck—?"

"You heard the first sergeant," said Colonna. This was no time to let friendship interfere with duty. "Better grab some grub and get some rest. It's gonna be a long night."

After filling his canteen with sweetened coffee to help fight off fatigue, Wise rummaged through his haversack for the last of his daily allotment of food. Digging deep he found a piece of fried chicken, a smashed ham biscuit and a small slice of pie which he voraciously gobbled up. He then went inside the church and stretched out on a pew in an attempt to get some rest. He glanced at his pocket watch. 2:35. How could anyone sleep this early in the afternoon? While he lay on his back with his eyes closed and ears covered, cadets raced by, tossing bedrolls from pew to pew.

Finally, overcome by weariness, he slipped into the dream world.

Chapter 12

Breckinridge

Saturday, May 14, afternoon
Lacey Springs, Virginia

"When do you expect General Imboden," Breckinridge asked, as he glanced at his pocket watch. It was 2:31 p.m. He was looking forward to his first meeting with the "Defender of the Valley." In the past four days Imboden's small force of less than 1,600 cavalry had defeated two large Union detachments and now blocked the Federals' approach to New Market. Breckinridge was pleased to have someone in his command as knowledgeable about Valley geography, politics and people as Imboden. Because of Imboden's contacts, Breckinridge had been given space in a large, weather-worn, two-story house near Lacey Springs for his headquarters and sleeping arrangements.

"The courier said around three o'clock," replied Stoddard Johnston, as he tossed his bedroll on a bench by the kitchen. "Depends on the Yanks." For the past hour the faint sound of artillery had been heard in the direction of New Market.

The house where Breckinridge was staying was beside the turnpike and belonged to Braxton Bunting, a middle-aged farmer who lost an arm two years ago at Cross Keys. Since then Bunting had become a successful farmer at Lacey Springs with six field hands and enough fertile land to supply Richmond with ample grain, chickens, cows and hogs. In appreciation for Imboden's written order prohibiting Confederate procurement officers from impressing his animals and workers, Bunting was hosting an afternoon barbecue for the army's top officers. To prepare the feast, he and his crew had been busy since midnight slow-cooking two halves of a large pig.

While Johnston and an aide spread Jedediah Hotchkiss' maps on a table in the parlor, Breckinridge searched through his saddle bag for a pair of dry socks and a clean shirt. After changing clothes he stepped out onto the front porch and hung his wet coat across the back of a rocking chair.

Standing on the porch, Breckinridge again checked the time. Earlier, he'd sent a staff officer around to the various campsites informing brigade and regimental commanders of a meeting at Bunting's house for a late lunch and update.

Lost in thought, Breckinridge was startled when a twig snapped by the side of the house. It was Major Charles Semple, a 31-year-old Irishman from Kilkenny who was the brightest and most experienced officer on his staff. Semple had been in the army since 1861 and had earned recognition for bravery and leadership at Baton Rouge, Murfreesboro and Chickamauga.

"General, most of the men are already out back," said Semple. "They're drinking cider and watching Mr. Bunting cook the pig."

Without waiting for Johnston, Breckinridge put on his still-wet coat and followed the major to the rear of the house. Several officers were gathered around a table. All were laughing and seemed unconcerned about the approaching battle. Their attention was fixed on a large, hot iron grate holding two halves of a sizzling pig. Droplets of sauce and fat dripped from the meat onto the hot coals emitting small puffs of aromatic smoke. Pans of baked beans, cole slaw, hot cornbread and tubs of butter covered the table. Between the table and grill sat a thirty-gallon barrel of hard cider chilled by chunks of ice cut from the winter-time Shenandoah River.

When the men saw Breckinridge they lowered their cups and stood at attention. He immediately put them at ease with a wave of his hand. He didn't want to interrupt the festive mood, at least not for a while. There would be time enough for making plans and discussing tactics. Still new to the department he wanted to observe his leaders over cups of fermented apple juice and plates of roast pork.

Standing on a log, Bunting tapped a horseshoe with an iron rod. "Gentleman, welcome to the farm. First, I'd like to introduce Jed, the best barbecue man this side of Atlanta." With a flourish he pointed to a middle-aged, short, rotund black man who was mopping the pig with a cloth tied to a broom stick and dripping with peppered vinegar. "I know most of you—being Virginians—have never tasted real "down east" barbecue. That greasy salt pork the army doles out as rations comes from the same animal, but that's where the similarity ends. Jed here has been cooking porkers for politicians and church socials for over twenty years. He's been watching over this pig since midnight—and stayed mostly sober while doing it."

Jed turned, doffed his hat, and went back to grilling. With a long, two-pronged fork he punctured the rich brown skin in four places to test for doneness. Satisfied, he motioned to two helpers to move the halves onto two heavy, wide-board tables for use as chopping blocks.

Semple pulled Breckinridge aside. "Interesting story on how Bunting got his field hands. When he found out Richmond was returning captured black soldiers to their owners, he took Jed to the POW pen in Richmond and had him go among the prisoners looking for 'runaways.' Whenever he found someone willing to claim he'd been a slave on the farm, Jed would ask his name, then tell Bunting. Bunting would notify the officer in charge that he'd finally found 'Ole Joe, that no-good runaway,' and wanted him back in time to plant new crops for the Confederacy."

"You mean blacks actually volunteered to return to slavery?"

"The smart ones did. Better to be on a farm working in the fields than locked up as a prisoner in a hell-hole like Andersonville."

"Didn't the authorities check on his claims?"

Semple shook his head. "Nope. He had forged papers, but they didn't care. Just knowing the man's name and having the black answer to it was enough. The authorities were more interested in having a working slave than another mouth to feed in prison. Once the volunteer was brought here, Bunting drew up papers to set him free. He then offered him a job as a sharecropper on the farm. That way he didn't have to worry about his field hand running off to rejoin the Union army whenever they passed through. System seems to have worked well."

Breckinridge admired Bunting's ingenuity. It reminded him of the way politicians cut deals in Washington before the war.

After sharpening his knife, Jed cut long strips of crispy skin and meat from the shoulder of the nearest pig. Piling a plate with fragrant, steaming barbecue, he sprinkled on some "special sauce," and passed it around for testing.

"There's lots of vinegar and pepper in the sauce," said Bunting. "It's a mite hot, so be careful." When Bunting's wife stepped out from the kitchen, he introduced her. "This is Maisie. She's the officer-in-charge of this operation."

When Maisie signaled that all was ready, Bunting again hit the horseshoe with the iron rod. "Gentlemen, pig's on. Plenty to eat, so help yourselves."

Trying to be polite, the officers stepped aside to let Breckinridge be first in line.

Breckinridge waved them on. He would wait and eat with Imboden, plus he was interested in watching them interact without interruption. He'd met most of the officers in Dublin or Staunton, but some were strangers. A majority were Virginians who had worked together as a team for years. It was Breckinridge and his staff who were outsiders and had to learn to fit in.

While Jed chopped the meat into bite size chunks, the officers eagerly stacked their plates high with the succulent meat. They'd learned long ago to eat whenever the chance arose.

While Breckinridge chatted with Major Semple, Stoddard Johnston walked up.

"Maps are ready, Breck. When the men finish eating, they can go make copies."

"Charley, who's that officer beside Colonel Patton?"

"Lieutenant Colonel Edgar," replied Semple, who had made it a point to get to know all regimental officers and their staffs. "Good reliable man in charge of the 26th Virginia. Bright. Energetic. Self-motivated. Graduated from VMI in '53. He taught Tactics at the Institute for a couple of years. Been wounded twice."

"And the Captain?" asked Breckinridge, as he studied a young, tall officer standing beside Edgar.

"Now there's an interesting story. His name's Charley Woodson. He's Captain of Company A, 1st Missouri Cavalry. They're attached to Colonel Smith's battalion. The whole company is made up of former prisoners of war from Missouri who were exchanged at City Point but didn't want to go back west. They're designated cavalry but don't have horses, so they're fighting as infantry. They call themselves the 'Missouri exiles.'"

"A lot like my Orphans," said Breckinridge, as he remembered the 1st Kentucky "Orphan" Brigade he'd commanded at Stones River and Shiloh. Since both units were from border states still in the Union, they couldn't return home on furlough without facing arrest and imprisonment.

While waiting, Johnston and Semple walked over to the cider barrel. Johnston poured an extra cup for Breckinridge.

When Johnston returned, Breckinridge said in a low voice, "Stoddard, you know I can't drink alcohol. I promised Mary—"

"Better take it, Breck. Mary would understand. It's bad form not to accept your host's hospitality. Besides, it might make the men uncomfortable seeing you bone dry while they're helping themselves. You know the old saying, 'Never trust a man who won't share a drink with you.'"

"Suppose you're right," said Breckinridge, glad for an excuse to indulge. While sipping the refreshing cider, he noticed Colonels Patton, Edgar and Derrick standing by one of the pig halves, stripping out choice pieces of loin. "Stoddard, without too much fuss, go over and ask Colonel Patton to come here for a second?"

Happy at the chance to indulge in some premium cuts for himself, Johnston strolled over to the three officers.

Breckinridge watched Johnston engage in animated conversation with Edgar and Patton. Finally, with a full plate, Johnston returned with Patton.

"You wanted to see me, General?"

"I'm concerned about General Echols. I see he's not here. Major Semple thinks he may not be feeling well."

"He's lying in his tent, resting. I'm afraid the past few days have been a strain on his heart."

"Too bad. I was afraid that might happen. As senior officer I want you to take over the brigade until he's feeling better. Tomorrow's going to be rough and I need someone in charge who can lead the men."

"Understood, General."

"Stoddard will explain to General Echols why we're making the change now."

"Since that's taken care of," said Johnston, grinning broadly, "Colonel Edgar brought up an important matter that needs to be settled."

"What's that?" asked Breckinridge.

"Well, to put it plainly, Lt. Colonel Derrick is not a VMI graduate."

"But he *is* West Point," interjected Patton.

"True, and that's in his favor," said Johnston. "The way Colonel Edgar sees it, the coming battle is going to pit VMI trained officers against German mercenaries and it's not clear how Derrick fits in."

"How many VMI graduates do we have?" asked Breckinridge.

Furrowing his brow, Patton tried to look serious, "Well—your two generals, Echols and Wharton, are both graduates. I'm class of '52. Edgar's '53 and Smith, up at New Market, is '52. Even Imboden attended a few classes at the Institute."

"But what can *I* do?" asked Breckinridge.

Johnston scratched his head as if deep in thought. "Edgar suggested that you brevet Derrick an honorary member of the Corps. But since it's a state school, I have a better solution. When Norton I, Emperor of the United States and Protector of Mexico appointed you governor of his province of Virginia, that gave you authority over all state schools. *Ipso facto* as governor you can just grant Derrick an honorary degree from the Institute."

"Consider it done," said Breckinridge. "But, since it's your idea, Stoddard, you'll have to draw up the papers."

As the laughter subsided, Patton pointed to two riders approaching from the turnpike. "The one on the left's General Imboden. The man on the right's Captain Hanse McNeill.

"Is that the partisan who wrecked the B&O depot?" asked Breckinridge.

Patton nodded, "He's quite a character. No formal education but has a keen sense of humor and is smart as a whip. Unfortunately, he's a little slack on discipline. General Imboden had to court-martial him twice in the past month—nothing personal, just business."

"What was the outcome?" asked Johnston.

"Secretary of War Seddon and General Lee both like McNeill—and the spring campaign's underway—so the court found him innocent of all charges."

The court-martials and battle of egos reminded Breckinridge of Bragg's army. In the winter when things were slow, tempers flared and charges of insubordination and dereliction of duty started making the rounds. First, it was Gilmor. Now, McNeill. But since Grant was on the move, all sins were forgiven—if not forgotten.

Returning to the front yard, Breckinridge and Johnston waited for the riders to arrive. Watching Imboden and McNeill swing out of the saddles, Breckinridge was impressed by their vigor and nimbleness.

Tying their mounts to a hitching post the two men walked over. Breckinridge stuck out his hand, "General Imboden. It's a real pleasure."

Imboden smiled. "I've been looking forward to it, sir. I've followed your career ever since you first went to Washington. I must say, I was extremely disappointed when Lincoln won. How differently things would've turned out had you been elected President." In pre-war Staunton, Imboden had two passions, politics and railroads. Like Breckinridge, he was a lawyer and energetic campaigner. He was also excellent at public speaking. Those talents led to his being elected twice to the Virginia House of Delegates. However, as crosscurrents from a changing political scene swept the Valley, in 1858 he lost his bid for a seat in the US Congress to John Letcher, Virginia's eventual war governor.

Stepping aside, Imboden introduced the man behind him. "General Breckinridge, this is Captain Hanse McNeill from Hardy County, West Virginia. His rangers are the best guerrilla fighters in these mountains. His hobbies are tearing up railroad tracks, burning depots and giving Sigel nightmares."

"I've seen the reports," said Breckinridge, as he grasped the hand of the strongly built figure. "Quite impressive. I understand you were with General Price at Wilson's Creek in Missouri."

"I was. It was my first run in with Herr Sigel and his Dutchmen," replied McNeill, with a twinkle in his eye. "We go back a long ways. At Piedmont, me and the boys were just doing our Christian duty." A former lay minister and member of the Knights Templar, McNeill liked quoting chapter and verse to justify his actions. "The Good Book tells us, there's a time to kill and a time to break down. Piedmont was the time and place to break down. So, we just put our faith into practice. Fortunately, we didn't have to kill no Yanks to spread the Gospel."

Breckinridge chuckled. He'd never heard the Bible interpreted quite so literally. He immediately took a liking to this resourceful, unpretentious mountaineer whom Lee had called "bold and intelligent."

Walking beside Imboden and McNeill, Breckinridge led the men to the back of the house. "Help yourselves to food and drink. When you're ready Captain McNeill, I'm sure the officers would like to hear of your adventures at Piedmont. And, General Imboden, tell us about your run-ins with the Federal cavalry."

As the officers crowded around Imboden and McNeill, Bunting brought both men large mugs of cider. While Imboden sat on a stump, McNeill, never bashful about spinning a good yarn, began the saga on how he'd caught the Federals with their pants down and muskets unloaded. When he got to the part where the partisans were retreating into the mountains, he rapped his mug lightly on the table, hoping for a refill.

When his cup was full, he continued. "We had no idea there were so many Yanks after us. When we got to Moorefield, we relaxed a little too much. We'd been in the saddle for a while and I have to admit I was caught napping. The boys had unsaddled their horses and were having fun reading captured Yankee mail. All of a sudden, we looked up and there came a whole line of Yankee blue. I ordered the men to fire a quick volley, then retreat. Lieutenant Dolan and eleven rangers stayed behind to cover the withdrawal. Fortunately for us, the Yanks weren't in a fighting mood and didn't chase after us. They must've been saddle sore, so they just pitched camp and spent the night at Moorefield. Next day, they sent out a scouting party, but we was long gone."

"Any of your men killed?" asked Patton.

"Nope. John Fay and Sam Daughterty were captured." He threw back his head and burst out laughing, "The Yanks had to pull Fay out of a barrel of flour—must've been a sight. But that was it. Next morning when the bluecoats was gittin' ready to go back to the Valley, the tables were turned. Instead of being the hunters, they become the hunted." He waved his cider mug at Imboden, "Your story, counselor."

Rising to his feet, Imboden, who had already received a congratulatory telegram from Lee for the Piedmont raid, picked up where McNeill left off. "The last thing the Yankees expected was for us to be right on their heels. They'd received reports a large group of our cavalry had left the Valley, but they figured they had at least a full day's head start. On the night of the ninth we reached the outskirts of Moorefield and laid a trap. At daybreak, we struck."

"How many men did you have?" asked Edgar.

"Eight hundred. They had 500. But surprise was on our side, and that's all it took. They made several brief stands but our men were fired up. It was nip-and-tuck, head-down, tail-up all the way to Old Town, Maryland. I reckon we ran 'em over forty miles. By the end of the day they had lost more than fifty men and eight wagons, plus horses and equipment. We also caught up with Fay and Daughterty who joined the chase."

The officers signaled their approval by banging their mugs on the table beside the cider barrel.

"Tell 'em about Boyd," said McNeill. "How you run 300 Yankee cavalry back into the briars on Massanutten Mountain.

Imboden nodded gratified by the interest in his stories. "Craziest thing I ever saw. About this time yesterday some of my men were camped just below New Market. I was on Shirley's Hill with Colonel Smith when someone noticed a detachment of cavalry about six miles away, filing out of New Market gap. They were in columns of two's and heading straight for us. I knew right away they were Yanks since we didn't have any men east of the gap. The weather was bad, rainy and misty, so they couldn't make us out. They were expecting Colonel Moor and his infantry to be in New Market by then so they took us for Federals. Big mistake. I ordered the 23rd to mount up and head 'em off. The 18th took 600 men down Smith Creek to a small ford where they crossed and circled behind the column.

We had them boxed in and outnumbered two-to-one. I was hoping to bag the whole lot."

"When did they find out you were Rebels?" asked General Wharton.

"That's the funny part. Smith's Creek lies halfway between the gap and town. Because of the rain and high water, the Yanks had to use the bridge on the Luray road to reach New Market. The casual way they approached told me they didn't expect a thing. I dressed some of our men in Federal uniforms and posted them at the bridge as pickets. When Colonel Boyd saw the uniforms he was convinced we were friends. They trotted across the bridge like they were going to church. When they were half way over, we pounced."

"Like cats on a barrel of field mice," said McNeill.

"It was a rout. We shot a few and captured over a hundred. The rest jumped off their mounts and scurried into the mountains."

"Probably still running," said McNeill.

Breckinridge was pleased with the way things were looking up. A third of Sigel's cavalry had now been eliminated, his own flanks were secure and Imboden still held New Market. He pulled Major Semple aside, "Have General Wharton and Colonel Patton join us in the parlor."

When the men were gathered around Hotchkiss' maps, Breckinridge asked, "General Imboden, what's the status of Sigel's infantry?"

"Don't have a clear picture of what's going on at Woodstock. The weather closed down our signal station on Massanutten. We captured a couple of Yankee cavalrymen, who claim three regiments of infantry and a battery of artillery under Colonel Moor left Woodstock this morning at eleven. They're headed for Mt. Jackson."

"That's a lot for a reconnaissance-in-force," said Patton.

"Does Sigel know we're here?" asked Wharton.

"Doubt it," replied Breckinridge. "If he did, he wouldn't be sending men piecemeal up the pike. General Imboden, where's the best place for a line of defense?"

Imboden tapped the map at a point half a mile south of New Market. "We could put it here. By anchoring our left flank on Shirley's Hill and the right at Smith's Creek, we would have high ground with a good field of fire. Our left flank would be exposed, but I can cover that with my cavalry. Rude's Hill would be better but it's four miles further north."

"Any chance the Yankees will try to establish their defenses at Rude's Hill?" asked Patton.

"Probably not. They would have their backs to the river with only a small bridge for an escape. If that bridge was knocked down, they'd be trapped."

"And you don't think we could make it there?" asked Wharton.

"The Yanks will beat us to it," said Imboden. "Some of their cavalry are already probing Mount Jackson which is only three miles north of the hill. Better to take our time and set up a strong line at New Market."

"I agree," said Breckinridge. "General Wharton, Colonel Patton, have your men prepare to move out early tomorrow morning. I want to be in position by daybreak. When we get to New Market have your men throw up earthworks. If we can get Moor to attack before the rest of the Federal army comes up, we can defeat them in detail."

There was the clatter of hooves along the pike as a courier galloped up. "General Imboden, big force of Yankee cavalry's at Rude's Hill. Colonel Smith says to tell you that we don't have enough men to hold them. We're skirmishing and falling back on New Market."

With the faint sounds of McClanahan's cannons heard in the distance, Imboden and Captain McNeill piled extra barbecue into empty haversacks and mounted up.

Breckinridge called to General Imboden, "Try to hold your position until dark, then fall back until you find us."

Chapter 13

Strother

It was 5:35 p.m. by the time Strother finished packing his bedroll, saddlebags and haversack for temporary storage in a tool shed beside the Cheney house. He wasn't pleased at having to vacate the hospital tent that he and Major Lyon had shared for the past three nights, but the teamsters had orders to prepare for an early morning departure.

With nothing to do until Lyon located new accommodations, Strother ambled over to the telegrapher's tent to check on incoming messages. The number of cables from Washington had slowed to a trickle since the War Department's attention had shifted to Grant's struggles with Lee at Spotsylvania Courthouse. However, couriers were arriving hourly with news from Colonel Moor's detachment, which left at 11:00 a.m. and was now at Mount Jackson. The last courier brought word that Major Quinn's cavalry was at Rude's Hill and was driving the Rebels steadily back toward New Market. While this was good news, the exact number and composition of the Confederate force was still unknown.

At least Strother didn't have to stand in the driving rain while he waited. Major Theodore Lang from Sigel's staff had erected a spacious canvas topped lean-to between the cipher tent and headquarters. This shelter was now the de facto message center for anyone wanting information on Colonel Moor's progress and Sigel's plans for heading south with the rest of the army.

At six o'clock Strother was joined by Colonel Jacob Campbell, the regimental commander of the 54th Pennsylvania. The full bearded, physically imposing Campbell was one of Strother's favorite officers. Having spent the past three years guarding the B&O railroad and fighting guerillas in the mountains of western Virginia, Campbell knew the rough terrain and which citizens were loyal and which were hard-core secessionists. Like Strother, he had traveled widely before the war and was a first class raconteur of amusing tales about travels in the deep-south and along the California Trail. In 1840 he had worked briefly for the *Literary Examiner* in Pittsburgh, then moved to New Orleans for employment as a reporter for *The Daily Crescent*. After that, he became part owner of a steamboat on the lower Mississippi, and, bitten by the gold bug, traveled to California aboard a Conestoga wagon as a "Forty-Niner." By the time war broke out the restless Campbell had returned to Johnstown, Pennsylvania, where he'd helped construct the Mammoth Iron Works. Still seeking adventure, in 1861 he was among the first to volunteer for Mr. Lincoln's "ninety day" war.

Pulling a wet cigar from his jacket, Campbell tried to light it before the tobacco unraveled. As the match sparked and sputtered, he heard the faint sound of cannon fire coming from Mount Jackson, twelve miles away. "Well, Strother, looks like Moor's made contact with the Rebels." The scowl on his face clearly showed he was agitated. "Tell me again why Sigel put Colonel Moor in charge of the detachment that left this morning. The 34th Mass and 1st West Virginia are part of Thoburn's brigade."

Since his pony had been taken away before daybreak for a scouting party, and his dinner companions, Colonel Wells and Lt. Colonel Lincoln had left with the 34th, Strother was in no mood to make excuses for the commanding general. "It's pretty obvious Herr Sigel wants a Dutchman in charge so the Germans get all the glory."

"To *hell* with glory," snarled Campbell. "Colonel Moor doesn't know a damn thing about this part of the country, nor how to deal with partisans and bushwhackers. You can't juggle regiments around just to satisfy a whim."

"Well, Moor *was* reluctant to take the assignment. He asked for maps and scouts, but got neither." It bothered Strother that the hastily assembled reconnaissance-in-force had been sent twenty miles into enemy territory under a new commander. If they got into trouble it would take hours before support could reach them. Just that morning, cavalry patrols had reported that Breckinridge had joined forces with Imboden and was now approaching New Market with over 5,000 men. But Sigel had relied on his civilian scouts and was convinced the bulk of the Confederate army was still at Staunton. Now Sigel had made the mistake of splitting his army in the face of the enemy and risked being defeated in detail.

Suddenly, the front door of the Cheney House burst open. Out popped General Sigel, hatless and with the tops of his high top boots hanging down and flapping against his legs with every step. Behind him two bewildered guards fumbled with their muskets while trying to attach bayonets.

"Ver is dey! Ver is dey! shouted Sigel as he ran past the startled officers. *"Haff you seen dem beoples, Strodare? By Gar, I vill catch dot dam tiefs!"* Eyes wide with excitement, the general stumbled through the mud, headed for the servants' camp.

"What the hell was that?' asked Campbell.

Again the door banged open and out came Major Lang, followed closely by Madame Cheney, mistress of the house. When Lang saw Strother, he ran over and crouched behind him.

Stopping just short of the lean-to, Mrs. Cheney stood in the rain, the water splashing over her face and running down her dress. Her nostrils flared with anger as she screamed, *"Did you hear what that—that man said? That—foreigner?* That I was a *thief.* Accusing me! In my *own* home! Saying *I* stole his liquor bottle!"

"He's just upset," replied Lang, as he backed further away.

"Upset? Is that what you call it? Me a Christian lady—a *thief!"* Lifting her hands to the heavens, she exclaimed, "May the *vengeance* of the Almighty follow that man. He has wounded me too deeply for healing or apology." With that, she spun on her heels, and with her head held high, marched back inside her house.

"I wouldn't want that women's curse on me," said Strother, as he watched Major Lang still cringing from the tirade. Lang was a close friend of Strother's. Both were West Virginians and had been assigned to Sigel's staff on a temporary basis. They had met in Martinsburg when Strother was given the job of writing a report on the campaign and Lang was placed on Sigel's staff to advise him on the conditions in the Shenandoah Valley. For his new position Lang had been christened with the creative title, "chief-of-headquarters" which Strother had instantly turned into, "chief-of-hindquarters."

"That was quite a show," admitted Campbell, still unsure of what he had just witnessed.

Lang wiped sweat and rain from his brow, "The general thinks someone stole his favorite brandy flask. When he started to pack for the move south, it was gone. Now he's accusing everyone he sees of stealing it. I've never seen him so agitated."

Campbell sneered at the ludicrous image of the commanding general of the army bounding through camp chasing a brandy flask. "Major Lang, would you kindly inform me what the plans are for the rest of us? I've heard 'We're going to stay in Woodstock.' Then—no, 'We're moving to the attack.' Then again, 'We're heading to Front Royal to march across the mountains and strike Lee's left flank.' I've got a regiment to look after and need to prepare."

"I overheard General Sigel tell General Stahel to be ready to move out at 5:00 tomorrow morning," said Lang. "He mentioned something about going to Mount Jackson and waiting there until Colonel Moor develops the situation at New Market."

While the men talked, Lieutenant Colonel John Linton, Campbell's second in command, galloped up. Before the war, Linton had been a successful attorney in Schuylkill County, Pennsylvania, but caught up in war fever volunteered in '61. Breathing hard, Linton leaned forward in the saddle, "Colonel, one of our details collecting firewood down by the creek was attacked by mounted Rebels. One man was killed and two wounded."

"How many Rebels?" asked Campbell, untying his horse from the hitching rail.

"Ten to fifteen. Sergeant Colbert said it looked like they were chasing someone on the other side of the creek. When they saw we were infantry they high-tailed it back into the woods. Thought I'd better come tell you."

Without a word, Campbell climbed into the saddle and the two men rode off.

Major Lang turned to Strother, "Jim Lyon said you're looking for a place for the night."

Strother's ears perked up. "Nothing fancy, a small corner in a dry shed will do. I also need a spot for Tom, my helper."

"I know just the room." Leading Strother to the rear of the Cheney house, Lang pointed to the door of a root cellar. "It's tiny, but dry."

Pleased to have accommodations in the headquarters building, even if it was a cellar, Strother invited Lang to join him and Major Lyon for dinner that evening at the Inn at Narrow Passage. Now that Colonel Wells and Lt. Colonel Lincoln were gone, there would be two empty spaces. "Food's outstanding. We can ride over—you wouldn't happen to have a spare horse I could borrow? Mine's out on a scout."

"Actually, I have six. General Sigel wants me to take a dozen couriers to Mount Jackson early tomorrow morning to keep him informed on Moors' progress. How far's the inn? I can't be gone long."

"A couple of miles. We eat at seven thirty. You can be back by nine o'clock. Trust me, Lang, it'll be the best meal you'll have on the campaign. Bring a haversack for leftovers."

As the Major turned to head back upstairs, a buckboard clattered up. On the seat beside the driver slumped a hatless, disheveled officer, whose face and hands were covered with bruises and scratches. Behind the wagon rode Lt. Colonel Linton.

Linton waved to Major Lang, "This is Colonel Boyd. He was in charge of that cavalry detail attacked by Imboden at New Market. Our men found him and two of his men in Edinburg. He's wounded and needs a doctor, but wants to report to General Stahel first."

Looking at the dejected cavalryman, Strother was troubled by the ease with which Imboden had defeated the 300 man detachment. It was a bad omen of things to come.

Chapter 14

Cadets

The orange glow from the setting sun filtered through the windows of Mt. Tabor church, casting pale shadows on the walls. Lying on his side on the hard, wooden pew Wise was awakened by someone dripping water from a canteen into his ear.

"Time to rise and shine, sleeping beauty," said Stanard.

Reluctantly Wise stood up, hooked on his belt and grabbed his musket. It would be hours before he got another chance to rest. After posting Stanard, Woodlief and Redwood at key locations around camp, he took his place by the baggage wagons. Resting his musket against a wagon wheel, he poured himself a cup of sweet coffee from an extra canteen. It was going to be a long, boring night. As the hours crept by he could hear frogs croaking in a nearby pond and see bivouac fires twinkling in the distance. Were the fires from Yankees bedding down for the night? Overhead, a few stars blinked through the haze of clouds drifting across the moon. If only Polly were here with him he might even consider the view romantic. Gradually, the coals from nearby campfires burned into ashes as darkness closed in. Thirty feet away he could hear the *chomp, chomp, chomp* of Lt. Colonel Ship's horse noisily eating its rations of corn and hay. Occasionally a light shower passed over, pattering softly on the canvas stretched across the boxes in the wagons. He wondered if the Yanks were still awake, thinking of girl friends, family and mortality. Several cadets slumbered nearby, curled up under blankets and lost in dreams of home and happier times. How many would be missing tomorrow night when the rolls were taken?

Sunday, May 15

Shortly after midnight, he heard hoof beats approaching along the turnpike. Then he heard Woodlief issue the challenge. It was Major Semple from General Breckinridge's staff.

"Where's Colonel Ship?" asked Semple.

"In the church," responded Wise, pointing toward the dark outline of a building eighty yards away.

"I need to see him at once. Orders from General Breckinridge."

Holding a lantern in front, Wise made his way over the soggy ground to Mt. Tabor church. Inside, among the jumble of bodies lying on the floor and in pews, was the Commandant. He was stretched out on a pew with his sword at his side and his head resting on his knapsack.

"Courier from headquarters, sir," Wise whispered, as he gently shook the Commandant's shoulder.

Still dressed in full uniform, Ship blinked, rubbed his eyes, then swung his legs around to a sitting position. It only took a few seconds for him to get his bearing and pull on his muddy boots. Following Wise outside, the Commandant walked over to where Semple was drying his hat over the dying coals of a campfire. After a brief conversation, Ship beckoned to Wise. "Inform all company commanders to prepare to move out in twenty minutes. Keep it quiet. No drums.

"Is there enough time for coffee?"

"Not yet. We don't want any fires. When we get to New Market we can heat water.

Sleeping peacefully on the floor of the church, Moses Ezekiel was startled when Sprigg Shriver, Second Captain of C Company, shook his foot. He had been dreaming of Alice. They were playing house and having a tea party. "Grab your gear and fall in. No noise," said Shriver.

When the four companies were formed into three rows and the rolls checked, they marched onto the pike and halted. Before starting on the last leg of their journey, Lt. Colonel Ship asked Captain Frank Preston, the staunch, one-armed Presbyterian in command of Company B, to offer a prayer for the day ahead.

With the cadets at parade rest, Captain Preston stood in front of the Corps and rested his one good hand on the pommel of his sword. "Before we go into battle I think it proper to offer a prayer to God Almighty and ask His aid and protection for what lies ahead."

With heads bowed, the cadets listened while Captain Preston spoke of home, of father, of mother, of country, of victory and defeat, of life and death. He ended with a heartfelt petition, "May we all be safe in the coming battle, but if any should die we ask that You grant them salvation and take them into eternity with You. Amen." As an afterthought, he added, "And may we show mercy to our enemy."

Although most cadets were deeply moved by Captain Preston's heartfelt words, in the back row of Company A, Clarke Howard heard someone half-jokingly say, "Maybe we're actually going to get into this fight if they're going to pray over us."

"Battalion! Attention!" called Ship. *"Left Face! Right Shoulder—Shift Arms! For—ward—March!"*

In the pitch-black the three columns of cadets began to wind their way north along the pike, each person following in the footsteps of the one in front. Sloshing through puddles the columns snaked along at a snaillike pace, stopping, starting, stopping, starting. Squinting into the gloom, Howard searched for the cadet in front but had to reach his hand out to touch his back. There was a file of cadets on his left, and one on his right with whom he occasionally touched elbows, but couldn't see. He heard them splashing and talking, but they were as invisible as if miles away.

At the rear of the column, Johnny Wise and the three other members of the guard kept up by holding on to the sides of supply wagons as they creaked along.

After five hours of stop-and-go the Corps finally reached the outskirts of New Market. As the eastern sky gradually turned light, the cadets could see the looming outline of Massanutten Mountain three miles on their right. Lost in morbid thoughts and concerns of how they would stand up against regular Union infantry, the cadets were unusually quiet as they passed the veterans of Wharton's brigade. The regulars were squatting by the road, cooking breakfast and smoking pipes. "Ho, there! Here come the bombproofs! Hallooo wagon dogs!" joshed the regulars. Now, the veterans' light-hearted banter and verbal gibes, mixed with their total indifference to the coming battle, helped lighten the mood and restore the cadets' confidence that all was well.

A tall, thin regular with an angular face, protruding nose and long, skinny legs trotted over to Company A. In his right hand he held a pair of shears. In his left was a pack of playing cards. "Say thar young gentlemen. Would you like fer me to cut off some love-locks and send them to yer poor ma after yer daid?" With a bony hand, he waved to his comrades who were doubled over laughing. "My friends call me the 'Deacon' cuz I always enclose a special Bible verse to yer mammy with each snip of hair. If you'll jest put yer name on one of these here cards an' pay me a single dollar, I'll take keer of it."

Behind the Deacon shuffled a short, scruffy private from the same company. Respectfully removing his hat, he lowered his head and held out a piece of paper. "Howdy, young gents. I'm the 'Undertaker.' Me an' the Deacon always works as a team. We're offerin' a one-day special to you keydets fer only *two* dollars. If you'll jest let me know how old you are and if you wants a rosewood coffin—satin-lined—we has all colors—I'll make sure yer ma knows 'bout it when she gits what's left of yer body. Fer no extree charge we'll put yer name an' age on the silver colored plate that goes on top of the box—since she ain't gonna be able to recognize what's left." Trying not to grin, he added, "Better sign up now while yer still alive! Ain't no use comin' back when yer daid sayin' 'Please, Mr. Undertaker, sir, I'd now like one of them fancy coffins.'"

When the Corps reached their assigned place on the pike two miles south of town, they halted and moved off the road into an open field to await further orders. They could hear the occasional *pop-pop-pop* from a musket near New Market, but the intervening hills blocked their view.

While waiting, John Hanna, first lieutenant of Company D and Andy Pizzini, first sergeant of Company B, walked among the ranks trying to calm nerves and check equipment to make certain each person had the required 40 rounds of ammunition. One hundred and eighty-two cadets were armed with the newer, Austrian rifles which fired Minie balls. The remaining forty-seven still had the old model smoothbore, which used round lead balls.

When Hanna inspected Winder Garrett's musket, he found so much rust and crud on the bayonet locking mechanism that it was difficult to snap into place.

"Better scrape that off," admonished Hanna, handing Garrett a wire brush. "You might need that bayonet."

Garrett, a private from Williamsburg, Virginia, and direct descendant of Sir George Yardley, first colonial governor of Virginia, nodded and went to work. Technically a third classman, he had failed several courses in his first year and been required to repeat them. His low grades were due to a lack of formal education before entering the Institute and not a shortage of native intelligence. Quick witted, strong, and something of a class clown, his fellow cadets had nicknamed him "Sir Yardley, Court Jester."

Shortly after 8:00 a.m. Breckinridge ordered an artillery duel with Federal batteries to hold them in place while he established a strong defensive line. One six gun Union battery was stationed among the tombstones in the cemetery at St. Matthew's Church. Another four guns were located on the Federal right flank at Manor's Hill. Fortunately for the cadets, the rolling terrain protected them from the cannon fire.

After waiting for over three hours in the pouring rain, the cadets began to grow restless. Some sat on the ground and rummaged through knapsacks looking for something to eat. Others stood in small groups, listening to the artillery duel and wondering if and when they would be sent in. Tired from the lack of sleep, George Lee, grandson of Light Horse Harry Lee and nephew of Robert E. Lee, ignored the noise and rain and promptly fell asleep on a bed of wet grass. To prepare for what lay ahead, several older cadets sent fourth class Rats to a nearby stream to fill canteens.

When it seemed like nothing would happen, cheering was heard from troops along the pike south of town. Looking for the cause, the cadets spotted General Breckinridge and staff riding their way. His head was uncovered and he was bowing left and right to acknowledge the applause. As the entourage passed, Carter Randolph called out, "Boys! Three cheers for General Breckinridge!" Joining in the wild huzzahs, Johnny Wise watched from his seat on top of a supply wagon and marveled at the soldierly appearance of the army's commander. To Wise, he appeared to be El Cid. The noble way he held his head, coupled with his erect bearing and aura of command sent a rush of pride through Wise, elated at being part of such a grand spectacle.

After the general and his staff disappeared, Stoddard Johnston, Breckinridge's chief-of-staff, rode over to Lt. Colonel Ship and dismounted.

"Colonel, we're ready to establish the battle line."

"Where do want the cadets?"

Johnston showed Ship a hand-drawn map. "We'll form a single line with a reserve. It'll be staggered into three echelons to make it appear like we have more men. Your battalion is attached to General Wharton's brigade as part of the reserve. Echol's brigade under Colonel Patton will be across the road on the right. Colonel Edgar's 26th Virginia will be to your immediate left." With a ramrod, Johnston pointed to Shirley's Hill, a quarter of a mile on the left. "General Wharton's brigade will be placed on the top of that hill as the first line. Position your Corps 250 yards behind them."

"What about our artillery?"

"Keep the cannon with you if possible. The ground's a bit miry in spots and may not support gun carriages. If they can't keep up, send them over to Major McLaughlin." As Johnston climbed back into the saddle, he added, "The general wants all officers dismounted. No need to make targets for Yankee sharpshooters." With a salute, he said, "You may move the Corps forward."

While the cadets formed for a flank movement toward Shirley's Hill, skirmishers from the 30th Virginia rushed by, heading for the front. As they passed there were no more taunts, only calls of encouragement, *"Give 'em hell, boys! Show the Yankees what you can do!"*

Sitting dejectedly on the seat of a baggage wagon, Wise and the other three members of the guard watched the Corps march off. As Company D disappeared into the rain and haze, he became obsessed with a single thought. If he remained with the tents and cooking pots while the Corps fought their first, and perhaps only engagement, he would never be able to look his father in the eye again. For months he'd annoyed him with pleas to be allowed to leave the Institute and enter service. Now that he finally had a chance to fight, here he sat, guarding barrels of pork, boxes of flour and tents. His father, a Confederate general, had a satirical tongue sharp as a scorpion's sting and wouldn't hesitate to use it if his son turned out to be a wagon-dog. While Johnny watched the last of the cadets fade from view, he knew what he had to do.

Hopping up on the seat, Wise called to Stanard, Woodlief and Redwood. "Boys, we have the enemy in front. The Corps has left us behind. I don't like fighting any better than you do, but I have an enemy at my back far worse than anything out there," he said, waving his hand toward a hill north of town. "If I go home and tell my father that I sat on a supply wagon while the rest of the cadets fought a battle, I know what he'd do. He would kill me with ridicule. I'm going to rejoin my company. Any of you who think it's your duty to remain with the wagons may do so."

With that, he jumped to the ground and grabbed his musket. Although Stanard was reluctant to desert his post, he finally agreed to join the others. After leaving the wagons in charge of the black drivers, the foursome started off at a trot and were soon in ranks.

Before the battalion had gone a hundred yards, Lt. Colonel Ship noticed that the soggy ground made it impossible for the two artillery pieces to keep up. He ordered Captain Minge to take the guns and report to Major

McLaughlin. With whips cracking and hooves flying, the 32-man section made its way back to the hard surface of the pike.

When the Corps reached Shirley's Hill, a courier galloped up to the Commandant. "General Breckinridge wishes to see you, sir. He's over there with General Wharton," said the courier, pointing to the crest of Shirley's Hill.

"Slight change of plans," said Breckinridge when Lt. Colonel Ship rode up. "We're going to form two battle lines. The Cadets will remain left of the pike 250 yards behind General Wharton's first line. When the first line advances, move with it, but maintain your distance."

"General, I hope you'll use the cadets," said Ship. "They've been called out several times in the past two years and still haven't seen action. The veterans call them wagon dogs and momma's boys. They're most eager to prove themselves."

"My compliments for their enthusiasm," replied Breckinridge. "But, I don't want to expose them to combat if it can be avoided. However, if necessary, I plan to use them freely."

Chapter 15

Breckinridge

Sunday, May 15
New Market

Standing on the forward slope of Shirley's Hill, Breckinridge, General Wharton and Stoddard Johnston tried to count the number of Federal troops arrayed against them three-quarters of a mile in front. In spite of patches of morning fog and drifting clouds of smoke they could see flags for three regiments of infantry and two batteries of artillery. Pacing back and forth, Breckinridge took out his pocket watch. 10:35. It was getting late.

"Well, Gabe, I don't think they're going to attack," said Breckinridge. He had hoped to fight a defensive action, but the Union commander, Colonel Moor, was an old hand at tactics and was staying put. Until one side took the initiative and launched an assault, all they could do was stand in the rain and stare at each other. Breckinridge knew that the longer he waited, the greater the danger Sigel would reinforce Moor with the rest of his army.

Wharton studied the Federal position with his field glasses. "I think Moor knows he's outnumbered. He can also see we have better ground."

Looking over his shoulder, Johnston spotted Major Charles Semple, approaching from the turnpike. Because of the pools of water and deep mud, the Major's horse only moved at a slow trot.

When Semple drew alongside, he waved a piece of paper back and forth. "Great news, General. Courier from Staunton just brought word on Crook and Averell." Jumping off his horse, he handed the telegram to Breckinridge, "It's from McCausland. He's at the Narrows and sent it late yesterday afternoon."

While Breckinridge read, relief spread across his face. He turned to Wharton and Johnston, "Well, gentlemen, the salt works and lead mines are safe. Morgan and Grumble Jones stopped Averell at Wytheville. The Federals lost over a hundred men before they turned back. Averell's cavalry is heading to West Virginia to join Crook at Meadow Bluff."

"So, Crook's no longer a threat," said Johnston.

"Not at the moment. All we have to do now is stop Sigel."

"What about the rail depot at Dublin and New River Bridge?" asked Wharton.

Re-reading the telegram, Breckinridge said, "They wrecked Dublin and burned the wooden part of the bridge but couldn't bring down the supports. Local workers think they can have it back in full operation within three weeks."

Johnston smiled, "Hardly worth their sweat and powder. All that bluster and hurrahing for damn little benefit."

While the four men discussed their next step, Imboden rode up and dismounted.

Breckinridge nodded toward the Federal troops. "They're still there."

Imboden frowned, "I ran through my whole bag of tricks, but Moor refused to take the bait. My men charged his line several times, then fell back, but Moor wouldn't budge. He's a sly old fox. It's a good thing he's not in charge of their army." The 50-year-old Moor had received his early military training in Germany and had been, like Sigel, on the losing side in the '48 Baden Revolution. But, unlike Sigel, Moor had commanded US troops during the Second Seminole War and under Zachary Taylor in Mexico. An apt student, he understood and got along well with the American military culture.

"The signal station on Massanutten just sent word that the rest of the Federal infantry left Woodstock this morning at five," said Imboden. "My guess is they're at Mt. Jackson by now. From there it's only a couple of hours to New Market."

"How many men you reckon Moor has with him?" asked Breckinridge.

"Scouts report around 2,300, a third of the total Yankee force." With binoculars Imboden surveyed the Federal line. "Not bad. He's got his artillery on high ground at Manor's Hill and his battle line stretches to the turnpike. It *looks* strong, but his flanks are in the air. Wouldn't be hard to get around behind him."

"Any idea where he's hiding his cavalry?" asked Semple.

"One of my patrols spotted three cavalry regiments behind that rise to the left of Manor's Hill."

Studying Moor's formation, Breckinridge asked, "What's the backside of Manor's Hill look like?" Although he had Hotchkiss' maps, Imboden had been in the area for several weeks and knew every inch of terrain and the location of every major obstacle.

"From the crest it slopes gradually northward for quarter of a mile. Then it flattens out for another half-mile until it reaches Bushong farm. The fields between here and the farm are a combination of wheat, clover and grass. The whole area's a quagmire of mud."

"If we attack do you think Moor's will stay put?" asked Major Semple.

Imboden thought for a moment, then pulled out a rough sketch he'd made of the area. Holding his hat over the paper to protect it from the rain he showed it to Breckinridge and Semple. "He can't stay there. His flanks are too vulnerable. He's outnumbered two-to-one and will soon know it. As soon as he counts our infantry he's going to fall back. If we drive him hard, he'll probably make a stand at the Bushong farm."

"Any chance he'll try to make it to Rude's Hill?" asked Wharton.

"Not if we stay on him. With all this rain, they'll have to use the pike which will slow them down. At the farm, the river and creek come close together, giving them good flank protection. They'll also have high ground."

Breckinridge turned to Major Semple, "Charley, you know the situation. What's your recommendation?" The General trusted Semple's military judgment without reservation. In addition to having an eye for terrain, and an understanding of tactics the major was blessed with the luck of the Irish. Not only had he survived two near-fatal wounds at Fort Donelson and Baton Rouge, but had escaped serious injury at Chickamauga when a bullet heading for his heart was deflected by a Bible in his breast pocket.

"Well, General, if it was up to me, I'd attack *now*. We've got Moor outnumbered and we don't want to give Sigel time to bring up the rest of his infantry."

"You're right, Charley. It's up to us to make the first move." Studying Moor's position one last time he turned to Imboden, "By god, General, if we attack at once we can whip them right here—and I'll *do* it!"

With his blood up, Breckinridge called to Johnston, "Stoddard, go tell Major McLaughlin to take his guns to the turnpike and be ready to move forward."

Calling General Wharton over he said, "Gabe, start the attack in fifteen minutes. Keep the alignment you have now with Wolfe, Woodson and

Smith in front. Echol's brigade under Patton will be echeloned slightly behind you on the right. They'll have to go through town, so don't get too far ahead. Edgar's battalion and the cadets are your reserve. We'll make adjustments as the battle progresses."

Turning to Major Semple, Breckinridge continued, "Charley, ride over and tell Colonel Patton to move forward when General Wharton's brigade advances. Remind him we're still in echelon and to keep 250 paces behind the first line."

Finally, Breckinridge pulled Imboden aside. "I want you to cover the right flank. Take the 18th across Smith's Creek and patrol along the east side to make sure Sigel's cavalry doesn't try an end run."

"What about artillery?" asked Imboden.

"Take four guns from McClanahan's battery."

"And if there are no Yanks east of the creek?"

"Then see if you can slip behind Sigel's army and destroy the bridge over the North Fork. If you can knock that bridge down we can trap them this side of the river."

"I'll try," said Imboden. "But, it's going to be tricky. The creek's flooded and we'll have to re-cross near Mount Jackson to get to the bridge. When Boyd's men tried to swim across the creek two days ago they either drowned or had to turn back." He looked skyward at the storm clouds. "My guess is the water's up at least a foot since then."

"Well, General," said Breckinridge, "you know the area better than I do, but it would be quite a coup if we could capture Sigel's army."

"We'll do our best," said Imboden, as he saluted and rode off.

Breckinridge called to Johnston, "Stoddard, send a courier to Major Gilmor. Tell him to destroy that bridge. If anyone can do it, it'll be Gilmor."

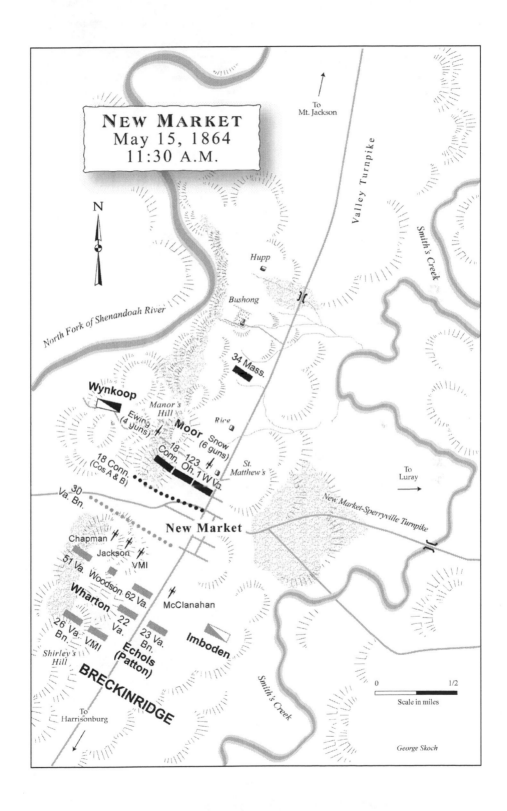

Capt. Frank Preston
VMI faculty
VMI Archives

Capt. Henry Wise
VMI faculty
VMI Archives

Col. George S. Patton, CSA
Portrait ca. 1861
VMI Archives

Brig. Gen. Gabriel Wharton, CSA
Picture ca. 1863
VMI Archive

Cadet Oliver P. "Big" Evans
VMI Archives

Dr. Robert L. Madison
VMI Post Surgeon
VMI Archives

Cadet Collier H. Minge
VMI Archives

Cadet John C. Early
VMI Archives

Capt. Charles H. Woodson, CSA
Postwar photo
VMI Archives

Bushong House, New Market Battlefield
Photo ca. 1920-30
VMI Archives

1st Lt. Henry A. DuPont, USA
Hagley Museum and Library

Maj. Gen. Julius Stahel, USA
Library of Congress

Capt. Alfred von Kleiser, USA
Photo ca. 1865
VMI Archives

Col. George D. Wells, USA
Library of Congress

Chapter 16

Cadets

Karoomph! Wise flinched as the concussion from a stray shell swept the ranks of cadets standing two rows deep on Shirley's Hill. Tightly gripping his musket he looked left, then right at fellow students massed shoulder to shoulder, jaws clinched, eyes set, nervously waiting. They could hear the deep-throated concussions of cannon fire as Wharton's first line disappeared over the crest of the hill. Clouds of smoke, held close to the ground by dense, moist air, drifted into his face burning his nose with its acrid stench. Maybe he had been a little too hasty in wanting to see the elephant. This was no circus, at least not the kind he'd seen in Richmond as a young boy. As more and more spent bullets and shell fragments fell among the cadets his enthusiasm for a face-to-face encounter with the enemy began to waiver.

Whoosh! Another shell whizzed by, trailing vapor. Through gritted teeth, Wise let out a low whistle, thankful the Yankee artillery was still over the hill and out of sight. With his left hand he checked the wooden canteen hanging loosely by his side. Shaking it slightly he listened for the reassuring slosh of sweetened coffee scavenged from last night's leftovers. Since there had been no breakfast, it would have to last until after the battle. Next he patted the small, leather pouch attached to a silver chain around his neck. Inside were his lucky rabbit's foot and Polly's four-leaf clover. He hoped the fragile leaves hadn't been mushed into a lump by the rain. If she could only see him now, musket in hand, bravely facing the enemy, there would be no more talk of "insipid" cadets.

Tucked away at the bottom of his haversack was his treasure trove of lemon cake, yellow cheese, Apple Jack brandy, biscuits and country ham. These were carefully hoarded goodies to be shared with Jack Stanard and Louis at tonight's campfire while rehashing the day's adventures. At least he wouldn't be on guard duty—what if he was arrested for deserting his post guarding the baggage wagons? He pushed the thought from his mind. No time to worry about that now.

While large rain drops splashed on the visor of his forage cap, Wise removed an engraved, silver hunting knife that hung in a scabbard attached to his belt. It was reassuring to have an extra weapon close by—just in case. The knife wasn't big and intimidating like a Bowie, but it was useful in camp for cutting meat and whittling wooden pegs. He slid his fingers over the etchings. It had belonged to his maternal grandfather, the Honorable John Sergeant of Philadelphia. If he were still alive, what would the former candidate for Vice-President think of a grandson now standing in the pouring rain waiting to attack U.S. troops? Wise looked down at the shiny, six inch blade with the outline of an eagle holding a banner proclaiming "Duty, Honor, Country." It was his most prized possession, the only memento of a mother who died when he was only four. Slipping it back into its sheath he dug further into the haversack for his pocket watch. 11:45. Sunday. He'd almost forgotten it was Sunday. What did God think about fighting on the Sabbath? Stonewall Jackson, a devout Presbyterian and true believer had waged many of his most successful battles on Sunday—so it must be alright. As rain ran down the back of his neck, Johnny's daydreams drifted to home and family. Were they thinking of him while they attended morning services at St. Paul's in Richmond? The mobilization of the Corps had happened so suddenly that none of them knew he was in the mud on a Virginia hillside waiting for the order to charge.

A heavy foreboding gnawed at the back of his mind. Last night Stanard had told him of a premonition of being killed today. But, that was just nerves. Heck, they probably wouldn't even be anywhere near the real fighting. At least when he got back home he would be able to claim he'd been on a battlefield where there was a real danger of being killed. Tonight, when the campfire chatter got going, everyone would brag how *they* hadn't been scared at all, not one little bit. He wished he'd snuck an extra canteen of Apple Jack into his knapsack while in Staunton, but Pizzini had threatened to court-martial anyone substituting alcohol for water. That might not apply to extra canteens, but Pizzini wasn't someone to trifle with. He'd been at First Manassas and had repeatedly warned, "The only drink called for by the wounded and dying was *water*."

Thump! Someone in the front row got hit. Wise turned to see who it was. Marshall? Reid? Too far to tell. Probably just a spent ball. In a second the word rippled down the line, "George Spiller, George Spiller." Wise saw a cadet stumbling to the rear, bright-red blood streaming down his face.

Wise bit his lip and stared straight ahead. A week ago he'd been safe in barracks, bored and complaining about school work and missing all the "fun." Now the thought of being shot and permanently crippled, or killed, caused his stomach to knot and churn.

"Color Guard-d-d, front and cen-ter-rrr!" shouted Lt. Colonel Ship. In the hushed silence Big Evans marched the guard into position between B and C companies. All eyes followed as he faced the Corps and unsheathed the large cream-colored silk flag. A loud *Hurrah!* rose from the Corps as Evans shook out the folds and waved the banner aloft. A lump rose in Wise's throat as a strong breeze caught the flag and made it flutter and snap as if alive. With grim determination, Evans turned to face the enemy. From this point on, the flag would only go forward. There would be no retreat.

As the last row in Wharton's first line disappeared over the crest of the hill, General Breckinridge and two staff officers rode up. When the cadets recognized him, they raised their kepis and cheered. Remaining on his horse, Breckinridge talked briefly with Lt. Colonel Ship, then turned to address the Corps. "Young gentlemen, I hope there'll be no occasion to use you today, but if there is, I trust you will do your duty."

Clarke Howard listened incredulously, "What did he mean by that? No occasion to put us in? Here we are, already part of the second line, and when the first line advances, we have to go with it."

The Commandant raised his sword, *"Atten—shun! Port—Arms! For—ward! At the double—quick! March!"*

As they followed behind the veterans it didn't take long to reach the crest of Shirley's Hill. Here, for the first time, Wise had a panoramic view of the battlefield. In awe, he watched Confederate skirmishers darting from side to side as they made their way toward the long row of Federal infantry. On both Federal flanks artillery batteries discharged small clouds of white smoke into the air. While the cadets descended the hill, tiny black dots came screeching and howling toward them, exploding in front of, above and behind their formation. Although Wharton's veterans had broken ranks and rushed down the slope, the Corps, new to the business of battlefield maneuvering, marched down in formation.

After having adjusted their artillery fire on Wharton's first line, the Yankee cannoneers now had the exact range of the cadets and the number of little puffs of white smoke rapidly increased.

Barooomph! A shell exploded in front of Company C sending razor-sharp fragments hurtling out in all directions. The shock wave, along with a piece of shell, hit Wise in the face. His senses reeled and the earth rocked as his musket flew from his hands. Semi-conscious, he stumbled to his knees, then fell face forward onto the soggy ground.

From his position in Company A on the extreme right of the cadet line, Clarke Howard was looking down the front row when he saw the shell explode. He watched Archibald Hill, first captain of Company C, pitch forward and fall, stiff as a log.

Seeing Wise's crumpled body, First Sergeant Will Cabell had no time to stop and help but ordered, *"Close up, men!"* Without hesitating, cadets filled the five empty spaces in the formation and the Corps moved on.

When they reached a shallow ravine at the bottom of the slope, the cadets came to a halt. They could breathe easier now that they were protected from enemy fire by a small hill. Crossing a dirt road they climbed a four-foot fence and re-formed on the other side.

Before the Corps could resume its advance, the whole army was brought to a standstill. To keep Federal forces off balance, Breckinridge ordered an artillery barrage while he repositioned the regiments into a single battle line. The adjusted line now stretched from the southern slope of Manor's Hill to the turnpike on the right. With a two-to-one advantage in manpower, the Confederate infantry overlapped both Federal flanks, forcing them to retreat or be captured. To confuse the enemy as to his strength, Breckinridge continued to have the brigades remain in echelon. The only regiment not part of the battle line was the Corps of cadets, which remained in reserve behind Wharton's brigade.

Before going forward, Lt. Colonel Ship had the cadets strip for action. Company by company the orders were given to discard everything but muskets, cartridge and cap boxes, and canteens.

"Ground knapsacks! Ground haversacks! Ground bed rolls!" yelled First Captain Frank Preston.

Attached to Company B, members of the color guard heard the command and began shedding excess equipment. Stepping back six inches, Moses lowered his blanket roll onto a small patch of wet grass. With the toe of his shoe he eased the end out of the mud, then balanced his knapsack on top. Although the blanket was wrapped in an oilskin, the continuous rain from the past few days had worked its way inside and soaked his extra socks and underwear.

"Center ammunition and cap boxes!" shouted Preston.

There was the squeak of leather on leather as cadets slid wet ammunition boxes around to the front of their belts.

"Load—Muskets!"

Moses removed the wood plug from the end of his rifle, took out a cartridge and bit open the paper. The bitter taste of powder stung his tongue, causing his lips to pucker. He leaned over the end of the barrel to keep the rain out, then tried to withdraw the wooden ramrod. It wouldn't budge. The wet weather had warped the wood. He remembered the article in the library that told how Austrian troops carried their ramrods in a loop on their belts. Propping the butt of the musket on a small clump of grass, he tugged and grunted. When the ramrod finally broke free, his right arm went flying in the air. Removing the lead bullet from its paper sleeve he tamped it down on top of the powder, then replaced the wooden plug. After several futile attempts at slipping the ramrod back in place, he gave up and wedged it under his belt.

Moses noticed several cadets struggling with their weapons. Two feet away, Monty Fulton hunched over his musket, twisting and jerking on the wooden ramrod. Moses placed his musket on his knapsack and stepped over to help. While Fulton held the stock, Moses grabbed the ramrod with both hands and pulled. It was no use. Removing his own ramrod from his belt, he loaned it to the frustrated cadet. At least Monty would be able to fire one shot. But the lack of a ramrod wasn't going to be a problem. By the time Fulton needed one again, there would be plenty available from the dead and wounded.

Back in place with the color guard, Moses knocked clods of mud from the soles of his shoes with the butt of his gun. Listening to the firing up ahead, he wondered if he would finally see action. The Corps was in reserve, but if the Yankees attacked with all their men, Breckinridge would need every musket on line. Moses shivered. What was that? Nerves? It certainly wasn't cold, in fact it had become muggy and he was sweating.

Reaching in his pants pocket, Moses removed the prayer his grandfather had given him the last time he was home. It was a special prayer composed for Confederate soldiers by Rabbi Max Michelbacher of Congregation Beth Ahabah in Richmond. His grandfather had made him promise to carry it if he went into battle. Normally his grandfather wasn't religious and had often declared that there was only one true religion and that was "*Do unto others as you would have them do unto you.*" But these weren't normal times. Moses seldom dwelled on the hereafter and wasn't superstitious enough to believe a prayer written on a piece of paper would magically protect him from harm. But now he found the prayer comforting. Silently mouthing the words he read:

> *O most merciful Father, although unworthy through my many transgressions, I approach Thee to seek Thy mercy and protection. Behold me now, Thou who art near when all other aid faileth. Guard me from the impending evil. Arrayed before us is a menacing enemy who intends, by force of arms, to deprive us of our rights, liberties and freedom in this, our Confederacy. The foe intends to desecrate our soil and rob and murder our people. Here I stand with the other sons of the South, to face the foe, to drive him back and defend our natural rights. O Lord, God of Israel, be with me in the contending strife, protect and bless me and give me the courage to bear the hardships of war. Bless my mother, my father, my grandmother, my grandfather, my brothers and my sisters. May they find in Thee their trust and strength. Show me the way. Be with me always and grant me Thy salvation. Amen.*

Folding the prayer, he returned it to his pocket. The sound of musket fire was growing more intense as the skirmishers disappeared over a small rise.

When the veteran regiment on the right began its advance, the cadets witnessed a sight that surprised them. With pistols and swords the officers and file closers were forcing skulkers back into ranks.

With nerves taut, Moses began moving forward with the color guard. Before long it would be his turn to charge the dark line of Yankee infantry.

Chapter 17

Woodson

"*Get down! Get down!*" shouted Charley Woodson, captain of the company of Missourians anchoring the center of the Confederate line. Temporarily assigned to General Wharton's staff, Woodson had slogged over to check on his men. Now he didn't want to leave while they were in such danger.

For the past three and a half hours the Missourians had helped drive the Yankees out of New Market, pausing only when they encountered stiff resistance. The opposition had been light and they experienced only four casualties—one dead and three wounded. The company still had 58 effectives and now faced a battery of five 12-pounder Napoleons firing canister and a long line of Federal infantry. To Woodson it looked like the Yankees were making their final stand. Located on a slight rise, the Federal infantry line stretched from the North Fork of the Shenandoah River on the left to the Valley Turnpike on the right. To take such a strong position would require a frontal assault by the Missourians which meant heavy casualties.

Woodson had learned from bitter experience at Pea Ridge how deadly canister could be at close range. Like a giant shotgun, each round raked the line with 27 iron balls weighing 7 ounces each. Traveling at 1,500 feet per second, each ball contained enough energy to bore through three men, and still penetrate 3-inches of live oak. The cannon didn't even have to be aimed, just pointed in a general direction and the lanyard pulled. It was the perfect weapon for close-in fighting with limited visibility.

Finding it difficult to make himself heard over the roar of battle, Woodson used hand signals to get his men to lie down on the muddy ground. The company was in an advanced position with only thin stalks of knee-high wheat for protection. To their immediate left a slatted, wooden fence separated an apple orchard from the wheat field. The field was ankle-deep in mud churned up by four days of constant rain and the back-and-forth movement of artillery horses, cannon wheels, and marching feet. Any attempt to charge across the field before the cannon were silenced would slow his men to a deadly walk. Woodson watched as Sergeant Jacob Norris stood and tried to rally the troops only to be struck down by a canister ball. The sergeant was dead before he hit the ground as blood gushed from a huge, gaping chest wound which tore into his heart.

"Shoot the horses," yelled Woodson as he peered under the clouds of drifting smoke at the legs of artillery horses and cannoneers. If they could just disable enough animals, the battery would be forced to retreat.

On the left, behind the fence, men from the 30th and 51st Virginia regiments were stunned into disorder by the withering fire of the Napoleons and fragmentation shells from a dozen cannon perched along the bluff near the river. While the men milled about, a steady stream of iron and lead scythed huge gaps in their ranks. Unable to withstand the murderous barrage, they began to gather in small groups, then drift rearward, leaving dead and wounded littering the ground. Woodson frowned as he watched shell-shocked veterans abandon their position.

Whoomp! An air burst from an exploding shell slammed Woodson into the ground, smashing his face in the mud. Temporarily dazed, he sat up, shook his head and tried to focus. When he regained his senses he heard moans from nearby wounded. To check his legs, he ran his right hand over the torn fabric. They were still there and undamaged. Next, he gingerly felt his upper body for wounds. His clothes were wet, but it wasn't the warm, sticky-wet of blood. With his left hand he reached for his canteen. "*Ohoo!*" A sharp pain shot through his arm. Unable to bend his arm, he stared at a tear in the sleeve and the red stain spreading along his wrist. When he tried to move his fingers, he was relieved to see them wiggle. It was only a flesh wound.

There was a tug on the back of his jacket. It was First Lieutenant Ed Scott, his friend and second in command.

"You all right?" yelled Scott.

"Yeah. Think so."

"We've got to move back," shouted Scott, as a load of canister roared past, the balls trailing wisps of blue smoke. He pointed to the Bushong

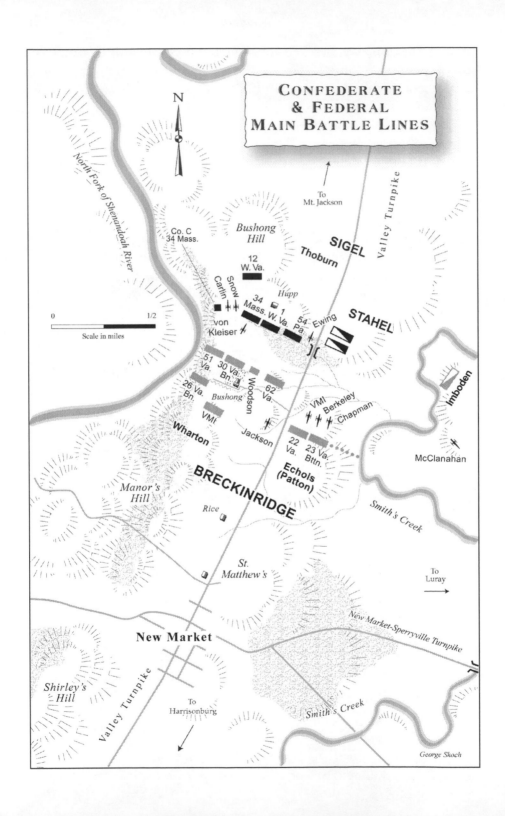

house, a two-story white, clapboard building fifty yards to the rear. "We can rally behind that building."

Woodson leaned close to Scott's ear, "Better stay here. At least 'till those cannon are knocked out." He had no intention of retreating and getting shot in the back. He didn't want word to reach the McCampbell brothers back home that he'd been killed running from the enemy. Anyway, it wouldn't be long before the Federal infantry made its move, and when they did, their artillery would have to stop firing in order not to hit their own men.

The Missourians, who were fighting dismounted, were armed with second-hand pistols, breech-loading carbines made in Richmond, and .69 caliber infantry muskets. How they had wound up fighting as infantry in the Army of Northern Virginia was a convoluted tale. Woodson's odyssey began a year earlier when he was captured in northern Missouri fighting as a guerilla under Colonel Joseph Porter. In a section of the country where it was "War to the knife and knife to the hilt," he was lucky to have escaped summary execution as a bushwhacker. Instead, he'd been court-martialed and sentenced to hard labor for the duration of the war. Sent to prison at Alton, Illinois, he was mixed in with the general population of POW's and paroled along with 1,000 other Confederates when overcrowded conditions resulted in outbreaks of smallpox, malaria, typhoid, rubella and dysentery. After being exchanged at City Point, Virginia, the never-shy 22-year-old petitioned James Seddon, Confederate secretary of war, for permission to form a company of cavalry made up entirely of Missouri ex-POWs. Once organized, he requested that they be allowed to stay in Virginia and not be sent back west. When his petition was granted, Woodson and Scott easily recruited seventy other young men to form Company A, First Missouri Cavalry. It was the only Missouri unit in the Army of Northern Virginia. The company elected Woodson captain and Scott first lieutenant. In prison they had heard fellow inmates talk about the Shenandoah Valley and the colorful exploits of Turner Ashby, John Mosby, Harry Gilmor and Hanse McNeill. The free-wheeling lifestyle of partisan rangers appealed to Woodson's and Scott's sense of adventure and dreams of glory.

As a teenager in Missouri, Woodson, an orphan, had been adopted by a neighbor and sent to school until he was seventeen. Trained as a carpenter, the war came along just in time to save him from a lifetime of drudgery building barrels and constructing outhouses. In addition to heart-stopping excitement, the war offered the penniless youg man an opportunity to become a respected cavalry officer and mix socially with members of the landed gentry. An additional bonus was that by fighting in the Valley, Woodson and company would get a second chance at facing Franz Sigel and the same Germans they had fought in Missouri at Wilson's Creek and Pea Ridge.

To gain Lee's approval, Woodson, Scott and the "Missouri Exiles" offered to enlist for 40 years or the duration of the war. Impressed by their enthusiasm, Lee assigned them to the Valley as part of General Imboden's 62nd Virginia Mounted Infantry regiment. This was exactly what Woodson and Scott wanted except for one rather important detail. On paper Company A was cavalry, but they had no horses. In an army where cavalrymen had to furnish their own mounts, this meant they had to fight as infantry until they could beg, borrow or capture enough mounts.

Whack, whack, whack. The sound of Minie balls striking the wooden fence on Woodson's left reminded him of a hail storm in Missouri. Looking to his right he saw the color bearer of the 62nd slump to the ground. It was the second member of the guard he'd seen struck down in less than ten minutes. Without hesitation, a corporal scooped up the flag and waved it high. Still watching the colors, Woodson noticed Major Hall approaching, running in a low crouch, dodging and weaving.

"Colonel Smith says to hold your position at all hazards."

Woodson pointed to the colors, "Looks to me like the regiment's retreating."

"No, no," assured Hall, pointing to a slight depression thirty yards to the rear. "We're just moving back to that ravine. The canister's tearing us apart. Why don't you—"

"We'll stay here," said Woodson. "If we retreat we'll be out of pistol range of those damned cannon."

"I'll tell Colonel Smith," said Hall, tipping his hat and heading back along the line, as shell fragments and iron balls whined and hissed by.

Woodson clasped Scott's arm. "Pass the word to concentrate on that battery."

Working his way along the front line, Scott instructed the men to aim at the horses. If no target was visible, they should shoot at the muzzle flashes of the cannon. On reaching the last man, he pointed his pistol at a cannoneer sponging the barrel of a Napoleon and pulled the trigger. The man's kepi flew into the air as he pitched forward onto the barrel of the cannon. Scott noticed a man on his left staggering toward him. The blood was gushing from his chest and back. It was First Sergeant Will Day.

Day reached out with a trembling hand, "Lieutenant, I'm almost gone. Please help me off."

Whump!

Scott staggered back from the shock of a nearby explosion. A severe pain racked his right arm. Looking down he saw the sleeve turning bright red. When he tried to move his hand there was no movement. A piece of shell had disabled his arm. Close beside him, Lieutenant Jones, his best friend, fell face down in the mud, struck by a jagged fragment from the same shell. Blood and brains oozed from Jones' forehead. Just last week Scott and Jones had strolled together in the forest near Woodstock admiring the scenery. On spotting some wild flowers Scott had woven them into wreaths for their hats. After handing Jones a band of flowers, he noticed one in the mix that he'd often seen in the hands of the dead at funerals. He tried to remove it before it brought bad luck, but was too late.

With his good arm, Scott led the mortally wounded Will Day a few feet to the rear and laid him down. Noticing Will's ashen-white face, Scott called to him, but there was no answer. Placing his mouth close to Day's ear, the former minister, who led weekly Bible classes for the Company, pleaded with the dying man, "Will, call on the Almighty Father to pardon you for your sins and receive you into His Kingdom." There was no response.

A frantic voice called from behind, "Lieutenant, Lieutenant!" It was young Tommy Cave, blood spurting from his chest and neck. Two years ago, when only fourteen, Cave had enlisted in Scott's unit against his father's wishes. Captured and sent to prison at Alton, he had been exchanged along with Woodson and Scott. Grasping Scott's hand, in a strained, youthful voice, Cave said, "Goodbye, Lieutenant, I am killed."

Scott took Cave by the arm and eased him to the ground. Placing a canteen of water to the youngster's lips, he whispered in the boy's ear, "Tommy, repeat after me, 'Our Father forgive me and receive me to thy Kingdom.'" There was no reply. The eyes were already fixed in a deathly stare.

On the other side of the company Woodson looked at his left flank. All the men in the 30th Virginia and part of the 51st were gone. The gap between the Missourians and what remained of the 51st had widened. His left flank was now wide open. It wouldn't take long for the Federals to realize what had happened and launch their attack. If the gap weren't filled quickly the battle might be lost. While rallying the men, Woodson saw more topple to the ground. It was too late to order a retreat.

Chapter 18

Breckinridge

"Quick, Charley, ride over and check on Wharton's men." Through field glasses Breckinridge could see men huddled in small groups behind the Bushong house and barn. Some were sitting, others kneeling, still others leaned dejectedly on their muskets. The driving rain and shifting smoke made it difficult to tell what was taking place. Early that morning he had ordered all officers to fight on foot, but there wasn't time for Major Semple to make the trip without a horse. He'd have to run the gauntlet. "They'll be gunning for anyone mounted, so keep low."

Standing with his staff on a small knoll beside the turnpike, Breckinridge asked Stoddard Johnston, "How many you reckon they got?" The general had chosen this area for his command post since it was close to his artillery and provided a sweeping view of the battlefield. There was also a low, broken stone fence in front which provided limited protection. Inside the fence, thirty yards away, was VMI's section of two, 3-inch rifled guns commanded by Captain Collier Minge. Because of their accuracy the rifled cannon had been concentrating fire on the Union batteries along Bushong Hill. Breckinridge had also ordered Minge to keep a sharp lookout for any Federal cavalry emerging from the cedars.

With his left hand, Johnston adjusted the focus on his telescope. "There're two—three regimental flags—and another one further back, close to that house with two chimneys." He adjusted the eyepiece for a clearer picture, but the rain kept fogging the lens. "That's it."

"Only four?" The lack of infantry puzzled Breckinridge. With approximately 600 men per regiment, that meant Sigel had about 1,800 men on his front line with another 600 in reserve. It had been three hours and forty-five minutes since he launched the attack, plenty of time for Sigel to bring up the rest of his army. Was this some sort of trap? The day before, scouts had reported eight Federal infantry regiments between New Market and Woodstock. "Where do you think he's hiding the rest?"

"Maybe—behind those buildings, or in the woods," suggested Johnston.

"Or, across Smith's Creek," said Breckinridge. "They may try to get behind us." Breckinridge was relieved that Imboden was on the other side of the creek with 600 cavalry and four field guns. If Sigel tried to gain their rear, Imboden could hold them off long enough for Breckinridge to send reinforcements. Since all the Confederate infantry, except for VMI's small battalion, were on the main line, the army was vulnerable to any surprise attack from the rear or right flank.

"Are those the same three regiments we've been fighting all day?" asked Breckinridge. Since launching the attack, his men had been chasing three Union regiments from New Market to the Bushong farm. The Federals had tried twice to slow down the Confederates, but had been overwhelmed and driven back by superior numbers. Now it appeared this was Sigel's final defensive line.

"Strange," said Johnson." The number of flags is the same, but the banners are different."

"What's that brick building behind the Federal line?"

"The Hupp house," volunteered Colonel Patton who was standing nearby. "Belongs to Dr. John Rice, the man who built the turnpike. Some of his kin live there. When he's in town, Dr. Rice stays at Stanley Hall, that fancy mansion we passed half a mile back."

Breckinridge studied the sturdy structure. A chimney adorned each end of the square, two-story, brick building which was uncommonly fine for a second home. The usual scattering of out-buildings: a large barn, a hog pen, an ice house, a corn crib, and three large hay stacks were enclosed in a four acre tract encircled by picket fences. Breckinridge shook his head. It was a shame to damage the farm with artillery and small arms fire, but it was in the wrong place at the wrong time.

Breckinridge lowered his binoculars, "We need to launch an attack before Sigel brings up the rest of his troops."

"*General!*" called Captain Minge. He pointed toward the cedar trees directly in front. "The Yankee cavalry's filing onto the turnpike." Although this was Minge's first time under fire, the 19-year-old was as calm as a seasoned veteran. The highest ranking cadet officer at the Institute, he had been at VMI since the start of the war and had learned artillery tactics directly from Stonewall Jackson.

Between clouds of smoke, Breckinridge saw Federal horsemen drawing sabers and crowding onto the pike's hard surface. He beckoned to Major McLaughlin, chief of artillery, and Lt. Colonel Clarence Derrick, regimental commander for the 23rd Virginia.

"Well gentlemen, it looks like they're going to charge." With a ramrod, Breckinridge pointed toward a narrow, stone bridge 275 yards down the pike. "They'll have to cross that bridge in columns of two before forming into squadrons on this side. That'll give us a few minutes to blast them with artillery."

"That's a damn heap of horseflesh," observed Patton as he watched more and more cavalry emerging from the woods. "How many—?"

"Close to 1,800 if they use both brigades," replied Breckinridge.

"We can take them if the men don't panic," said Patton. He knew how unnerving an all-out cavalry charge could be, even to veteran troops. He glanced at the cadet cannoneers, "Hope those boys stay calm."

Picking up a clod of wet mud, Derrick ran the slippery muck between thumb and forefinger. He studied the pools of water standing in the fields and watched horses and men at the edge of the trees stumble back and forth trying to gain solid footing. "The Yanks couldn't have chosen worse ground," he said, with casual distain. "Nothing but sludge." He scraped the mud from his fingers with the back of his sword. "They'll stay on the pike as long as possible." A student of British tactics, the West Pointer had already decided how to position his regiment.

"Into the valley of death rode the six hundred," said Patton. "They're clinging to old tactics, but what can you expect from Dutchmen trained in Europe?" Ever since the introduction of rifled muskets and improved canister, most military tacticians considered it foolhardy for cavalry to attack artillery positions strongly supported by infantry.

With no time to waste, Breckinridge began to issue orders. The charge would be quick, close, and brutal. "Colonel Patton, keep your men left of our artillery. Have them concentrate on cavalry coming up the road. Colonel Derrick, stay on the right and guard the flank. We don't want them at our backs."

"Unless you object, General, I plan to form two of my companies into squares," said Derrick, whose regiment stretched all the way to

Smith's Creek. "I'll swing my skirmishers around to hit their flank as they approach."

"Excellent," responded Breckinridge. "Gentlemen, don't let your formations drift in front of the artillery. Visibility's going to be poor and we'll be firing double canister. Try to funnel their horses into the muzzles of our cannon."

As the officers headed back to their commands, Breckinridge walked over to Major McLaughlin and Captain Minge. "When the action starts, you'll have support from Patton's and Derrick's infantry. I've ordered extra canister brought up. Good luck and good shooting."

McLaughlin nodded, then jogged over to Chapman's battery on a rise fifty paces to the right. The six-gun battery had two 3-inch rifled cannon nicknamed "Maggie" and "Katie," and four 12-pound Napoleons named "Bettie," "Nannie," "Sue," and "Mollie." Although only 23, Chapman was a veteran officer with over two years experience fighting in the Valley. For the past three hours his battery had been leapfrogging the infantry in the advance, sending round after round of case shot into the ragged ranks of retreating Federals.

Minge ran back to his two-gun section and gathered the cannoneers in a semi circle. "Men, we're gonna be facing cavalry. You know the drill. It'll be loud and things will happen fast. This is the chance we've been waiting for." By drilling his crews two hours at the end of each day during the march from Lexington, his cannoneers had learned to fire a round every 30 seconds. When both guns functioned smoothly they could sweep the field with over two hundred half-pound iron balls every minute. "Do your duty and bring honor to the Institute."

As the cadets splashed back to their stations, Minge motioned for second lieutenants Fred Claybrook and Levi Welch to join him in a huddle. Prior to the war, Stonewall had named the Institute's four cannon, "Mathew," "Mark," "Luke," and "John." Now, there were only two 3-inch guns left. To keep the tradition alive the Cadets had dubbed them "Mathew" and "Luke." "Their cavalry will come straight at us," said Minge. "Fred, aim Mathew so it's shooting directly down the pike. Levi, aim Luke 40 yards to the right. That'll give us a good spread."

"We're getting low on case shot," said Welch. The year before, while on furlough from VMI, he had served on Colonel Patton's staff as a courier during the battle of Dry Creek. His coolness under fire had earned him recognition and a letter of appreciation. It was this proven steadiness in the heat of battle that had induced Minge to request him for the artillery detail.

"We won't need much case," said Minge. "As they're crossing the bridge, hit them with shell and whatever case you have left. When they're ready to charge, we'll switch to canister." He pointed at the stone bridge, "That's your marker. Set your fuses for 275 yards."

"Single or double loads?" asked Claybrook.

"Visibility's gonna be poor. The riders on the pike will be moving fast, but the ones in the field will be slowed by the soggy ground. We'll start with single loads, then switch to double at 100 yards. Go ahead and place your aiming stakes." Knowing how to use aiming stakes to align cannon when visibility was poor was a trick Minge had picked up from Stonewall.

"At what elevation?" asked Welch.

"Minimal. Just enough to keep the shot out of the mud. You can set the screws now."

"Any infantry support?" asked Claybrook.

"Colonel Patton's on our left with 600 men. Colonel Derrick's on the right with another 600. Arm your spare men with fixed bayonets and put them on the flanks." With 16 cadets available for each gun crew and a total of 32 in the section, Minge had enough spare men to provide limited protection in case a few cavalrymen broke through.

Whump!

A cadet standing next to Mathew's carriage spun around and fell to the ground. A crimson blotch spread across his right shoulder.

"It's Whitehead!" yelled Claybrook. As cannoneer number 4 it was Whitehead's job to prime the piece and pull the lanyard.

"Switch in Morgan," said Minge. "Have your 5's and 6's bring all the canister close to the guns."

Claybrook nodded then ran over to the cannon to round up his eight man crew. After issuing instructions he tapped Otis Glazebrook on the shoulder. "OK, Gunner, your show."

As gunner it was Glazebrook's job to aim the piece and give all commands for its operation. The artillery field manual specified that cannoneers should be "intelligent, muscular, active, and not less than five-feet-seven." At five-eleven, wiry and 162 pounds, Glazebrook easily met those criteria. The manual also recommended that cannoneers be "good at handling horses and knowledgeable about mechanics." First in his class academically Glazebrook had grown up on a horse farm.

Four days ago when Glazebrook selected his crew he had requested

John Webb for his Number 1. It was Number 1's job to muscle the heavy, wooden rammer into position, sponge the bore after each round, then ram home a 14-pound shell. Glazebrook had also selected 15-year-old Lewis Davis as a driver for his horses. Davis, at 5-feet-4 weighed only 128 pounds, but loved animals. Now, he was on the flank as a spare man to help guard against cavalry.

As smoke rolled across the battlefield, Minge watched the Yankee cavalry approach the bridge and form into a double column. In a loud voice he ordered, "*Sec—tion! Commence firing!*"

Claybrook nodded to Glazebrook, who turned to his crew. "*Load—shell!*"

With a swift, well-practiced motion Webb sponged the barrel, then shoved in a shell with a short fuse. Standing behind the tube, Glazebrook sighted the piece on the bridge which was only fleetingly visible through the haze. Tapping the side of the trail he signaled his Number 3 to use the hand spike to shift the cannon slightly to the left. After a final check, he stepped aside and raised his right arm. "*Matthew!—Ready!—Stand clear!*"

With everyone at a safe distance, Glazebrook dropped his arm, "*Fire!*"

With a roar, Matthew discharged its cargo, the recoil sending the carriage four feet to the rear.

Communicating by grunts and hand signals, and with feet slipping in the mud, the crew quickly rolled Matthew back into position while Glazebrook centered the barrel on the aiming stake.

Kneeling on the wet ground and peering under the smoke, Minge watched the cavalry form into squadron formation. Jumping up, he shouted, "*Load—canister!*"

"*Load canister!*" Claybrook repeated to his crew.

On the right, explosions from Chapman's six-gun battery shook the earth while to the left, sheets of flame erupted from the muskets of Patton's infantry. Heavy smoke covered the field, while overhead streaks of lightning, mixed with thunder, added to the confusion.

Minge kneeled again and peered under the smoke. Between patches of vapor he saw the horsemen moving toward them. At 100 yards, he stood up, "*Double—canister!*" Finally, "*Prepare to receive cavalry!—Stand to your guns!*" Drawing his sword he braced for the onslaught of animals and riders.

Like well-oiled machines, the crews of Matthew and Luke sweated and grunted as commands snapped by.

"Load!"
"Ready!"
"Stand Clear!"
"Fire!"

Clouds of caustic, suffocating smoke rolled over the cannoneers as they gasped for breath and fed canister into the gaping maw of the two cannon. Now Matthew and Luke were the cadets' sole means of survival. Reduced to a world a few feet square full of smoke, powder, and concussions, the cannoneers bent to their work. To Webb, who was sponging the barrel and ramming home shells, it seemed that Mathew had taken on a life of its own. In exchange for survival he had become the willing slave to a demanding piece of iron.

On the left flank, covered in the smog of battle, Lewis Davis stood fast, his hands gripping the stock of a captured Springfield. With fixed bayonet and the butt of the musket grounded in the spongy earth, he faced outward, his bloodshot eyes straining to pick up any signs of enemy activity. To his front he saw the ghostly shapes of Colonel Patton's men loading and firing. Behind him, Matthew and Luke erupted every 30 seconds, his body shaking with each discharge. As he tried to spit the bitter gunpowder from his mouth, he was startled by a mounted figure lunging at him from the fog. His muscles tightened as he braced for the collision, but the horse, its eyes wide with fright, reared at the last second. Stumbling backwards, Davis raised his left arm to ward off the slashing hooves pawing the air inches from his face.

Regaining his footing, Davis jerked his musket up and pointed the barrel at the horse's head, ready to pull the trigger—but hesitated. The rider was a young, bareheaded cavalryman who stood in the stirrups, pulling on the reins with all his might, trying to regain control of the runaway animal. Davis exhaled when he saw that the rider had no weapon. He opened his mouth to yell for the cavalryman to surrender, but his throat was parched dry and nothing came out. For a fraction of a second, his eyes locked with those of the rider's. He saw the fear, the panic.

Unable to remain suspended in air, the horse's hooves came crashing down making the ground tremble while the horse snorted with terror. With a final tug, the rider wheeled the animal's head around and started back for the bridge.

"Run, horse, run!" shouted Davis, as he closed his eyes. Pointing his musket in the air, he pulled the trigger.

Moving from cannon to cannon, Minge sought to calm the jangled nerves of his crews. On the left he could see Colonel Patton's regiment surging forward, yelling like demons as they poured a wall of lead into the exposed flank of the retreating enemy. Relieved to have survived, Minge looked over the field now covered with writhing horses and wounded men. As musket and cannon fire increased, the remaining horsemen turned around and headed at full gallop for the safety of the trees.

"We've whipped them!" whooped Stoddard Johnston, throwing his hat in the air. "By damn, the Yanks are running!"

"Rider approaching!" shouted Captain James Norquet, Breckinridge's engineering officer. From west of the pike, Major Semple emerged from the smoke, riding hard.

Reining in his horse, Semple jumped from the saddle. *"General, our line's collapsing!"*

"How bad?"

"There's a wide gap in front of the house," he said, pointing across the turnpike at the Bushong farm.

Raising his field glasses, Breckinridge saw more Confederate troops seeking shelter behind the house. "Charley, you've got to go back and turn them around. If we can just contract the lines—"

"Too late," replied Semple, vigorously shaking his head. "I've tried, but the men won't rally."

"Where's Edgar's regiment?"

"They're moving up, but he's only got 400. We'll need another 200 to close the breach." Removing a handkerchief from around his neck, Semple wiped mud from his face and hands, "You can fix it if you put the cadets in. They're *right* there."

Breckinridge shook his head, "No, Charley. They're just children." He thought of Mary and his promise to himself to keep the cadets out of action. "I can't expose them to that kind of fire. It's the center of the line. If the veterans can't hold it—"

"If you don't, we might lose," warned Semple. "If the Yankees break through, they could roll up the whole line."

This was the decision Breckinridge had been dreading ever since calling the cadets to his army. Again, he scanned the Bushong farm with his binoculars.

Semple continued to fidget with his hat, "General—if we move *now* . . ."

"Will the boys stand?" asked Breckinridge, trying to delay having to make a decision. He was hoping Semple would say he didn't know, or wasn't sure, anything to give him an out.

"As well as our own men," came the quick reply. He pointed to the grim, powder-blackened faces of the cannoneers in VMI's artillery section. "There's your answer."

"But, Charley—"

"You've got no choice. Think of the disgrace to the Institute and cadets if you don't use them."

Breckinridge looked at the flags of the Federal infantry. It wouldn't be long before they started moving forward. The Major was right. Earlier that morning on Shirley's Hill, VMI's Commandant had asked for a chance to take part. To hold them back now might mean defeat. He owed General Lee more than that. If he didn't commit his reserve it would mean he didn't consider the cadets real soldiers, and that would be a serious blow to their manhood.

"OK, Charley. Put the boys in." Breckinridge turned away so his staff couldn't see his anguish. As Semple rode off, he lowered his head. "May God forgive me for that order."

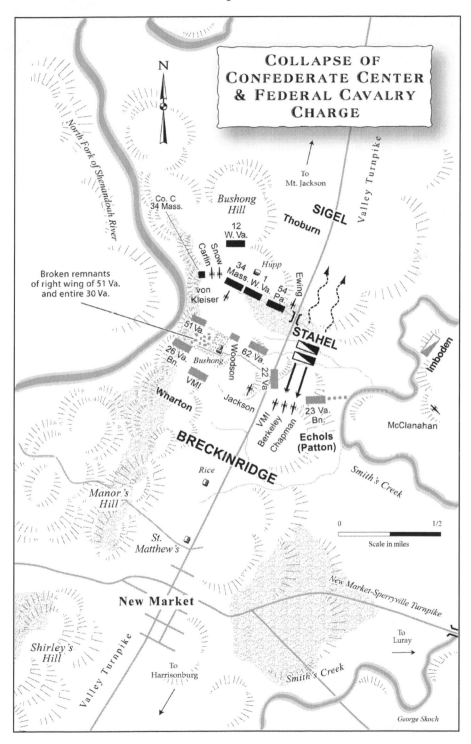

N

To
Mt. Jackson

SIGEL

Valley Turnpike

North Fork of Shenandoah River

Co. C
34 Mass.

*Bushong
Hill*

12
W. Va.

Thoburn

Snow
Carlin

34
Mass.

Hupp

1
W. Va.

Ewing

54
Pa.

Broken remnants
of right wing of 51 Va.
and entire 30 Va.

von
Kleiser

STAHEL

Imboden

51 Va.

26 Va.
Bn.

Bushong

Woodson

62 Va.

22 Va.

VMI

Jackson

VMI

Berkeley

Chapman

23 Va.
Bn.

McClanahan

Wharton

**Echols
(Patton)**

BRECKINRIDGE

Rice

Smith's Creek

*Manor's
Hill*

*St.
Matthew's*

0   1/2

Scale in miles

New Market

New Market-Sperryville Turnpike

To
Luray

*Shirley's
Hill*

Valley Turnpike

To
Harrisonburg

Smith's Creek

George Skoch

COLLAPSE OF
CONFEDERATE CENTER
& FEDERAL CAVALRY
CHARGE

Chapter 19

Cadets

Moses picked through the pile of muskets stacked on the ammunition cart pulled up behind the Corps. The Commandant had encouraged all those having trouble with ramrods to exchange their guns for a discarded Yankee Springfield or Confederate Enfield. Most of the rifles were caked with mud and all had minor battle damage, but at least they worked. Not wanting to be away from the colors for long, Moses quickly selected an Enfield with a cracked stock that still had its bayonet attached. He filled his cartridge box with forty .577 caliber rounds.

While other cadets rummaged through the discards, Moses hurried back to his place on the left of Evans. The *zip, zip, zip* from Minie balls and *karumph* of artillery reminded him they were under fire. Although the battalion was in reserve, it was less than 500 yards from the Federal front line and within easy reach of enemy rifle balls and artillery shells. Partly shielded from the infantry by the trees and buildings on the Bushong farm, the formation was in plain view of Federal artillery along the high ground on the left.

As Moses examined his new rifle he noticed the percussion cap was missing. Withdrawing the Enfield's metal ramrod, he checked to see if the weapon was loaded. It was empty. Removing a round from his cartridge box, he bit off the end, and carefully poured the powder down the barrel. After snapping a cap in place he noticed a horseman approaching from the turnpike. In a flurry of mud and lather, Major Semple galloped up to Lt. Colonel Ship who stood by the colors.

Major Semple saluted, "Compliments from General Breckinridge." He removed his hat and waved it toward the Bushong farm, "The general wishes you to move your battalion forward and occupy the gap in our line on the other side of that house."

This was the order Ship had been waiting for. Finally, the chance to prove his well-trained cadets were first rate soldiers. Peering at the farm through binoculars, he could make out a large barn on the left, the main house straight ahead and what looked like an orchard beyond the house. "Is the gap left or right of the house?"

"It runs from the house to the barn. There's a zig-zag fence beyond those trees. That's your objective. Station your men at the fence and prepare to receive an attack by their infantry. We're stretched thin so put your men in a single line." When he was about to leave, he turned back, "As soon as you reach the fence, have your men lie down. The artillery fire's hot as blue blazes in that orchard. Don't expose yourselves more than necessary." He gave a final salute, and rode off.

Moses was pleased at being called a man. Although still a teenager, he was older than some of the regulars in the main army and bristled with resentment whenever anyone referred to cadets as "boys"—or worse, "children."

Ship ran along the front row of the battalion looking for the company commanders. "Fix bayonets and get ready to move out."

"Company C, Ten—shun!" shouted Second Captain Sprigg Shriver, as a shell shrieked overhead. *"Fix—bayonets!"*

The clatter of metal on metal filled the air as cadets removed bayonets from scabbards and twisted them onto the ends of muskets. Now Moses felt queasy about actually going into battle. He thought of Leonora and wondered if she would be upset if he were killed—or maimed. He closed his eyes, "Please, God, don't let me lose an arm or leg." But, he was determined to do his duty no matter the cost. He checked the bayonet to make certain it was secure, and grimaced when the sharp point pricked the palm of his hand. At eighteen inches it was long enough to penetrate a body and rip through lungs, arteries and brains. He hoped he wouldn't get close enough to find out.

As a member of the color guard Moses would be in front of the cadet line, a perfect target for sharpshooters. At least he wasn't six-foot-two, like Evans. He'd heard that marksmen aimed for the tallest and biggest soldiers. Maybe if he hunkered down a little he wouldn't be so noticeable.

Standing in front of the cadets the Commandant raised his sword. *"Battal—yun! On cen—ter dress! For—ward! At the double-quick! March!"*

The Corps started off, but not at the double-quick. Every step was slowed by ankle-deep mud which sucked at their feet. Looking ahead Moses saw the farmhouse only 250 yards away, but it seemed like a mile. When he stepped into a depression, the sludge rose over the top of his right shoe. With a *slurp*, he pulled his foot free, but left the shoe behind. Should he go back? No. As a member of the color guard he had to stay with the flag. Besides, he might be killed or wounded and he didn't want other members of the Corps to think he was running away.

The closer the battalion got to the farm the more shell fragments they encountered and the louder the battle noise became.

Whooomph! The explosion from a shell lifted Lieutenant John Hanna off his feet, toppling him sideways into the mud. Temporarily stunned, he opened his mouth and worked his jaw back and forth until his ears popped and his vision cleared. Placing the flat of his sword on a patch of clover, he pushed himself up. Jogging back to his place in line he passed the crumpled body of Henry Jones, sprawled in the mire. Then he saw Charlie Crockett, lying in the mud with part of his skull missing. He heard Jones moaning and saw him twitch, but he couldn't stop to help. "Maybe they're just wounded," he told himself, knowing it wasn't true.

With his next step, Hanna almost tripped over First Sergeant William Cabell lying face down in the sludge, his head pierced by a lead ball. With outstretched hands, the grandson of a former governor of Virginia and Breckinridge's cousin, was tearing up clods of mud and tuffs of grass. Hanna blanched. How quickly that had happened. Just seconds ago, Cabell had been the bright, academic leader of the second class with hopes of becoming a successful physician like his father. Now, he was convulsing in the muck in his death throes. Soon he would be just another decaying corpse. "Ashes to ashes," Hanna muttered as he crossed himself, regretting that he hadn't gone to confession before leaving the Institute. What if he were killed while not in a State of Grace? Had he committed any sins since his last confession? How much time would he have to spend in purgatory to atone? He clutched the Crucifix on the chain around his neck, "Holy Mary, Mother of God, pray for me now at the hour of my death."

"Close up!" shouted Colonna. The gap in Company D quickly filled as the line moved on.

Now when the Corps passed wounded veterans on the ground there was no more "Rock-a-bye baby," but shouts of *"Go get 'em, boys! Give the Yankees hell!"* As they marched forward, the wings of the battalion advanced faster than the center. When he noticed the lack of alignment, Lt. Colonel Ship called out, *"Battal—yun, mark time! Cen—ter dress!"* Once it was straightened out, he shouted, *"For—ward! March!"* He was glad his voice hadn't cracked.

"Mark time under fire?" muttered Porter Johnson, who'd been a cadet for nine months. "That's crazy. Those Yankees are trying their damnedest to kill us and we're worried about alignment?" He glanced at the Commandant who was white as a sheet and sweating profusely while dodging Minie balls and shrapnel. "Even a commandant ducks when the lead starts flying," he mumbled.

Marching beside Lt. Colonel Ship was Big Evans, the color bearer. Johnson noted with approval that there was no hint of fear on Big's face. Evans kept looking over his shoulder every few steps to check on the progress of the Corps—and was actually smiling. It was obvious that Big wasn't worried that holding the flag made him *the* primary target for every Yankee with a gun. Johnson shifted as far away from the colors as possible. He would let Big have all the glory. All Johnson wanted to do was survive.

Johnson's his best friend, Johnnie Cocke from Tennessee, marched on his right. Cocke was a veteran who had been with General John Hunt Morgan on his famous raid through Kentucky. Whenever Cocke drifted to the right, leaving a space between their elbows, Johnson would nervously call out, "Close up Cocke, close up." Finally, when it was Johnson who shifted too far left, Cocke got his revenge. In a voice loud enough to be heard down the line, he demanded, *"Now, dammit, Johnson, you close up!"*

Whumph! While Johnson watched a wounded officer on the ground wave his sword to rally his men, a shell landed in the mud, twelve feet in front. The explosion spun Johnson around like a top, flinging his musket over his head and hurling him to the ground. A small piece of shrapnel struck his chest, cutting his jacket and shirt, but not his skin. A second, larger chunk smashed into his left arm causing him to black out.

As the Corps trudged on, a bullet hit James Darden in Company C in the left thigh. The impact hurled him sideways against Moses who stumbled but managed to keep his feet. Although suffering from shock and bleeding profusely, Darden pulled himself up, grabbed his musket and hobbled after his company. As soon as he was back in line, a second Minie ball sliced through his left arm, severing an artery. Dropping to his knees, he clutched at his arm, trying to stop the bleeding.

Behind Darden marched Tom Jefferson, who saw the blood gushing out in spurts. Realizing his friend would bleed to death if the hemorrhaging weren't stopped, Jefferson ignored the standing order to keep moving and eased Darden to the ground. Ripping open Darden's shirt sleeve, Jefferson unhooked his canteen strap and wrapped it tightly around the cadet's wounded arm. Twisting the strap until the flow of blood stopped, Jefferson tied it into a firm knot, then grabbed his musket and ran to catch up.

No sooner had he taken his place, than Jefferson heard a loud *thump* as Will McDowell was hit squarely in the chest by a Minie ball. The 17-year-old North Carolinian fell back, writhing in agony as he tore open his jacket and shirt, blindly groping for the source of pain. Just last October McDowell's mother had sent the Superintendent ten dollars to have a daguerreotype made of her eldest son. She wanted a good picture so, "should any misfortune befall William, I will have some likeness of him preserved." Her presentiment had come true.

When Jefferson started to go to McDowell's aid, Andy Pizzini grabbed his arm. "No, Tom. There's nothing you can do."

As the cadets approached the two-story, white clapboard house, for the first time they saw veterans retreating. The vets were breaking for the rear in ones and twos, then fours and more until it became a steady stream. Some rushed through the cadets' formation, throwing parts of the battalion into confusion.

"Steady, men. Steady," called Ship, concerned that seeing regulars run might cause panic. "Open ranks and let them through."

From his position in the first row of Company C, Louis Wise watched an officer wave a pistol trying to stop his men from retreating. Then he heard him yell, *"Rally men and go to the front! Here you are running to the rear like a bunch of frightened sheep. Look at those children going to the front. Rally and follow those children!"* Louis flinched at the word, but at least no cadets were retreating. Now he was more determined than ever to prove himself equal to any veteran.

On his left, Louis noticed a color bearer from a regular regiment bravely standing in plain sight of Federal artillery and waving the battalion's flag. This act of defiance quickly attracted the attention of Federal gunners on the hill who fired several shells in his direction. When the smoke cleared,

Louis saw the flag droop, then rise again as another man grabbed the staff. Slowly, the veterans began to rally and head back to the front.

As he plodded along with Company A, Clarke Howard busily made resolutions for the future, promising God to live a clean, Christian life if only he was spared. Suddenly, he noticed the dark thunderclouds swirling overhead. He marveled as the bolts of lightning streaked to the earth followed by loud claps of thunder. Amidst the noise and flashes of light he saw dozens of little sparrows darting about, frantic with fright. He remembered the Bible verse, "Fear ye not therefore, ye are of more value than many sparrows." He wondered how many sparrows he was worth. Finally, the little birds recovered their senses and fluttered above the chaos. As they disappeared into the clouds he wished he had a pair of wings so he could join them.

As Moses dodged explosions and Minie balls, he noticed Carter Randolph looking around and grinning. At Second Manassas and Antietam, Randolph had carried dispatches for Stonewall Jackson. In an after-action report J.E.B. Stuart wrote, "I would like to commend a young lad named Randolph who brought me messages from General Jackson under circumstances of great personal peril. He delivered his dispatches with great clearness and intelligence." Amused by all the bobbing and weaving, Randolph called out, "There's no use dodging, boys, if a bullet's going to find you, it'll hit you anyway." No sooner had the words left his mouth than he was struck a glancing blow on the forehead, sending him sprawling. Moses was close enough to hear the sickening *plunk* of lead striking bone.

Last night, Moses and Randolph had made a pact that if either were killed the other would take his pocketbook and letters and send them home to his mother. Seeing the blood running down Randolph's face and no sign of life, Moses bent over and collected Randolph's personal effects. Gritting his teeth, he lowered his head and moved on.

Peering ahead, Moses saw the Bushong house looming directly in front. Wounded veterans were crowding behind the building, lying on the ground and moaning with pain. As the Corps neared the house, Companies C and D filed around on the left side while A and B circled on the right. The patter of Minie balls and shell fragments striking the side of the house could be heard above the roar of battle.

Slowed by the remnants of a picket fence, C and D Companies were delayed in reaching their place in the orchard on the other side of the house.

A and B Companies were already waiting, marching in place, marking time. After the alignment was corrected Lt. Colonel Ship shouted *"Corps! For-ward! March!"*

When the Corps had gone ten steps, Lt. Colonel Ship was struck hard on the left shoulder by a heavy piece of shrapnel. Swept off his feet, Ship crashed to the ground. Stunned and unable to speak, he lay on his back and stared at the sky while the rain splattered his face.

As Moses moved around the trunk of an apple tree he was hit in the chest by a spent piece of shell. Knocked to the ground, he gasped for breath. When he was finally able to breath, he sat up and searched for wounds. There were none.

Noticing the Commandant go down, the cadets hesitated, unsure of what to do. Seeing the colors move forward, they ran the last fifty yards to the fence, dodging around and over bodies of wounded and dead veterans. When they reached the fence, First Captain Frank Preston, shouted, *"Com—pany B! Halt! Rea—dy! Aim! Fire!"*

For the first time, the cadets were able to return fire at a foe who had been killing and wounding them for the past three hours. Elated at the chance to vent their frustrations, they gave a shout and sent a volley of lead smashing into the line of blue 200 yards away.

Crouching low and moving along the fence, Preston ordered, *"Lie down, men! Aim low! Fire at will!"* He then eased down onto a small patch of grass, cautiously tucking his one good arm under his body. Having spent the past two years feeding and dressing himself with only one hand, he was determined to save what was left.

When he recovered from the initial shock of being hit by a spent fragment, Moses staggered to his feet, grabbed his musket and hobbled to the zig-zag fence where Evans stood with the flag. Moses' chest tightened as he looked at the long lines of enemy forces. He could see flashes of muzzle blasts from twelve cannon 300 yards on the left as fragmentation shells and case shot crashed into the orchard. Directly in front, less than 170 yards away, a battery of five Napoleons showered the orchard with canister. Moses ducked as Minie balls fired by the infantry whistled past his head like swarms of angry hornets.

An overwhelming urge for survival gripped Moses as he saw cadets lying flat on the ground, their faces buried in the mud. There would be no loss of honor if he joined them and simply hunkered down until the shelling stopped. After all, he had advanced with the colors and hadn't run. But, one look at John Stuart, first sergeant of Company C, told him that if he didn't start shooting it would be noticed, and there would be no promotion to sergeant in July.

Moses dropped to one knee and started loading his new Enfield. His hands shook as he spilled a few grains of powder while removing the Minie ball and ramming it down the barrel. Leaning forward, he balanced the musket on a fence rail and took careful aim at a patch of blue. Holding his breath, he slowly squeezed the trigger. *Blam!* The explosion slammed the butt of the nine pound rifle hard against his shoulder. The sharp pain made him cringe—but it felt good. Now he was a real soldier.

In Company C, Nelson Noland watched Second Captain Sprigg Shriver step over a broken fence and go forward. With all the smoke and confusion Noland couldn't tell if this was a general advance, but rising to his feet he followed. When they'd gone thirty paces, Noland saw Shriver drop to the ground. He hesitated. Had Shriver been hit, or was he just seeking cover? Lowering himself into a muddy furrow, Noland tried to keep his face and musket out of the mud. Unsure of what to do, he raised his head a couple of inches and peered under the dense layer of smoke blanketing the ground. A hundred and fifty yards ahead were the feet of enemy cannoneers and spokes of carriage wheels. His pulse raced as he rolled on his back and clutched his rifle close to his body. Overhead, pieces of paper swirled about, then darted forward, caught in drafts by canister rushing past. To his right, the limbs of a large tree swayed back and forth with each discharge. Not wanting to be killed out of ranks he waited for a lull in the firing, then sprinted back to the fence, scuttling in between two cadets lying behind a rail.

On the far left, the battle noise kept cadets in Company D from hearing the order to lie down. When he reached the fence, Captain Benjamin Colonna, followed by Eddy Berkeley and Preston Cocke, kept going until they reached a large poplar tree where they stopped and began firing. As they searched for suitable targets a shell burst in the tree limbs directly overhead, sending hot metal fragments shooting through the air.

One shard smashed into Cocke's right arm, causing a painful, but not disabling wound. Another piece struck Berkeley a glancing blow to the right temple, gouging out a strip of flesh and flinging him sideways to the ground. Bleeding profusely he staggered back to the fence where Lieutenant John Hanna, seeing all the blood, ordered him to a field hospital.

Berkeley was about to head for the rear when he spotted Jack Stanard sitting with his back against a tree trunk, his head lowered, his arms hanging loosely by his side.

"Eddy, Eddy. Help—water—" pleaded Stanard.

Berkeley ran over, "Jack! Jack! Where're you hit?" He removed his canteen and held it to Stanard's trembling lips.

"My legs—they—they're shot off," said Stanard, as he pointed weakly to the shredded remnants of bloody pants pasted to his legs. "Find Johnny. He'll know what—help me—"

"Johnny?" Berkeley didn't have the heart to tell Stanard that Wise had been hit at Shirley's Hill.

"He—he'll know—"

Berkeley almost gagged when he lifted the cloth from Stanard's gaping wounds. Pieces of bone jutted through torn flesh as blood ran in rivulets onto the ground.

"Is it—bad?" asked Stanard.

"You'll be all right," Berkeley lied as he searched for something—anything—to use as a tourniquet.

"Fall back and rally on Edgar's Battalion!" someone yelled.

When two cadets stood as if to obey, First Sergeant Andy Pizzini jumped to his feet, and with the veterans' taunts still fresh in his mind and his Corsican blood at the boiling point, cocked back the hammer of his rifle. *"I'll shoot the first person who tries to run!"*

Locating a muddy towel, Berkeley stripped off two long pieces and knotted them together. He tried to wrap the makeshift tourniquet around Stanard's right leg, but it was no use. The bones in both legs were shattered and the arteries ripped apart. Throwing the tourniquet aside, Berkeley tried pressing the towel against the wounds. Nothing worked.

As the color drained from Stanard's face, he tried to speak, "Tell mother—that I—Mother? *Mother*—?"

"It's all right, Jack," Berkeley said, patting the dying cadet on the shoulder. His battle to save Stanard's life now over, Berkeley sat down beside him and held the shaking hand until it stopped moving.

Holding the towel to the cut on his own forehead, Berkeley examined Stanard's expressionless face, then reached over and felt his neck. There was no pulse. After wiping his fingers on his shirt, Berkeley closed Stanard's eyes.

Chapter 20

Wells

"*Open ranks! Open ranks!*" shouted Colonel Wells, as he rode along the front line, trying to keep his regiment from being overwhelmed by panic-stricken soldiers retreating through his formation. The 18th Connecticut and 123rd Ohio had tried to make a stand west of the turnpike, but outnumbered three-to-one had been easily driven back.

When the last man stumbled through, Wells had his officers and file closers re-establish their battle line. On the right, Company A was anchored on Snow's and Carlin's 12-guns atop the bluff on Bushong Hill, beside the North Fork of the Shenandoah River. These batteries had a clear field of fire which they used to great effect in bombarding the Confederate line. On the left, Company H connected with Lt. Colonel Wheddle's 700 man regiment of West Virginians who stood two rows deep waiting for the order to attack. Thirty-five yards in front, Von Kleiser's five 12-pound Napoleons were firing canister into the Rebel position.

Satisfied with the disposition of his men, Wells patted Boston Bar's neck and tweaked his right ear. Turning in the saddle he looked behind the artillery batteries at General Sigel who was wildly gesturing with both hands to Colonel Thoburn and Major General Stahel. Wells checked his watch. When was Sigel going to launch the assault? Fifteen minutes had passed since the artillery barrage blasted an opening 200 yards wide in the center of the Rebel line. And now? Nothing. When his men saw the Rebels retreating they had cheered loud enough to wake the dead, but still no response from Sigel. He *must* have heard and seen what was happening. Now Rebels were returning to the fence rails in front of the house. It wouldn't be long before the whole Rebel line was as strong as ever.

The rumbling of cannons combined with thunder and musket fire had become so overwhelming that Wells could no longer use bugle calls to issue commands. All communications had to be visual and could only be done with hand signals. While the rain splattered his raincoat, Wells watched his men for signs of panic. He marveled at how unruffled and self-possessed they seemed—at least on the surface. Would they still remain so calm when they heard the Rebel Yell? He'd heard the high-pitched *yee-haa-eee* several times and it always sent chills up his spine. No one who fought the Rebels ever forgot the banshee like wail. Most of his troops were new to the chaos and carnage of war and he was concerned how they would hold up. Had he done enough to prepare them?

After posting a couple of extra file closers behind each company, his concentration was interrupted by a lone rider galloping toward him from the right. Shielding his eyes from the rain and clouds of smoke blowing in from Von Kleiser's Napoleons, Wells tried to see who it was. The horseman wore a dark, rubber raincoat with a wide-brimmed hat pulled low. When the rider got closer, he saw it was Lt. Colonel Lincoln.

"Found Colonel Curtis—*whomp*—them—*ka-blam*—cease firing!" yelled Lincoln, as he trotted alongside.

Wells cupped his hand to his ear, *"Say again!"*

Lincoln leaned closer, *"I finally got the West Virginians to stop shooting at us!"* By posting his reserves less than 60 yards behind the front line, Sigel had exposed the 930 men in the 12th West Virginia to heavy Rebel fire with no way of protecting themselves. Frustrated, they had started shooting back over the heads of Wells' regiment which was causing numerous casualties among the Massachusetts troops.

Wells noticed another horseman approaching from the same direction. He could tell by the pony that it was Colonel Strother. Thinking it might finally be the order to advance, he and Lincoln rode over.

After dismounting, Strother pointed to the two Federal batteries on Bushong Hill. "General Sigel wants you to send a company of infantry to support those cannon. Rebel sharpshooters are raising hell over there. They've already killed three cannoneers and ten horses."

"From my regiment?" asked Wells, incredulous at such an order. "He wants support from my regiment? Can't he see that all my men are in battle formation?" He waved a hand behind him at the 930 soldiers in the 12th West Virginia who were lying on the ground dodging Minie balls. "Send them instead. Colonel Curtis has twice as many as I have, and they're not doing a damn thing."

"General Sigel tried," admitted Strother. This was the breakdown in communications he had been so worried about. "The General ordered Colonel Curtis to send two companies to support the guns but only two squads actually went. The rest wouldn't budge." Strother removed a cotton towel from around his neck and squeezed out the water. "Whenever the General changes position, the West Virginians rise up out of the mud and follow him like lap dogs. They think he's retreating and they certainly don't want to be late for *that* movement. So, there Sigel sits, held in place by a regiment of overgrown children. If it weren't so tragic, it would be comical."

"Where's his staff? Can't they help?"

Strother shrugged, and nodded to the brick house behind the artillery batteries. "Most are waiting at the Hupp house for instructions, which, of course, haven't come."

Wells stared at Strother in disbelief. How could Colonel Curtis refuse a direct order? But, if Sigel was babbling at him in German, then Curtis simply hadn't understood what was wanted. Now, Sigel was stripping a full company of riflemen from Wells regiment to baby-sit for a couple of artillery batteries. "Where's Moor's brigade?" asked Wells, his face flushed with anger. "They charged through my lines ten minutes ago, upsetting the men. There must've been at least a thousand."

"Most kept going," said Strother. "The rest are somewhere in the rear."

Wells pointed to his left where the 1st West Virginia and 54th Pennsylvania were standing in line, waiting to attack. "I only see two other regiments on line, plus Curtis' 12th West Virginians in reserve. That's just half the infantry. I know it's a ridiculous question to have to ask, but where the hell are the rest?"

"The 28th Ohio and 116th Ohio are on their way. General Sigel thinks they'll be here any moment."

"Any moment?" snapped Wells. "*Any moment's* going to be too late."

Strother nodded. "It's a madhouse over there. Ten minutes ago, General Stahel rode up shouting, *'Mein Gott General Sigel! Vare ist mein cavalrie?'* Can you imagine? A Major General in charge of cavalry and he doesn't know where his troops are? Now they're jabbering at each other in German…"

"The Rebels are re-forming!" exclaimed Lincoln, as he scanned the fence line in front of the Bushong house with his field glasses.

Agitated, Wells grabbed the sleeve of Strother's raincoat. "Colonel, go tell General Sigel if he's going to attack, he's got to do it *now*."

"I'll tell Colonel Thoburn. He's the only one who'll listen."

"What kind of flag is that?" asked Lincoln, pointing to a new stand of colors at the orchard fence.

Wells raised his binoculars, "Can't say. Never seen it before." He'd encountered dozens of Rebel flags at First Manassas and during the Peninsular Campaign, but never a large white banner with the seal of Virginia on one side and George Washington on the other. He handed the binoculars to Strother, "Do you recognize it?"

Strother waited for the smoke from the last volley of Von Kleiser's cannon to drift by, then focused the binoculars. "Definitely some kind of Virginia flag. On the front—e—pluribus—unum. And the back—yup. I know it. It belongs to the Institute."

"The what?"

"Virginia Military Institute."

"We're fighting youngsters?" asked Wells, who didn't want to tarnish his reputation by fighting schoolboys.

"Not exactly," replied Strother. "They're disciplined and well trained. Same as West Point cadets. Don't be fooled by their youth, they're extremely dangerous."

"If Breckinridge put them in, then he considers them soldiers," said Lincoln. "My suggestion is to head straight for their flag. That's the Achilles' heel of the Rebel line. My guess is they'll turn and run before we get within a hundred yards of that fence. If we can break through there, we might be able to roll up the whole Rebel line."

As a strong breeze cleared more smoke, Wells observed movement along the fence to the right of the farm. A second battle flag had appeared. He glanced back at the orchard. The gap in the Rebel line, which fifteen minutes ago had looked so inviting, was now filling up with cadets and veterans. He turned to Strother, "Colonel, for God's sake, tell Thoburn to order a charge."

As Wells remounted Boston Bar, he shouted to Lt. Colonel Lincoln, "Send Company C to support the cannon. Tell them to get between the guns and the river. The Rebels will try to flank the batteries from the bluff." With the loss of a full company, the 34th Massachusetts regiment was now down to only 450 men.

"What about the dogs?" yelled Lincoln. The troops had tethered the regiment's pets to a tree, hoping to keep them safe. But in the confusion the dogs had slipped their leashes and playfully romped in and out of formation, thinking this was just another drill.

"Can't worry about them now," said Wells. "Order the men to fix bayonets. You take the right, I'll take the left." With his sword, he pointed toward the Bushong farm, "When we go in, head straight for that barn. I'll take the orchard and house. When the Rebel line collapses, we'll signal Thoburn to send in the reserves." Having to depend on Colonel Curtis's 12th West Virginians to exploit a breakthrough was unsettling. If the regiment couldn't perform a simple task like guarding twelve cannon they certainly weren't going to be of much help supporting a general breakthrough.

Wells took his place on the left of the regiment. Twenty yards away Lt. Colonel Wheddle, Commander of the 1st West Virginia, paced back and forth. Wells hoped his low opinion of the West Virginians' fighting ability wasn't justified, but their lack of experience, training and enthusiasm bothered him. He'd found that many were reluctant to wage war against a state to which they had recently belonged. Most still pointed with pride to Stonewall Jackson's birthplace in Clarksburg and spoke highly of their neighbors in the Rebel army.

Wells continued to study the battle line looking for a weakness. From stragglers he'd learned that the person in charge of the First Brigade was Brigadier General John Echols from Lynchburg. He'd met the tall, imposing Echols sixteen years before when both were studying law at Harvard. If they met on the battlefield would they still recognize each other? Would they try to kill each other?

Wells shifted uneasily in the saddle. Maybe he should've ordered his officers to fight on foot like the West Virginians. Anyone perched on a horse was wearing a bull's-eye on his raincoat. He'd also noticed that no Rebel officers were mounted.

Last night he'd tossed and turned while trying to grab a few hours sleep. Thoughts of mortality and home had kept him awake, staring at the ceiling of his tent. During the day, the activities and distractions of camp life held the hobgoblins at bay, but at night, when it was dark and quiet, phantom fears often crept in. His biggest nightmare was being confined to a bed in some backwater hospital or prison, wasting away to nothingness from dysentery or camp fever. Or having his spark snuffed out along some dirt road by a bushwhacker up a tree. No. There was no glory in any of that. If he was destined to die he wanted it to be at the head of his men—these men—in a desperate charge.

When he had finally drifted off, it happened again. That recurring dream of Miss Daisy Ruddell. When the campaign was over he planned on revisiting the Inn to continue their conversation. He felt like a schoolboy, infatuated with this beautiful southern belle. He wondered if she had any interest in him, or had the war erected too big a barrier? She was only 28 and he was 38, not too great a difference in ages. Wouldn't Boston society be surprised if he returned home with Daisy on his arm?

Leaning forward, Wells again tweaked Boston Bar's right ear for good luck. "Well, old fellow," he murmured, "Maybe she does and maybe she doesn't. But we're going to find out." Lost in his private reverie, the explosion from a nearby shell jerked him back to reality. He patted Boston Bar's neck, "Let's get through this little scrape and it'll mean extra apples for you tonight."

There was a commotion on the right as Colonel Thoburn and two staff officers came trotting behind the lines. When they were fifteen yards away, Thoburn leaned forward and shouted an order to Wells which was drowned out by battle noise. As Thoburn headed over to Lt. Colonel Wheddle's regiment, he sent an aide galloping down to Von Kleiser's battery. When the guns fell silent, Wells knew what it meant. He watched the West Virginians come to attention, dress on the colors, then slowly begin to advance.

Removing his hat, Wells rode to the front of his regiment. He wanted the men to know that he was going in with them, that he would share their fate. On reaching the colors he turned to face the troops. With his sword, he pointed to the Bushong house. *"For Massachusetts!"* he shouted, and signaled the color guard to start out. With a *"Hurrah for Massachusetts!"* the grim faced soldiers slowly began to advance.

As the men moved forward the regiment's pet dogs frolicked in front of the formation, jumping and barking with delight. One big, black bob-tail nicknamed John Brown, who had distinguished himself in camp by catching pigs and charging Wells' grey horse during brigade drills, gleefully bounded ahead. By the time he'd gone fifteen paces, John Brown was lying on his back, coughing up blood and kicking at empty air with all four paws.

Whoomp! Wells felt Boston Bar shudder as a bullet slammed into his shoulder. The blood poured down the horse's right leg, covering Wells' boot.

Maybe it wasn't too serious, he told himself and leaned over to—*Zipp*—a Minie ball ripped through his hat, grazing the top of his head. He felt liquid running down the back of his neck. Gingerly removing his hat, he ran his fingers through his hair, then held them in front. He sighed with relief when he saw only water.

Amid a blizzard of lead, the men leaned forward as if caught in a hail storm and solemnly tramped on. As the line passed around Von Kleiser's battery, Wells could see bright flashes coming from the cadet muskets along the orchard fence. No longer kneeling, they were standing while loading and firing. On the right, a veteran Rebel regiment was closing in on his exposed flank. As his men went forward, they began falling like jackstraws, on their backs, faces, and sides.

Thump! Whack! Two more bullets struck Boston Bar. One in his chest, another in the neck. The startled animal jerked his head up, took two steps, sank to his knees then rolled on his right side. Unable to pull his right boot free of the stirrup, Wells was pinned under the horse. Seeing the Colonel struggling to remove his foot, Sergeant Haddon rushed up and helped yank the boot out from under the animal. After making sure his leg wasn't broken, Wells stood and returned his sword to its scabbard.

Staring down at the beautiful bay, blood pouring from its wounds, legs wildly thrashing about, Wells dreaded what had to be done. He had often thought of this moment with a heavy heart. After a quick inspection of the injuries to make certain they were fatal, he drew his pistol and with both hands held in twelve inches from the intelligent forehead. "Goodbye old friend. You'll get all the apples you want in Valhalla." Tears filled his eyes as he squeezed the trigger.

Not waiting for his other mount, Wells ran to catch up with the regiment. Now the orchard was less than 100 yards ahead. As Wells walked behind the color guard, he saw Corporal Pepper, who was carrying the regimental flag, hurled back. A red mist exploded from the back of Pepper's head. Rushing over, Corporal William Wishart grabbed the staff and marched on.

As the regiment approached the farm, Wells turned to the left and was surprised to see the West Virginians *retreating* at the double quick. Since they began their advance before the 34th was ready, the West Virginians had attracted the concentrated fire from the whole Rebel line. Now, thoroughly demoralized, they were falling back, leaving Wells' left flank unprotected.

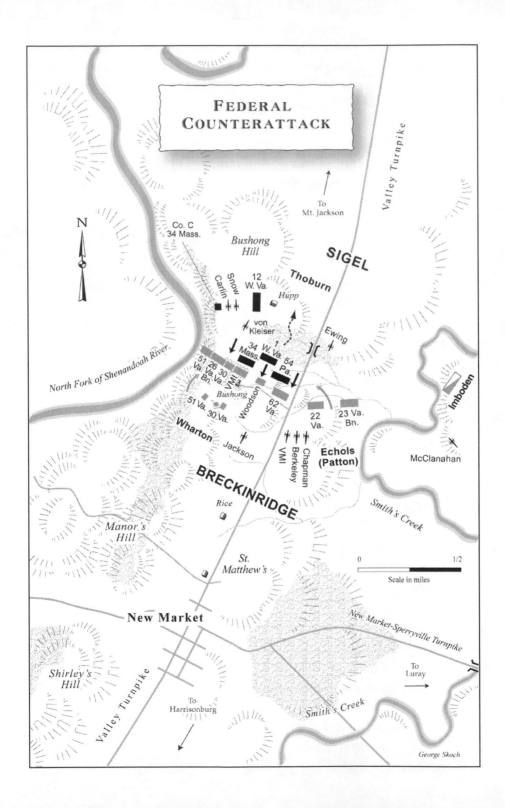

FEDERAL COUNTERATTACK

N

To Mt. Jackson

Valley Turnpike

Co. C
34 Mass.

Bushong
Hill

SIGEL

Snow
Carlin

12
W. Va.

Thoburn

Hupp

von
Kleiser

Ewing

North Fork of Shenandoah River

51, 26, 30,
Va. Va. Va.
Bn.

34
Mass.

1
W. Va.

54
Pa.

VMI

51 Va. 30 Va.

Bushong

Woodson

62
Va.

22
Va.

23 Va.
Bn.

Imboden

Wharton

Jackson

VMI

Chapman
Berkeley

Echols
(Patton)

McClanahan

BRECKINRIDGE

Rice

Smith's Creek

Manor's
Hill

St.
Matthew's

0   1/2

Scale in miles

New Market

New Market-Sperryville Turnpike

Shirley's
Hill

Valley Turnpike

To
Luray

To
Harrisonburg

Smith's Creek

George Skoch

When less than 80 yards from the fence, Captain Daniel Willard, commander of Company D, spun around, a surprised look on his face. A shell fragment had smashed his left shoulder, ripping open an ugly gash. A second later a Minie ball shattered his left knee cap, knocking him to the ground. Moving to Willard's aid, Wells saw that the wound would be fatal if the flow of blood weren't stopped. Turning around he yelled for Sergeant Haddon to bring up the grey. "Sergeant, take this man to the field hospital. Tie him across the saddle if you have to—and hurry!"

As the 34th closed on the Bushong orchard, the musket fire increased in intensity. Gaps were opened in the formation which couldn't be filled. The regiment was close enough now that Wells could see the fierce determination on the faces of cadets as they peered down the barrels of their muskets. Wells watched in awe and concern as the cadet line stood firm, trading volley for volley.

On the right, the Rebel regiment Wells had spotted before, closed in on his flank. Through the haze he could see bright flashes blinking from their muskets, telling him they weren't far away. Now pressed on both flanks by regulars and in the front by unyielding cadets, Wells realized he had to call off the attack or face annihilation. *Whump!* A piece of shrapnel ripped through the sleeve of his rubber raincoat striking his left arm. Dropping his sword he pulled open the raincoat. There was no feeling in his hand and the arm was numb, but there was no blood.

Retrieving his sword with his good hand, Wells shouted for the troops to halt, but his command was lost in the din of battle. When the color guard slowed for a broken fence, Wells ran up to Corporal Wishart, grabbed him by the shoulder and turned him around. The wings of the regiment continued to surge forward until the men lost sight of the colors. With hand signals, Wells managed to turn the regiment about and head back toward their starting position. Retreating at an orderly pace, the men halted every forty paces, wheeled around and fired. He could hear officers saying, *"Don't run, Massachusetts! Keep your line! Common time!"* As he passed Boston Bar's corpse, Wells averted his eyes. The sight of his companion lying in a pool of blood was too much to bear. When the regiment finally reached its starting point, Wells halted the men, turned them around and resumed firing.

Looking over the ground they had just covered, Wells frowned at the sight of so many of his soldiers littering the field. Glancing to the right, he was surprised to see Carlin's and Snow's batteries limbering up, preparing to abandon Bushong Hill. On the left he saw stragglers from the 1st West Virginia, disappearing over the hill into the fog. Only Colonel Campbell's Pennsylvanians in the cedars bravely soldiered on.

Chapter 21

Cadets

K neeling behind a broken fence rail, Captain Henry A. Wise watched the Yankees in front retreat to their old position. Much to his relief, the Federal charge had been broken. With so much smoke it was difficult to tell, but it looked like the Federal regiment on the right had not stopped, but kept going. The attack had come within 45 paces of the fence, but the cadets had stood firm, trading shot for shot with the cool steadiness of seasoned veterans.

Once again the five Napoleons were pounding away at the orchard with canister and shell. Fortunately, a southwesterly breeze blew the low-lying cannon smoke back into the gunners' faces, making it difficult to gauge distances and pick targets. The rain, which had paused briefly, again swept the field in waves.

Looking left, Captain Wise noticed the fog lifting in front of the two Union batteries on Bushong Hill. He could see cannon barrels turned sideways and cannoneers scurrying back and forth, feverishly cutting dead horses from harnesses and hitching panicked animals to limbers. From the river, two Confederate battle flags approached the batteries. The twelve field pieces that had caused so much damage were now silent.

As the last person on the far right of the cadet line, Captain Wise was unable to estimate the number of casualties suffered by the Corps. He looked at his watch. They'd been in the orchard only eighteen minutes, but it felt like hours. While he continued to search for the missing Yankee regiment, a load of canister crashed into the fence line on his left, lifting

Lee Smith off his feet. When Wise saw Smith wasn't moving, he sent First Sergeant Erskine Ross over to see what could be done.

When Ross examined the wounded cadet he found the buttons on his jacket smashed into his chest and blood gushing from his face. A splinter from the fence had struck him, crushing his collar bone. In addition, a Minie ball had entered his mouth, shattering the jawbone and coming out the side of his neck. After a cursory inspection, Ross determined that no arteries had been severed, but the wounds would be fatal if not treated immediately. Looking for help, he noticed Lucien Ricketts, calmly sitting on a horse among the apple trees, twenty yards to the rear. He motioned him over. "Cooney, what the hell are you doing on a horse?"

"Helping Colonel Ship. I'm his courier." Although only 16, Ricketts had been at Gettysburg as special courier for General Albert Jenkins, and wasn't frightened by the turmoil in the orchard.

"Didn't you hear the order to dismount?"

"Yeah. But that was for officers, 'an I ain't no big bug."

"Never mind, where's Colonel Ship?"

"Back there on the ground," said Ricketts, waving toward the Bushong house.

"Is he seriously hurt?"

"Don't think so. Just shook up. He told me to ride over and tell Captain Wise that he's in charge."

"I need your help," said Ross, as he lifted Smith into a standing position. "Take this man to a field hospital, pronto!"

It only took a few seconds to wedge the unconscious cadet firmly into the saddle between the pommel and Ricketts. With Smith secure, Ricketts galloped off.

Captain Wise watched the Napoleons in front as they continued to blast away. Something had to be done. He knew that the longer the Corps remained in the orchard, the harder it would be to get them to charge the cannon and infantry.

Ka-bloom! Wise flinched as a shell exploded in the tree limbs directly overhead. The concussion slammed him hard against a fence rail, sending his sword spinning into the mud. After checking for damages, he bent over to retrieve the sword—then felt a strange, cold sensation on his back side. Running his hand behind him, he felt skin.

A voice shouted, "*Captain Wise!*"

Looking back, he saw Lieutenant Bill Hardy, his face strangely contorted. With his sword, Hardy pointed at Wise's back.

"Are you hurt?" asked Wise.

"It's—it's—not me," blurted Hardy, convulsed with laughter. "It's *you.*"

Turning to the side, Wise grabbed his belt and twisted his pants around. Blushing beet red, he stammered, "Oh, d—damn!" A shell fragment had torn away the back of his coat as well as the seat of his pants, taking not only part of his uniform, but his dignity.

"Message from Colonel Ship," said Ross, running up. "He's out of action and says you're in charge."

Whoomp! Another shell exploded fifteen yards in front, the concussion blowing a cadet sideways. Wise knew the time had come. "Lieutenant Hardy, take command of the Company." Hopping over the fence he ran along the front line toward the colors. Pausing every few steps, he turned to the cadets and shouted, *"Get up men! Let's give the Yankees hell!"*

A wild cheer rose as cadets scrambled over the railings, swiftly forming into ranks on the other side of the fence. Private Clark Howard, who had been lying behind a small apple tree, got to his feet and stared at the section of fence he would have to climb. The double-rail, four foot high fence was the tallest he'd ever seen. Summoning all his courage he quickly pulled himself to the top as Minie balls snapped by, only inches from his head. His heart pounded when he reached the top rail, convinced that all Yankeedom was targeting only him. Holding tightly to his musket, he jumped to the other side, landing with a splash in a soupy puddle of brown water.

By the time Wise reached Company B, Captain Preston was already on his feet, issuing orders. *"Company B! Cease firing! Get up! Form into line!"* When Preston saw Wise, he waved his sword at the Yankee guns on Bushong Hill, "Henry, they're gonna run!"

Tom Jefferson reached through the fence rails, carefully balancing his musket against a post on the other side. He put his left foot on the bottom rail and swung himself up. When he reached the top a tremendous explosion knocked him backwards into the mud. As he tried to rise to his knees he fell back as a feeling of total helplessness engulfed his whole body.

Gasping for air and dazed, Jefferson was only vaguely aware of Andy Pizzini hovering over him. Unable to focus he felt Pizzini shaking his shoulder.

"Tom! Tom! Where're you hit?" asked Pizzini.

All Jefferson could do was mumble, "I—I thin . . ." With the rain pelting his face and clothes, a dull, heavy sensation filled his chest. Looking down, he saw a red stain spreading over the front of his jacket. Staring blankly at the blood he thought of his mother and how upset she would be when she found out he'd been killed. He hoped they would tell her he died facing the enemy.

Ripping open Jefferson's jacket, Pizzini bit his lip when he saw the wound. On the right side of Jefferson's chest bubbles frothed out of a dark hole. Pizzini had seen this kind of wound before and knew there wasn't much hope. He pulled a bandage from his pocket and pressed it firmly against the wound, trying to staunch the flow of blood. "Hold this in place until you see Doc Madison. I'll send help as soon as I can."

At the opposite end of the line, Benjamin Colonna, second captain of Company D, slid his sword back into its scabbard and grabbed a rifle. At this distance he could do more damage with a musket than a sword. While aiming at an artillery horse, he was jolted by Bill Dillard falling heavily against him. Stepping back, Colonna watched Dillard sink to the ground, blood seeping from wounds in his neck and shoulder. Colonna ran over to Captain Robinson. *"Captain! Captain!* Colonel Shipp's down. You're in command."* As Minie balls whined by, he exclaimed, *"My God,* Captain, we can't *stand* this much longer. *Order a charge!"*

Jumping over a section of broken fence, Robinson faced the cadets, *"Company D! On your feet! Fall in!"*

As Corporal of the Color Guard, Moses watched Evans step through a hole in the fence and wave the flag. Following closely behind, Moses took his place beside Evans. On Moses' left, Sergeant Louis Wise, brother of Captain Wise, threw up his hands, staggered back and fell. Moses started to run over, but Wallace Nalle pulled Louis to the relative safety of a pile of rails.

With the clamor of battle drowning out commands all eyes were riveted on the colors. Standing by the flag and covering the hole in his pants with his hat, Captain Wise raised his sword. *"Battalion! Load muskets! Ready! Aim! Fire!"* Although only those within a few feet could hear him, the rest saw what was wanted and sent a volley of lead flying across the field into the enemy formation. While the cadets reloaded, a breeze blew the smoke from the volley into the faces of the Yankee cannoneers and infantry, providing a screen for the Corps' advance.

Using the roof of the Hupp House with its two chimneys as a guide, Captain Wise shouted, *"Battalion! On Center—Dress! At the Double—Quick! March!"*

With a loud cheer the Corps sprang forward, the colors leading the way. The field in front was a sea of ankle deep mud, but that didn't dampen the cadets' enthusiasm.

"Look! Look!" yelled the regulars in Woodson's company of Missourians on the right. *"Look at the seed corn go!"* Encouraged by the cadets' example, the veterans on the left formed a ragged battle line and joined the charge, splitting the air with the Rebel Yell.

Swept up in the excitement, Moses screamed out his own version of the Rebel Yell which ended with *Lee-nor-ree!* He felt that by invoking her name he would be protected from harm. He wondered if she could sense the danger he was in. He'd read that people who were extremely close could often tell when the other was in peril.

As Moses plunged into the smoke, he no longer felt fear. Instead, he was overcome by a sense of elation. He'd heard veterans talk about the exhilaration of combat and now knew what they meant. *Slurp!* Before he'd gone twenty steps, the muck pulled off his last shoe. But with no shoes to worry about he could move faster, and the cool mud squishing between his toes felt good.

When Moses glanced to his left, he saw a new cadet who'd been at the Institute for only nine days, suddenly turn and head for the rear. Moses was shocked. He tried to remember his name. Clin…Klen…Clendinen. That's it. Thomas Clendinen. Jefferson had pointed him out last night as they sat around the campfire. A native of Baltimore, Clendinen had enlisted in Alabama at fifteen, been captured, and sent to a POW camp. Although Moses didn't know him personally, he was surprised that someone with that record would show the white feather. Still shaking his head, Moses felt a tug on the back of his jacket.

"Found them," said Clendinen, sheepishly holding up a pair of new shoes. The brogans had been tied around his cartridge box and had fallen off when the laces came loose. Moses understood. A pair of good shoes was worth more than gold, and it took a brave person to retrieve them under fire. Now Moses regretted not having removed his own shoes and hanging them around his neck when he had the chance.

After the Corps had gone 50 yards they descended into a slight depression, which briefly shielded them from artillery and infantry fire. For the first time, Moses noticed the mutilated bodies of dead and wounded Yankees littering the ground. Some lay face down, others sat up or lay on their sides, still alive, begging for water. Still others sullenly watched the cadets move past. Pizzini, no stranger to combat, kept a sharp lookout for any wounded who might try to shoot him in the back as he passed by. At Manassas a good friend had been shot by a Yankee playing dead.

When they'd gone another 30 yards, the Corps began the final ascent up the slope leading to the cannon and infantry. To keep the smoke screen rolling forward, Captain Wise ordered a halt to fire another volley. During the pause the veteran regiments on the left and right caught up with the fleet-footed cadets.

When the advance resumed, a fragmentation shell burst overhead hurling Frank Gibson back five feet. Lying on his back he tried to sit up, but couldn't move. Seven pieces of shrapnel had hit him at the same time. One shattered his right leg below the knee. Another passed through his thigh. A third clipped two fingers from his left hand, and a fourth ripped open his cheek, exposing bone. Not stopping, the Corps raced on.

Preparing for the final assault, Captain Wise ordered one last volley. Unable to see through the smoke, the cadets sent a barrage of Minie balls streaking toward ghostly images in the haze. When the noise died down, Captain Wise noticed a lack of cannon fire coming from the front. Suddenly, there was wild cheering on the left. Not sure what it meant, Wise dropped to the ground and peered under the smoke. Through brief clearings he caught glimpses of cannoneers cutting wounded horses from broken harnesses and tugging on ropes attached to limbers in a desperate effort to escape.

"Forward, men!" shouted Wise. *"Capture those guns!"*

Breaking ranks, the cadets raced to see who would be first to claim a cannon. With his musket primed, Andy Pizzini reached the area where the battery had stood. Only one cannon was still in position, its horses dead in their traces. The other four guns were rapidly disappearing into the haze.

The gunner of the disabled cannon had his back to Pizzini and was sponging the barrel when he heard a shout to surrender. Whirling around, he swung the heavy rammer at Pizzini's head.

"Look out!" shouted Hank Cousins rushing up. With the barrel of his rifle he deflected a sword thrust aimed at Pizzini's head by a Yankee officer trying to save the last cannon. As the tip of the blade glanced off Pizzini's jawbone it tore a long gash in his cheek. Crouching low, Pizzini lunged, plunging the bayonet deep into the officer's groin. Kicking his bayonet free, Pizzini searched for the gunner who had tried to kill him with the ramrod.

In the confusion, the gunner had jumped on the last unwounded horse and was desperately trying to free it from its harness. The sweat poured down his face as he managed to cut a leather strap attached to a limber. With a *whoop* he dashed for freedom. Raising his rifle, Pizzini rushed off a shot, but the bullet merely clipped the cannoneer's ear. Frustrated, Pizzini hurled his rifle at the man who ducked and rode off. Grabbing the next three cadets who came running up, Pizzini yelled, *"Help me wheel this gun around!"*

Grabbing the trails, the cadets turned the heavy cannon toward the Federal infantry. Pizzini hastily ran a vent pick down the fuse hole to make certain the cannon hadn't been spiked. "Hank, you and Patton check the ammo chests for canister."

Flinging open the lid of the nearest box, Cousins shouted, *"None here!"*

Ripping back the copper sheet on a second chest, Bill Patton yelled, *"Four rounds!"*

"Double canister!" shouted Pizzini as he raised the barrel's elevation. Out of the smoke, two second classmen trained in artillery came running up. Pressing them into service Pizzini grabbed the ramrod and sponged the barrel.

Standing on top of a caisson, Bill Patton searched through the mist for a target. While the canister was being loaded, a gust of wind blew a hole in the clouds exposing the top of a Union flag 35 yards away. With his right arm Patton directed Pizzini where to shift the trail until the barrel was lined up with the flagstaff. To guard against killing their own men, Hank Cousins lay flat on the ground looking for the feet of any friendly troops in front of the cannon.

"Field of fire?" called Pizzini.

"Clear!" yelled Cousins.

"Fire!" shouted Pizzini and pulled the lanyard. With a roar the cannon jumped a foot off the ground and bounced back ten feet.

"Re-load!" shouted Pizzini.

Straining against the heavy weight, the cadets pushed the Napoleon back into position. Not stopping to sponge the barrel, another double load of canister was rammed home.

Raising his arm, Pizzini shouted, *"Ready!"*

"Field of fire?"

"Clear!"

"Fire!"

Again, the gun discharged its deadly cargo at the Union colors.

"*Cease firing!*" yelled Cousins as shadows moved around the cannon on the right. "*Cadets in front!*"

"*Cease firing!*" repeated Pizzini.

While Pizzini retrieved his musket, the color guard ran up. Clambering onto the caisson, Big Evans shook out the regimental flag and waved it back and forth. A cheer went up from nearby cadets. The battery had been stormed and a cannon captured.

Chapter 22

Wells

*K*arooomph! A cannon blast struck the line, rocking Wells back on his heels. *"Everyone down!"* he shouted as iron balls shredded two men less than ten feet away. Standing with the color guard, Wells peered into the driving rain, searching for the source of so much destruction.

Karooomph! Another explosion erupted, sending five balls ripping through Captain William B. Bacon, commander of the color company. One struck him squarely in the jaw, blowing out the back of his neck. Another ripped off his right arm. A third hit him in the stomach, severing his spinal column. Bacon, a tall, thin, clean shaven Bostonian had been with the 34th for two years and twenty-one days. Educated, jovial and polite he had written "Gentleman" when the recruiting officer asked for his civilian occupation.

"Where's that damn gun!" demanded Wells of no one in particular. The muzzle blast had hit with such force that it had to be close, but with all the noise and smoke he couldn't tell how far off or in which direction. Had the Rebels captured one of Von Kleiser's guns?

"Colonel, Colonel!" came an excited voice from behind. Wells turned to see Lieutenant Cobb racing up. With him was Lieutenant Ephraim Chalfant from Carlin's battery.

"We need help!" said Chalfant, pointing behind him at a gun carriage stuck up to its axle in mud. Four of its horses had been killed and the cannoneers were furiously switching out dead animals for the living. "We've lost two cannon already. Now, Number five's stuck. If we can't pull it free—"

With his ears still ringing, Wells interrupted, "Where're the West Virginians? Go get them."

"The few we had ran off," replied Chalfant. Only two squads of West Virginians had responded to Sigel's order to support the batteries. When the battery started limbering up, they retreated with everyone else.

"What about the men I already gave you?" After having sent Company C to guard Carlin's and Snow's batteries, Wells hadn't heard from or seen them since. With his regiment now down to fewer than 325 men he wasn't about to sacrifice more troops to pull a hunk of useless metal out of the muck. It amused him to see that one of the men grunting and tugging on the cannon's wheels was General Sigel. His boots were caked with mud, his fancy coat was unbuttoned, and his shirt was soaked with rain and sweat.

"They're somewhere on the bluff by the river," said Chalfant. "I think they're surrounded."

Wells groaned with disgust. He'd sent a whole company to protect the guns and they had been abandoned.

Now Wells' only concern was survival of the rest of his regiment. In front, several dark shapes headed his way in the haze, the flashes from their rifles drawing nearer. Ignoring the pain from his bruised left arm, he mounted his horse and stood in the stirrups for a better view of the battlefield. In the place where Von Kleiser's battery had recently stood, VMI's flag waved back and forth. Twenty feet further away the battle flag of a veteran Rebel regiment fluttered. If he didn't act fast his whole regiment would be surrounded and captured.

Brushing Chalfant aside, Wells dismounted and leaned close to Lt. Cobb, "Have Corporal Wishart stand by with the colors." He wasn't waiting for permission from Generals Sullivan or Sigel, or anyone else, to fall back. He would retreat on his own authority and consequences be damned.

Wells had no intention of being taken prisoner and hauled off to Andersonville or some other Rebel hellhole as a POW. It was a fate worse than death. Trying to survive the rats and camp diseases without going insane or ruining his health would be almost impossible. Already it looked like most of Company C had been captured and it was his fault for sending them to guard the cannon. During a recent visit to the Armory Hospital in Washington he'd seen the pitiful human wrecks returning from Andersonville. What bothered him more than the stench, oozing sores and emaciated bodies were the blank, empty, soulless stares. At the end of April, Grant and Stanton had announced a new policy of ending all POW exchanges. They blamed the draconian policy on the Confederates for refusing to exchange black prisoners. But Wells knew better. The sad truth was they were willing to sacrifice the lives, sanity and health of Union soldiers simply to reduce the number of soldiers available to Lee. Whenever Rebels were exchanged, they were immediately sent back to the front lines. When Federal prisoners were exchanged, they packed up and went home. Who could blame them? They'd done their duty and suffered enough. Stanton's and Grant's lack of respect and sympathy for their own men and families disturbed Wells. No. He wasn't going to stay here to be led like a lamb to the slaughter.

Standing beside the color guard, Wells yelled, *"Fall back, Massachusetts! Fall back!"* But the battle noise drowned out his commands. Glancing left, then right, Wells saw Rebel regiments closing in. In ten minutes they'd be cut off with no means of escape. Running up to Corporal Wishart, Wells grabbed him by the shoulder and faced him to the rear. *"Follow me!"* he ordered, then began walking the colors toward the pike. Seeing the regimental standard leaving, the rest of the 34th slowly began to withdraw.

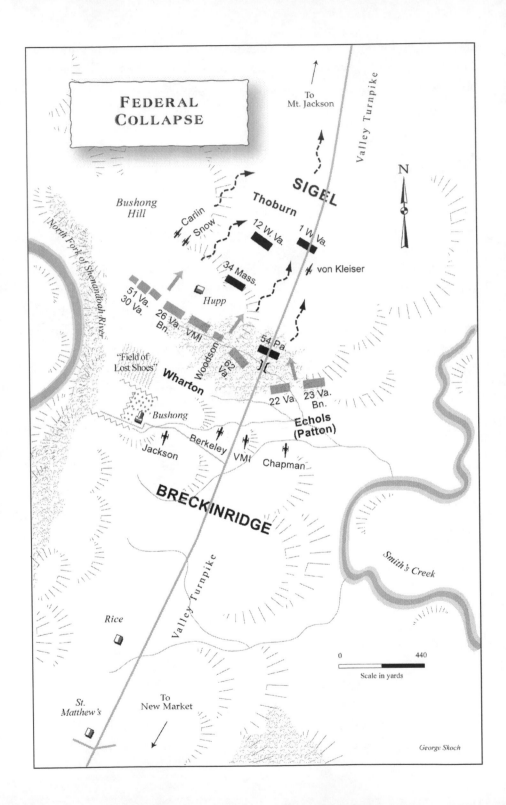

FEDERAL
COLLAPSE

To
Mt. Jackson

Valley Turnpike

SIGEL

N

Bushong
Hill

Thoburn

Carlin

Snow

12 W. Va.

1 W. Va.

von Kleiser

34 Mass.

51 Va.
30 Va.

Hupp

26 Va.
Bn.

VMI

54 Pa.

North Fork of Shenandoah River

"Field of
Lost Shoes"

Wharton

Woodson

62
Va.

22 Va.

23 Va.
Bn.

Bushong

Jackson

Berkeley

VMI

Chapman

Echols
(Patton)

BRECKINRIDGE

Smith's Creek

Rice

Valley Turnpike

0   440

Scale in yards

St.
Matthew's

To
New Market

George Skoch

Chapter 23

Cadets

Now everything was forgotten but the excitement of pursuit. The tide of battle had turned and the fleet-footed cadets chased the disheartened Yankees, stopping only long enough to load, fire and scoop up prisoners.

When First Lieutenant John Hanna charged around the captured 12-pounder Napoleon he spotted a Yankee officer on foot leading a horse by the halter. The officer was preoccupied with rallying his men and helping a wounded soldier lying on the ground. With his attention diverted, the officer failed to notice he was being closely monitored. Seizing the chance to bag an officer, along with a prized horse, Hanna splashed over. Gripping the heavy cavalry saber in both hands, he closed in. He hoped his target wouldn't put up too much of a fight and he wouldn't have to hurt him.

"Watch out, Colonel Lincoln!" shouted the wounded man as he caught sight of the fast approaching cadet.

Startled, Lincoln wheeled around and reached for his pistol. Hampered by a bulky rain coat, he tried to pull the gun from its mud-spattered holster, but lost control of the slippery grip. Holding tight to the reins, he stared in dismay as the sidearm tumbled barrel first into the mud. Ducking under his horse's neck, Lincoln switched the reins to his left hand and reached for the handle of his sword. Again, the raincoat got in the way but he finally managed to withdraw the weapon from its scabbard.

"Surrender!" yelled Hanna, as he ran up, grabbing the horse's reins. *"You're my prison—"*

"No, sir! You're my prisoner!" shouted Lincoln, waving his sword high above his head. Although surprised, he hadn't come this far to meekly give up to a college student without a struggle.

Both combatants tugged on the reins as they jockeyed for position. Neither had enough space for a clear strike. Nearby cadets and Federal troops stopped fighting long enough to watch the unusual duel. Neither Hanna nor Lincoln were natural born killers, but here, on this overcast rain drenched field, the bright, young cadet from Philadelphia was locked in mortal combat with the grandfatherly Massachusetts lawyer. Hanna, a former altar boy who liked music and poetry, had recently noted in his diary, "I regret very much the sin I have committed today in getting angry and do not want to be looked on by fellow cadets as a fighter."

The two antagonists dodged, slashed and parried. Both sweated and grunted as sparks flew from metal striking metal. The loud clanging and jerking on the reins caused the horse to rear, knocking both combatants off balance. Regaining his footing, Hanna swung the heavy saber over the saddle at Lincoln's head, but narrowly missed when his foe ducked at the last second.

Reaching under the horse's chest, Lincoln tried a chopping cut at Hanna's legs. But the hilt of his sword became entangled in a stirrup.

When an artillery shell exploded nearby, the panicked horse reared again, its front legs thrashing wildly in the air. Caught off guard, Hanna's foot slipped and he stumbled backward.

When Lincoln saw his opponent jab the tip of his saber in the ground for balance, he drew back his sword for the kill.

"Uhuu!" grunted Lincoln, as a searing pain shot through his right shoulder. The sudden blow paralyzed his arm, propelling him face forward into the side of the sweating horse. Dropping his sword, he looked to the side and saw the tip of a bayonet sticking out from the front of his raincoat. Letting go of the reins, he tried to grab the saddle for support, but couldn't raise his arm. When his attacker finally jerked the bayonet free, Lincoln sank slowly to the ground, a steady stream of blood turning the ground red.

Standing behind the stricken officer was Winder Garrett, his chest heaving and eyes wide with excitement.

Exhausted, Hanna was unable to speak. All he could do was nod to the cadet he'd reprimanded earlier that morning for a rusty bayonet. Seeing the handle of Lincoln's pistol sticking out of the sludge he retrieved the hard-won prize. It was a richly engraved Navy Colt with a walnut handle. After wiping off the mud with the sleeve of his jacket, he ran a stick through the barrel to clear out any debris. He then checked the cylinder to see if it was loaded. Good. Ready to fire. At last he had the weapon he so desperately needed.

As cadets and Confederate regulars surged onto the crest of the hill they stepped over and around the mangled bodies of Union dead and wounded. Two hundred yards ahead, Union artillery wagons and cannon lumbered toward solid ground on the pike. Hundreds of infantrymen and cavalry mixed in with the caissons and ordnance wagons in a mad dash to escape. Discarding everything that might slow them down, soldiers abandoned rifles, haversacks, cartridge boxes and clothes. On the left, along a sloping hill, and on the far right in the cedars, two ragged lines of Federal infantry stubbornly resisted the Rebel onslaught.

Directly in front of the Corps stood the two-story Hupp house. A large barn, a log cabin, a hog pen and a stone springhouse surrounded the house. All were enclosed by a white picket fence. Most of the buildings had been heavily damaged by exploding shells. All the windows in the house were shattered and the white brick walls were pockmarked from hundreds of Minie balls. Frantically trying to avoid capture, dozens of Yankees hid under haystacks, inside and under buildings, and one even dangled from a rope tied to a pulley in a shallow well.

When Jacob Imboden, General Imboden's brother, reached the picket fence in front of the barn, he saw Benjamin Colonna standing stock still, sword in hand. As the smoke lifted, Imboden could see a Yankee officer in a pigsty on the other side of the fence, pointing a pistol at Colonna's head.

"Jacob, are you loaded?" asked Colonna in a low voice, while keeping a wary eye on the officer.

"Yeah," replied Imboden, as he cocked back the hammer of his newly acquired Enfield.

"Then get ready to shoot that damn Yankee!" Cupping his hands into a megaphone, Colonna yelled, *"Surrender! Or be killed!"*

"Nein!" came the reply as the officer squeezed off a quick shot, sending a ball zipping past Colonna's ear.

Crouching low, Colonna turned to Imboden, *"Shoot him!"*

Raising his rifle to his shoulder, Imboden aimed at the man's chest, but couldn't pull the trigger.

"For God's sake, shoot the sonofabitch!" yelled Colonna, as the German prepared to fire again.

Feeling sorry for the officer, Imboden pointed his rifle at the man's legs, and pulled the trigger. Unfortunately for the officer, the Minnie ball struck high, doubling him over like a rag doll and slinging him back into the hog wallow.

As Cadet James Preston sprinted toward the log cabin, a spent ball struck him in the chest, temporarily rendering him unconscious. When he regained his senses, his musket was upside down with the bayonet stuck in the ground and he was washing his hands in a mud-puddle. In his left breast pocket a thick copy of the New Testament had absorbed most of the shock from the slug. Picking up his musket, he started forward, then noticed little Charlie Faulkner leaning over, peering under the cabin. Beside him Hugh Fry peeked cautiously around the corner of the building.

Suddenly Fry raised his rifle. Fifteen yards away, a mud-smeared Federal crawled out from under the cabin. *"Surrender!"* demanded Fry.

Standing up, the huge German smirked at the small cadet. He aimed his musket at Fry's head. When he pulled the trigger there was the dull click of a misfire. *"Bockmist!"* grunted the German as he fumbled for another cap.

Cocking the hammer of his Springfield, Fry, who harbored no qualms about killing an enemy in self defense, aimed for the man's belt buckle. *Blam!* The bullet struck four inches high knocking the Yankee off his feet and spiraling him into a haystack.

"They're hiding under the cabin!" yelled Faulkner as six more cadets rushed up. Circling the cabin, they pointed their muskets at five burly Yankees who crawled out from their hiding place. Mumbling curses in German, the Yankees reluctantly raised their hands.

When cadets and veterans surrounded the nearby barn and threatened to set it on fire, eight more bluecoats grudgingly climbed down from the rafters. Fry snickered at the soldiers' appearance. They looked like scarecrows with straw stuck to their faces, hair and wet wool uniforms.

Sixteen-year-old Charlie Faulkner, whose father had been one of John Brown's court appointed attorneys, lined up twenty-three prisoners, all big enough to swallow him whole. Puffing out his chest and standing as tall as he could at five-feet-three, he marched the captives to the rear.

Now rested after watching over the dying Stanard, Eddy Berkeley looked around the orchard for the rest of his company. Between gaps in the smoke he saw them two hundred yards in front, disappearing over the crest of a hill. Still bleeding from the gash in his head, he took his musket, stepped over the broken fence, and started off to join his comrades.

Trudging through the muddy wheat field, he passed General Breckinridge and two staff officers riding over the field checking on the progress of the attack. Struggling to walk in the ankle deep mud, Berkeley stopped. Dizzy from loss of blood he began to sway back and forth.

Taking one look at Berkeley, General Breckinridge rode over. When he saw the flickering eyes and fresh blood, he called to a member of his staff. "Captain Snyder. Put this boy on a horse and take him to a field hospital—and hurry."

As the color guard passed the Hupp farm, Moses saw a Union cavalryman with drawn pistol heading for Evans and the flag. Fortunately the spongy ground slowed the animal to a trot. As the horseman approached, Moses leapt forward, grabbed the horse's bridle with both hands and yanked hard. The frightened animal reared, ruining the rider's aim. Running up behind the rider, Garland James, another member of the color guard, lunged over the horse's rump and plunged his bayonet into the rider's back.

Marching beside Evans along the edge of a stand of cedars, Moses spotted a Yankee infantryman limping through the trees. His back was turned and he was dragging his musket through the mud. The wounded man was less than thirty yards away and an easy mark. Moses raised his weapon—but couldn't fire. It was one thing to kill someone attacking you, quite another to shoot an injured man in the back. He was relieved to see a Confederate regular run up and capture the man without firing a shot. As the color guard descended into a ravine, Moses was startled to see a figure lying face down in a small stream. Moving closer he saw the Yankee was desperately trying to hold his face out of the water.

Turning his head, the soldier spied Moses, "Johnny. Johnny Reb. Help. *Help me!*"

Moses' first inclination was to keep moving, but seeing the man's head drooping back in the water, he stopped. Grabbing the soldier's legs he pulled him away from the stream. Rolling the man on his back, Moses examined his clothes for signs of wounds. An ugly hole was ripped in the right side of the jacket. The soldier's face was drawn and pale with the haggard expression of someone who'd seen too many troubles. In his calloused right hand he clutched a colored tintype of a woman in a mourning dress. His left hand held a silver locket containing a few strands of child's hair.

"Are . . . are you a Mason?" the man gasped. Raising his bloody hands in supplication, he asked, "O Lord, my—my God, is there no—no help for a widow's son?"

Moses felt a rush of pity. The contorted face was no longer that of a hated enemy but a fellow human in great distress. Laying his musket aside, Moses dragged the man to the safety of a nearby cedar. When he released his grip he felt warm, sticky blood between his fingers.

"Water, water," pleaded the man, still holding tightly to the locket and tintype.

Reaching for the soldier's canteen Moses noticed that a fragment of shell had ripped open the lower half. Without hesitating, he removed his own canteen and held it to the man's lips. The soldier took two sips, coughed up blood, then lowered his head. Leaning his canteen against the man's side, Moses placed the soldier's haversack under his head for a pillow. He could do no more for him. Seeing the flag thirty-five yards ahead, Moses picked up his musket and ran to join the guard.

It didn't take the Corps long to pass beyond the cedars, through briar patches, across a deep ravine, to the eastern slope of Bushong Hill. From there they had their first view of a steady stream of Yankee troops and equipment heading north along the pike. Here and there small clusters of infantry still resisted, buying time for the wagons and wounded to escape.

When the Confederates reached the turnpike, they halted to replenish cartridge boxes and regroup. To keep up the pressure, Captain Chapman's 6-gun battery, the two-gun section under Lieutenant Berkeley, and the two VMI cannon under Collier Minge went into battery beside the pike and began shelling the fleeing columns. While the Confederate regimental commanders pondered their next move, two Union cannon hidden by smoke, wheeled into position 300 yards down the pike and started returning fire. Concerned that this bombardment meant that Sigel was establishing a new line, Colonels Edgar, Patton and Derrick decided to wait for General Breckinridge before resuming the attack.

When the cadets neared the pike, a courier galloped up to Captain Wise. He pointed to the Hupp house, half a mile back. "Sir, your battalion is ordered by General Breckinridge to break off the engagement and return to the two captured cannon in front of that farm. You are to wait there for further orders."

Rounding up as many cadets as he could find, Captain Wise directed Evans to take the flag back to the Hupp house. As the cadets walked along the ground they had just crossed, they became light-hearted and jocular. Scattered among the dead horses and wounded men were abandoned haversacks and knapsacks full of food, Bowie knives, Springfield rifles, cartridge belts, and oil cloths. All free for the taking. Running from prize to prize, the cadets scooped up as many treasures as they could carry. One veteran from Woodson's company of Missourians rummaged through knapsacks and blanket rolls searching only for shirts. By the time he met the cadets he already had more than two dozen stuffed in a knapsack and draped over his shoulder.

Sprinting ahead, Johnnie Cocke found a new cavalry poncho wrapped around a checkered shirt. Now, he could stay dry when marching in the rain. Twenty feet away, he spotted a tarred, canvas haversack lying on its side. Eagerly yanking open the straps, he yelped with delight at the generous supply of coffee, sugar, crackers and cheese. Before he could buckle the flap back in place he spied another object in the mud fifteen feet to his left. Racing over he found a knapsack with an engraved silver cup—obviously stolen—a matching set of bone-handled silverware, a deck of playing cards decorated with scantily clad women, two pairs of socks, a housewife with buttons, needles and thread, and best of all, a bottle of brown whisky. While showing his booty to James Preston, a stray bullet cut the strap of the haversack with the crackers and cheese, dumping the contents into the mud. In disbelief, Cocke stared at the sodden crackers. "Damn it, Preston, did you see that thing take my rations?"

On reaching the two captured cannon, the cadets examined the guns that had caused them so much trouble. One was a 3-inch rifled cannon left behind when its wheels became mired in the mud. The other was the 12-pounder Napoleon captured in the charge on Von Kleiser's battery. On the barrel of the Napoleon was scratched "62nd VA." The cadets were in the process of scraping off the veteran regiment's claim to their hard won prize when they heard Captain Wise call out, *"Battalion! Atten-shun!"*

Heading their way was General Breckinridge and a staff officer.

As the cadets formed two ragged lines, Captain Wise called out, *"Present arms!"* With as much precision as they could muster, the cadets brought their muskets to the front.

Breckinridge removed his hat, "Young gentlemen, you can be proud of what you have done today. I have *you* to thank for our success." Waving his hat in salute, he said, "Well done, Virginians. Well done, men."

Breckinridge then ordered Captain Wise to release the Corps from further duty. When he turned to ride away, the cadets, now veterans baptized in blood, raised their kepis and shouted, *"Hurrah for General Breckinridge! Hurrah for VMI! Hurrah for the Confederacy!"*

Chapter 24

DuPont

New Market

"Take these guns back to Mount Jackson," ordered the young, disheveled captain. His poncho was ripped and one bandaged foot dangled against the stirrup. Nervously glancing over his shoulder, he added, "And don't stop till you get there."

"On whose authority?" quizzed First Lieutenant Henry A. DuPont. This was the second harebrained, conflicting command he'd received in the last fifteen minutes from a frightened officer headed for the rear. Since Sigel hadn't bothered to appoint a chief of artillery, there had been little coordination among batteries and random staff officers kept imagining themselves in charge.

"It's—it's an order. From General Sigel," sputtered the captain, who didn't wait for a reply, but dug a spur into his horse's flank and galloped off.

DuPont rolled his eyes. He wasn't about to retreat without firing a shot—unless personally ordered to do so by his superior, General Jeremiah C. Sullivan. Especially not on the word of some panic-stricken headquarters' sycophant who knew nothing about artillery. DuPont, first in his West Point class of 1861, had never been under fire, and was determined that this would be the first test for his battery.

It was clear from the masses of disorganized Federal troops streaming to the rear, that Sigel's lack of generalship had resulted in an overwhelming defeat.

This morning, after advancing up the pike as part of General Sullivan's command, DuPont had been ordered to halt at noon for a leisurely, half-hour lunch. They were only a mile and a half from the front, and the booming of artillery and crackle of small arms fire could be heard clearly, but General Sullivan refused to be rushed. The last official directive he'd received from Sigel had been to fall back to Mount Jackson where the main defensive line would be established. As Sigel's only non-European, non-German speaking high-ranking officer, Sullivan had been ignored and systematically excluded from war councils. This breakdown in communications now made him reluctant to move without specific orders.

When an order finally arrived at 12:41 p.m. to send forward two artillery batteries, General Sullivan chose Von Kleiser's and Carlin's. Twenty minutes later when a second order was delivered to bring up the infantry, General Sullivan interpreted it literally and told DuPont to stay behind with his artillery until called for.

After waiting two more hours, DuPont finally received a directive from Sullivan to move his six guns to the front. Although he tried to remain calm, he could barely contain his excitement. This was his chance to make a good impression. Unless he could prove he was a competent, aggressive battery commander there would be no promotion. He'd be stuck in the lowly grade of first lieutenant for the rest of the war. George Custer, who had graduated last in the class of '61, was already a brigadier general. DuPont was finding it more and more difficult to explain to his father why he wasn't at least a captain. True, his battery was regular army and not part of a state militia, and advancement in the regular army, especially artillery, was glacial. But if he didn't get a promotion soon his father would think it was due to some major defect in ability or character, and that would reflect poorly on the family name.

As DuPont's men maneuvered their six 3-inch cannon toward the front, they had to thread their way through a flood of terrified infantry and cavalry headed for Mount Jackson. In addition, there were dozens of broken-down artillery caissons, limbers, supply wagons and ambulances blocking their path. As his cannon rumbled along, DuPont noticed a difference in the morale of Union forces depending on which side of the pike they came from. Those east of the pike were in total rout, throwing away muskets, accoutrements and haversacks. Those west of the pike, the 34th Massachusetts under Colonel Wells and the 54th Pennsylvania under Colonel Campbell, still gamely fended off repeated Rebel attacks and were retreating in good order.

When DuPont's number three cannon was forced off the hard surface by an overloaded ambulance, the gun's carriage sank axle deep in a muddy rut. While the cannoneers tied ropes and hitched two extra horses to the trails, a dismounted cavalry major, covered in muck up to his waist, limped over. His imported, high-heeled, polished Wellingtons were caked with mud and his mood was as dark as the stains on his fancy boots.

"Lieutenant, I vant you shud gif me one of dem horses."

"Sorry, Major," said DuPont, surprised at the audacity of the request. As it was, he was short ten horses and had been forced to leave the battery ambulance behind. "These are artillery horses."

"Den, I orders you to gif me a horse!" shouted the major, waving an ivory handled riding crop wildly in the air. *"I been eine very important mann on General Stahel's staff."*

Seeing the commotion, Colonel David Strother, who was passing by on his pony, trotted over to see why Major Oscar Weber was yelling at DuPont. He knew all of Stahel's staff and considered Major Max Weber a pompous blowhard who cared nothing for the Union and was unworthy of being called an officer. He also recognized his personal friend DuPont. Before the war, Strother and his father had been occasional guests at Eleutherian Mills, the DuPont family's estate in Delaware. Strother's father and the 53-year-old Henry DuPont Sr. were both ardent Republicans and strongly anti-secession. During their time together they had enjoyed sharing Cuban cigars, good brandy and planning ways to defeat the Democrats in the next election. Recently, the senior DuPont had been appointed by the governor of Delaware as major general in charge of the state's militia. This in addition to his job as President of DuPont Company, *the* chief supplier of black gunpowder to the Union army. Like his son, General DuPont had graduated from West Point where he'd been a roommate of Francis H. Smith, VMI's Superintendent. Because of this close association, General DuPont had asked Smith to allow his son to attend the Institute. Since only Virginians could be cadets in 1855, Smith had been forced to decline the request.

It didn't take Colonel Strother long to pull rank on Major Weber and send him hobbling back to the turnpike in his fancy boots. Seeing that DuPont was determined to go to the front, Strother informed him that Sigel, Stahel and General Sullivan were heading four miles north to Rude's Hill. There, if hard pressed, they planned to establish another defensive line. The geography of Rude's Hill offered high ground and protection on both flanks by the Shenandoah River and Smith's Creek. The only drawback was the lack of an escape route if the bridge over the North Fork of the Shenandoah was destroyed.

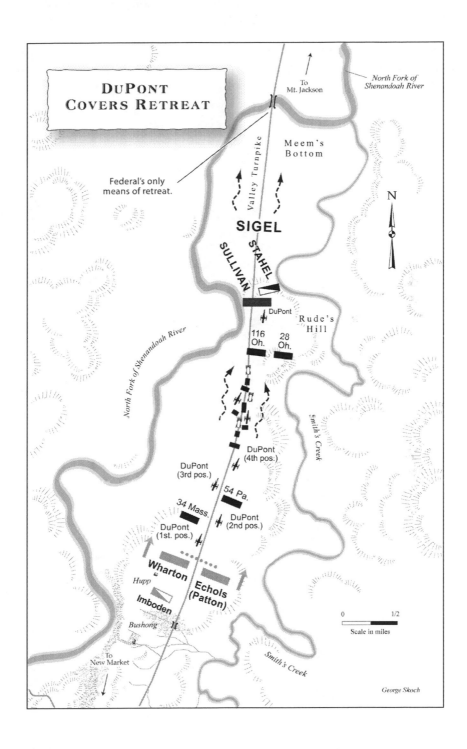

DuPont Covers Retreat

To Mt. Jackson

North Fork of Shenandoah River

Meem's Bottom

Valley Turnpike

Federal's only means of retreat.

SIGEL

SULLIVAN

STAHEL

DuPont

Rude's Hill

116 Oh.

28 Oh.

North Fork of Shenandoah River

Smith's Creek

DuPont (4th pos.)

DuPont (3rd pos.)

54 Pa.

34 Mass.

DuPont (2nd pos.)

DuPont (1st. pos.)

Wharton

Hupp

Echols (Patton)

Imboden

Bushong

To New Market

Smith's Creek

N

0   1/2
Scale in miles

George Skoch

After Strother departed, DuPont's gun crews wrestled cannon number three back onto the hard surface and continued their trek south. Now that General Sullivan and his staff were gone, DuPont was on his own. When the battery reached the area DuPont estimated was the main battle line, he ordered the guns off the road onto a slight rise west of the pike. The location offered a clear field of fire but placed the battery in the open with no natural cover. The only protection was the thick layer of smoke blanketing the battlefield.

The lack of infantry support and exposed position didn't faze DuPont. He was determined to provide covering fire for the retreating men and equipment even if it meant losing one or more of his cannon. In order not to risk losing all six guns at once, he divided the battery into three platoons of two guns each. These sections would be stationed in echelon down the pike at 500 yard intervals. When the last retreating Federal passed the forward section, it would cease firing, limber up, and leapfrog to a new position on the pike.

To lead the sections DuPont selected his top three cannoneers. In charge of the first section, he chose Second Lieutenant Chuck Holman, a bright, energetic college graduate from Baltimore who had been with the battery since the beginning. For the center platoon he picked First Sergeant Samuel Southworth, a seasoned veteran from New York who had fought with distinction at Malvern Hill during the Seven Days Battles where he'd been seriously wounded in the right leg. He put Second Lieutenant Benjamin Nash, a former coal miner from Pennsylvania who had recently joined the battery and was eager to prove himself, in charge of the third section.

The thick blanket of smoke and mist on the pike was both a blessing and a curse. The lack of visibility made it difficult to see the enemy but it also prevented the Confederates from discovering how disorganized the Union army had become. With any luck, the Rebels would consider the fire from DuPont's guns part of a new defensive line which would slow them down.

Pointing to the pike, DuPont told his platoon leaders, "You won't be able to see your targets so use the road for reference. The Rebels will stay close to the hard surface so place your shots anywhere along the pike. No canister, just case and shell. We don't want to hit our own men."

While DuPont helped Holman position his two guns, Colonel Wells emerged from the swirling smoke twenty yards west of the pike. He was riding his grey, fifteen paces ahead of the colors. DuPont watched an excited officer run up to the color sergeant and turn him around, facing south. As if on cue, when the men saw the colors stop, they wheeled about, formed a ragged line, and fired a volley at the approaching shadows.

DuPont jogged over and saluted, "Sir, Battery B, Fifth Regular Artillery."

"Regulars?" queried Wells, surprised at his stroke of luck. Removing his hat, he wiped gun-powder-streaked-sweat from his brow. After seeing so many troops running away, it was a relief to find someone ready to stand and fight. "I'm pleased there's at least one feisty battery left."

"Are any other cannon still engaged?" asked DuPont.

"You're it," replied Wells. "The Rebels are regrouping for their final push, so do what you can to hold them back. We've got to get the wounded and wagons over the river."

"I'll keep firing as long as I can."

"Sorry I can't offer infantry support, but the Johnnies are hot on our heels."

"I understand. Can you give me an estimate of their strength and location?" The instructions he'd received at West Point had covered dozens of situations but none where the battery commander had no idea where the enemy was located or its numbers.

"They've got at least six regiments on both sides of the pike. If you concentrate your guns on the road, you can't miss." Wells peered over his shoulder at dark figures moving toward them. "Be careful. With all this smog it's hard to tell friend from foe.

"I'll set the fuses for 100 yards."

Noticing that his color guard had stopped again, Wells dismounted and ran over. His left arm was still immobilized by the blow from the shrapnel that struck him during the charge, but he managed to grab the color bearer by the shoulder and turn him around. As he walked the flag past DuPont, he beamed with pride, "That's the sixth time I've had to go back in the fire to get them moving. Those rascals simply don't know *how* to retreat." Placing his good hand on the pommel of his saddle he pulled himself up. He called to DuPont, "If the Rebels overrun us before we reach the bridge—minutes count, Lieutenant. Minutes!"

DuPont shouted to Lieutenant Holman, *"Section one, fire at will!"* Jumping on his horse, he waved his hat at the next two section leaders, "Follow me!"

As Holman's two guns blasted away, DuPont led the other platoons onto the pike. Weaving in and out of columns of retreating troops and vehicles, the two sections bounded down the road. When they'd gone 500 yards, Southworth swung the second platoon onto a small rise beside the pike.

Pumping his hand in the air to signal approval, DuPont led Nash's platoon 500 yards further down the road to a stretch of level ground protected by a stone fence. After posting the last platoon, he hurried back to Holman's section. For the next thirteen minutes the gunners ignored accuracy for quantity and furiously hurled shell after shell into the smoke.

When DuPont no longer saw any retreating Federals on the pike he ordered the guns to cease firing. As the fog lifted, he surveyed the road. It was empty. Holman's platoon was all alone. Hitching both cannon to limbers, the section moved to the pike and raced northward. When they'd gone 145 yards they passed the rear guard of the 34th Massachusetts, still covering the retreat. In five minutes, DuPont reached the middle platoon which was already in action. As Holman's two-gun section rattled to its new location, DuPont rode over to help Southworth.

By the time Holman's section had finished firing for a second time, the last Federal soldier had disappeared over the horizon toward Rude's Hill. An eerie silence settled over the battlefield. When a gentle breeze blew the smoke away, DuPont mounted his horse and rode to the pike where he searched for enemy activity. Four Rebel guns were going into position 400 yards up the pike, but there were no signs of cavalry or infantry. He watched tiny puffs of smoke erupt from the muzzles of the Rebel guns, but the shells were poorly aimed and landed harmlessly in nearby fields. Satisfied there was no immediate pursuit, he gathered his sections together and set out for Rude's Hill.

When he reached the hill, he crossed a new line of defense manned by the two Ohio regiments which had been absent at New Market. Taking a position on the backside of Rude's Hill, DuPont waited for orders from General Sullivan. There were none. Concerned about being trapped by the river, General Sigel had decided to continue his precipitous retreat across the bridge to Mount Jackson. By the time the Confederates discovered that the Federals had abandoned their new defensive line, the last of the Union infantry and wagons had crossed Meem's Bottom and safely passed over the bridge.

It was 7:05 and growing dark by the time DuPont's battery reached the bridge. To his surprise, both banks of the river were deserted. Sigel had failed to assign a demolition crew to destroy the bridge.

Realizing the danger, DuPont had his officers and cannoneers remove the wood flooring and stack the planks north of the river. After dousing the wet wood with kerosene they set the planks on fire. No sooner had the flames started billowing skyward than a patrol of Rebel cavalrymen raced up to the far side of the bridge.

Even if Breckinridge managed to reach the bridge they would have to wait until morning to make repairs. With his job done, DuPont lined his battery up on the pike and set off for Mount Jackson. When they had gone a quarter of a mile they met Colonel Wells and an officer riding behind a wagon heading south.

"Has everyone crossed the bridge?" asked Wells.

"There may be a few stragglers, but that's all," said DuPont.

"No wagons or ambulances with wounded?"

"Don't think so," replied DuPont, noting the concern in Wells' voice. "Are you looking for someone in particular?"

"Colonel Lincoln, my number two. I've searched every vehicle on this side, but there's no sign of him—or his horse. Someone said he'd been killed. Another claimed they saw him dueling with a Rebel, then captured, but nothing definite." With the light from a lantern casting shadows across his face, Wells said, "I hate to think of him seriously wounded and lying in a ditch."

"I'll check the other artillery caissons and limbers when we get to Mount Jackson," said DuPont.

Wells saluted, "Lieutenant, you're to be commended for the way you handled your battery today. You and your men helped save the whole command."

Chapter 25

Wise

Earlier that day – 1:33 p.m.
New Market

A bolt of lightning streaked across the sky followed by a jarring clap of thunder. Startled, Johnny Wise opened his eyes and blinked as large drops of rain splashed on his face, sending cool water cascading into his nose and ears. Where was he? Why was he lying on his back in the mud?

A sharp pain shot through the top of his head when he tried to sit up. All he could do was roll on his side and try to keep from passing out. In the distance, he could see bright orange flashes lighting up low hanging clouds.

Using an elbow he pushed himself into a sitting position. Holding his head with both hands he stared at the ground. There it was again. Someone calling his name. Looking up he saw a dark form looming over him. Wiping rain from his face with the back of his hand he tried to focus. It was that Rat from Richmond, Charlie—Charlie Read, the Presbyterian pastor's son. What was he doing here? There was a long gash over Read's right eye and blood was dripping into Wise's face. What was that all about?

"Mr. . . .Mr. Wise!"

Wise could see Read's lips moving, but was having difficulty hearing any words. His ears felt like they were stuffed with cotton. Gradually, bits and pieces of sound broke through as if coming from the bottom of a well.

"Mr. Wise!" shouted Read, his voice quivering. *"Are you hurt? Can you hear me?"*

Now Wise was able to make out a few words, but could only answer in grunts. His jaw refused to form sentences. He was sitting on a hillside and Read was hovering over him like a specter from another world. Slowly, memory came drifting back. They were marching down a hill—a terrific explosion directly in front—the earth shook—his musket leapt from his hands. Noticing Read frowning while looking at the top of his head, Wise hesitantly raised his hand to his forehead and felt along the hairline. His head was numb and slippery. Lowering his hand he stared at the fingers. *Blood! Beautiful blood!* He was wounded and *not* dead. *Hurrah!* Now he could write his father and brothers that he had been in a real battle and been honorably wounded. He'd seen the elephant—and survived. With his right hand he fumbled for the leather pouch on the chain dangling around his neck. Still there. The lucky rabbit's foot and Polly's four-leaf clover had saved him.

"That's a nasty cut," said Read, as he wiped a mixture of grass and sludge from Wise's face with a dirty rag. Looking closely at Wise's forehead, he cringed. The sight of blood made him nauseous. "Don't see any bone, but there's lots of blood—everywhere."

Wise grabbed the leg of Read's pants, "Rat—uh, Charlie. What happened?"

"Don't rightly know, sir. Last I recollect there was a real loud *bang*. Next thing, I was lying face down in the grass. I looked around and there was nobody here but you, Captain Hill, Merritt, Woodlief and me."

"Where's the rest of the Corps?"

Read pointed to a line of trees on a rise three hundred yards in front. "Out there somewhere. When I came to, they were gone. I could hear cannon—or maybe thunder—and lots of musket shots, but couldn't see a thing."

"Where's Captain Hill?"

"Over yonder," said Read, pointing to a motionless body thirty feet away, stretched out on the ground.

"Is he...?"

"Don't think so. I heard him moaning a couple of minutes ago. Let's go see."

When they reached Hill he was on his back, comatose. His kepi had been blown off and his hair was matted with dried blood. A long ugly cut crossed his temple. In a state of shock, his unseeing eyes fluttered and he gulped air like a fish out of water. A fleeting thought crossed Wise's mind. Since Hill was his French professor, when they returned to classes he wouldn't have to worry about failing the French exam. Removing the blanket roll from the officer's shoulders, Wise fashioned a pillow to make him as comfortable as possible.

"Who's that?" asked Wise, nodding at another body twenty feet away, lying on his side in a fetal position.

"Jay Love—Jay Love Merritt," said Read. In a low voice, he added, "I don't think he's gonna make it. He's gut shot."

When they approached Merritt they were relieved to see his arms and head moving. At least he wasn't dead—yet. Wise stepped closer, "Jay Love. Where're you hit?"

"I'm a goner for sure," came the hoarse reply. "It's all up the spout for me. Gut shot..."

"Let's see," said Wise, rolling Merritt on his back. Pulling open the torn jacket, he searched for signs of a wound. Merritt's mid-section was bruised and discolored, but there was no blood. Whatever had struck him hadn't penetrated the skin. "Is this the only place?"

"Uh—think so."

"Don't see any blood," pronounced Wise, shaking his head for emphasis. He took Merritt by the hand, "See if you can stand up."

"I can't—no blood?" Merritt was dumbfounded. "But, that—that thing kicked me like a mule."

With Read on one side and Wise on the other, the two cadets managed to pull Jay Love slowly to a standing position.

Still bent over in pain, Merritt stared at his stomach. With both hands he worked his fingers around his waist, then up and down his sides, then over his chest searching for a hole. Hesitantly, he took a few faltering steps. "I—I'm gonna live!" he said, tears of relief streaming down his face.

Wise turned to Read, "Where's Woodlief?"

"Gone to the hospital. Had a leg wound. There was lots of blood. He could hardly walk. But, it didn't look too bad."

"Hospital? That's where we need to go," said Wise, as he picked up his haversack and searched for his musket. "Better take our guns. We might need them." After a brief hunt he found his musket, fifteen feet away, caked in mud. "We'll have to send someone back for Captain Hill."

"Well, I'll be darned!" exclaimed Read. Retrieving his rifle from a shallow gulley he showed it to Wise. A shell fragment had struck the barrel, bending it into a 45 degree angle. "Glad that chunk of iron missed my head."

"Bring it along," said Wise. "Or they'll think you threw it away." He already planned to claim bragging rights by showing the damaged musket around the campfire that evening.

After collecting their gear, the three cadets trudged down the hill for the short walk to town. Merritt, still giddy from his close call with the Grim Reaper had to walk bent over, but still managed to keep up with his comrades. When they reached Main Street, which ran through the middle of town, they were astonished at the frenzied activity and confusion.

Civilians scurried back and forth, dodging explosions and carrying wounded. Stray shells screeched overhead while musket balls peppered the sides of buildings. Groups of German prisoners were being herded into a vacant lot on the south side of town. Some laughed and appeared relieved to be out of the fight. Others were sullen and dejected and glowered at the cadets as they passed by.

Halfway down the street Wise saw two Confederate regulars driving a mule-drawn cart. They were on their way to a field hospital near the front to drop off splints and bandages and pick up casualties. Wise ran over to tell them where to find Captain Hill, then asked where to locate Dr. Madison, VMI's surgeon.

"Doc Madison's up at the Rice farm. It's on the pike 'bout half-mile north," said a large, rough looking sergeant with a bloody bandage wrapped around his neck. "He's in the barn patchin' 'em up. There's another one of your docs at the Henkel house right over yonder," he said, pointing to a wooden, two story building 45 yards away. "It's the house with a white picket fence in front and wounded all over the yard. Cain't miss it."

Dodging horses and carts, the trio made their way along the street to a clapboard house where wounded lay under trees and against fence rails. Some waited quietly to be examined, others were praying, and a number thrashed about in delirium. On the back porch a long kitchen table had been appropriated for operations. At the bottom of the steps a doctor and two orderlies separated the hopeful from the hopeless. Those with serious concussions and shot in the head, chest or stomach were directed to a stable at the back of the lot where they were given laudanum and made as comfortable as possible. Such wounds were usually fatal and there was nothing that could be done for them except wash away the blood, clamp off arteries, and wrap the wounds in bandages. Lacerations, cuts and minor shrapnel damage to the face, neck, feet, arms and legs were cleaned, probed and sewed. Those with smashed bones were given morphine and lined up for amputation.

Wise recognized the doctor wearing a blood soaked apron. It was VMI's Assistant Surgeon, George Ross, brother of cadet Erskine Ross. Dr. Ross, an 1859 graduate of the Institute, had received his medical training at the University of Virginia and, although young, was an old hand at treating battlefield casualties. A former member of A.P. Hill's medical staff, he had operated on hundreds of patients at Bristow Station, Mine Run and Culpeper Court House. With practice came speed and Ross could amputate a shattered leg or arm in less than ten minutes.

When Ross noticed the three cadets, he motioned them to the front of the line. They were the first wounded students he'd seen. Fortunately, he had brought enough medical supplies from Lexington for members of the Corps. After washing out the dirt and mud from Wise's and Read's cuts he quickly sewed them up. Next, he wrapped their wounds in clean bandages and with an eye on the overhead clouds advised them to keep the dressings as dry as possible. Worried that Merritt might have serious internal injuries, he had him taken to a tool shed across the street and placed on a cot for further observation.

After treatment, Wise and Read were assigned the task of carrying water from nearby wells to the men in the yard. In spite of the wet weather, the wounded were suffering from exhaustion and thirst. As each new batch of casualties came in, the two cadets rushed over for news of the Corps. After twenty minutes lugging water, Wise began to feel dizzy. Using his bucket as a chair, he sat down next to a soldier lying on a pile of straw. First Sergeant Amos Slaughter, from Woodson's company of Missourians, had a shattered ankle and foot and calmly awaited his turn for amputation. To help pass the time the sergeant listened to the sounds of battle coming from the front a mile away. When he learned that Wise was a cadet, he told him he'd seen the Corps marching towards the Bushong house to fill a gap in the line.

After a series of heavy, dull explosions, the sergeant said, "Hear that, boys? Them's Yankee cannon firing canister and pounding the hell out of our men. Canister's a real killer. That's what got me. Guess your group's gittin' hit pretty hard 'bout now."

After a brief rest, Wise returned to carrying water. When he again passed Sergeant Slaughter, the Missourian grabbed Wise's pants leg. "Listen close now," he said. "Do ya hear that?"

"No sir . . ." replied Wise, whose ears were still ringing.

"That's just it. Things has gotten real quiet. There's no shells flying over our heads here in town. Them Yankee cannons has stopped shooting. That means their infantry's gittin' ready to charge."

Wise and Read listened carefully, but their untrained ears were unable to interpret the few sounds they could hear. Mixed in with musket fire came the faint roar of whooping and hollering.

"Here they come!" yelled Slaughter, his face transfixed as if still on the firing line. "Those cannon you hear now are our'n." He raised a fist. *"Give 'em hell boys!"*

Wise felt his chest tighten as he thought of his fellow cadets facing an assault by seasoned Yankee infantry.

In a few minutes, the hollering stopped and sounds of the Rebel Yell drifted in. Slaughter pumped his good leg up and down while lying on the bed of straw. *"Goddamn, boys! Hear that? We're attacking!"* His eyes danced and his face beamed with delight.

"*Water! Water!*" pleaded a wounded man lying on a blanket by the road. His right arm was missing below the elbow and he reached for the bucket with a bloody stump.

For the next thirty minutes Wise and Read continued to carry water. As time passed, the number of casualties coming in for treatment steadily increased. Looking up, Wise noticed two cadets approaching from the front. On closer examination he recognized Louis, clutching an arm and walking slowly. Wise rushed over, "Are you hurt bad?"

"Afraid so, Johnny," replied Louis, grimacing with pain. "Golly, I'm glad to see you're still alive. Someone said your head was knocked clean off by a cannon ball."

"Takes more than a cannon ball to kill a Wise. How's the Corps doing?"

"We stopped 'em cold. They tried to make us run, but we stood there and took it."

Johnny took Louis to see Doc Ross. Johnny was relieved, and Louis greatly disappointed when the doctor pronounced the cut on the shoulder merely a flesh wound and the piece of shrapnel in his arm "painful but not serious."

After Louis was patched up and given laudanum, the two cadets left the porch. While Louis rested, Johnny picked up a bucket, then saw Read heading his way. "Johnny, there's an old woman at the Baptist Church shoveling out turnover pies and buttermilk to the wounded. Let's go git some before they're gone."

Hungry and tired, Johnny, Louis and Read immediately set out for the magical source of food. There was a sign on the front of the brick building, "Smith Creek Baptist Church." As they approached they could see wounded being carried inside on stretchers. A spring-wagon was parked behind the building. It was loaded with two 10-gallon cans of buttermilk and six wooden crates crammed full of half-moon apple pies and ham biscuits. Gum blankets covered the crates to ward off flies, rain, and greedy soldiers. After eating their fill, and stuffing extra biscuits in their pockets, the cadets returned to the hospital.

As more cadets trickled in, Wise asked if they had seen Jack Stanard. Johnny Bransford said he saw Jack in the orchard right before the charge, and he wasn't injured. When Notty Upshur was brought in on a cart, he told Wise he'd seen Stanard fall, but didn't know if it was serious. Asked where Stanard was now, Upshur answered, "He's probably at Stanley Hall. Doc Madison's taking care of the wounded in a barn out back."

"Let's go, Louis," said Johnny, now deeply concerned.

Retracing the path he'd just taken, Louis led Johnny north along the turnpike. When they'd gone half a mile, they approached a large, colonial style mansion west of the road. The ornate sign in the front yard proclaimed "Stanley Hall." Constructed of brick, the sturdy, three-and-a-half story building had four chimneys and a large platform on the roof. A signal station had been set up on the platform. From there flag messages could be received from Massanutten Mountain and relayed to a signalman on the top floor of the Presbyterian Church in town. Dozens of wounded in every stage of distress filled the mansion yard.

Behind Stanley Hall seven wooden shacks functioned as sleeping quarters for the house servants. These were crowded with wounded lying on cots and beds of straw. In addition a large, two-story bank-barn had been converted into a hospital. Two operating tables manned by a team of three doctors and seven orderlies had been set up inside the barn. On the north side lay a pile of corpses, beside them a growing stack of arms and legs.

While asking for information about Stanard, Louis and Johnny had to be careful not to step on hands or feet of the injured. When they met Dunny Christian, a cadet from Company B slightly wounded in the left side, they asked about Jack.

"Check with Eddy, Eddy Berkeley," said Christian. He pointed to the back porch of Stanley Hall. "Eddy's somewhere inside. He's pretty doped up but he may be able to help. When I saw him thirty minutes ago, all he could say was, 'Poor Jack, poor Jack.'"

Dreading what they might learn, Johnny and Louis slowly climbed the back steps and entered the wide, noisy hall, which bustled with activity. An overworked orderly directed them up the winding staircase to the second floor. In the first room on the right they found Berkeley on a cot, his head swaddled in bandages and his eyes closed.

Gently shaking his shoulder, Johnny asked, "Eddy. Eddy. What happened to Jack? Jack Stanard?"

Berkeley's eyes fluttered as he struggled to overcome the loss of blood and effects of opium. Unable to sit, he mumbled, "Uh. Stanard? Poor Jack . . . in orchard . . . legs shot up . . . against tree . . .tried to stop blood . . . couldn't . . . had to leave." Then he closed his eyes and fell silent.

"Come back later, boys," said an orderly rolling another bed into the room.

When they got outside, Johnny said, "We've *got* to find him, Louis." After a moment's hesitation, he mumbled to himself, "He should've stayed with the wagons."

Heading west, Louis led Johnny to the open field the Corps crossed to reach the Bushong farm. Louis winced as he watched orderlies near the barn unloading wounded from a cart.

The first dead cadet Johnny and Louis encountered as they neared the farm was William Cabell, first sergeant of Company D. He lay face down in the mud, his arms stretched out, his hands clutching tufts of earth and grass. A large hole gaped in the back of his head. Gingerly, Johnny turned him over and wiped the mud from his mouth and nose. Cabell's eyes were open and fixed in a deathly stare.

Closer to the farm they found Hugh McDowell from Company B. In his death agony he had ripped open his jacket and blindly clutched at the red hole in his chest where a musket ball had entered. Despite his torn jacket, his face was relaxed and as peaceful as if he had simply fallen asleep.

Crossing a picket fence beside the house, they met Washington Redwood helping a wounded classmate limp to the Bushong barn for treatment. Wise ran over, "Have you seen Stanard?"

Redwood shook his head and simply pointed toward the worm fence at the far side of the orchard.

When Johnny and Louis found Stanard's body, he was still in a sitting position, propped against a tree trunk. His eyes were shut and he looked like he was resting, but the ashen face and bloody pulp from the waist down told a different story. With his heart in his throat, Johnny knelt beside his roommate and held his hand as memories from happier times came flooding back. Tears cascaded down his cheeks as he said in a voice choked with emotion, "Farewell, Jack. Farewell, friend."

Chapter 26

Ezekiel

"I'll trade you," said Moses, eyeing the large, gold locket on a silver chain that Jim Minor so carelessly twirled around his index finger. The 16-year-old was obviously disappointed with only finding a locket, two bags of dried beans, a pair of dirty socks and several packets of hardtack in the scramble for discarded knapsacks.

In the search for booty, one of the treasures Moses had stumbled across was a knapsack with a new .36 caliber Navy Colt tucked inside. The cylinder was richly engraved with a naval scene and the back strap and trigger guard were gold plated. The revolver had been carefully lubricated, and wrapped it in an oil cloth cushioned by a thick wool shirt. Also in the knapsack was a bullet mold, two boxes of cartridges and a tin box full of caps.

In addition to the pistol Moses had found two cavalry ponchos—one for himself and one for Jefferson—plus a bone-handle Bowie knife with a razor-sharp, 11-inch blade. He put the knife in an empty haversack to hide it from the prying eyes of veterans still searching for loot. What he really needed was a pair of good shoes, but footwear was in short supply. Some cadets and veterans had stripped shoes from Yankee corpses, but the thought of robbing the dead filled Moses with revulsion. Now, he wanted Minor's gold locket as a souvenir for Leonora.

"Whatcha got?" asked Minor, sneaking a peek at Ezekiel's mysterious bags

"What *everybody* wants *most*," said Moses, slowly pulling the knife from the haversack and holding it up for inspection. "Better than some old woman's locket." He tried not to appear *too* interested, but his eyes kept drifting back to Minor's locket. "That old doodad you've got is probably made of brass anyway," he mumbled. If he was right, Minor was too young to have a girlfriend and didn't place much value on a lover's memento.

"Is that a real Bowie?" asked Minor, his face lighting up at the prospect of a trade.

"Sure is. Same kind Jim Bowie used in Louisiana to fight all those duels. See the top of the blade?"

"Lemme—lemme hold it!" said Minor, eagerly reaching for the handle.

"Be careful," said Moses, as he passed it over. "Top of the blade's as sharp as the bottom. Yep. A Bowie is a mighty dangerous weapon. Could save a man's life in a showdown."

Thrusting the knife back and forth like a sword, Minor slashed away at imaginary enemies, a broad smile spreading across his boyish face.

"'Course, if it was anybody but you, Jim, I'd have to ask for a lot more'n just a small locket," Moses said, dismissively. "But, since you're in the same company as me …"

"Done!" said Minor, tossing the locket to Moses before he could change his mind.

"Battal-yun! Fall—in!" shouted Captain Wise. Now that General Breckinridge had released the Corps from further duty it was time to call the roll to find out who was missing.

Since Evans had furled the flag and dismissed the color guard, Moses lined up with his regular company. Standing in ranks, he kept glancing over at Company B, searching for Tom Jefferson. He was looking forward to tonight's bull-session around a campfire with all the bragging about the day's events.

As soon as the first sergeants finished making their reports, Moses trotted over to Company B. He wasn't too concerned about Jefferson's absence since cadets were still streaming in from the cedars and hills.

"Hallooo, Moze," called a familiar voice. It was his roommate, Monty Bludon. Wearing a new pair of Federal brogans, Bludon had been rifling the pockets of dead Yankees and checking abandoned knapsacks. It was obvious he had no reservations about scavenging the dead. With him was Hardy Dinwiddie, a member of the color guard who had been delayed taking a wounded cadet to a field hospital.

"Saw Lucien Ricketts at the hospital," said Dinwiddie. "He's still trotting around on that horse."

The image of Ricketts riding around on a borrowed horse like a high-and-mighty officer amused Moses and Bludon who broke out laughing.

"He says there's a lady on Main Street passing out really good grub. Let's check it out."

With nothing to do before settling in for the night, the threesome headed for town. Along the way they met veterans joking and carousing as if on holiday. Now there were no more taunts of "toy-soldier" or "children," but genuine murmurs of admiration and affection for the "boys" who had stood up to canister and held firm against a direct assault by the best regiment in Sigel's army. In recognition of their bravery, the regulars offered canteen cups filled to overflowing with every kind of alcoholic concoction.

After politely taking a sip from a dented cup, Moses gagged and spewed, much to the delight of the vets. While Bludon and Dinwiddie took their turns, Moses spotted a young girl standing close to a wounded, teenage Yankee prisoner. She was giving him water from a dipper and staring at his forehead. While he gulped water she lightly ran her hand along the back of his shoulder.

"Go away, little girl," snapped a guard. "This here's a mighty dangerous Yankee. They swallow small people like you—in one bite."

The girl jumped back, but kept staring at the prisoner. When she spied Moses and the other cadets she jumped up and down, and waved a small Confederate flag.

Moses walked over. "Young lady, can you tell me where to get something to eat?"

She beamed with pride at being addressed as "young lady." "Over there," she said, pointing to a wood frame, three-story building fronting Main Street. "That's Mrs. Rupert's house. It's next to the Seminary. I'm a student at the Seminary. Are you a cadet?"

Moses nodded, "Can you take us?"

"Mrs. Rupert's our principal," said the girl, trotting beside Moses and twirling in half circles. "My name's Elizabeth May. Elizabeth May Byrd. My friends call me Chatty—Chatty Byrd 'cause I talk too much. What's yours?"

"Moses—"

"Like in the Bible? Are you biblical, Moses? Is that why you're named Moses? Can you name all 27 books in the New Testament? I can. Do you want to hear?" When they reached the front door, Chatty whispered into Moses' ear, "Mrs. Rupert's a Yankee—but she was born in Scotland. That's on the other side of the ocean. She only went to school in Massachusetts, so maybe she's not a *real* Yankee. Mama says Yankees have horns—and tails—but I don't think so. Mrs. Rupert doesn't have horns. Maybe it's just the men—the older ones." She pointed to the Federal prisoner, "Robert doesn't have horns—or a tail. I looked."

As they started up the steps, Chatty continued, "I'm ten, almost eleven. How old are you, Moses?"

"Nineteen."

"Oh," she replied, pursing her lips. "That's old. Do you have a sweet-heart? Is she pretty? Do you have a tintype—?" She stopped mid-sentence, "See that, Moses?" Chatty pointed to a weathered, wooden cross stuck in the ground beside the front porch. On it was a hand lettered sign. "*In extremis all men are brothers. God loves us all.*" "Mrs. Rupert says it means 'to do unto others.' It's Latin. She reads a lot. She says Latin confuses ignorant people who haven't been saved."

Without knocking, Chatty opened the door and scampered in. She quickly reappeared with a tall, dark-haired, pleasant faced middle-aged woman.

"Come in, boys. There's plenty to eat. I'm Jessie Rupert."

Removing their hats, the barefoot cadets wiped their feet on a muddy rug at the entrance.

"Never mind that. Come in, come in," coaxed Mrs. Rupert.

The cadets shuffled in, embarrassed by their wet clothes and scruffy appearance. A large wooden table stood in the center of the room. On the far side a fire roared in a stone fireplace.

"Hang your wet clothes by the hearth and take a seat," said Mrs. Rupert.

After propping their muskets against the wall and draping their soaking jackets on a wooden rack, Moses, Bludon and Dinwiddie sat down. Four classmates already sat on a bench at the table. The cadets' waited patiently as platter after platter of bread, butter, sandwiches and preserves were laid in front of them.

Mrs. Rupert raised her hand, "Before we eat, let's give thanks to the Almighty for his merciful deliverance of everyone here." After a brief prayer, she signaled for the cadets to begin.

With Chatty's help Mrs. Rupert kept the glasses full of milk and cool spring water. When all the platters were empty the conversations shifted from food to accounting for the dead and wounded.

When Moses told his story about standing next to Carter Randolph when he was shot and killed, Walter Jones, his arm in a sling, said, "Oh, he's not dead. I saw him at the hospital."

Surprised, but relieved, Moses asked, "What hospital?"

"The one at the barn. Stanley Hall. It's down the pike just a short way."

There was a knock on the door. Chatty rushed over and two more tired, hungry cadets entered. One was Duck Colonna, the other, Andy Pizzini. As they hung their jackets on the drying rack, Moses asked if either had seen Jefferson.

Placing his hand on Moses' shoulder, Pizzini said, "Bad news, Moze. He was hit in the chest by a Minie ball just before we left the orchard. It's pretty serious."

Thunderstruck, Moses felt weak in the knees, "Wh—where is he?"

"In a hut on the Bushong farm. I haven't seen it, but Clack Lewis said it's close to the main house."

"I've got to find him," said Moses, as he stood up.

"Hold on, Moze," said Colonna. "I'll go with you soon as I eat."

When they were ready to leave, Chatty dashed up to Moses. "Can I have a button? One that says VMI? Something to show the other girls? They won't believe I know a real, live cadet."

Reluctantly he twisted off a button already hanging by a thread. It was the only one on his jacket imprinted "Cadet-VMI." When he dropped it in her outstretched hand she clutched it to her heart and beamed with excitement. Standing on her tiptoes, Chatty kissed Moses on the cheek.

Moses felt his face heat up. What would Leonora think if she knew he'd been bussed by a cute little student from the New Market Female Seminary?

Before they departed, Mrs. Rupert took Moses by the hand. "When you find your friend, bring him here. I'll locate a bed."

It was getting dark by the time Moses and Colonna reached the battlefield. On their approach to the farm they saw Robert Cabell sitting on the ground, rocking back and forth, tears running down his face as he cradled the mutilated head of his dead brother, William, in his lap. Thirty yards further on, they came across McDowell. His two roommates, Ed Tutwiler and Alex Stuart, grimly lifted the lifeless corpse onto an oil cloth.

When they reached the farm a corporal from the 30th Virginia, hobbled up using a rifle as a crutch. "I seen one of your boys inside that small building over yonder," he said, pointing to a hut a hundred yards from the main house. "Knowed he was a cadet by his clothes. He's shot up pretty bad. He tried to say something, but all he could do was mumble. I was on my way to git some help when I seen you two."

Moses and Colonna raced to the hut and swung open the door. Inside Tom Jefferson lay all alone with his head resting on a flour sack of corn husks near a stove. When Moses shook his shoulder, Jefferson's eyes slowly opened.

"Moze—it's you. I knew . . . you'd come."

"How bad is it," asked Moses. When Jefferson groaned, he had his answer.

With difficulty, Jefferson explained that he'd been carried to the house soon after being wounded. The small, ramshackle building was the living quarters of an old woman. Before she left she accidentally kicked over the only medicine he had. Since that time he'd been lying on the floor with nothing to drink and no attention. "Water . . ." pleaded Jefferson.

Moses lifted Tom's head. From the metal canteen he'd found on the battlefield, he gave him all the water he could drink.

"Can you stand?" asked Colonna.

"Think so," Jefferson said in a low voice. When he tried to rise, he collapsed. "So—so—tired…"

Supporting Jefferson between them, Moses and Colonna carried him outside and flagged down two orderlies collecting the seriously injured on a mule drawn limber.

"Put him in the cart," directed one of the men. "Doc Madison wants all badly wounded cadets brought to Stanley Hall."

Walking beside the limber, Moses and Colonna helped pull the cart out of ruts whenever the wheels got stuck. After reaching the pike it took fifteen minutes to travel to the barn at Stanley Hall.

The cart pulled up to the front door and stopped. One orderly, a husky six-footer, jumped down, "Wait here till I fetches the Doc."

Five minutes later, dressed in a crumpled, blood splattered smock, Madison came out. Opening Jefferson's jacket he examined his chest. Frothy bubbles rose from a gaping hole on the right side. The frown on Madison's face told them there wasn't much hope. He called to the orderlies, "Put him on a table. I'll have to probe."

The Institute was fortunate in having a surgeon as skilled as Madison in charge of its medical staff. Born into a distinguished family in Orange County, Virginia, his grandfather was the youngest brother of President James Madison. Graduating from William and Mary at nineteen, he received his medical training at Jefferson College in Philadelphia. After practicing in Baltimore for eight years he joined VMI's faculty in 1859 as Post Surgeon and Professor. When the Corps was temporarily disbanded at the start of the war, he served as a surgeon in the Confederate army.

After service in the field at First Manassas he was put in charge of a large hospital at Orange Court House where he specialized in trauma wounds and amputations.

Inside the barn, near the doorway, two makeshift operating tables had been located close to the entrance to help ventilate chloroform fumes. While a pair of orderlies sloshed water over a table to remove blood and pus, Madison scraped pieces of tissue from a long, porcelain-tipped probe. When all was ready, he nodded to an assistant to administer just enough chloroform to keep the patient unconscious for twenty minutes. More than that would cause nausea and possibly death.

Without delay, Madison went to work. There was no exit wound so the ball was still inside. With any luck it hadn't damaged the lung too severly. With sweat dripping from his forehead Madison probed and searched. Two . . . three . . . four . . . minutes. Finally, contact! The slug was in Jefferson's back, near the surface. Unfortunately it had severely damaged the lung and smashed a couple of ribs. The doctor glanced at a pocket watch dangling from a hook attached to the table. Ten minutes to go. With the help of an assistant he rolled Jefferson on his stomach. Feeling between the shoulder blades he located the slug. With a scalpel he deftly sliced through muscle until he found the bullet. He was relieved there wasn't more trauma to the muscle and shoulder blade. After picking out bone splinters he sprinkled the wound with opium.

Rolling Jefferson on his back, he re-examined the hole in the chest. Removing bits of shattered rib and muddy uniform, he sewed the flesh together, leaving a small opening for the pus to drain. With any luck, the wound wouldn't become infected with pyemia or hospital gangrene. For pain, Madison mixed half a grain of morphine with water and injected it beneath the skin.

After wrapping Jefferson's chest and back in clean dressing, Madison directed the orderlies to place the patient on a cot at the rear of the barn. Taking Moses and Colonna aside, he handed Moses a bottle of opium pills, "We've done all we can for now. Go into town and find him a bed, somewhere quiet where he'll get attention. If the wound doesn't become infected there's a chance he might recover." As he started to leave, Madison added, "Let me know where he is and I'll come by early tomorrow morning. Your friend's going to be in pain so give him as many pills as necessary to help him sleep."

When Moses and Colonna were alone, Colonna said, "I'll wait here with Tom while you find transportation."

"Think he's gonna be make it?"

"Doc Madison's done his best," was all the encouragement Colonna could muster. From here on, Jefferson's life was in the hands of Providence.

Barefoot and exhausted, Moses headed for the turnpike. Even though it was late, the road was busy with ambulances, limbers and cavalry so he had to walk beside the road in water filled ruts, but he didn't mind. The soft mud was easier on his feet than the rough pike. When he reached the outskirts of town he saw a buckboard being pulled by two mules and headed north. Flagging down the driver, he asked if he would go to Stanley Hall, pick up Jefferson, and carry him to town. Moses knew he was asking a lot, but he had no choice.

The man shook his head. "Sorry, son. Can't help. I'm on my way to collect any wounded still out there." What he didn't tell Moses was that he'd been sent by his wife to find injured Federals.

"I'll pay you," said Moses. "It won't take long."

"I really don't have time…"

Moses reached in his knapsack and withdrew the engraved pistol. "I don't have any money, but this gun's worth a lot."

The man leaned over and took the revolver, shifting it from hand to hand. With an admiring grunt he held it close to a lantern and began spinning the cylinder. "Mighty fine Colt. Looks brand new."

"Comes with bullet mold, cartridges and caps."

The man handed it back. "I can't take your handgun just because you need to help a friend. My wife would kill me." Again, he looked at the pistol. It was just what he needed to keep away roaming bands of renegades and bushwhackers. "Tell you what. If you'll sell it—"

"Yes, sir," said Moses, not waiting for him to finish the sentence. Not only had he now found transportation but money to help care for Jefferson.

"Is four dollars, gold, enough? I know this thing's worth a lot more, but that's all I have." When Moses nodded, the man pulled out a worn, leather purse and counted out four small coins. "Now, where's your friend?"

"At Stanley Hall, in the barn. I need to get him to town. Mrs. Rupert said she'll find him a place to stay."

The man threw back his head and bellowed with laughter, then stuck out his hand. "I'm Solomon Rupert, Jessie's husband." He pulled Moses up on the seat beside him and continued his journey north. Solomon turned to Moses, "So, you're a cadet?"

"Yes, sir. I'm Moses Ezekiel."

"From Lexington?"

Moses nodded.

"My wife used to be principal of the Ann Smith Academy in Lexington."

Moses' face lit up, "I know lots of girls at Ann Smith."

"Jessie was there until '58 when she moved to New Market." Solomon hesitated, "She liked Lexington well enough, but had to leave town when word got out that she was teaching colored children to read the Bible."

"What's wrong with that?" asked Moses who, at twelve, had taught the family slaves, Aunt Mary and Jane Eliza, to read from the Old Testament.

"It's against the law," sighed Solomon. "Some people don't want slaves reading, even the Good Book. Knowing how to read and write is powerful medicine. Might start them thinking." Reaching in a vest pocket, he pulled out a plug of tobacco and bit off a corner. "Let me tell you a funny story. Three years ago, when Virginia seceded, some locals in New Market decided to have some fun with my wife. They knew Jessie was strong minded and anti-secession. Anyways, soon as Virginia left the Union they hung a brand new Confederate flag on the porch of the Seminary." Solomon guffawed, tobacco juice running down the corners of his mouth. "When Jessie looked out the window she noticed the local e-lites gathered across the road, staring in her direction. She went out on the porch and there was a Confederate flag, just a-flapping in her face. *Well*, she whirled around, marched back inside and grabbed some matches." Solomon glanced at Moses to make sure he was listening.

Solomon continued, "Jessie jerked down the flag, struck a match—*whoosh*—it went up in flames." He spat a stream of tobacco juice into the mud. "When you're facing a herd of wild bulls, you don't go waving a red flag in their faces—unless you're Jessie." Solomon shook his head. "The crowd started yelling, *'Get her!' 'Kill the Yankee traitor'* Two men rushed up, grabbed her elbows and hustled her over to the town jail where I was justice of the peace. To keep them from lynching her I locked her up. We weren't married then."

Solomon shifted the wad of tobacco in his mouth. "Well, the locals didn't know what to do with her now that they had her. Here was this woman who had been teaching their children. She'd lived in New Market for three years and they were neighbors, but the locals couldn't just ignore what she'd done to the new flag. The town council called an emergency session. When someone mentioned that there was a Confederate camp at

Rude's Hill, they decided to hand her over to the military for her comeuppance. They tied her hands behind her back, dumped her in a buckboard like a sack of 'taters, then drove to the camp." He shook his head. "Things looked pretty bleak for my Jessie. Well, when they marched her into the tent of the commanding officer, who do you think was there?"

"General Imboden?" asked Moses.

Solomon grinned. "Close. But better. Stonewall Jackson. When he saw her he rose from his chair, stepped over and extended both hands in welcome. Jessie and Stonewall were old friends. Both believed in the Holy Ghost and were members of the same Presbyterian church in Lexington. Every Sunday afternoon Jessie and Stonewall held classes to teach colored children to read Scripture."

"Well, I'll be darned," said Moses.

"After reminiscing about old times, Stonewall sent her home with an armed guard and told her to keep it as long as she felt threatened." Solomon stared into the dark, "I tell you, son, life's full of little surprises."

When they reached Stanley Hall, the house, yard and barn glowed from the flickering light of lanterns and torches as treatment of the injured continued at a brisk pace. The shifting shadows, mixed with groans and screams from the dying and wounded presented a macabre scene.

As they headed for the barn Moses averted his eyes from a pile of arms and legs. The severed limbs only reminded him of Jefferson's suffering. Out of the corner of his eye he noticed someone waving their arms to attract his attention. It was the corporal from the 30th Virginia he'd met at the Bushong farm.

"Did ya find yer friend?" ask the soldier, still limping along with a rifle for a crutch.

"Yes, sir," answered Moses.

"Don't 'sir' me. I ain't no officer." With a bandaged finger he pointed to Moses' bare feet. "Still ain't got no shoes?"

"No, sir."

"I kin fix that." The corporal crooked his finger for Moses to follow him, "Let's go shoppin' at my commissary."

"Here?"

"Yup. Corporal Haywood G. Thompson's dry goods and notions. Open day and night. No red tape. Silent testimonials from satisfied customers, and, best of all, everythin's free." Leading Moses to the back of the barn, Thompson raised his lantern over a pile of corpses stacked like cordwood against the side of the barn. Tapping the foot of the nearest dead Yankee, he asked, "How 'bout this un?"

Moses tugged at the shoe, but glanced up at the Yankee's face. The eyes were wide open and seemed to be warning him not to disturb the dead. Moses quickly dropped the foot.

Thompson held the lantern over the feet of a second soldier who had on a pair of nice, new brogans. "How 'bout these? They looks only slightly used. May be a tad stinky and muddy, but the former owner didn't have no complaint." He swung the lantern over the face which had a large hole between his eyes. "Do you, son?"

The shoes appeared to be the right size. Moses hesitated, making sure not to look at the man's face. The idea of stealing from the dead was still unsettling, but necessity is a hard master. Pulling off the right shoe, he tried it on. It was a little large, but with an extra pair of socks, it would fit. Quickly tugging off the other shoe, he hurried back to the front of the barn before slipping it on. Beside the buckboard, Solomon Rupert conversed in hushed tones with a Confederate captain.

"That one," said the captain, pointing to a seriously wounded Federal lying on the ground with his neck and right arm wrapped in bloody rags. "And these two," he continued, tapping the feet of a couple stretched out on a bed of straw.

Entering the barn, Moses saw Carter Randolph on a cot in a stall. Doc Madison was examinig him by waving a lantern in front of Randolph's face to measure his response to light.

"How's he doing?" asked Moses.

"He's very lucky," said Madison. "The ball struck his head at an angle and didn't penetrate the skull. It passed completely around, just under the skin, and lodged at the back of his head. It was easy to remove, but he's suffering from a severe concussion."

Moses took out the letters and pocketbook he'd saved for Randolph and slipped them into his pants pocket. Bending close, he said, "Carter, I'll be back as soon as I can." But Randolph didn't respond.

Walking to the rear of the barn, Moses found Colonna on the floor beside Jefferson's cot, fast asleep. By the time they got Jefferson bundled into a poncho and moved out to the wagon, there were already three wounded Federals on board. Moses fashioned a cushion of hay for Jefferson, then sat down beside him on the floor of the wagon. Before they started out, Solomon confided to Moses and Colonna that the Yankees were Masons selected by Captain Taylor for transportation to the Seminary for special treatment.

With a minimum of prodding and a couple of well-placed taps from the buggy whip, Solomon persuaded the two mules to amble back to the turnpike. When they reached the Seminary, he parked the rig at the front door. A young student peering from a window spotted Moses and the wounded Jefferson. Seconds later Jessie came running out, followed by Chatty and two curious friends.

"The Clinedinsts have agreed to take him in," said Jessie, pointing across the street to a two-story, wood-slatted house with walkup steps and seven windows facing Main Street. Give me a second and I'll let them know he's here."

Although it was 2:00 a.m., there were lights on inside the house when Jessie knocked on the door. After going inside, she soon returned with a young, petite woman who extended her hand to Moses. "I'm Eliza Clinedinst. Please call me Lydie. Miss Jessie told me all about your friend."

Moses removed his kepi, "Thank you kindly, Miss Lydie, for taking him in. His name's Tom Jefferson. He's from Amelia County and he's hurt real bad. Doc Madison thinks he'll recover if he gets good care."

Colonna and Moses carried Jefferson inside and laid him on a bed in a downstairs room.

When he felt the warm, feather mattress Jefferson opened his eyes and looked at Eliza. "Thank you, Sister. What a good, soft bed."

Chapter 27

Wise

Lying on the damp ground, Johnny pulled the blanket tightly around him. As pink clouds began to appear in the east over Massanutten Mountain, he pulled the loose end of the blanket over his head to ward off a cool breeze blowing in from Smith's Creek. Since they had no tents, the cadets had dubbed their bivouac area "Mount Airy." With a finger, Johnny opened a corner of his cocoon and peeked out. At least it wasn't raining. He could hear the snap of twigs and crackle of fires as the camp gradually stirred to life. The smell of burning oak and freshly brewed coffee tickled his nose. The thought of hot coffee was almost enough to entice him out of his warm bed. The usually boisterous morning chatter had been replaced by conversations in hushed tones as yesterday's events were relived and an inventory taken of classmates killed, wounded or missing.

Still half asleep, and fully dressed, Wise lay where he was. That last dream had seemed so real. In it he and Stanard were planning to leave the Institute and join Mosby's Rangers, but they couldn't find any horses. As the dream faded, the realization that Stanard was dead, came as a shock. To make matters worse Johnny felt partly to blame. If Jack had only stayed with the wagons, he would still be alive.

"Up and at 'em," said a sprightly voice close by, as a foot jostled the end of Wise's blanket. Slowly pulling the cover from his face, Johnny focused on the intruder. It was Louis, bandaged on the arm and shoulder, but otherwise as annoying as ever.

"Some of the boys say they're dishing out fresh eggs, ham and flapjacks at a girls' school in town," said Louis. "All the molasses and real butter you can eat. If we don't get a move on we'll miss out." He'd seen what Judge, VMI's cook, was preparing—greasy pork and beans—and had decided to take his chances in town.

When Johnny heard "girls' school" he perked up. He wondered if Polly Logan knew any of the girls there. He didn't want word to get back to Polly that he'd been flirting. As he rose reluctantly to his feet the lump on his forehead began to throb. Sloshing canteen water over his head and face, he adjusted the bandages and tried to comb the knots out of his hair. Brushing dirt and grass from his crumpled uniform, Wise raised an arm and took a quick whiff. He hadn't taken a proper bath since leaving school and hoped the rank smell wasn't too noticeable.

"I gotta go get my knapsack and bedroll," said Louis. "Pizzini says they're in a storehouse on Lime Street. Goodykoontz is standing guard but not for long." Louis also wanted to see Stanard's body one last time before it was placed in a coffin. It would be his only chance to snip a lock of hair for Stanard's mother.

As Louis and Johnny walked toward town they saw a group of cadets gathered around two veterans holding their heads in their hands and hopping about from leg to leg. Now that the cadets had been tested in battle and found worthy, they could mingle with regulars as equals and were taking full advantage of their new status. When Louis and Johnny drew closer they heard the cadets howling with laughter.

When he saw them, Erskine Ross waved them over. "You've got to hear this," he said, wiping tears from his eyes. Turning to a vet, he said, "Tell us again what the Dutchman said."

The sergeant's eyes twinkled with impish delight as he rocked back and forth. "Der Dutchmens said, *'Dem leetle tevils mit der vhite vlag was too mutch fur us. Dey shoots und smash mine head, ven I vos cry Zurrender' all der dime.'*"

When the laughter died away, Ross motioned Louis and Johnny to the side. "Thought you might want to know, they put Stanard, along with the other four, in a small warehouse at the end of Water Street. It's a one-story building with a rusty orange roof. They're making coffins next door at a woodshop. When they're finished they're going to put the bodies inside and nail them shut. The funeral's scheduled for two o'clock this afternoon."

Louis and Johnny decided to swing by the girls' school before going to the makeshift morgue. Better to eat breakfast while they still had an appetite. Sprinkling canteen water on the bandage covering his head, Wise pressed hard, but it was no use. He couldn't squeeze out any more blood. He thought about picking open a scab, but Louis was in a hurry.

"Come on, hero," chided Louis as he shifted his own bandages so that the dark, dried blood was more visible. "You might get more sympathy if you limped a little."

When they reached the Seminary, there were cadets on the porch and front steps wolfing down multiple helpings of eggs and pancakes while basking in the admiration of pretty, fawning girls. Lining up behind Charlie Wesson for a trip to the food table, Louis and Johnny smiled at two young girls, who giggled and shyly averted their eyes.

After flirting and eating their way through two helpings of fried eggs sandwiched between flapjacks and slathered with butter and molasses, Johnny and Louis reluctantly departed.

By the time they reached Water Street, Johnny's resolve for saying farewell to his roommate had vanished. He knew that if he saw Stanard's mangled corpse in a dark, dingy, smelly warehouse it would give him nightmares for the rest of his life. The double door leading into the storage room was open and he could see bodies laid out on the floor. The sights and stench of death coming from the building left him weak and nauseous. Taking Louis by the arm, he shook his head, "I can't go in, Louis. Tell Jack I'm sorry. He'll understand."

Five minutes later Louis returned to the street. He was pale and holding a handkerchief over his nose. It had been an ordeal but he had the lock of hair.

Their next stop was the storehouse on Lime Street where Goodykoontz stood watch over the cadets' bedrolls and knapsacks. With shoulders drooping from fatigue, Goodykoontz looked bedraggles and acted disoriented.

"Could you ask Colonel Ship to relieve me," pleaded Goodykoontz. "I've been here all night." His eyelids fluttered. "Can't stay awake any . . . any longer."

While Louis pawed through the pile of bedrolls and knapsacks, Johnny searched for Stanard's belongings. If he didn't take them now, they would be stolen by scavengers and camp followers. Wise knew Jack would want him to have any edibles and expendables in the knapsack and to remove any embarrassing items that might upset his mother.

When they got back to Mount Airy, Johnny decided to write a letter of condolence to Stanard's mother. While rummaging through Jack's knapsack for pencil and paper, he had the eerie feeling he was trespassing. But, in the past thirty-six hours his world had been turned upside down and old rules no longer applied. After removing a sheet of paper and a stub of a pencil, he took out a ham sandwich, a wedge of cheese, a used bar of soap, a small rum cake and a half-empty bottle of peach brandy. Digging further he found a deck of poker cards and what looked like a love letter from Becky Gregory. He would keep the cards, soap and food, and when he got back to barracks return the letter to Becky—unread. He didn't know her address so he'd just send it in care of the Virginia Female Institute in Staunton.

While he sat on a wooden crate composing the letter, two nearby cadets began shouting at each other. Glancing over he saw Charlie Marks and Dave Peirce, both red faced and gesturing wildly. Peirce, his left arm in a sling, wave his good hand in Marks' face.

"I *dare* you!" declared Peirce.

"I *double* dare you!" shot back Marks.

"Then I double-*dog* dare you!" retorted Peirce, a look of satisfaction crossing his face.

Drawing himself up to his full 5-foot-4, Marks glared at Peirce. Summoning all his strength, he hissed, "Dave Peirce—I double-*black*-dog-dare you, and bet you a dollar in gold you ain't got the grit to do it!"

Stunned into silence, Peirce did an about-face and stalked off. The verbal gauntlet had been thrown. No one could back away from a "double-black-dog-dare" and keep his self-respect.

"What was that?," Wise asked a nearby cadet who had witnessed the confrontation.

"They heard that some veteran regiments south of town had fresh eggs, milk and baked bread this morning, but the commissary ran out before they got this far. Marks said he was going to march up to General Breckinridge and demand the same good food that other units were getting. Peirce dared him to do it, but now it looks like Peirce got himself trapped."

Wise grunted and turned back to writing. *"Dear Madame."* He hadn't met Jack's mother but felt like he knew her. *"It is with heartfelt grief that I sit down to offer you all the consolation that one of the best friends of poor Bev can offer."* In barracks Stanard was known as Jack, but his family called him "Bev."

"I roomed with him for eight months before his death and during that whole time I never heard him utter an oath or do anything that was not becoming a Christian man . . . " Well, not often anyway. *"Every night while we were on the march—notwithstanding the noise and confusion—he prayed regularly. He told me the week before we started out that he would have been confirmed if he had stayed at the Institute and not gone on furlough."* Johnny knew Jack's mother wanted him baptized, but Jack wasn't interested—that is until he met Becky Gregory. *"His last request was 'whoever wrote his Mother should tell her he died a Christian.'"* What harm would a little white lie do if it soothed a grieving mother?

"Bev was a noble-manly boy; high-minded, honorable, and a Christian and had one of the best tempers I ever saw. He was very calm and when he fell it was with as calm a smile as if he was sinking into a placid slumber. Madame-many may grieve for your Boy-many may shed hot tears over his dear body-but none more than your sympathizing friend, John S. Wise."

"Whew," said Wise, glad the chore was behind him. Writing a letter of sympathy was harder than he thought. Looking up he saw Andy Pizzini heading his way, a bandage plastered over a wound on his cheek.

Pizzini pointed to where Hanna and the Commandant were standing. Colonel Stoddard Johnston, Breckinridge's chief-of-staff, stood with them. "Hanna's looking for you. He's planning the funeral and wants all room-mates of dead cadets to take part."

"What do they want us to do?"

"Recite part of a poem during the burial service," said Pizzini. "It was written by Colonel Theodore O'Hara, an officer from Kentucky and a close personal friend of General Breckinridge. He wrote the poem after the Mexican War. It's called, 'The Bivouac of the Dead.' Where's Suggs-L?"

"Fetching water," said Johnny.

"Go get him, and report to Hanna."

"That was quite a reception you boys gave the Yanks yesterday," said Johnston, as Louis and Johnny trotted up. "I don't think they like your brand of southern hospitality."

Wise and Louis smiled then glanced at the Commandant who was grinning broadly.

Hanna had done such an outstanding job organizing last week's flag raising ceremony that Lt. Colonel Ship had put him in charge of today's detail. Now Colonel Johnston wanted to know the order of service.

Hanna began ticking off his checklist. "The Corps will form at Mount Airy at 2:00 p.m." He glanced at the Commandant, "There'll be a lot of absentees, so we may have to consolidate into three companies." Reaching over, he brushed flakes of dried mud from Wise's sleeve. "See if you can clean off some of the crud before we form up." He continued, "The Corps will march into town in a double column along the pike. When we reach Water Street we'll meet two caissons with the coffins. Next, we go to reverse arms and escort the coffins to St. Matthew's cemetery." He nodded to Louis and Johnny, "Each of you will be assigned a verse to read at graveside." Noticing the wound to Louis' arm, he added, "Leave your musket here Suggs-L. The wounded won't carry muskets."

"What's the order of procession from town?" asked Johnston.

"Colonel Ship and his staff will lead off in slow time. Next comes the color guard followed by the coffins. The drummer and fifer will play an appropriate dirge from Water Street to the cemetery. Wounded men unable to walk will ride in wagons at the rear of the column."

"If you want a riderless horse, you can use mine," said Johnston.

"That *would* add a nice touch," said Hanna. "I don't think there'll be many bystanders, but the more pomp, the better. We want something that cadets can tell their children and grandchildren."

"I'll get a pair of black riding boots for the stirrups," said Johnston.

"Excellent." Hanna motioned to Louis. "Suggs-L, you take charge of the horse. Walk him at a slow pace behind the caissons and make sure to tie the boots firmly in the stirrups with the toes facing backwards."

"And the graveside service?" asked Ship.

"Unless there's some objection, I thought that when we reached the cemetery we would form a semi-circle around the grave. All five coffins will be placed in one grave. Since the interment will probably only be for a short time, I've instructed the gravediggers to make the hole shallow. A local matron, Mrs. R.L. Wickes, has a daughter with an excellent singing voice. I've agreed to let her start the service with 'Somebody's Darling.' She'll be accompanied by her brother on the violin."

The Commandant and Johnston nodded approval.

Hanna continued. "When she's finished, we'll have the twelve cadets who lost roommates recite a verse from Colonel O'Hara's poem. Reverend Cline will say a few words, then the honor guard will fire three volleys as the bodies are lowered into the grave. One for duty. One for honor. And one for country."

Colonel Johnston, who had attended dozens of military funerals, patted Hanna on the back, "I must say, Lieutenant, your grasp of funereal protocol and pageantry is most impressive."

Hanna handed Johnny and Louis their verses. "Each verse has two quatrains. Try to memorize them so it doesn't sound like you're just reading words."

It was 11:00 a.m. by the time Wise got back to camp. With a wet towel he tried to scrub some of the grime from his uniform.

Although a third of the Corps was absent, Hanna corralled enough cadets from the artillery section to fill out four, thin companies. Since Cabell, First Sergeant of Company D, was among the dead, Hanna detailed Wise to take his place. As acting first sergeant, it was Wise's job to organize the undermanned company into a functioning unit.

Five minutes before two o'clock, the drums, draped in black cloth, began beating the call to ranks. When the last tap sounded Wise was standing on the right of the first column. He hoped his efforts would impress company officers enough to win him promotion to first sergeant at makeovers in July.

As the Corps moved onto the pike, General Breckinridge and four staff officers rode up. Trooping the line, he removed his hat, and turned to address the battalion.

"Boys, the work you did yesterday will make you famous."

Dave Peirce took a step forward and saluted. "General, fame's all right, but for *Gawd's* sake, where's your commissary wagon?"

Breckinridge smiled while members of his staff laughed heartily. He was pleased to see the cadets still had a sense of humor. After saluting the colors and waving his hat, Breckinridge and his staff galloped off.

Wise chuckled at Peirce's audacity. Not many people would've had the pluck to address the commanding general in such a bold manner. He sneaked a peek at Charlie Marks whose face was contorted in a grimace. Peirce had clearly won the double-black-dog-dare, along with a new gold coin.

With raised sword the Commandant commanded, *"Right Face! Forward! March!"* As the Corps moved along the pike the fife began playing a sprightly version of "Dixie."

Positioned at the head of the column, Wise could see hundreds of soldiers and civilians in the road ahead. In addition to veterans and citizens, the color guards from two regiments of regulars stood by the pike. All veteran units, except for Imboden's command, had been ordered to leave for Richmond at once. Wise hoped the Corps wouldn't have to march around the crowd in the mud. Much to his relief, as they approached, the groups parted, leaving a clear path into town.

All chatter and background noise stopped as the Corps drew near. Some soldiers pointed at the cadets, others just stared. Wise braced for the usual taunts and ribbing. When they reached the first group of soldiers, there was a low murmur. With broad grins on their tanned, battle-scarred faces, the veterans began removing their hats and waving them over their heads. Then shouts of *"Three cheers for the cadets! Way to go, boys!"* Finally the shrill *"Yip! Yipee! Yip!"* of the Rebel Yell filled the air. Wise was amazed. The cadets were being hurrahed by the veterans. Ladies in mourning dresses, their shoulders draped in black shawls, waved handkerchiefs and fought back tears as the cadets marched by. When VMI's colors passed in front of the color guards of the two regular Confederate regiments, the guards snapped to attention and dipped their tattered flags in salute.

A lump rose is Wise's throat. He glanced left and right at the wildly cheering crowd. It was the proudest day of his life.

When they marched past the Seminary, girls with long hair held in place by black ribbons leaned from windows while others stood on the porch waving small flags at their schoolboy heroes. *"Hurrah for the cadets! Hurrah for VMI!"*

Slipping loose from Mrs. Rupert's grasp, Chatty Byrd darted across the road and skipped alongside Wise. "Moses and Tom are my best friends. They're in that house over yonder," she said, pointing to the Clinedinst residence. "Moses gave me a button. What's your name? Are you from Virginia? Are you a general?" Johnny stifled a laugh, and kept his eyes straight ahead.

When the column reached Water Street they were met by two caissons draped in black, each hitched to a team of fine horses. One caisson held three coffins, the other held two. Tacked to the front of each casket was a handmade laurel wreath woven by Seminary students with the name of the deceased cadet painted in black. After the caissons had taken the place of honor and the column was ready to head for the cemetery, the Commandant gave the command, *"Battalion! Reverse arms!"* The rattle of muskets echoed through the crowd as cadets swung their rifles under their left arms, butts forward, barrels pointed back and down. Reaching their right hands behind their backs they grasped the inverted barrels.

"Forward! In slow time! March!" In perfect unison, the Corps started off, marching north along the turnpike toward St. Matthew's cemetery. The veterans at the side of the road stood at attention and saluted the colors and coffins. Women wept openly with their handkerchiefs covering their eyes. Men bowed their heads and held their hats over their hearts. When the column moved past the Seminary, even Chatty, a rope tied around her waist and held tightly by Mrs. Rupert, was silent. But her big brown eyes were wide open, taking in the whole spectacle.

On reaching St. Matthew's cemetery, the column wheeled left, filing onto the grounds and facing the freshly dug grave. The honor guard stood to the right, prepared to fire three volleys at the end of the service. On the left stood Miss Amanda Wickes and her brother, Jonas, who was tuning his violin. Louis handed the reins of the riderless horse to Colonel Johnston's orderly, then joined Johnny with the eleven other cadets scheduled to recite the poem.

While the coffins were carried from the caissons to the grave, Miss Wickes began to sing:

> *Into the ward of the clean white-washed halls,*
> *Where the dead slept and the dying lay;*
> *Wounded by bayonets, sabers and balls,*
> *Somebody's darling was borne one day.*

Wise was impressed with the clear, angelic quality of her voice. He admired her jet-black hair set off by a beautiful, radiant face. The bodice of her mourning dress was cinched tightly around her waist, revealing a trim, delicate figure. Stanard would have approved.

> *Give him a kiss, but for somebody's sake,*
> *Murmur a prayer for him, soft and low,*
> *One little curl from his golden mates take,*
> *Somebody's they were once, you know.*

Wise glanced down at the sheet of paper with verse eleven scribbled in pencil. Surprised at the emotion tugging at his throat, he fought for control, hoping he wouldn't choke.

When Miss Wickes had finished, Hanna lined the twelve cadets on the far side of the grave. Louis went first:

The muffled drum's sad roll has beat
The soldier's last tattoo;
No more on life's parade shall meet
That brave and fallen few.
On Fame's eternal camping-ground
Their silent tents are spread,
And Glory guards, with solemn round,
The bivouac of the dead.

Next up was Ed Tutwiler, Hugh McDowell's roommate. Tutwiler had found McDowell on the field shot through the heart, and from the pained expression on his face, it was clear he hadn't gotten over it. While Wise tried to listen his mind began to wander back to the good times he had spent with Jack, happily wandering the grassy hills in Lexington, hunting quail and rabbits, playing games, sharing hopes and dreams of times to come.

Looking at the coffin with Jack's name, Wise fought back tears. When it was finally his turn, he stepped to the edge of the grave. Holding the piece of paper in front, he bit his lip. There was no need to look at the words. The verse was burned into his memory. In a voice trembling with emotion, he spoke to his friend for the last time:

Rest on, embalmed and sainted dead!
Dear as the blood you gave
No impious footsteps here shall tread
The herbage of your grave
Nor shall your glory be forgot
While fame her records keeps,
For Honor points the hallowed spot
Where Valor proudly sleeps.

Chapter 28

Ezekiel

Tuesday, May 17
New Market

After treating Jefferson's wound with bromine and changing the dressing, Doc Madison walked Moses and Evans out to the street. It had been two days since the battle and Jefferson still couldn't hold down acidulated water or eat food. He'd been restless all day, but with enough pills had finally gone to sleep.

"Tom says it doesn't hurt as much," volunteered Moses. "That's a good sign isn't it?"

"Too soon to tell," replied Madison. The fatigue from working two days straight with only three hours sleep was slowing the doctor down. "I've seen recoveries from injuries a lot worse than his." He didn't want to dishearten Moses, but in his experience fewer than forty percent of soldiers with penetrating chest wounds survived. And of those, only a handful had lung damage as severe as Jefferson's. The numbness, the internal hemorrhaging, the discoloration, the difficulty breathing—all bad signs. Some doctors, out of desperation, operated on chest wounds. But Madison had found that such surgery only caused more pain and hastened death. In his opinion, Jefferson was sinking fast and wouldn't last the night. The most he could do now was ease the suffering with opium. Before leaving he handed Moses another two dozen pills. "When he complains, give him as many as it takes."

It was dark now, and neither Evans nor Moses had eaten since breakfast. "I sure could use some coffee," said Evans. "I'll trot over to Mrs. Rupert's to see what I can rustle up."

When Moses went back inside, he heard Jefferson coughing. The cough, dry, hacking sound, had developed in early afternoon and caused him a great deal of discomfort. Turning up the wick in the lantern on the mantel, Moses asked, "Can I get you anything? Sweet coffee? Lemonade?"

"Thanks, Moze. I . . . I'm feeling much . . . better now. Another . . . one of those pills . . . might help."

Moses held a cup of water to Jefferson's parched lips as he swallowed two tablets. "While you were asleep, Alex Redd and Will Duncan came by to see how you're doing. They're all pulling for you. I told them you're getting better and it won't be long till you're back in ranks." There was no answer. It bothered Moses that Jefferson had lost all interest in talking about the battle and the Corps. His only thoughts now were of his family and growing up at Winterham.

As the calming effect from the opium gradually took effect, Jefferson raised his head, "Moze . . . please get a . . . Bible and read me the . . . the part where it says 'In my Father's house . . . there are many mansions . . .'"

In the parlor Moses found a well-worn Bible. Not being familiar with the New Testament he took it upstairs and asked Lydie to identify the passage Tom wanted.

"That's John 14," she said, as she located the verse and marked it with a slip of paper. "It's one of my favorites."

Returning to Jefferson's room, Moses opened the Bible and sat at the foot of his bed. In a soothing voice he began, *"Let not your heart be troubled: ye believe in God, believe also in Me. In my Father's house are many mansions: if it were not so, I would have told you. I go to prepare a place for you."*

Moses glanced at Tom and saw that his eyes were closed. Although his breathing was labored, he didn't seem to be as restless. He continued, *"And if I go and prepare a place for you, I will come again, and receive you unto myself; that where I am, there ye may be also."* Now Moses could hear Jefferson lightly snoring. Closing the Bible, he placed it on the stand by the bed. He would finish the passage when Jefferson woke up.

Twenty minutes later Evans returned with a mug of hot coffee and some sandwiches made especially for Moses by Chatty Byrd. After checking on the patient, Evans went into the next room for some much needed sleep. Sitting in a chair by the bed, Moses tried to stay awake, but his eyelids grew heavy. Soon he was in a deep, dreamless slumber. Then he heard Tom calling.

"Moze—Moze!"

Rubbing his eyes, Moses glanced at the clock on the mantel. 10:55 p.m. "I'm here Tom."

"Moze. Please light . . . a candle. It's so dark!"

The hairs on the back of Moses' neck bristled. Two lighted candles on the table and a lantern on the mantel already lit the room. His grandmother had told him that when someone was about to die, they would first lose their sight. For the first time, Moses realized that all hope was gone and Tom was slipping away. Moving to the bedside, Moses took his friend's hand.

Jefferson gripped Moses' fingers. "Lucy? Is that you? It's been so— I'm glad you're here. Mother? It's me, Tom—"

As Jefferson moved his head from side to side, his eyes half closed, Moses eased his hand back down. Going next door he woke Evans. "Big, go upstairs and get the Clinedinsts. Tell them the time has come."

Dressed in nightgowns, Lydie, Anne and their mother silently filed into the room. They held lighted candles and clutched prayer books. Standing at the foot of the bed they silently prayed.

As Jefferson's breathing became more labored, Moses sat beside him and held his dying roommate in his arms. Gradually, the breathing subsided, then quietly, without a sound, stopped.

When they saw that Jefferson had passed away, Mrs. Clinedinst began reciting the 23rd Psalm.

> *The Lord is my Shepherd; I shall not want*
> *He maketh me to lie down in green pastures…*

With a damp cloth, Moses wiped the sweat from Tom's forehead then felt for a pulse. There was none. Holding a mirror to Jefferson's nose he checked for any sign of breathing. The mirror didn't fog. A lump rose is Moses throat as tears ran silently down his cheeks. With trembling fingers he closed Jefferson's eyes.

> *Yea, though I walk through the valley of the shadow of death*
> *I will fear no evil…*

While the praying continued, Lydie stepped over to the mantel and stopped the clock. 11:23 p.m. With a black cloth she covered the dressing mirror in the corner of the room.

> *Surely goodness and mercy shall follow me all the days of my life,*
> *And I will dwell in the House of the Lord forever.*

Epilogue

THE CORPS

Temporarily assigned to Imboden's command, the Corps remained in New Market while Breckinridge and the rest of the army joined Lee in Richmond. After the first couple of days of caring for wounded and burying the dead, the euphoria of having seen the elephant and survived began to wear thin. On May 19, with hearts weighed down by thoughts of deceased and maimed comrades, the Corps left for Staunton. As they approached Harrisonburg they were surprised to be hailed as victors and conquering heroes. Their somber mood quickly vanished as they were greeted with ovations at every stop. When one matronly woman saw the raggedly dressed, shoeless boys, she asked, "Where are the cadets?"

In his autobiography Moses Ezekiel wrote, "When we reached Staunton one group of young ladies and hundreds of citizens greeted us enthusiastically. One of the girls placed a laurel wreath on our cadet flag," which he kept as a souvenir. Again fawned over by students from the female academies and feted by the townswomen, the cadets revelled in the attention. In his autobiography, *The End of an Era*, John Wise noted, "The dead and the poor fellows still tossing on cots of fever and delirium were almost forgotten by the selfish comrades whose fame their blood had bought."

In Staunton, VMI's Superintendent, General Francis H. Smith, greeted them with a supply of new shoes for the one-third who were still barefoot. Instead of returning to Lexington, the Corps received orders to proceed immediately by train to Richmond to help guard entrances to the city.

On Sunday, May 22 the cadets crowded into freight cars for the trip to Richmond. While waiting on a spur track in Ashland, they encountered the remnants of the Stonewall Brigade, which had been decimated at the

Bloody Angle during the Battle of Spotsylvania. The brigade's commanding general, James A. Walker, was the cadet who had challenged Stonewall to a duel. It flattered the cadets that their idols had heard of them and their victory.

In Richmond, while Grant and Lee maneuvered only miles away on the banks of the North Anna River, the cadets, " . . . garlanded, cheered by ten thousand throats, intoxicated with praise unstinted, wheeled proudly around the Washington Monument, to pass in review before the President of the Confederate States, and to receive a stand of colors from the Governor of Virginia." (Wise, *The End of an Era*). While in Richmond they were given new uniforms. In recognition of their fighting ability the cadets were also equipped with top-of-the-line, new Enfield rifles imported from England. On Friday, May 27, the Corps again paraded around Capitol Square and listened to a resolution by the House of Representatives thanking them for their service at New Market.

When word reached Richmond that General "Black Dave" Hunter with a force of 18,000, was on the outskirts of Staunton, the Corps was ordered back to Lexington. They arrived by canal boat on June 9 but could only watch as Hunter burned the Institute.

CASUALTIES (KILLED AND WOUNDED)

While there are conflicting claims by battlefield participants as to whom bore the brunt of the fighting, the percentages of killed and wounded tells the story. VMI's 24% (10 killed and another 45 wounded) was only exceeded for the Confederates by Woodson's company of Missourians.

Union		Confederate	
34th Mass	32%	Woodson	64%
54th Penn	23%	VMI	24%
1st W. Va.	8%	62nd Va.	20%
12th W. Va.	3%	51st Va.	15%
Total Union	7%	Total Confederate	13%
Killed	96	Killed	43
Wounded	520	Wounded	474

THE INSTITUTE

After the rout at New Market, Grant quickly replaced Sigel with 61-year-old Major General David Hunter. Hunter, a West Pointer, was ordered to proceed immediately up the Valley, capture Staunton, then cross the Blue Ridge and attack Lynchburg. After defeating General "Grumble" Jones at the Battle of Piedmont on June 5 (Jones was shot in the head and killed while leading a charge) Hunter headed to Lexington. He arrived there on June 11. On June 12, Colonel David Strother saw Federal looters exiting barracks, " . . . loaded with beds, cadets' trunks, carpets, cut velvet chairs, mathematical glasses and instruments, stuffed birds, charts, and hats in a most ridiculous confusion." Hunter asked Strother if he thought the school should be burned and Strother replied in the affirmative. His reasoning was that VMI was, " . . . a most dangerous establishment where treason was systematically taught . . ." On orders from Hunter, all buildings associated with the Institute were torched, except the Superintendent's quarters, which Hunter was using as headquarters.

Both General George Crook and First Lieutenant Henry DuPont protested such wanton burning, ". . . the destruction of the cadet barracks was fully justified by the laws of war, but the burning of the buildings containing the library, the philosophical apparatus . . . and other objects used solely for education purposes, was entirely unnecessary. Such destruction was contrary to the conventions of civilized warfare which requires respect for the property of institutions of learning" (DuPont). One of the homes set ablaze was Colonel Gilham's quarters. DuPont and several other officers helped the distraught Mrs. Gilham, whose brother was an officer in the Federal army, carry personal effects outside her home before it was set on fire. One of the volunteers who helped Mrs. Gilham was Captain William McKinley, future President of the US.

In his pyrotechnic application of General Grant's new policy of waging war against private property, Hunter ordered the burning of the home of John Letcher, Virginia's War Governor. His excuse was that Letcher had incited citizens to resist the invasion of Federal troops. In Old Testament eye-for-an-eye retaliation, General Jubal Early carried the "scorched earth" policy to the north. On July 30, his men burned 150 homes in Chambersburg, Pennsylvania, effectively destroying the town.

Greatly outnumbered at Lexington, Confederate forces under General John McCausland offered only token resistance to Hunter's advance. The cadets were ordered to withdraw toward Lynchburg and spent the night of

June 11 on top of the Blue Ridge Mountains. With no school left, classes were canceled until further notice and the Corps went into camp at Camp Lee and Poe's Farm. On December 28, those who hadn't secured positions with active commands, resumed studies at the Alms House in Richmond. This time, the Corps remained in the capital until the evacuation of Lee's army on April 1, 1865. On April 2, the student body was disbanded. The school reopened on a limited scale for classes in Lexington on October 17, 1865.

FEDERALS

Disgraced by his poor showing at New Market, **Major General Franz Sigel** was shunted off to Harper's Ferry to take over Hunter's reserves. In a snide comment on Sigel's precipitous retreat, David Strother was overheard saying, "We are doing good business in this department. Averell is tearing up the Virginia and Tennessee Railroad while Sigel is tearing down the Valley turnpike." When Sigel learned of the remark, he blurted, "By gar! I vill not haff beoples zayin' dem kind o' tings! I pelief dere are beoples on mein staff who are not griefed to zee me dearin' down de' pike! By gar! Colonel Strodare must not zay dem kind o'tings or he veel be court-martial."

When word of Sigel's defeat reached Madame Cheney, the woman he had accused of stealing his brandy flask, she thanked God, declaring that her prayers were always answered, and that she never cursed anyone who didn't presently come to grief. In an attempt to shore up his fading reputation, Sigel went so far as to write an anonymous, glowing report of the campaign to the Congressional Committee on the Conduct of the War. It didn't help when Hunter later discovered that Sigel had been under the influence of a crooked civilian trader named Robbins.

Sigel's dismal performance as a commanding general continued at Harper's Ferry. When Jubal Early approached Martinsburg on his raid toward Washington, Sigel was unable to delay the Confederate advance or protect the B&O Railroad. His rapid retreat from Martinsburg provided Early with some much need supplies. Now known as the "Flying Dutchman," on July 8, Sigel was again replaced by General David Hunter. This time a furious Grant made certain he would have no more field commands. Moving to New York, Sigel spent the rest of the war waiting for an assignment that never came. On May 4, 1865, he resigned his commission. Remaining in New York after the war, he served in various minor political positions while trying in vain to salvage his military reputation. He died in 1902.

Major General Julius Stahel remained with Hunter's command until wounded at the Battle of Piedmont. For his actions he later received the Medal of Honor. But personal bravery didn't save his command from Hunter who was determined to purge the army of Sigel's influence. When he learned of Sigel's dismissal at Harper's Ferry, Stahel sent him a note, *"Heute dir, morgen mir."* (Today you, tomorrow, me). It was an accurate reading of the tea leaves. On the same day Sigel was relieved, Stahel was transferred out of the field to court-martial duty. He resigned his commission in February, 1865. After the war, Stahel held various consular posts in the Orient, then returned to New York to work in insurance. For twenty-five years he resided at the Hoffman House where he was known simply as "The General." Stahel died in 1912.

When General Hunter took command of the Department of West Virginia, he appointed **Colonel David Hunter Strother**, a distant cousin, as chief of staff. Strother was with the army at Lynchburg where it was soundly defeated by Jubal Early. When General Philip Sheridan took charge of the Army of the Shenandoah, Strother submitted his resignation and moved to Baltimore. After the war, he was brevetted a brigadier general and briefly appointed adjutant general of Virginia. In this post he served for a year on the Board of Visitors of VMI. Faced with the need to earn a living, he tried to re-start his career writing for *Harper's Monthly*, but the public was no longer interested in tales of backwoods mountain folks or articles about his service in the military. An appointment as Consul General to Mexico in 1879 saved him from poverty. Strother died in March, 1888, at Charles Town, West Virginia. His relatives and other Virginians never forgave him for taking part in the plundering and burning of the Shenandoah Valley.

After New Market, **Colonel George D. Wells** remained in the Valley and fought in the Battles of Piedmont, Third Winchester, and Fishers Hill. On October 13, 1864, in a skirmish leading up to the Battle of Cedar Creek, he was shot from his horse and mortally wounded. With Rebels rapidly closing in, he ordered his men to leave him on the field, "It's no use, I can't live. Gentlemen, save yourselves." When General Jubal Early discovered that the wounded officer was Colonel Wells, he sent for his own ambulance, but it was too late. His remains were forwarded to the Union lines under a flag of truce and are interred at Greenfield, Massachusetts.

Seriously wounded in the shoulder and taken prisoner, **Lieutenant Colonel William S. Lincoln** remained in New Market from Sunday until Thursday when he was transferred to Harrisonburg. There his wound was properly examined and dressed for the first time. A frequent visitor to his room on the upper floor of the courthouse was Captain Hanse McNeill. When the partisan captain asked if he'd written home, Lincoln said he had, and had sent his letter to Washington by flag of truce boat. McNeill replied, "Pshaw! Your folks will never hear from you by that route. Here's some paper. Write a letter if you want. Pay for a Confederate stamp—you have to contribute at least that much to our cause. Give me your word you won't write anything you ought not to, seal it and give it to me. I'll put it in one of your post offices, though I don't promise I won't rob it first." It was the only letter of Lincoln's to reach its destination during his time in captivity.

Caught up in the confusion over paroles and exchanges, Lincoln was scheduled for shipment south to a POW camp. Aware that such a move would prove fatal with his wound, he decided to escape. In his informative book, *Life with the Thirty-fourth Massachusetts Infantry,* he recounts the perilous adventure that took seventeen days of "toil, exposure and danger" to finally reach Union lines at Cumberland, Maryland. After being mustered out of the army in June, 1865, he was brevetted a brigadier general. At 78 he died in Worcester, Massachusetts.

The important part taken by **First Lieutenant Henry A. Dupont's** battery in slowing down the Confederate advance was overlooked in Sigel's after-action report in the *Official Records*. Due recognition was given in Edward R. Turner's *The New Market Campaign*. More importantly, the significance of the part he played was reported by an eyewitness, cadet-Captain Benjamin Azariah Colonna, in a 1912 article in the *Journal of the Military Service*. Colonna wrote, "The audacity of this battery caused us to think that it had strong infantry support, and we paused to form a line before advancing further. This caused a delay of fifteen or twenty minutes, and allowed the Thirty-fourth Mass., the Twelfth W. Va. And the Fifty-fourth Pa. and perhaps some other troops, time enough to slip through to freedom." When Hunter took command of the Department of West Virginia he promoted DuPont to captain and appointed him chief-of-artillery. At Cedar Creek DuPont earned a Medal of Honor for "distinguished gallantry" and was brevetted to lieutenant colonel. He remained in the service until 1875 when he resigned to work for the family firm. In 1906, as a US Senator from Delaware, he introduced a bill to help compensate the Institute for damage caused by Hunter. Signed into law by Staunton-born President Woodrow Wilson, the government granted VMI $100,000, which was used to construct Jackson Memorial Hall. DuPont died on New Year's Eve, 1926.

CONFEDERATES

Two days after the battle, **Major General John C. Breckinridge's** small force, except for the Corps of cadets and Imboden's cavalry, left to join Lee's army on the North Anna River. From there he led a Division to Cold Harbor where they helped hold the line against Hancock's corps. When word reached Lee that General Hunter had captured Staunton and was heading for Lynchburg, he sent Breckinridge and General Jubal Early to stop him. Soundly defeated, the Federals hastily retreated into West Virginia, leaving the Valley open for Early's raid on Washington. Breckinridge performed well at the Battle of Monocacy and got as far as Fort Stevens on the outskirts of Washington before having to turn back. When Secretary of War Seddon resigned in February, 1865, Davis replaced him with the Kentuckian. After Lee surrendered 27,805 men at Appomattox on April 9, 1865, Breckinridge and Joseph E. Johnston met with Sherman at Bennett Place, Durham, NC, to discuss the surrender of an additional 89,270 troops. On April 26, the agreement was signed, effectively ending the war. In a harrowing escape to Cuba chronicled in the December, 2001, issue of *Civil War Times*, Breckinridge left the United States before he could be tried for treason. He and Mary lived in Canada and Europe until 1868 when he was granted amnesty. They returned to Lexington, Kentucky, where he devoted his energies to reconciliation. Because of his interest in bringing the country together, President Grant urged him to run for office but Breckinridge was finished with politics. He never forgot New Market and the boys he called, "my cadets." While in Canada, Lieutenant Bennett Young, a fellow exile, wrote, "I pleaded with him to tell the story to me many times and when he did it was with reluctance. Invariably, irresistibly, the tear would start in his eye and sadness overspread his face as he recalled the scenes of that memorable day in May, 1864." Breckinridge died in 1875 at 54.

While General Philip Sheridan was busy torching the Valley from Harper's Ferry to Staunton, **Captain John "Hanse" McNeill's** 60-man ranger command continued to harass his supply lines and gather intelligence. On October 3, while leading an attack against a small camp of Yankees guarding a bridge, McNeill was mortally wounded. When his identity was discovered by General Sheridan, a Federal surgeon walked up, "Captain McNeill, I thought it was you, but I wasn't sure. Last year I was your prisoner and your treatment of me was so kind that I now hold myself ready to render you any service in my power to give." Not only did the doctor tend to his medical needs but also left him with a bottle of fine liquor to ease the pain. McNeill lingered on until November 10 when he died in Harrisonburg, surrounded by his wife, daughter and two sons. Command of the loosely organized rangers then shifted to his 23-year-old son, Jesse McNeill. To prove himself a worthy successor of his father's legacy, Jesse organized a daring raid to Cumberland, Maryland, in February, 1865. Dressed in Yankee uniforms, the rangers captured Major General George Crook and Brigadier General Benjamin Kelley. Imprisoned in Richmond, both embarrassed generals were exchanged in March, 1865.

After Cold Harbor, the Missourians under **Captain Charles Woodson** returned to the Valley and joined McNeill's rangers in their hit-and-run tactics. In December, General Early attempted to place Woodson's and Jesse McNeill's rangers under the command of Lt. Colonel Harry Gilmor. Both refused. When Gilmor tried to arrest Jesse, the young McNeill simply ignored him and continued to operate as an independent command. Woodson wrote to John C. Breckinridge, the new Secretary of War, to plead his case for staying independent. The issue became moot when Gilmor was captured on February 4, 1865. At war's end, Woodson returned to Missouri where he became a successful contractor, bridge builder and part-time politician. To avoid retaliation for bushwhacking, and to polish his resume for political purposes, he reinvented the story of his wartime services. Woodson died in 1909 at 67. His second in command, **Lieutenant Ed Scott** stayed behind in the Valley, attended medical school and started a practice in Randolph County, West Virginia. After a brief illness Scott died in 1872 at 32.

After the war, **Harry W. Gilmor** moved to New Orleans where he married Miss Mentoria N. Strong. In 1866 he published his memoirs, *Four Years in the Saddle.* Later, he returned to Baltimore where he served for five years as City Police Commissioner. Gilmor was 45 when he died in Baltimore in 1883.

After taking command of Echol's brigade, **Colonel George S. Patton** applied to Richmond for promotion to brigadier general. It was approved, but before it reached him he was killed at the Third Battle of Winchester. Wounded in the hip by a shell fragment, he kept a pistol by his bedside to prevent a surgeon from removing his leg. He commented, "What would I look like stumping through life with a wooden leg?" Seemingly on the road to recovery, he contracted gangrene and died a week later. His cousin, **Colonel George H. Smith,** continued fighting in the Valley until war's end. He then moved to Mexico to try his hand at cotton farming. Unsuccessful at hoeing cotton, he moved to California in 1868. Already a well-known attorney, he enjoyed a distinguished career as a jurist in the Golden State and was instrumental in the establishment of the University of Southern California School of Law. In 1870 he married his cousin George Patton's widow, who had a son named George S. Patton. This son was the father of WWII's famous four-star General George S. Patton Jr. When George Smith died in 1915, his adopted son paid him the ultimate compliment, "He did not have the military mind in its highest development because he was swayed by ideas of right and wrong" (*Blue & Gray, Magazine Special Issue*).

CADETS

When the Corps returned to Richmond and went into camp at Camp Lee, **Corporal John "Johnny" Wise** was promoted to fourth line sergeant in Company B. Instead of remaining with the Corps, he accepted a commission as Second Lieutenant and drill-master with the Reserve Forces. For the rest of the war he was assigned to various staff positions. When General Johnston surrendered at Bennett Place, Durham, North Carolina, Johnny was in Greensboro with President Davis and witnessed the closing act of the Confederacy. In the summer of 1865 he visited his uncle, Union General George C. Meade, in Philadelphia. While at Meade's home, despite having been a Confederate officer, he was, " . . . regarded as such a mere child that he was not invited to the table when company came, but dined with the other children in the nursery." (Wise: *The End of an Era*)

From 1865-67 Johnny studied law at the University of Virginia then went into partnership with his father. Interested in maintaining close ties with the Institute, he briefly served on VMI's Board of Visitors and was a frequent speaker at school reunions. Attracted to politics, in 1885 he ran for Governor of Virginia as a Republican, but was defeated by General Fitzhugh Lee. In 1888 he moved to New York to practice law and was quite successful. An excellent writer, he published his autobiography, *End of an Era,* in 1902. Part of this classic covers his experience as a cadet in Lexington and the part of the Corps at New Market. Johnny never saw Polly again but married a woman from Nashville, Tennessee, with whom he had five sons. All five were cadets at the Institute. John S. Wise died at the home of his son, Henry, in 1913.

First Lieutenant John F. Hanna, the cadet from Philadelphia who dueled with Lt. Colonel Lincoln on the battlefield, graduated from VMI on June 17, 1864. Commissioned a Second Lieutenant in the Confederate army, he served on the staffs of Generals Imboden and Echols. For a short time he was a captain of infantry in the trenches in front of Fort Harrison. After the war, Hanna attended law school at George Washington University and practiced in the Court of Claims and before the Supreme Court. In 1885 he was injured in a riding accident and died six days later at his home in Mt. Vernon, Virginia. He never married. His diary covering the period April 17 to May 9, 1864, is available on the VMI archives website. In it he gives an account of daily cadet life just prior to the battle at New Market.

Cadet **First Sergeant Andrew Pizzini Jr.** remained with the Corps when it moved to the Alms House in Richmond. Promoted to Second Cadet Captain, Company D, he helped guard the city until the Corps was disbanded on April 2, 1865. He remained in Richmond, eventually becoming president of the city's Electrical Street Railways Light and Power Company. He died in 1913.

Cadet **Franklin Gibson** survived his seven wounds. He became a lawyer and teacher and moved to Missouri. He died in 1903.

Lieutenant Colonel Scott Ship continued as Commandant at VMI until becoming Superintendent in 1890. He was appointed a member of the board of visitors for both West Point and the US Naval Academy at Annapolis. Ship retired in 1907 and died at his home in Lexington in 1917.

On June 27, 1864, **Moses J. Ezekiel** received his much desired promotion to Sergeant in Company C. Offered a commission as a second lieutenant in the Confederate army he turned it down and remained with the Corps at the Alms House in Richmond. Sometime during the summer of 1864 his ardor for Leonora Levy cooled and by the fall he noted in his autobiography, "The young girl with whom I was now in love and whom I intended to marry was a blonde, the adopted daughter of a prominent doctor in Richmond." In August, 1866, Leonora Levy married the former Confederate Major, Alexander Hart, from New Orleans.

Moses returned to Lexington in October, 1865, when classes resumed. While a first classman he was a frequent visitor at the home of Robert E. Lee, then president of Washington College in Lexington. In 1866 he gave Mrs. Lee a painting, *The Prisoner's Wife*. Impressed with Moses' talent, General Lee advised, "I hope you will be an artist, as it seems to me you are cut out for one. But, whatever you do, try to prove to the world that if we did not succeed in our struggle, we are worthy of success." In 1867 he moved to Cincinnati with his family to study sculpture. After receiving recognition for a statuette labeled *Industry*, he moved to Berlin to work with Rudolf

Siemering and Albert Wolff. In Rome he opened a studio in the Baths of Diocletian where he produced bronze and marble sculptures. Visitors to his studio included presidents U.S. Grant, Theodore Roosevelt and William H. Taft. Among the many awards he received were The Cross of Merit from George II, Grand Duke of Saxe-Meiningen, The Golden Cross from Keiser Wilhelm II, Emperor of Germany, and the title, *Cavaliere* from Victor Emanuel III of Italy.

Deeply influenced by his life as a cadet and his experience at New Market, Moses sought commissions for monuments with Confederate and southern themes. One of his first major works was *Virginia Mourning Her Dead*. He later presented a bronze replica of the statue to VMI where the classical, allegorical life sized figure of "Virginia," perpetually mourns over the body of Thomas Jefferson, the roommate who died in his arms. At the 1903 dedication while gazing at the fresh young faces of the cadets, he noted, "Something arose like a stone in my throat and fell to my heart, slashing tears to my eyes."

In 1876, his daughter, Alice, and her mother, Isabella, travelled to Europe to visit Moses. After a brief reunion they returned to Washington where Alice finished school and became a teacher. In 1898 Alice married Dr. Dan Williams, a famous African-American physician in Washington, D.C. Dr. Williams was noted for having performed the first successful heart surgery in the US. He also founded Provident Hospital, the first non-segregated hospital in the US. (*Moses Ezekiel*, Cohen & Gibson). Moses never married and his lineage went extinct when Alice's only child died at birth.

One of Moses' most impressive sculptures is the thirty-two foot tall *Confederate Memorial* in the Confederate section at Arlington National Cemetery. Before he died in 1917 he asked to be buried among his southern comrades at Arlington. His grave marks the east compass point of the monument. The simple inscription reads:

Moses J. Ezekiel
Sergeant of Company C
Battalion of the Cadets
Virginia Military Institute

Acknowledgments and Further Reading

We are grateful to the many people who helped with this book. Our families and friends have been patient and understanding throughout the years required to bring the work to publication. We are grateful to all of you for cheering us on.

Special thanks to Jill Hoffman and John Hoffman for their unfailing support of yet another of our projects.

Zika Wolfe, Fred Wolfe and Shannon Currey asked good questions and provided insights and focus. We thank them for their encouragement and senses of humor.

The editorial service of John Perlin, CM, CVO, ONL, LLD, St. John's, Newfoundland, was extremely valuable in catching inevitable errors, omissions and inconsistences.

We are grateful to William Andrew Powell for his editorial suggestions.

Special thanks to L. F. M. Jones.

We owe a debt of gratitude to those mentioned in the sections which follow. We could not have written this book without their assistance. Reference sources and suggestions for further reading are listed below.

VMI ARCHIVES AND MUSEUMS

The extensive and well maintained **VMI Archives** and **VMI Museums** are in special categories all their own. The archives are available through a user-friendly web site and offer windows into daily cadet life prior to the Battle of New Market. The archives contain additional information about other people and topics concerning the Institute during the Civil War era. The authors especially thank Colonel Keith Gibson, class of '77, Executive Director of Museum Programs; Diane B. Jacob, Head, Archives & Records Management; and Mary Laura Kludy, Archives & Records Management Assistant. Their help and willingness to answer questions and provide photos is appreciated.

In addition, we thank Major Troy Marshall, Director of New Market Battlefield State Historical Park at New Market, for providing valuable information and photos.

We are grateful to Jon M. Williams, Andrew W. Mellon Curator of Prints & Photographs, Hagley Museum and Library, for his help in furnishing a photo of First Lieutenant Henry A. Dupont, a key character in the novel.

MUSEUMS
Lexington, Virginia:

To anyone interested in the history of VMI's participation in the Civil War, the authors recommend a visit to the excellent museum located on the VMI campus in Jackson Memorial Hall.

New Market:

Not to be missed is the Virginia Museum of the Civil War at the New Market Battlefield State Historical Park in New Market. This museum is located on the site where the battle actually took place. It includes exhibits on the Corps of cadets and includes the Bushong Farm as it was on May 15, 1864. The positions of some Confederate and Federal artillery batteries and infantry regiments are marked.

SPECIAL PLACES
Inn at Narrow Passage

We recommend that anyone interested in Valley history spend a night or two at the carefully restored Inn at Narrow Passage, a historic B&B near Woodstock, VA. Our thanks to Ed and Ellen Markel, Innkeepers, for digging up extensive information on Miss "Daisy" Ruddell, proprietress during the war. It was here that Stonewall Jackson said to Jedediah Hotchkiss, "I want you to make me a map of this Valley from Harper's Ferry to Lexington, showing all the points of offense and defense in those places."

Winterham Plantation

Winterham Plantation is another historic B&B of note. This mansion was the childhood home of cadet Thomas G. Jefferson, who was mortally wounded at New Market. It's located in Amelia County and is ideal for civil war buffs interested in Richmond, Lee's retreat, Sailor's Creek battlefield, and Appomattox. It took Gary and Kathy Hadfield three years to restore the plantation to the condition Tom Jefferson would have recognized when he was alive. We are grateful to Gary and Kathy for sharing with us their knowledge of the history of the Jefferson family, the property and the surrounding area.

REFERENCES AND FURTHER READING

We list here some of the many works we consulted in writing this book The list is not complete or exhaustive. We provide it as a convenience for readers who are interested in learning more about the 1864 VMI cadets, the battle, and the times.

General Background

Davis, William C. *The Battle of New Market*. Harrisburg, PA: Stackpole, 1993. The definitive account of the battle. Has been printed by various publishers since 1975.

Knight, Charles R. *Valley Thunder, The Battle of New Market and the Opening of the Shenandoah Valley Campaign, May 1864*. New York: Savas Beatie, 2010. An informative update on the battle by a former Historical Interpreter at the New Market Battlefield State Historical Park at New Market. Includes maps and photos of the participants and places.

Additional General Background

Colonna, Benjamin A. "Battle of New Market," *Journal of the Military Service Institution of the United States*, vol. LI, 1912, pp. 344-351.

Duncan, Richard R. *Lee's Endangered Left, The Civil War in Western Virginia, Spring of 1864*. Baton Rouge: Louisiana State Univ. Press, 1998.

Holsworth, Jerry W. "VMI and the Battle of New Market," Special Issue, *Blue & Gray*, Spring, 1999, Vol. XVI, Issue 4. An extremely helpful publication on the battle which includes a roster of all the cadets who were at New Market. Also lists the complete Order of Battle and the officers in charge. This issue contains numerous illustrations and maps.

Turner, Edward R. *The New Market Campaign, May, 1864*. Richmond, VA: Whitter & Shepperson, 1912.

Whitehorne, Joseph W.A. *The Battle of New Market*. Washington, D.C: U.S. Army Center of Military History, 1988.

Wise, Jennings C. *Virginia Military Institute History*. Lynchburg, VA: J.P. Bell, 1915.

Cadets

Couper, William. *The Corps Forward, Biographical Sketches of the VMI Cadets who Fought in the Battle of New Market.* Buena Vista, VA: Mariner Publishing, 2005. A reprint of the important 1933 book by Couper with extensive biological information on all cadets and professors who took part. Includes Preston Cocke's brief account of the battle, *The Battle of New Market,* as well as a chronological table of the main events in the history of the Institute during the war.

John S. Wise

John S. Wise, *The End of an Era.* New York: Houghton Mifflin, 1901. A classic.

John S. Wise, "The West Point of the Confederacy," Century Magazine, vol. XXXVII, Jan. 1889, pp. 461-471.

Moses Ezekiel

Cohen, Stan and Keith Gibson. *Moses Ezekiel, Civil War Soldier, Renowned Sculptor.* (Missoula, MT: Pictorial Histories Publishing, 2007). This biography of Moses' life contains full-color pictures, with thoughtful explanations, of his major works.

Gutman, Joseph and Stanley F. Chyet, eds. *MOSES JACOB EZEKIEL Memoirs from the Baths of Diocletian.* Detroit, Wayne State Univ. Press, 1975.

Jack Stanard

Barrett, John G. and Robert K. Turner Jr., eds., *Letters of a New Market Cadet: Beverly Stanard.* Bay Shore, NY: Evergreen Press, 1961.

Confederates

John C. Breckinridge

William C. Davis, *Breckinridge: Statesman, Soldier, Symbol.* Baton Rouge: Louisiana State Univ. Press, 1992. The definitive biography of this important statesman.

Charles W. Woodson

Curran, Thomas F. "Memory, Myth, and Musty Records: Charles Woodson's Missouri Cavalry in the Army of Northern Virginia," *Missouri Historical Review,* Oct. 1999, vol. XCIV, No. 1, pp. 25-41.

Monacello, Anthony. "Strange Odyssey of the 1st Missouri," *America's Civil War,* March 1999, pp. 26-33.

John D. Imboden

Tucker, Spencer C. *Brigadier General John D. Imboden, Confederate Commander in the Shenandoah.* Lexington, KY: Univ. Press of Kentucky, 2003.

Woodward Jr., Harold R. *Defender of the Valley, Brigadier General John D. Imboden, CSA.* Berryville, VA: Rockbridge Publishing, 1996.

John H. McNeill

Delauter Jr., Roger U. *McNeill's Rangers.* 2nd ed. Lynchburg: H.E. Howard, 1986.

Duncan, Richard R. "The Raid on Piedmont and the Crippling of Franz Sigel in the Shenandoah Valley," *West Virginia History*, vol. 55, 1996. pp. 25-40

Bright, Simeon M. "The McNeill Rangers: A Study in Confederate Guerrilla Warfare," *West Virginia History*, vol. 12, Number 4 (July 1951) pp. 338-387.

Harry Gilmor

Gilmor, Harry. *Four Years in the Saddle.* New York: Harper & Brothers, 1866.

Achinclose, Timothy R. *Sabres and Pistols, The Civil War Career of Colonel Harry Gilmor, CSA.* Gettysburg: Stan Clark Military Books, 1997.

Claudius Crozet

Hunter, Robert F. and Edwin L. Dooley Jr., *Claudius Crozet, French Engineer in America, 1790-1864.* Charlottesville: Univ. Press of Virginia, 1989.

Federals

Franz Sigel

Stephen D. Engle, *Yankee Dutchman: The Life of Franz Sigel.* Fayetteville, AR: Univ. of Arkansas Press, 1993.

William S. Lincoln

Lincoln, William S. *Life with the Thirty-fourth Mass. Infantry in the War of the Rebellion.* Worcester, Mass: Noyes & Snow, 1879. An entertaining, informative autobiography.

Clark, William H. *Reminiscences of the Thirty-Fourth Regiment Mass. Vol. Infantry.* Holliston, Mass: 1871.

George D. Wells

East Carolina Univ., J.Y. Joyner Library, Greenville, NC, *George D. Wells Letterbook.* Collection #241.

Henry A. DuPont

DuPont, Henry A. *The Campaign of 1864 in the Valley of Virginia and the Expedition to Lynchburg.* New York: J.J. Little, 1925.

Colonna, Benjamin A. "Light Battery B, Fifth U.S. Artillery, May 15, 1864," *Journal of the Military Service Institution of the United States*, vol. LI, November-December 1912.

David H. Strother

Eby Jr., Cecil D., ed., *A Virginia Yankee in the Civil War: The Diaries of David Hunter Strother.* Chapel Hill, NC: UNC Press, 1961.

——. *"Porte Crayon": The Life of David Hunter Strother.* Chapel Hill, NC: UNC Press, 1960.

——. *The Old South Illustrated by Porte Crayon.* Chapel Hill, NC: UNC Press, 1959.

Places

Winchester

Mahon, Michael G. ed. *Winchester Divided, The Civil War Diaries of Julia Chase and Laura Lee.* Mechanicsburg, PA: Stackpole, 2002.

Holsworth, Jerry W. *Civil War Winchester* Charleston, SC: History Press, 2011.

Cloyd's Mountain

McManus, Howard R. *The Battle of Cloyds Mountain: The Virginia and Tennessee Railroad Raid, April 29-May 19, 1864.* Lynchburg, VA: H.E. Howard, 1989.

About the Authors

John S. Powell is a graduate of the Virginia Military Institute, 1960; Tulane University, MBA, 1965; and Duke Law School, JD, 1963. From 1963-1965 he served as a first lieutenant, artillery, US Army. He is the author of *The Nostradamus Prophecy*, a techno-thriller (1998). Powell co-founded Biomedical Reference Laboratories, Inc. and is past president of Carolina Biological Supply Company. An avid student of Civil War battles, he is especially interested in those fought in the Shenandoah Valley. His great-grandfather, John B. Powell, was a lieutenant in the 43rd NC Infantry, and surrendered with the Army of Northern Virginia at Appomattox in 1865. In the past twenty-five years, the author and his wife, Martha Hamblin, (co-author of this novel) have visited Andersonville, New Market, Gettysburg, Cold Harbor, and dozens of additional sites, studying the tragic phenomenon that was the American Civil War.

G. Martha Hamblin is an award-winning photographer and poet. She earned her BA in biology from Randolph-Macon Woman's College in Virginia, holds an MA from Duke University, and an MS from Marlboro College Graduate School. Her keen interest in the Civil War started with a visit to Appomattox while at R-MWC. Her business career includes positions as vice president of Nova Scientific Corporation, co-founder of the NC Family Business Forum, and owner of Photophish Imaging & Art. Currently she is part of the management team of Hoffman Nursery, Inc. She lives in North Carolina with her husband, John Powell, and their cat.

Made in the USA
Lexington, KY
04 October 2014